What people are saying about ...

Grand Tour Series

"Bergren, award-winning author of nearly 40 books with two million–plus sold, launches readers into a sumptuous world of wealth and world travel with the first in the Grand Tour Series featuring Cora Diehl Kensington. Cora learns she is the illegitimate daughter of Montana copper baron Wallace Kensington, which sets her on a journey of discovery and healing when she joins her half siblings and their wealthy friends on a Grand Tour of Europe. Will McCabe, their guide, worries over the precarious family dynamics and his own developing feelings for Cora, who must face her own demons when her siblings sabotage her every move. The family must come together, however, when danger threatens all of them. Readers will come to love Cora as she struggles over her feelings for Will and the dashing Frenchman Pierre de Richelieu, and they'll delight in the scenes of England and France in pre-WWI Europe. This is a worthy beginning to the series."

Publishers Weekly

"A fascinating mix of travel and intrigue, heartache and romance, *Glamorous Illusions* sweeps you away on the Grand Tour, exploring London and Paris through the eyes of a young woman who longs to find her place in the world. The title captures the story perfectly, as Cora delves beneath all that glitters to discover what is real and true, while not just one man but two vie for her affections ... ooh, la la! A grand start to a new series from a seasoned author who writes from the heart."

"Who am I and where do I fit in this world? These are just two of the important questions addressed in this poignant story that takes the reader from an impoverished farm in Montana onto an opulent cruise across the Atlantic to stately England and finally to the city of love, Paris. With fresh characters, a touching story, and plenty of adventure and romance, you'll get swept away in this lavish world of the young and wealthy."

"From a bankrupt farm in 1913 Montana to the glitter and glamour of a European Grand Tour, *Glamorous Illusions* is the trip—and the read—of a lifetime. Absolutely one of my favorites ever, this book is a stunning adventure from first page to last. A truly masterful storyteller, Lisa Bergren has penned a magical journey of the heart and soul that will leave you breathless and longing for more."

"A Cinderella story lingers in the pages of *Glamorous Illusions*. Open the book and be swept into a story of heartache, strength, and romance. Add in the sweeping beginnings to a Grand Tour of

Europe, and I found all the ingredients for a story I couldn't put down."

GLITTERING PROMISES

GLITTERING PROMISES

THE GRAND TOUR SERIES

LISA T. BERGREN

David C Cook®

transforming lives together

GLITTERING PROMISES
Published by David C Cook
4050 Lee Vance View
Colorado Springs, CO 80918 U.S.A.

David C Cook Distribution Canada
55 Woodslee Avenue, Paris, Ontario, Canada N3L 3E5

David C Cook U.K., Kingsway Communications
Eastbourne, East Sussex BN23 6NT, England

This story is a work of fiction. All characters and events are the product of the author's imagination. Any resemblance to any person, living or dead, is coincidental.

LCCN 2013946263
ISBN 978-1-4347-6428-7
eISBN 978-0-7814-1085-4

The Team: Don Pape, Traci DePree, Amy Konyndyk,
Nick Lee, Caitlyn Carlson, Karen Athen
Cover Design: JwH Design, James Hall
Cover Photographer: Steve Gardner, Pixelworks Studios

Printed in the United States of America
First Edition 2013

1 2 3 4 5 6 7 8 9 10

080113

CHAPTER 1

~Cora~

"If you spot him again, shoot him on sight," my father said. "I shall deal with the repercussions myself."

I gently pulled off my gloves and felt Will's grip on my elbow tighten. I looked about the room—at my younger sister, Lil; my brother, Felix; and one of our guards, Pascal, standing with Antonio and my father.

"What's this?" Will asked, leading me closer to the others, deeper into the Venetian palazzo's grand salon. I was thankful that the long windows were wide open, allowing the brine-laced breeze to waft through. "What's happened?"

"Oh, Cora!" Lillian cried, rising and entering my arms. She clung to me a second and then pulled back to look at me. "It was Nathan Hawke! I'm certain I saw him across the piazza today!"

"Truly?" I asked. "Nathan? If you're right, he's far less clever than I thought." I looked to my father, his words about *shooting him on sight* making far more sense now. Nathan Hawke was dangerous, instrumental in our kidnapping a week past, thwarted only because Will and Art had used other nefarious men to double-cross him. I lifted a hand to my temple and shook my head. "It makes no sense. He should be on a steamer to Greece by now. Not lollygagging about where one of us might spy him, report him. He risks imprisonment!"

"Unless he *wants* to be seen," Antonio grumbled, thick chin in hand.

"For what purpose?" Felix asked.

"To make certain that we know who is behind the next kidnapping," bit out my father, throwing up a hand in frustration. "So that we might pay the ransom without hesitation."

"His partners are in jail," I said. "What true threat is one man when we are so many?"

"It took only one to take our Lillian," my father said, his blue eyes steel cold as he leveled them at me. "And another to nab you as well."

"We are far less naive than we were when we began this journey. We never go out alone—"

"Not that that resolves our concerns," my father said. "What would you do if he leveled a gun at you? Or your sister? Or young William here?"

"Presumably our armed guard would protect us."

He paced back and forth, flicking one hand in the air. "So he draws his pistol, Antonio draws another, and you are caught in the cross fire?"

I bit my lip, stymied by both his logic and the sudden reminder that he might care for me and my future, regardless of the bad blood that had passed between us. I pinched my temples between thumb and ring finger. "We've been through this, Father. We cannot live in fear the rest of our lives. Like it or not, after that *Life* article, we'll be recognized wherever we go. Even more so once the next issue is off the presses and reaches Europe."

"Which will be soon," said Hugh Morgan, one of our traveling companions, his tone uncommonly gentle. "It'll be any day now."

I looked back at my father. Here, at last, was the gauntlet he'd warned me of—the trials of leading, of making choices. I had to show him I was up to the task. "If it's not Nathan Hawke, there will be others, yes? You have enemies. I, apparently, have enemies. This is our present reality. And we all must deal with that threat, here, now, so that we can be done with it forevermore."

"It would be easier at home in Montana," my father said. "We wouldn't be so exposed."

I held a breath, defeated by the idea of turning tail and running after all we'd endured. We'd fought to be here, earned the right to finish our trip, even if it was against Father's wishes. Hadn't we? But I recognized his fear, his concern for the others—my siblings, Felix, Vivian, and Lil, as well as the Morgans—even if I couldn't trust what he felt for me. I sighed and looked to Will.

"When is the earliest we could leave, if we wished to?" Father said.

"The *Charleston* ships out in a couple of weeks from Pisa. We might secure passage on her. But given that it's high season, she's likely sold every stateroom, and getting us all aboard, even if you all agreed to travel second class…" Will shook his head. "No, it's highly unlikely we'd find anything above steerage. There's a slim chance we could find accommodations on the *Charlemagne*, the following week out of Naples."

"Oh, but the *Charlemagne's* a miserable ship," Pierre de Richelieu said, entering the room, his keen eyes covering each of us but resting on me. "Trust me. You'd never wish to board her wretched gangplank." His eyes narrowed as he took in the dour mood of the room. "What's happened?" he asked, his French accent growing thicker. "What is it?"

Antonio bent to whisper in his ear, and Pierre's handsome green eyes shifted to me, his brows furrowed in alarm—and then his gaze traveled down to Will's hand on my elbow. I knew he'd remained, even once Will and I began openly courting, hoping I might change my mind. He pinched his lower lip, then turned to a chair and sat down, heavily, as if beaten. He was due to leave for Paris within hours. I knew that this was perhaps the last time I'd ever see him, which made me alternately relieved and sad.

My father strode to the window and put a hand on the frame as he stared outward. "It is you that Nathan Hawke is after, Cora. An heiress, a millionaire in her own right, now. That's the story the press shall propagate. Luc Coltaire would've taken any of you. But a Montanan like Hawke? He's after you."

I let out a soft scoffing laugh. My sole inheritance—my claim on a portion of the Dunnigan mine—was in dispute. Father wished to hold it out before me like a carrot before a horse, forcing me to go in the direction he wished. I had secured an attorney and discovered I might have a chance at fighting for a portion, whether my father approved of my decisions—continuing the tour, allowing Will rather than Pierre to court me—or not.

"Perhaps you can flag Hawke down in the piazza," I said. "Explain to him that you are doing your level best to keep me and my parents from earning one dollar of our mine's bounty. That trying to wring a ransom from my banker will be as difficult as squeezing blood from a turnip since I have about three dollars to my name."

I heard the tiny gasp from my sister Lil. Everyone in the room seemed to take a collective breath, all eyes now concentrating on the two of us.

"Cora, this all mustn't be so trying," my father said, his blue eyes shifting in agitation to the others in the room. "And even if we weren't at odds about the Dunnigan mine, you know he'd come to me. Appeal to me as your father. I'm the known quantity."

"And we both know how far that would get him." I took a deep breath and looked to Will, then back to my father, feeling a wince of regret now over my harsh words and the shadow that passed through his eyes. "But if you feel it's me that Nathan is after, perhaps we should part company for a time. I don't wish to endanger the others."

"No!" Lillian cried, coming to me and taking my arm before looking back to our father. Her blonde ringlets by her ears bounced. "Please, Father. Don't allow her to go. It isn't safe!"

"We only have a few weeks left before the *Olympic* sails back home," I said, patting her hand. "We wouldn't be apart for all that long."

"But I agree with your family," Will said, surprising me. "It's far safer for you to be with the others, under guard, than on your own."

"Will, I—"

"No," my father said. "Listen to him. If we are to tarry here in Italy rather than return home immediately, it is imperative that we remain together."

Rising voices, floating down the marble staircase, drew our attention to the open doors. Vivian. And Andrew. They were getting closer, bickering, and then Vivian arrived, flushed and wringing her hands, Andrew directly on her heels. She looked up, belatedly realizing that so many of us had gathered and overheard them arguing.

I splayed out my hands and forced a smile, eager to relieve the pressure of the group's attention. "We were just discussing the possibility of parting ways for a time."

"Parting ways?" sputtered Vivian, her small features drawing together in a frown. "Who of us wishes to part ways with you?"

I almost laughed at Andrew's steady gaze behind her. He was one, for certain. Somehow, he seemed ready to pin their growing dissonance on me.

"I believe we are past that idea," my father said quietly. "Now we must plot our safest course."

I considered him and then cast my eyes about the room, thinking. "What if we changed course again? Get off the Grand Tour track. See Antonio's Italy together?" I gestured toward our guide and then folded my arms. "Nathan Hawke is resourceful, but I wager it was Luc Coltaire that kept them on our trail before. If we up and disappeared in the wee hours, this very night, would we not likely slip from the city without him knowing where we'd gone? And if we kept to the smaller towns and villages, rather than the grand cities, would we not be far less likely to encounter those that knew the first thing about us?"

My father's gaze shifted to me, his gray mustache twitching as he considered my plan. And it was then that I knew he agreed with me.

"But what of the big cities?" Nell whined. "I do so want to see Milan. Turin. And Florence!"

"We could stay outside of the cities. Come in for the day and disappear again," Will said, looking excited. He nodded his head, hope making his eyes sparkle. "It's far more difficult for a man to follow us on the small, isolated country roads than it is in the thick of crowded streets."

Pierre rose and nodded in agreement. "It is a good plan, to stay together and yet step off of Italy's stage for a time." He turned sad, warm eyes on me. "Regardless of how much you belong on it."

I colored under his steady gaze. Was there nothing I could do to dissuade him from his pursuit?

"You are off then, Richelieu?" my father asked, stepping up beside him. "To Paris?"

Pierre nodded, still staring at me. He forced his eyes to my father. "In a few hours."

"Then you have enough time for a proper farewell with Cora," my father said.

I started, straightened, and wondered what I could possibly say that wouldn't hurt Pierre's feelings further and—

"I did hope for that, yes," Pierre said. He turned toward Will, silently asking permission.

"That is up to Cora," Will said.

Will had my heart, but sending Pierre away *broken*hearted wasn't what I wanted. He'd done nothing to deserve such sorrow.

Will sighed, reading my expression. "May I have a private word with Cora?"

My father waved us out, and we turned around the corner and into the spacious, airy hall of the grand Venetian palazzo, every nearby room empty except for the salon behind us. In the center, the

palazzo was open to the skies above, and a small, tidy garden grew
below, as it had for centuries.

Will crossed his arms and leaned against the wall, facing me.
"Tell me," he said miserably. "Tell me," he repeated, an edge of anger
in his whispered tone as he pointed out the hall, "that you are not
hesitating saying farewell to him because you still *feel* something for
him."

"I care for Pierre," I whispered back. "How could I not? He has
been nothing but kind to me! But I love you, Will. I've always loved
you."

His expression was a mixture of relief and trepidation. "Then I
have no fear in giving the Frenchman a moment to say good-bye.
He'll undoubtedly try and make you look his way one more time.
You know that, right?"

"You have nothing to fear," I said. I gave him a rueful smile. "It
is Pierre de Richelieu. You know he'll do his level best." I stepped
toward him and wrapped my arms around his waist. "But I know
who is better for me than even the grand Pierre de Richelieu."

He reached down and tucked a strand of my hair behind my ear,
feigning ignorance. "Who? Hugh? Antonio?"

I smiled back up at him. "Why yes, either of them." Hugh
Morgan was a womanizing cad, half the time—though he'd seemed
to mature over the course of the tour—and Antonio was our sweet,
fatherly fellow guide.

"It's been lovely," Will said, wrapping his arms around me and
giving my forehead a careful kiss. "These last days, setting the tour
aside, simply enjoying Venezia and each other. But now we must
move forward. And we start by sending Pierre *home*." He put one

hand behind my neck, his touch gentle, reassuring, and with his other hand, he stroked my cheek.

I smiled up at him and nodded quickly. He leaned down to gently kiss me, once, twice, until we heard voices coming closer from the salon. Quickly, we drew apart, and I took his arm.

Pierre lifted a brow in question, along with his hand, and smiled as I walked toward him. "Excellent," he purred, tucking my hand around the crook of his arm. He was impeccably dressed, as usual, in a fine suit of a delicate summer weight, crisp white shirt, and cravat in a blue-green that enhanced his eyes. "This way, *mon ange…*" he said, gesturing toward the front of the palazzo, on the canal side.

"Pierre," Will growled. No doubt he'd heard Pierre's romantic name for me in French.

"*Je suis si désolé,*" Pierre said with an apologetic moan, lifting a hand and casting Will a look laced with remorse. "Force of habit," he said, staring down at me in adoration, as if there really could be no other name for me than *my angel*.

Will trailed behind us to the top of the marble stairs that led down to the canal-level *piano*, what the Venetians called each level of a building, right along the water. "You're going outside?" Will said, frustration lacing his tone. "Can you not share a quiet word of farewell in the safety of the palazzo?"

"Nothing to fear, my friend," Pierre said. "I only wish to take a ride on the water with Cora. Unless this Hawke walks on water, he will not get anywhere near us. And if he does…" He patted his jacket pocket, where he carried his pistol.

Will considered him. "See that you have easy access to that," he said at last. "And take Pascal with you. Those are my terms."

"Honestly, Will. Isn't that a bit much?" I asked. I considered it rather embarrassing, thinking of a private conversation in front of Pascal.

"Isn't it a bit much that Hawke dared come close enough for any of us to see him?" Will responded levelly.

I glanced with Pierre over to Pascal, the burly guard who was walking down the stairs behind us. He was so quiet, half the time I forgot he hovered near. And there would be no shaking my silent guardians, not after our kidnapping. And especially now, if Nathan Hawke was indeed lurking in the vicinity.

~Wallace~

Hugh and Felix left out the back door of the palace, most likely to find a place for an afternoon glass of wine and a chance to flirt with the local young women. Wallace bit back a demand for them to stay inside, unnerved by this latest sighting of Nathan Hawke, but he knew it would simply agitate the young gentlemen. Glancing out the window, he comforted himself with the sight of Stephen, a lanky detective, following the boys.

Sam Morgan came up to the window beside him. "They'll be fine, Wallace. We can't keep an eye on them every minute," he said, biting down on an unlit cigar.

Wallace gave him a rueful smile and then turned to sit heavily in a chair in front of the cold, unlit fireplace. "You're right, of course. But if anything happened to any of the children..." He bit his lip and looked over to the wide, empty doorway that led to the hallway.

"Perhaps it's best if you switch tactics with Cora now," Morgan said gently, taking the chair facing him.

Wallace stared hard at his old friend and business partner. Morgan didn't speak to him in such a direct manner often, but Wallace had learned it was wise to pay attention when he did. "Meaning?"

"Meaning," Morgan said carefully, stroking his short beard, "she is perhaps more like you than any of your other children. And the harder you press her, the more she'll press back."

Wallace waved his hand in agitation, encouraging him to go on, even while a good part of him wanted the man to remain quiet.

"She is naive in some ways, and yet wise to the ways of people. She understands what drives them, incites them. And she does not wish to be controlled."

Wallace studied him. "You think I've gone about it wrong. My desire to assert my authority as a father, guide her."

"She sees you more as a threat than a guide. When she did not come willingly, you tried to coerce her, which has only driven her further away."

Wallace sighed heavily and closed his eyes, rubbing them. "So? What do you suggest?"

"Care for the girl. Why not give her her due? She and her parents have worked that land for years. Take forty-nine percent, give them controlling interest. You'll still more than triple your fortune, and she'll have no choice but to see it as the gift it is. She'll have to come to you for advice. It's been some years since Alan Diehl considered such sums. In time, perhaps you can forge the sort of relationship you've sought all along. At *that* point, perhaps you can point her in Pierre's direction rather than William's."

Wallace considered him. "She has no experience. She might make poor decisions, endanger what we are on the brink of claiming."

"She might," Morgan allowed. "Or she might not. As I said, I believe she is more like you than any of the others. She is smart, Wallace. And if you give her free rein, I believe she'll seek you out for guidance before things get too far out of line." He leaned forward. "If you give her and her parents controlling interest, she has more incentive than ever to honor the gift. She'll understand it's work to manage a fortune, not simply an idle task." He sat back again and threw up his hands, the cigar now pinched between two fingers. "Who knows? Perhaps she'll inspire the other children to appreciate what they've been given and step up to some responsibility."

"Perhaps," Wallace allowed. He thought about Vivian, looking so unhappy. The girl needed Andrew to commit and put a ring on her finger at last. And Felix… How Wallace wished the boy would concentrate on his education and claim any part of the Kensington business as Cora appeared to be attempting a claim with the mine. She was acting more a man than his one and only son, who seemed to have nothing on his mind other than finding the next diversion. Lillian? He would soon need to turn his attentions to finding her a proper suitor and getting her settled.

But first…Cora. If he could simply find his way with her, perhaps the others would fall into line. And Morgan was right. There was no way to force Cora closer; she had to come to him on her own accord.

He considered Morgan's thoughts, testing them from one angle and then another. "I'll do it," he said quietly, feeling a little awestruck over such a momentous, instantaneous decision. "Make Cora and the Diehls more rich than they've ever dreamed."

"No strings attached," Morgan pressed.

"Well," Wallace said, cocking his head and steepling his fingers. "Let's just say no strings that are *obvious*. You and I both know that there are always strings. Always."

CHAPTER 2

~Cora~

We walked down the remaining stairs, and I forced my thoughts back to Pierre. For now, right now, on this languid summer afternoon on one of the prettiest waterways in the world, I needed to bid Pierre *adieu* once and for all. I took hold of the gondolier's hand and stepped gingerly into the bottom of the long, thin boat, then sat primly on the red brocade-covered seat in the back. The gondolier helped Pierre in, then Pascal, then offered me a parasol. I'd forgotten mine.

Pierre sat beside me, and I edged a couple of inches away, well aware that although Will had disappeared back inside, he likely watched from the windows. Pascal looked to his right, as if offering us privacy, even though his knees were but a foot away from ours.

"Where to?" asked the gondolier.

"Your normal route," Pierre said with a soft flick of his fingers.

"Pierre," I said, giving him a warning look.

"We won't go far, *mon ange*," he said, leaning back and giving me a catlike smile.

"Pierre."

"What?" He frowned, but there was still laughter in his eyes. "Is not your loyal guard dog right here with us? What could happen?"

I sighed and shook my head a little.

A lot could happen when it came to Pierre de Richelieu.

I saw what he was after when we turned one corner and then the next within the Rialto district, leaving one tiny canal for another. Here, in this passageway, there was no room for another boat to pass. The gondolier must've known that only one direction of traffic was allowed. Between the shadows of the buildings, the air cooled, a nice respite from the heat of the summer afternoon.

I set aside the parasol and swatted away a mosquito, breathing deeply for the first time since Will and I had returned from our afternoon outing. It was quiet, peaceful here on the water. Away from the bustle of the Grand Canal, in among the narrow, residential passageways, with people just now rising from their afternoon naps. Italians favored long, restful afternoons, work into the evening, and late-night suppers spent huddled around dripping candles. It was a natural cadence of life, particularly during the heat of summer, that I longed to adopt.

Pierre had been humming, and I leaned my head against the high back of our shared chair and looked at him, guardedly, not wanting him to mistake tenderness and companionability for second thoughts. Once I had entertained the idea of marrying him. But it had always been a fantasy, some other girl's tale, not my own. Because my heart had always been tied to Will's. But if I hadn't met Will McCabe? Certainly, turning away Pierre de Richelieu would have been the hardest thing I'd ever done. It was already difficult, even with my love firmly settled in my heart. Because Pierre was terribly…*dreamy*, as Lil and Nell often said in a breathy tone that matched the word. Handsome. Clever. Amusing. Refined.

"Is that a folk tune?" I asked.

"What?" he said, turning to me from his reverie.

"What you were humming. Is it a folk tune?"

"Yes, yes," he said, giving me a soft smile. "Something my mother hummed to me as a child." His eyebrows lifted. "I do not even know the words."

"It's lovely."

His eyes moved from me to the third canal we entered. "There. Up ahead," he said to the gondolier. "We'd like to pause for a bit."

"Certainly."

Pascal gave Pierre a long look.

"Don't worry, my friend, don't worry," Pierre said, trying to tamp down my guard's concern. "If Nathan Hawke wishes to get to us here, he'll have to come through you, no?" Pierre smiled at Pascal and then looked over at me. "I don't know whom he fears most— Hawke or me." He laughed under his breath. "He thinks I might try to run off with you," he said, nodding toward Pascal.

"Will you?" I asked with a sardonic smile.

"If you gave me half a hope, I would." He took my hand, and I stiffened. He paused, and his light brows knit together. "Come now, Cora, you've more than made your feelings plain. Trust me, won't you?"

I took a breath, studying his guileless expression. "All right," I said slowly.

The gondolier edged alongside a small gate and called upward. An old man appeared on a small balcony, standing beside a table set for two right above the canal. They shared a word in Italian, and the man invited us up.

I paused. "Pierre, I'm not really hungry." The farther we got from the palazzo, the more I feared that this was a bad idea. A very bad idea. Not because of Hawke. But because of Pierre. This was clearly his last attempt to persuade me to return to him, to turn away from Will.

"Nor am I," he said soberly. "But come. Share one last glass of wine, a last moment with me. That's all I ask." He frowned. "Come now. Can you not give me at least this courtesy?"

I sighed, guilt overcoming my concern, and then took his hand, ambling out of the gondola and onto an old rotting pier slick with green moss. "Careful," Pierre said, even as he slipped a little himself.

Pascal sought my eyes, silently asking me if I was all right. I gave him a firm nod. "We'll only be a little while," I said. Where could we go? I suspected what the men did—that the only way in and out of this tiny building was right here through this waterway entrance.

We moved up stairs so narrow that I wondered if Pierre would have to scrunch or turn sideways to get through. At the top, the ceiling lifted, and we turned left, walking through a cozy kitchen rife with the smells of supper simmering on the stove—heavily laced with garlic and oregano—and out to the small patio, where our host awaited us, proudly gesturing toward the cloth-covered table. He pulled out my chair, then helped me sit down. I glanced over the stone rail to Pascal, and the man visibly relaxed now that we were again within sight. I supposed I couldn't begrudge his tension—our guards had been put through the paces, watching us. But I hoped all that would be soon behind us.

"You eat?" said our host, gesturing toward his mouth as if he was uncertain about the word.

"No, no," Pierre said with a wave of his hand. "It's far too early. *Solo un po' di pane e vino, per favore*," he said. I guessed he'd asked for only wine and bread.

Clearly disgruntled, the man looked to me, as if hoping I'd interrupt and demand a four-course dinner, even though it was only three in the afternoon. Then, hopes dashed, he left for a moment before returning with the bottle of wine and a basket of bread that he practically slammed on the table.

Pierre grinned as he watched the man depart, then he looked over at me. "Perhaps I might have picked a more genteel locale," he said, picking up the bottle and uncorking it. He poured me a glass and then one for himself.

"No," I said softly, looking out over the quiet canal, the water so still that there was hardly a ripple. Our gondolier had settled into our seat for a nap, his broad-brimmed hat tipped over his face, legs perched on the edge, even while Pascal steadily perused the area. "It's actually perfect. A bit of respite after a very busy hour."

"Indeed," Pierre said, leaning forward across the table. He took a breath. "As you might suspect, this parting tears at me in a thousand ways."

"Oh, Pierre, you've given me so much." I impulsively reached for his hand and squeezed it. "I shall never forget you."

"But you are certain that our parting is the right decision for us?" he said, gazing from our entwined hands to my face. A shadow of sorrow in his eyes made me hesitate a moment.

"I am," I said, pulling my hand away. "If we'd met under different circumstances, Pierre, in a different time, a different place…"

"If we'd been different people," he said with a humorless grin.

"No. And yes," I said.

"And if there hadn't been a William McCabe."

"Most of all," I said quietly, "if there hadn't been him, too."

He gave me a lopsided grin, covering me with a tender gaze. "I never did have a chance against him. Who would have thought it? A pauper beating me."

I stiffened a little. "He's far more than the amount he has in his bank account."

Pierre nodded and took a sip of his wine, savoring it a moment before swallowing. He lifted his glass, as if toasting me. "And there it is again—why I am so madly in love with you, Cora Diehl Kensington."

My mouth was suddenly dry, and it was my turn to take a sip. Never had he come out and said it. So matter-of-factly. Without flirtation. "Pierre, I—"

He lifted his hand to shush me. "Never have I met a woman who was not first taken in by a man's bank account, or at least swayed by it. I want to win a woman like you. A woman who will see *me* for more than what I have."

"You deserve such a woman."

He took another sip and studied me, swirling the wine idly around his glass. "Tell me. Is there not some small part of you that believes you're that woman?"

"Pierre…"

"Truthfully," he said, giving his head a small shake, "with no worry about my feelings. Tell me that I hold not one part of your heart—not one tiny part—and I will leave and never bother you again. You can rest assured I will continue my business deal with Montana Copper so that your father cannot hold it over your head."

My eyes met his, quickly.

"Oh, yes. I understand that your father can be quite ruthless. But my dearest desire is for you to come to me, Cora, on *your* terms. Not as a dutiful daughter with an eye toward business holdings."

He reached across the table and took my hand again, lightly, in his. Something in his face, his demeanor, made me allow it.

"Pierre, I've told you. You honor me by your attentions, your pursuit. But my heart belongs to Will McCabe."

"Understood. But you didn't answer me," he said, staring into my eyes. He covered my hand with his other one, again carefully, as if afraid I'd shy away. "I need to know that I have no chance whatsoever. That *I* don't hold any portion of your heart, no matter how small."

I paused, considering. Looked across the narrow canal to the neighboring building, where I saw drapes moving back into place, as if somebody had just been there, then disappeared. I shoved away the paranoid thought of Nathan Hawke following us here, somehow. It was impossible. It was only a nosy neighbor… I focused again on Pierre. How was I to answer his question in all honesty—without giving him undue hope?

"You pause," he said, his voice little more than a whisper. "There is a chance for me."

"No," I said, finally pulling my hand from his and firmly placing it in my lap. I shook my head slowly. "It is Will who holds my heart, Pierre. I'm sorry. I paused because I care for you. I do. But it is Will that I love."

He studied me, grief lacing his eyes. "I will honor your choice. But, *mon ange*…Cora. I must come to see you in Roma, before you leave for America again. I need to know then that nothing has changed and you are certain that—"

"No. Don't come. I *am* certain, Pierre."

"But does Will have it within him to withstand the pressures of your father? Of society? With your newfound wealth?"

"My father still holds the purse strings. Unless he relents, or my attorney is successful in his suit—"

"He will relent," Pierre said. "Wallace Kensington is a gambler. He simply prefers to hold all the cards. You've dealt him a new hand he doesn't care for. But more than anything, Cora, he wants you. To know you, and you, him. As a father knows a daughter."

I sighed. *If only I were so certain of his intentions.* "I had all the father I ever needed. *Have*," I belatedly amended, wondering how Papa was faring this day in Minnesota. How Mama was…

"Do you?" He sat back and twisted the stem of his goblet in his fingers in a slow circle. "In some ways, you seem to me a fine woman, grown. In others, but a girl. A girl in need of a father such as Wallace Kensington, particularly as you negotiate the ways of society. As well as the press…"

I frowned. "Will and I shall address those pressures. Together."

"Is that what you want? From a man? How much of your inheritance will go to pay off his debts?"

"His uncle's debts. Not his."

"How much for his remaining education?"

"It matters not. Nor is it any of your concern."

"Perhaps not to you. But it *does* matter," he pressed. "A man does not favor being kept."

I shook my head, my agitation rising. What he implied…that if I did come into wealth, that Will would somehow resent it… "We shall see it through. We're strong, Will and I."

"Strong," he said, nodding and taking a slow sip of his wine. "For now. But I will come to Roma and call on you. Just to make certain that Will, or you, have not had a change of heart. Before a ship carries you across the sea again, I must know. I *must* know, *mon ange*," he said, leaning forward, his eyes filled with passion and concern.

I shook my head, unable to stop my frustration. "You will not be welcome, Pierre."

"No?"

"No."

"But Cora…you did not say it. You could not promise me that I did not still hold a tiny corner of your heart."

I stared at him. "You do not hold a piece of my heart, Pierre." Suddenly I wanted to hurt him, to wipe out his smug, knowing tone. I was so tired, so very tired of men in my life thinking they knew more than I did about myself.

He leaned back in his chair, his hand lifting to his chest. He stared at me. "That, Cora, wounds me. That you would lie to me."

I stared at him again, really angry now. "I…you…" But as I gathered my words, I knew I couldn't lie again. He was right. While

Will had my heart, while everything in me knew I belonged with him, there was still a tiny piece of me that acknowledged that if Will wasn't in my life…if things were different…

It'd be impossible to summarily send Pierre de Richelieu away. Forever.

And then the doubts he'd planted in my head crowded in. Were the obstacles for Will and me too fierce to get beyond?

I pushed back my chair and rose, nearly upsetting the tiny table between us. "I'd like to return to the palazzo now."

Pierre rose too. "As you wish, *mon ange*."

"Stop. Stop calling me that," I said, turning to him and laying a hand on his chest.

He looked down at my hand splayed across his chest, then back to my face as I tried to jerk away. But he caught my hand and placed it where it'd been, covering it with his own. "Ah, yes," he said lowly. "You feel my heart. It beats for you alone. Can you honestly leave Italy forever without thinking twice about what I feel for you? And you for me, regardless of what you claim? Is there not a part of you, especially now, now that you've become a woman of means? A woman all the more suited to be with a man of means?"

Feeling the blush heat my face, I pulled away from him and hurried down the stairs, rushing so that I nearly slipped again on the dark-green muck coating the canal walk surface.

Because he was right. Pierre de Richelieu had managed to pinpoint every small chink in my armor, all the things that both drew me to him as well as the things that repelled me.

CHAPTER 3

~Cora~

We returned to the palazzo in silence. Will was waiting for us out beside the pier. He straightened as we came into view, and his look grew stern as he noticed my stiff demeanor and refusal to look Pierre's way. As soon as we pulled up alongside the pier, I was rising, taking Pascal's hand instead of Pierre's, and then Will's. I bustled in, and Will was right on my heels.

"Cora, what happened?" he said, grabbing my elbow and trying to pull me to a stop.

"Please, Will, I don't care to discuss it. I have a dreadful headache. After I rest, we can chat."

"Did he—"

"Will! Please!" I said, rushing up the stairs. He let me go then, giving me the space my soul was crying for.

I approached Hugh Morgan in the hallway, and he paused, waiting for me to pass. Curiosity loomed large in his eyes, and I could see him working to find the right words, seeing my agitation.

"Not now, Hugh…" I said, holding up a hand. I scurried down the remainder of the hall and slipped into my bedroom, narrowly avoiding slamming the door behind me.

I leaned my forehead against it, panting, wanting out of my hot, confining gown and corset…and using every ounce of my strength to keep from screaming that if I didn't ever see another man in my life, that would be fine by me…

~William~

"What happened?" Will said lowly, grabbing Pierre's arm as he walked by. Both of them looked up at Cora's fleeing form, then back at each other.

Pierre pulled his arm away, straightening his jacket and then his cravat as he stared back at Will. "Rest assured, nothing untoward. I am leaving, William," he said with a slight bow. "Getting out of your way. But I shall come to Roma before you depart to make certain that you and Miss Kensington have not parted ways."

"What?" Will frowned. "Nothing shall divide us."

"You say that now. But the pressures upon you are many. And if either of you find them insurmountable…"

"There is nothing we cannot conquer. Do not bother returning, Richelieu. She is mine."

"You say that easily. But if Cora successfully wins her suit for a portion of the mine…" He squinted at Will and rubbed the back of his neck. "I've not seen a kept man who is a content man. Nor have I seen a woman who has become accustomed to much learn contentment with less."

Will stilled. A kept man? The thought had crossed his mind more than once. But each time he'd banished it. "Cora's wealth—or the loss of it—cannot sway our affections for each other."

"Perhaps," Pierre said doubtfully.

"We will rise above it."

"I hope so," Pierre said. "Truly, I do. Because, McCabe, she loves you."

His words gave Will pause. Studying the shorter, handsome man, he marveled that Cora had chosen him over Pierre at all. Pierre had it all—looks, wealth, and position. Her father would honor such a match. On Pierre's arm, she would want for nothing, regardless of what transpired in Dunnigan. And yet Will didn't have it in him to let her go. Not now. Not when they were so close.

"So...why rejoin us in Rome?"

"Because there is a tiny corner of her heart that is still mine." Pierre lifted a hand as Will began to bluster a response. "No, no. The lion's share of her heart is yours." He crossed his arms and studied Will. "But should the forces of our world—be they Wallace Kensington, the pressures of her potential wealth, whatever it might be—drive you two apart, rest assured that I will be there to convince her that that corner of her heart, in time, could grow to encompass it all."

Will paused for a breath, then two, never dropping his gaze. "I will give you no quarter."

"See that you don't, my friend," Pierre said, stepping past him and laying a hand on his shoulder. "See that you don't."

And with that he left, gliding over to his footman, who awaited him beside his luggage, and then out the door to the gondola.

~Cora~

I watched Pierre leave. He sat languidly against the red velvet cushions that we had so recently shared. He did not look up to my room or back to our palazzo, only stared at the water beside him as if lost in his own thoughts. My breathing returned to normal the farther away he got. *Is that You, Lord?* I prayed silently. *The reassurance is welcome. This is surely where I belong, with Will. Thank You. But now what, Lord? What to do about my father? My family? And the Dunnigan mine?*

Over and around my thoughts spun as I wondered what was right, what was wrong. I knew that Wallace Kensington could buy whomever he wished. How long until he found his way past my meager, temporary defenses, my weak claim that I could sue for my portion of the Dunnigan mine? Particularly once I was home in Montana? Wallace Kensington owned every judge of consequence. He'd allowed me this respite, this audacious claim, as an indulgent papa would, eager to see how far a toddler would go when given free rein. And yet if I didn't fight it, if I lost the Dunnigan inheritance, it wasn't just me who would lose…my parents would lose too. After all they'd put into that land, the thought was impossible to swallow. They deserved that money. I had to find a way to be certain they got their stake in it, regardless of what happened to mine.

How was I to make sense of it? Rise above the surface and see which direction I was to swim? I felt overwhelmingly weary. So weary from the constant travel and change.

I drifted off to sleep, my dreams filled with visits with Papa, his eyes sad and heavy with worry. Each time I awoke, I could barely open my eyes, and dimly I recognized Anna slipping in and out of my room, the summer sun setting over the city. Eventually, the stillness and quiet of the Grand Canal at night fell across me. Wearily, I made myself sit up. I swung my legs over the side of the bed and stared at the flickering light of an oil lamp outside until I was fully awake.

Then I dropped to the floor and went to the French door that led to the small portico and exited outward. The humid air, heavy with the smells of salt and fish and smoke, entered my nostrils. But I breathed it in with a glad heart, happy to be free of my room and the thoughts that crowded my mind. I set my hands on the cold stone rail and bowed my head, listening to the faint sounds of laughter drifting out a window on the other side of the canal. Someone was having a party; figures in fine clothing slid past the windows, hands holding champagne glasses.

A man cleared his throat. I looked up in alarm, then relaxed when I saw that it was Antonio sitting in a chair at the far end of the portico. I'd forgotten that the men had taken to positioning one guard here, along the exposed access to our rooms, be it day or night.

I gave him a small smile and eased in his direction.

"Feeling better, Miss?" he asked, rising and lifting a bushy black brow.

"I suppose so," I said, giving him a rueful smile. "My afternoon nap very nearly turned into an all-night sleep."

"You've endured a great deal of late. It's bound to make a body weary."

I smiled and looked outward, watching as lamps reflected in waving ribbons across the water. Once, I would've considered the things I'd endured on this tour trifles compared to the day-to-day trials of the farm. And yet I was exhausted, emotionally spent from the unique challenges of this trip. Was it ever proper to dismiss one life's difficulties as less of a hardship than another's?

I lifted a hand to my temple and massaged it. How was I ever to marry my old life to my new one? Who was I anymore? More Kensington than Diehl? Was it even possible for me to return to my old life, my old thoughts, given all that I'd experienced? This trip had molded me, changed me, strengthened me as well as weakened me...

I didn't want to return to my folks with anything but strength, gain. I wanted my mother to see that she'd been right to send me off with Wallace Kensington, that the struggle and pain had been worthwhile. But if I were to do that, I had to decide, once and for all, just where Wallace Kensington and I stood.

The door slammed on the level below us, so hard I wondered if the glass in the panels had cracked. Antonio and I shared a look. I could hear a woman weeping, but then the door opened again, quietly, and we heard a man speak right below us.

"Honestly, Vivian, have we not gone too far to turn back?"

My eyes narrowed. It was Andrew Morgan, my sister's intended. What was he doing in her quarters? I slipped my hands from the rail and stepped back, but I didn't leave. I looked to Antonio, who gestured toward the door, reminding me of what was proper.

"Is that what you call a proposal? What I've waited so long for?" she cried. I froze, then made myself turn the knob, knowing I shouldn't eavesdrop.

"Listen to me. *Listen to me.* Was it Nell or Cora who put these romantic expectations into your head?"

I paused again at the sound of my name.

"None that weren't there before! None that you didn't make me yearn for, once. But now? Honestly, Andrew—why do we even bother with the charade? If this is all there is between us, let's go to a judge, sign the papers, and begin our business arrangement in earnest. For that's what it is, isn't it? A business arrangement? Not a marriage?"

"You're acting most unsuitable, Vivian."

"Am I? Let go of me!"

I looked at my guard in alarm. Antonio glowered and pulled the door fully open as if he intended to rush downstairs and intervene. But I reached out and took hold of his arm. "Vivian?" I called out, turning and leaning over the railing, as if I'd heard just enough to wonder but not enough to be alarmed. "Is that you?"

They stilled below us.

"Yes," she called up a second later. "It's me, Cora. Forgive me for disturbing you."

"Oh, you didn't," I said. "I just thought I heard something. Are you all right?"

"Fine, fine," she said, each word laced with weariness.

"Are you alone? I thought I heard—"

"Yes," she said. I could hear the iciness in her tone gaining strength. "Andrew was just leaving. We've come to an understanding. We've decided to end our courtship."

Antonio and I held our breath and stared at each other. A few seconds later, the door below opened and then slammed shut.

This time, the sound of shattering glass was unmistakable.

CHAPTER 4

~Cora~

Antonio and I raced downstairs and could hear Vivian and Andrew yelling even before we reached her room. Will was at Vivian's door, beside Pascal, knocking and shouting, demanding they open up. Father hurried toward us, gray brows low over his eyes, one hand perched in a vest pocket.

We heard Viv cry out and Andrew shout—a thump against a wall, then another. Will and Pascal shared a quick look, then both took a step back and hit the door with their shoulders as one, cracking the doorjamb and lock off and leaving it open by a few inches. Will pulled back and kicked the door open.

Vivian was standing in Andrew's arms over by two chairs, her face wet with tears, and both looked at us in alarm.

"McCabe!" Andrew said, turning to face him, as if protecting Vivian. But I knew better. He didn't want us to see any more of her tear-stained face. "What on earth do you think you are doing?"

"We heard Vivian's cry," Will said, striding right over to him. "And you didn't respond to our summons at the door!" He tried to move around Andrew, but Andrew lifted an arm to block him. Will took hold of his jacket lapels and wrenched him away from Vivian. We could all see the dark fingerprints on her bare arms beneath her tidy capped sleeves.

Will let out a bellow of anger as he rammed Andrew against the wall. Andrew pushed back, but Will shoved him against the wall again, so hard that bits of plaster fell over the dark fabric of Andrew's jacket above his shoulder.

Vivian yelled, "No, no!" even as I moved to intercede.

We stood on either side of them, tugging at the men to get them to see their surroundings, anything other than the other one each sought to harm, but it was as if we were trying to pry magnetic plates apart.

"Enough!" my father bellowed.

Vivian looked over her shoulder and hurriedly wiped her eyes. "Father," she said, "it's all been a terrible misunderstanding."

I looked at her in wide-eyed frustration as Nell and Lil reached the doorway and entered, Felix and Hugh right behind them. "Wh-what do you mean, a misunderstanding?" I sputtered. "Viv, it's all right. It's perfectly acceptable to tell the truth. You don't need to pretend any—"

"Hush," my father said.

"But even you can surely see—" I began.

"Everyone simply *hush* before any more damage is done," he said, glowering at me and then up at the much taller young men. "Gentlemen, take a step apart. Now."

Andrew and Will took a last long, challenging look at each other, then dropped their hands and straightened their shirts and coats, never relinquishing their gazes.

My father looked at Vivian. "I take it this was a lover's quarrel? Nothing you two can't patch up?"

I sucked in my breath, finding it difficult to believe. Did he truly intend to ignore what was clearly so wrong between Andrew and Vivian? To what end? Simply because the patriarchs always thought the two of them would marry, unite the families? For appearances?

Vivian still stared at our father, and I could see her soften, give in.

"Viv," I began, hoping to encourage her to do what was right. What was in her heart and—

"No, Cora," she said, pulling her shoulders back and wiping her nose with a handkerchief. She gave her head a little shake and forced a smile. "It's as Father says. A lover's quarrel gotten out of hand. I'm terribly sorry, everyone," she said, looking around. "This is most humiliating. I've made such an awful mess, breaking all those panes of glass…" She took Andrew's arm, and he stiffened as if he loathed her touch…but he seemed as trapped as she in playing the expected part in the familial drama.

"Come, let us leave them to patch things up," my father said, lifting his hands and shooing us all from the room. Numbly, I turned and walked out to the hallway, waiting for him. But my father didn't look at me as he turned toward the stairs, probably intent on going to the salon and fetching himself a drink. I glanced toward Antonio, wondering if I had imagined what I'd heard, but all he did was give me a tiny rueful shrug.

There was only one man who could put a stop to this charade, this madness. I turned and hurried after my father, ignoring Lil's whispered warning to leave him be, that he wasn't in any mood for further discourse.

He was turning into the salon when I reached the bottom of the stairs, and I rushed in after him, pausing at the doorway to see him unstop a crystal decanter and pour a small glass half full. He took a sip, staring out a window that looked over a tiny garden.

"She doesn't love him, you know," I said quietly, walking toward him. He didn't startle. He'd known I was there, or expected me.

"She loves him enough. She's always loved him."

"Not as she ought a husband. Nor *should* she. He's a brute."

That brought him partially around. "Stay out of this, Cora. It is not your affair."

"Father, Will and Pascal had to break down the door. And did you see the bruises on her arms?"

He blew out a quick breath and turned back to the window, taking another sip, holding it in his mouth a moment before swallowing. "Andrew Morgan is…passionate. Spirited. He feels things… intensely. Always has. Even as a little boy. I can remember his face, beet red, furious because another child had gotten a finer toy top than he had received that very day from the mercantile."

He seemed amused by this memory. I looked around the room, wondering where Mr. Morgan was. I wished he were here. Perhaps if he'd been here, seen what transpired, he might've taken my side on this. Or at least seen the need for a private word with Andrew. I sighed and gathered myself. This was up to me.

"Has it ever occurred to you that Andrew is angry because he feels forced into this marriage?" I asked quietly. "I truly believe they care for each other. But over the course of this tour, Andrew has become more the dutiful beau than any sort of man in love." I knew I was right. The differences between Will and Andrew were marked.

My father leaned against the desk and stared at me mutely for a moment, looking confused at such a thought, then angry. "Any man would consider himself beyond fortunate to marry *any* of my daughters," he said. He lifted his glass in a gesture of dismissal. As if that said it all.

I swallowed hard, my mouth suddenly dry. Because he was clearly including me in that grouping. But was he also thinking of Will? Or Pierre, still?

I tried a different tack, stepping forward to stand beside him and then leaning against the desk too. The cavernous salon, crowned with a massive crystal chandelier and bedecked with luxurious furniture covered in tufted silk, stretched before us. I tried to gather my thoughts into one cogent argument.

"Granted, Andrew would be blessed to marry Vivian," I said. "But wouldn't they both be blessed to marry someone they love, someone God brought into their lives, who is uniquely right for them? Not simply the best choice from a business standpoint?"

My father was still for several moments. "Do you speak of Vivian and Andrew? Or yourself and Richelieu?"

I looked at him, beside me. He seemed older, more weary. Smaller, somehow. "Vivian and Andrew," I said.

My father took another long sip of his whiskey and crossed his feet at the ankles. "Cora, my dear, there is much you do not yet know, no matter how wise you believe yourself to be. Love, passion, those things fade in time. What remains is family. Honor. Loyalty."

I banished thoughts of him sending my mother away, heavy with child. Of him choosing "honor" by hiding us away. Pawning us off to another man, who thankfully became my papa and my mother's husband. "Is it not possible to have it all?" I asked softly. "Passionate loyalty? Honorable love?"

He blew out a scoffing breath. "Rarely." He took a sip and considered me, gesturing to me with his glass. "With their combined fortunes, Andrew and Vivian will never want for a thing. That is the most I can hope for my children."

Exasperation filled me, yet I dared not let it show. He was listening to me even if he didn't yet hear me; I didn't want to endanger that. "I disagree. There is so much more for a couple to aspire to… And don't you see? With *one* of their fortunes, they would not want for a thing." I shook my head and shoved off the desk, pacing. "And sometimes, *sometimes*, wanting things, wishing for, working for them, is a good thing. Otherwise, we become nothing but spoiled boys and girls frustrated that we don't get every new toy we see."

He was quiet for a breath, then two. "Leave me now, Cora," he said, taking the last long sip from his glass. "It is enough for today. Is it not?" He turned his dark blue eyes on me, and I stared back at him. Then I nodded and shoved away from the desk and moved out of the room, feeling his gaze on my back with every step.

~William~

Resting on the edge of a vast chair, elbows on his knees, face in his hands, Will waited for Cora to finish talking to her father. When she turned the corner and spied him, her whole demeanor seemed to lift. She slowed her pace. He rose and went to her, took her hands, then turned to lead her down the hall. "So?" he whispered, glancing back at the empty hall to the salon, then to her again. "Any luck in getting him to see what needs to be done about Andrew and Vivian?"

Cora shook her head and grimaced. "Perhaps a little. I fear I overstepped my bounds." She squeezed his arm and gave him a pained smile. "Sooner or later my father may well rue the day he ever brought me into the fold."

"I doubt that." They walked a bit in silence. "Perhaps that's what Vivian and Andrew are supposed to discover on this journey—how disastrous a union theirs would be. Nothing like the tour to show people how poorly they fit together."

"Or how well they do," she said, smiling up at him.

He grinned at her and led her to two matching chairs tucked together in an alcove, a tiny table between them. He gestured to one and she took it, and he the other. "Cora, before we leave Venezia," he said, reaching out to take her hand in his, "I must know. Forgive me, but I must know."

"What?"

"What transpired between you and Pierre?" He shook his head, frustrated with himself. "I mean, I needn't know all that was said. Just this: can you truly choose me over him without looking back? There are many battles ahead for me…*us*," he amended, "if you are on my arm. Life with Pierre…it'd be far easier for you, in some ways."

She leaned forward and covered his hand with hers. Her small fingers seemed to ignite his every cell, and he had to bodily resist the urge to lift her to her feet, to hold her, to kiss her. He concentrated on her beautiful blue eyes instead, willing her to say the words he longed to hear.

"Will, it is you I love. You. I don't care what we must face to be together. But we shall do it together. What we have is something so much more *true* than what Vivian and Andrew have," she said, dropping her tone and eyeing the empty hallway. "What we have is a gift from God Himself. I'm convinced it is right. Aren't you?"

He hated the glimpse of concern he saw in her eyes, and he shook his head vehemently, hoping to send her fear scurrying. "Oh, yes. Cora, I adore you. You've honored me far more than I could ever imagine, choosing me…" He glanced away, embarrassed by the sudden lump in his throat. He swallowed hard and then looked back to her. "I aim to do all I can to be worthy of that choice. But Cora, you know you have my heart. Everything I have and am is yours to do with what you wish. I only ask one thing."

"And that is?"

"If you ever have second thoughts. If you ever wonder—"

"I won't," she said, shaking her head.

"But if you do, I ask you…Cora, it's important to me that I not be the last one to find out. That I not become the goat in this group instead of the bear. Please. Come to me first if you have any desire to end our courtship. I'll try to win you back, of course," he said with a smile. "But it's important to me. That we be forthright. Honest with each other. Always and forever."

She laughed then, holding his hands. "Oh, Will. We've barely begun our courtship, and now you think we must work out the rules for ending it? Can we not simply move forward together, trusting the One that brought us together? Trusting each other?"

"Yes, of course," he said, wondering why it was so important to him that he'd nearly botched things before they'd truly begun.

She squeezed his hands. "I'm with you and for you, William McCabe. You are the one that has my heart."

He smiled at her and kissed her then. But try as he might, he could not still the small, stubborn voice in his mind telling him he might hold her for now, but he would never keep her.

CHAPTER 5

~Cora~

We left Venice in the wee hours of the following morning, riding in several long skiffs powered by steam engines, their quiet *tutt-tutt-tutt* sounds the only noise on the canal as we slid by the curving line of palazzos, boats, and gondolas tied for the night against their tall spiral-painted poles, as they had been for centuries. We were bleary-eyed as we silently said good-bye to the magical city, but I felt my pulse quicken at the thought of leaving Nathan Hawke behind forever. It made me smile, thinking of him awaking to find our palazzo empty, to discover that the servants knew only that we'd left for Firenze in the dark watches of the night.

As we'd explicitly told them.

There'd be no reason for Hawke to doubt their story, even if he might wonder at our secretive middle-of-the-night exit. A traditional Grand Tour route would normally track through Florence and Rome, but we were now on our own reimagined tour. We'd do as Will had outlined, staying outside of the cities and slipping carefully in and out, all the while watching for our potential nemesis and hopefully evading him all the way to Rome. In the spirit of staying out of the limelight, we made our way not to a grand hotel or palazzo but to a tidy two-story villa situated on a hilltop outside of Turin and owned by an older couple that Antonio knew.

They took one look at us and ushered us in as graciously and warmly as if we were penniless orphans, a thought that amused me, what with all our servants and our mountains of luggage piled on their doorstep that morning. We were exhausted from our sleepless night, so we decided to rest for the day in our spartan but clean rooms, not even venturing out to sup. Instead, we forced down bread and cheese and grapes, sitting about in silence. I was so weary I felt ill, as if my very bones were brittle and under threat of shattering if I taxed them too much. We retired before dark and rose late the next morning. It was only then that I started to feel the spark of life in my soul again.

Hope. It made me think of what I'd heard in the basilica in Venice. *Wait and trust. I remember, Lord. But for how long?*

I entered the small dining room and saw that my father, Mr. Morgan, Will, and two other men were sitting at the table. As usual, none of the other younger people were up yet. I paused, not wishing to interrupt but curious about what they were discussing, when my father caught sight of me and waved me in. "Cora," he said. "Please, come and join us."

"Are you certain?" I said, hovering in the doorway, my eyes moving to Will's. He had an odd expression on his face, as if he was stunned, confused. "I can simply take a cup of coffee in my room," I said weakly, now wanting to dodge what was to come, more than ever. If it unnerved Will—

"No, no. This pertains to you. Please. Join us," my father said, pulling out an empty chair.

The other men were rising, and I saw that there were stacks of paper on the table. My father introduced me to the men, an attorney and a banker from Turin. Each shook my hand, bowing and smiling. Clearly, neither of them spoke English. Perhaps that was why Will was there, to translate. I couldn't imagine another reason why my father would invite him into one of his meetings. But I was glad he was here since my father's words—"this pertains to you"—had set my heart to pounding.

I sat down, and a maid poured a cup of coffee and placed a basket of rolls in front of me. Distantly, I knew they smelled heavenly, just pulled from an oven, but my stomach roiled. I forced myself to pretend to take a sip of coffee, to appear calm, regardless of what I felt inside.

"I arranged for these men to meet us here, Cora," my father said, picking up his own white cup, steam dancing before his face. "They have drawn up papers to formally bequeath you and the Diehls controlling interest in the Dunnigan mine. Sign those papers, and you will be the wealthiest woman in America."

I stared at him a moment and then set down my cup, grimacing as I allowed it to clatter. But there was nothing for it; my hands were shaking. I glanced at Will, saw his nearly imperceptible nod and raise of eyebrows as if to assure me that this was on the up-and-up. Then I looked back to my father. "So…truly? No more arguments? No more games? You simply intend to *give* us the mine?"

"Well, fifty-one percent," he said, staring back at me. "I'll keep the other forty-nine."

"Wh-why?" I stammered. "Why now? After all…"

He shrugged lightly and took a sip of his coffee at last. "You wanted it on your terms. And I decided you were right. It had been Alan's land for all those years. It was the least I could do for them. For you. To honor how they raised you." He settled his cup in his saucer, his hand rock steady in comparison to mine. "And it sets you up properly as a Kensington."

So there it was at last. I stared at him, and he stared back. To accept this offer as a Diehl, on behalf of my parents, I had to accept my position as a Kensington, too. What did that mean?

I looked to Will with a question in my eyes.

"How can you say no?" he asked quietly. "He's offering you what you wanted—your share of a fortune. A *controlling interest* in a fortune. You're not only wealthy in your own right, Cora. You're in charge of that wealth."

I had to remind myself to breathe. I'd considered it but thought the opportunity was a long way off. Thought I'd have to battle my father for every cent, every portion. And now here he was, freely offering it to me. My eyes narrowed as I looked back to him. Wallace Kensington never offered anything freely. "You understand I don't know the first thing about running a mine."

"Yes. I will assist you if you wish, when you wish. But ownership involves steep responsibilities. Labor. Finances. Strategic, wise decisions. All of which I believe you can manage in time, with training. After all, you were first in your class in mathematics, science, history. In high school as well as Normal School, passing up every one of your male competitors."

I started, and then my eyes narrowed. How did he know that?

He smiled, catlike. "Ah, yes, it's long been clear to me that you have intellect that would be wasted in some country school on the plains of Montana. It simply took me some time to realize that my independent, smart daughter might very well run the Dunnigan enterprise better than I might myself." He shook his head, his eyes partially cold calculation and partially warm with admiration. "And it is not only book sense you have, daughter. You have people sense. It was you who helped me and Morgan evade the potential strike in Billings." He tilted his head. "That would've cost us thousands. Instead, all your predictions came true. With a small investment, our miners are more content than ever. We have no shortage of workers, and in turn, they have upped production, to the benefit of our bottom line."

"How much?" I asked evenly.

He shrugged one shoulder even as he smiled over my question. "See there? That's a businessman's response. And to answer, eighteen or nineteen percent. A sound investment. An investment I can track directly back to *you*."

I stared at him.

He huffed a laugh. "Why do you hesitate? Is this not exactly what you wanted?"

"I wanted a portion of the profits. I never anticipated…never thought…" I gathered myself and lifted my chin. "I never once thought you'd consider giving over charge of the entire *mine*."

"You were born on that soil. Your folks raised you right, there. And I shall teach you what you need to know to run the mine."

"I'm hardly a prospector," I said, lifting one brow.

"Aren't you? You ventured here with us. A bit of a gambler in you, I suspect."

"Not that I had much of a choice."

"Do you regret it?" His eyes slid to Will and back.

I studied him. He knew what I'd meant. But he was right. Even after our rough start, would I have honestly returned to a summer on the ranch as opposed to what I'd experienced, what I'd gained, the people I'd come to know? It was my turn to eye Will. He met my gaze with concern, clearly wrestling with the decision as I was. The banker and attorney simply watched us banter back and forth, waiting for Will to translate anything they needed to know.

Wallace Kensington rose and leaned over the table toward me. "Cora, it is uncommon for a woman to be in such a position. But you are a Kensington. I know you have what will be required. Or I shall help you discover it within you."

So there, at last, was what bothered me. He knew I'd have to turn to him in order to learn how to manage such a business. "I am a Diehl, too," I said, trying to buy time to think.

"That is why the Dunnigan mine will be known as the Kensington-Diehl Mine," he said, sliding a stack of papers in my direction. I looked down to the first page, and in the midst of all the verbiage, our names jumped out in capital letters: CORA DIEHL KENSINGTON, ALAN AND ALMA DIEHL.

I looked to Will, and he said, "Cora, how can you say no? You will find your way." He waved at my father and me.

"So that's it? The papers are all here?" I asked.

"They are," my father said, sliding the rest of the papers from his side of the table to mine. "They're in Italian, for expedience, and will be translated into English once we return. I'll leave you with Will, who can translate for you, and you may ask any question that arises as you go through the documents with these fine gentlemen. Summon me when you are ready to discuss it."

He turned to leave.

"Father," I called. He slowly turned around, waiting on me. "There is one other stipulation."

He paused. "Stipulation?" he asked, enunciating each syllable.

"I want you to forgive all of the McCabe debts." I said it quickly, before I lost my nerve, knowing I was pressing my luck.

"Cora, I—" Will sputtered.

"No," I said, continuing to speak to him even as I turned toward my father. "He has been using that to keep us apart. If he's honest in this endeavor to move forward in a spirit of reconciliation, it shall be no skin off his nose to release you from what was never your burden to bear in the first place." I took a breath, knowing I was pushing into dangerous territory. "Do it as an act of good faith, Father. If you are truly to treat me as a partner, don't sour that relationship by holding the man I love over a fire he can't hope to escape. It was Stuart's debt, not his. You lost in that gamble."

"Cora, I—" Will tried to interrupt.

But I was emboldened, feeling the power unfold within me. This was the right thing to do. The honorable thing to do. And I would see it done. "Please. Release Will from his bonds, Father. And honor what you agreed to pay him, if he completes his task as the bear of this tour. Despite what you think about our relationship, he has served our group well in leading us."

My father's eyes narrowed, and he sniffed, then readjusted his hands over the glass knob of his cane. I reminded myself to breathe. I couldn't portray every confidence in my entreaty if I fainted dead away.

"Very well," he said at last. "But anything of Stuart McCabe's of value, including his apartment, goes against the debt," he said to Will, drawing himself up straighter. "Men may accuse me of generosity, but never of stupidity."

"That's fair," Will breathed.

With that, my father turned on his heel and left the room. The banker and lawyer looked from his departing back to us, waiting expectantly.

"*Un momento*," Will said to them, holding up a finger and turning toward me with shock and wonder.

I looked up at him in delight, wondering if this day could possibly become any more miraculous. He gazed down at me, his expression a confusing mix of glee and consternation. "Oh, Cora. Did you just manage to do what I believe you have?"

"I hope so," I said with a nod, taking his hands in mine and squeezing.

He lifted my hands to his lips, his eyes shifting back and forth, his mind still working, then shook his head in awe and then reluctantly let go of one of my hands to lift the pages of the agreement. "I've glanced through them already. I'll translate every word for you so you can judge for yourself. But if you sign those, what your father said was true. You are about to become the wealthiest woman in America."

CHAPTER 6

~Wallace~

"It is outrageous," Andrew thundered in the library, pacing before the cold fireplace. "You've given a girl—a girl that knows not the first thing about business—control of the Dunnigan mine? Are you mad?"

"Watch your words, Andrew," Morgan said.

But Andrew ignored his father, swearing under his breath and shaking his head. "I have an MBA from *Harvard*," he spat out. "All these years, you two have bred me to believe that if I sowed the right seeds, married the right girl," he said meaningfully, "the combined family fortunes would be managed by me." He hooked a thumb to his chest and leaned slightly toward Wallace.

"Back away, lad, before you do something you regret," Wallace said, warily eyeing the young man.

"Indeed!" Morgan seconded. "You are behaving most abominably, Andrew! I insist you remember your place."

Andrew ripped his gaze to the right, still shaking his head, pacing a few steps and then turning back to the patriarchs, the veins

in his neck pulsing in fury. "My *place* is head of the Kensington &
Morgan Enterprises."

Wallace frowned. "Perhaps you've misunderstood. Nothing has
changed in that regard, Andrew. There is more than enough there for
you to handle, in time."

"But you have placed me in a subservient position to that…that
girl out there," Andrew said, pointing a shaking finger to the doorway. "A girl who knows nothing about the work that is ahead of her."

"That girl is my daughter," Wallace said, steeling his tone. "And
I shall not leave her side when it comes to running the mine until
I'm confident she can run it as well as any man. Now you must do
as your father encouraged, Andrew. Remember your place. You've
already said too much."

Andrew drew a long, shaky breath and stared at Wallace. "Forgive
me, Mr. Kensington. But you must know I become impassioned
because it is not only for me and my family that I feel the weight of
these issues, but also because I hope to provide well for Vivian when
we become man and wife. I cannot help but feel that you have taken
bread from her cupboard and placed it in Cora's."

"Andrew—" Morgan began.

"No! Absolutely not!" Wallace said, striding over to Andrew and
looking up at him. He jabbed at him, almost touching his chest. "The
Kensington-Diehl Mine has absolutely *nothing* to do with my other
children. The only reason I discovered gold and copper in Dunnigan
was *because* Cora was there. Had she not…well, we wouldn't even be
having this conversation. So I advise you to quit pouting over what you
don't have and instead be grateful for the significant sum that it will add
to the Kensington fortune and possibly, in the future, your own."

"Surely you see that I could manage the mine with ease," Andrew said, a slight whine creeping into his tone. "There wouldn't be much to learn at all."

Wallace drew himself upward, resting his hands on the end of his glass-knobbed cane. "I have made my decision. Now you have one choice. Move forward with the spirit of gratitude, the desire to help Cora, not hinder, and all will be well. For *all* of us." He stepped even closer to Andrew. "But if you broach this subject again, or do anything to harm my objective to aid Cora in becoming the most successful gentlewoman America has ever seen, you shall answer to *me*."

~Cora~

The papers were signed, and my father instructed a local banker in town to establish an account for me and then deposit an enormous sum that evening. In celebration, I invited the entire group and our hosts out to supper at a local *osteria*, and when the bill was presented to me, I paid more for the meal than my family had spent at the Dunnigan mercantile in six months' time. It took my breath away, and as we drove home, I felt numb, dizzy by what had transpired over the day. But I also felt free, giddy with delight.

Only when Will escorted me to my room and kissed me good night by the door did I feel the first twinge of unease, the slightest distance, from him. "Wait," I said, grabbing his hand as he turned to go. He turned back to me, but only partway, a question in his eyes. "Will, are you...all right?"

"Yes, fine," he said dismissively. "Just feeling weary." He cocked a half smile. "I always do about now on a tour, but few tours have been so…involved."

I smiled and played with his fingers, holding his big hand in both of mine. I looked up at him. "It's a lot to take in."

"It is," he said, moving to cover my shoulders with his hands. He leaned in and gave my forehead a soft, slow kiss, then pulled back to look in my eyes. "Let us speak more of it tomorrow, all right? I think a good night's sleep will aid us both."

I nodded and forced a smile, then watched him walk away a few steps before I slipped into my room. I closed the door and leaned against it, looking upward, praying. *Lord, help me find my way. Help us find our way.*

Anna came in and quietly helped me get ready for bed. "It was a big day, Miss, was it not?"

"Indeed," I said, sitting down. She unpinned my hair and then set to brushing it out with a wide ivory-handled boar's hair brush.

"May I speak frankly, Miss?"

"Do you ever speak any other way, Anna?" I asked with a small smile. I waved her on. "Please."

She returned my smile, looking at my reflection from over my shoulder. "It's been a big day for you. A grand day."

"That it has." It still seemed like a dream…was it all really happening? Her expression of concern pulled me back to the present. "But…"

She gave me a rueful smile. "I've worked for those of great wealth all my life. I've rarely seen money make anyone a better person, but I've seen it destroy many."

"How so?"

"From what I can see, happiness depends on how a body uses what the Lord gives them. Seek His will out, Miss Cora," she said, patting my shoulder and setting down the brush. "He'll show you how to live a contented life. So many people I've seen in the Kensingtons' set don't have that…that inner satisfaction. Because they try to buy what cannot be purchased. Do you understand what I mean?"

"I-I think so," I said.

And I thought I did. I just didn't know what it meant for *me*. Yet.

The next morning, Felix, Anna, and I arrived back at the villa before ten, after seeing to our errands in town. I'd convinced my brother to accompany us, trusting him to see us through, since he spoke some passable Italian. Though by his own admission, he knew mostly conversational words meant to woo beautiful Italian women or impress gullible American tourists we encountered in our circles. Given that we were out of the crowds in the city, Will and my father had eased on their stipulation about us having an armed guard at all given times. Here in the countryside, we'd all visibly relaxed within hours.

"*Buon giorno*," Will said in surprise, just reaching the bottom of the wrought-iron stairs of the villa as we entered. "Where have you three been?"

"Good morning," I said, taking his offered arm. "Felix accompanied us to a telegraph office," I said, "so I could tell my parents our happy news. Then we went to the bank. I wired them some funds."

He beamed down at me. "Oh, Cora. That must've felt wonderful."

"Indeed," I said, thinking for the thousandth time how glad I was. My mama and papa would not see another day in which they would worry about how they were to meet their bills or put food on the table. Papa could continue to seek out all the medical care he needed for his weak heart. And when he was better, they could do whatever they wished. Buy a cottage in the country. Or even a mansion filled with servants.

"The idea of them never worrying again about money makes me happier than almost anything," I said.

"I imagine so," Will said, smiling.

Lil and Nell appeared at the top of the stairway, and behind them, Andrew and Viv. "What makes you happier than almost anything?" Andrew said, his face and tone odd.

Hugh appeared too, catching our conversation.

"Are you still going on about the prospects in Dunnigan?" Andrew asked, his eyebrow lifting, his tone now clearly patronizing. They walked down the stairs.

Will cleared his throat in warning from my side.

"The prospects, as you call them," I said, "are not prospects at all. I've accepted Father's offer to run the Kensington-Diehl Mine."

Andrew's brow lifted higher. "You. A schoolmarm." He looked about at the others with a wry grin, then back to me. "My dear Cora. What did they teach you in Normal School that makes you believe you can run a mine?"

I swallowed one quick retort, then another. "I am by nature a learner."

"Well, that's good, my dear, because learning this will be difficult."

"You realize that you'll be stuck in a dull office all day, poring over numbers," Vivian added. She took my arm. "Do you *really* want to do that?"

My eyes narrowed. Of all the subjects in school, mathematics was my least favorite. And I much preferred novels to any other sort of reading… "I do enjoy learning new things," I put in. "The challenge of it." I straightened my shoulders. "I believe I can do it."

"That sounds dreadfully sensible," Hugh said as he reached the stair landing with the others. "Wouldn't you rather have time for shopping and balls and grand parties?"

"You're confusing my sister with yourself, Morgan," Felix said, sliding an arm around my shoulders and giving me a squeeze. "Don't let them talk you out of it. The Kensington-Diehl Mine is rightfully yours. I'm proud of Father for giving you this opportunity."

Hugh snorted. "You're only relieved it wasn't you that Wallace put in that managerial chair."

"Well, yes, there is *that*," Felix said with a smile.

"In any case, you need not worry your pretty head too much over it," Andrew said, giving me another patronizing smile. "I'll be there to answer any question you need ask, when your father isn't about." There was something else in his tone, something less than friendly.

"Oh, thank you," I forced myself to say, then slid my eyes to meet Will's. Working with Andrew Morgan every day wasn't something I'd considered.

"A necessary evil," Will said under his breath.

I nodded and thought it best to change the course of our conversation until I'd had ample opportunity to think it all through. Will led me through the wide front door and out to the front of the villa. "So…are we off to see the shroud?" I asked. "Is that what you said was on the docket today?"

We paused as the motorcars pulled up in the front drive before the villa, dust rising on the road behind them. The old home was rustic, with unkempt vines overtaking several stone walls. It felt homey and welcoming, and I wished we never had to leave.

"Would you prefer to merely take a morning drive and return to convalesce a bit more?" Will offered.

"I'm weary of succumbing to my weariness. Let us see this fabled shroud. And then I'd very much like to get to see the countryside of Tuscany that Antonio waxes on about every chance he has."

"That *does* sound restorative," Vivian said, coming outside with Nell and Lil. She finished pulling on her second glove and took a deep breath, smiling at all of us. "I feel better already, being in the country."

I tried not to stare when Andrew came out to stand beside her, but I couldn't help myself from sneaking peeks. Was I the only one who could see the forced nature of their relationship, how obviously wrong they were for each other? But how much more intolerable would he be toward me if they decided to part ways?

The others clambered aboard the cars—minus Mr. Morgan and my father, who had elected to remain behind to see to "non-Dunnigan business," they'd said—and then we traveled through picturesque green hills dotted with spires of Cyprus trees. I spotted farmers on wagons pulled by horses, the sight making me wistful for home. Gradually we merged onto a wider road that contained more and more motorcar traffic. Forty minutes later, we entered the city of Turin and soon pulled up near a grand cathedral made of white stone.

Rising high above it, in back, was a dome. A line of pilgrims extended out the door of the cathedral and around its corner. Some were barefoot. Some were on their knees. Some had obvious ailments. The pilgrims mixed with refined ladies and gentlemen, who tried to ignore the "riffraff" even as their faces pinched in impatience at having to wait to go inside.

"The priests here do not bow to the wealthy," Will said in my ear, nodding toward the line as we exited the car. "In other locations we can buy quick entry. Here, the holy men say that all are equal in God's sight."

I covered a smile over Viv's agitation at this news and boldly took Will's arm as we walked to our place at the end of the line, not caring if any of our touring party reported my familiarity to my father. Antonio and Pascal trailed behind us, warily watching the crowd as if any one of them might pounce. A woman of perhaps seventy, her head bulbous with monstrous cysts, waited in line ahead of us. She was hunched over, one shoulder higher than the other, her gnarled hands on the end of a cane as she shuffled forward.

Will glanced toward me, looking as if he wondered if the sight would overwhelm me or the other females in the group. For our entire trip, Will, Antonio, and the guards had done their best to keep the beggars from us, practically creating a human wall when needed to allow us to pass unencumbered. But we'd seen them, even if we'd pretended not to, before we'd looked away in discomfort. There was simply no feasible way to marry our extreme luxury with their desperate circumstance.

I was certain that Will was right when he told us there were a fair number who were out to take advantage of their sorrowful state. But now more than ever, I felt oddly separate from this woman. And I knew it had a great deal to do with the amount my father had put into my checking account the day before.

Happiness depends on how a body uses what the Lord gives them. Anna's voice rang as clearly in my head as if it were a bell high above me.

We turned a corner, and I glimpsed the terribly deformed beggar ahead of us again. "I want this time in Italy to be more than the culmination of our tour," I said to Will. "I want it to be a pilgrimage of sorts. To find out where God is leading me. What He wants from me. *How* He wants me to live my life. My whole future is suddenly so different than I imagined."

Will nodded and lifted my hand for a quick kiss. "Us," he amended. "Where He is leading *us*. While you may feel bandied about by your father, one moment pulled, the next pushed, your heavenly Father only longs to bring you closer."

I smiled up into his blue eyes, two shades lighter than my own. They were more like the sparkling Atlantic than the deeps of the Mediterranean. They held a spark of hope and wisdom.

We each got lost in our own thoughts then, but I took comfort in his proximity, the strength of his hand in mine, the warmth of it through the fabric of glove and sleeve. I grew more pensive the closer we got to the church entry, and as we left the growing heat of the afternoon and entered the shadowed cool of the cavernous sanctuary, I inhaled and exhaled with satisfaction.

Across marble tiles, we moved down one side of the cathedral as others left down the other. In the center were old pews, scratched and colored with decades of use. A few people sat and considered the gilt altarpiece extending upward and the sculpture of Mary and Jesus in front of it. But most were heading beyond it, to the chapel in the rear of the cathedral, beneath the great dome that sent three streams of light at an angle through small windows at its base.

"The shroud was in France until the 1500s," Will said in a reverentially quiet tone as we drew closer, watching as people knelt before a glass case with margins of gold. The case, like a king's glass coffin, held a cloth inside. Some people wept. Some went to their faces beside it. Others passed by it with a cursory look. Will looked around at all of us as we huddled in a tight circle so that we could hear him. "It was brought here to Turin after a fire nearly destroyed it. The holes you see were from melting silver. They've been repaired over the centuries."

Slowly, the line moved forward. In France, we'd visited churches that purported to hold the crown of thorns or a vial of Christ's blood or a nail from the cross. But as I drew near, I knew this relic would be far more moving.

At last we were directly beside it, and I had difficulty seeing anything more than the tattered, ancient yellowing cloth. But as the sun shifted and the rays of light moved in the chapel, I could make out the darkened images of two legs, then crossed hands as I neared the center of the case, then a rib cage.

My breath caught as I made out a beard, mouth, nose, eye sockets, and the bloody stains left from what must have been a thorny crown. I froze beside the end of the case, continuing to stare into the likeness of a man's face.

Could it possibly be true? Was I staring into a reflection of my Savior's body, the cloth that covered Him in the tomb…all that was left of Him when Mary Magdalene went to attend Him three days after the burial? I reached out and laid a hand on the glass, my eyes filling with tears.

A priest hissed a demand to *non toccare*, even as Will gently pulled me away with an arm around my waist, leaving room for other pilgrims. Seeing my tears, he reached for his handkerchief and handed it to me.

I took it but then pulled away from his grasp. "Wait," I said. I turned to face the case, now ten paces away. There was but one ray of sun cascading down inside the chapel. The others in our group stood to one side, respectfully silent. Even Hugh, always ready with a wisecrack. But I had hardly a thought for them and what they must be thinking of me and my odd behavior.

All I could think of was what Mary Magdalene must've felt in that moment in the tomb, lifting the cloth as if to make certain He wasn't there. Her friend and Redeemer, lifted from the cross and carried down, held in His mother's arms. The cold of death upon Him, yet now gone. No longer in the grave. Resurrected, as clearly as Lazarus had been, shaking off the stink of decay and entering life again. Up and gone. I gripped Will's arm, and he cast me a concerned glance. "Cora? Are you well?" he whispered. "You look wan."

I nodded and looked up at him. My stomach did seem unsettled, and my head ached, but he seemed to understand that I was more overcome with reverence than feeling ill. He paused, then slowly drew an arm tight around my shoulders. Together, we stared toward the glass case that seemed to me an iconic symbol of my Savior. No cage or coffin could hold Him. He was free...free, and so much mightier than I had given Him credit for being.

There was nothing I could not conquer—or at least manage to get through—if my God was beside me. Whether that was poverty or wealth. I giggled at that thought. When had I ever considered wealth a threat? Not once before I had money. But now? Would such a fortune change me? Mold me in ways that would be better not to be molded?

No. I would use it for good. Shape it, not allow it to shape me. I laughed aloud, as if I'd just beaten it in a round in the ring.

Will gave me a quizzical look, and Vivian and Andrew frowned at me, which made me giggle more. But directly behind Andrew, I glimpsed the older woman—the one covered in cysts—shuffling toward the door. My heartbeat seemed to pause, then pounded in my chest.

The least of these. Inasmuch as ye have done it to the least of these, ye have done it to Me. My eyes moved from the woman to the shroud's glass coffin and then back to the woman now disappearing among the crowds. I squeezed Will's hand. "Will, I need you to do something for me," I said, looking up into his eyes.

"Anything."

I pulled him along, edging past a group of tourists. The others awkwardly followed behind us. "Cora, what is your hurry?" he asked.

"Her," I said, only slowing when we again had her in sight.

He frowned quizzically at the woman. "Her?"

"Yes. I want you to give her this," I said, pulling open the drawstrings to my purse and then unclasping my wallet. From it I brought out a wad of *lire*. Everything I had withdrawn that morning from my new account.

His concern deepened as he took it from me. "But Cora, this is a great sum of money." He lowered his volume as the others drew nearer. "I mean, I know you have a great deal more at your disposal, but you cannot simply be giving it all away…"

"Can't I?" I said, laughing again, feeling slightly hysterical, manic in my generous state. I fought the urge to take it from him and give it to her myself. But I wanted him to explain to her, since he spoke her language. "Tell her it's so she can see a doctor, have a meal, find lodging." My eyes narrowed on the wad, wondering how the lire compared to dollars. "It is enough, isn't it?"

A beautiful Italian woman in a fine dress passed behind Will. She glanced at me as if she'd overheard our conversation. She was wiping her eyes as she held on to a man's arm, apparently as moved as I was by seeing the shroud. But I focused again on Will, waiting on his answer.

He frowned again. "It is more than enough. But Cora, are you certain? She could be one of the many people who prey upon rich young tourists—"

"Will," I implored, "please. It's the right thing to do. Look at her. I must come to her aid."

"Certainly," he said. He pulled away, moving quickly through the crowds to do as I'd asked.

"Miss Cora?" Antonio asked, offering his arm. But I couldn't abate his curiosity, only wait with excitement to see how the woman would receive the gift. We edged closer. Will was gesturing back toward me, and I gave her an embarrassed smile. The beautiful Italian woman who had paused earlier, who looked a little older than I, hovered near the woman. She looked back at me, too, listening as Will explained my intent. The young woman's piercing dark eyes unnerved me, and I looked to the floor. Would she see me as I was? A miserable sham of a pilgrim, belatedly remembering Whom I owed most?

I looked up again. The woman and her companion were gone, but Will and the beggar approached me. She grasped my hand, chattering excitedly in Italian and gazing at me as if I were as wondrous as the shroud.

"She's thanking you. Saying you are an angel from God," Antonio said as Will beamed behind her.

"Tell her she's most welcome," I said, staring into her small brown eyes hooded by aging flesh. "Tell her it wasn't me but God caring for her. I am but His servant."

Antonio paused, as if digesting my words, then he translated as I'd asked. The woman squeezed my hand, nodding again and again, half bowing, then turned away, the beatific smile still on her face. I was struck by the beauty of that smile. It showed missing and rotting teeth, but there was such joy—such pure joy—in it. I grasped Will's arm, and we made our way to the door.

Outside, the heat enfolded us, and perspiration immediately beaded at my temples. After the dim interior of the church, I blinked against the bright sunlight. Antonio went to the sidewalk and flagged our drivers, who'd parked a block away. They immediately pulled out and into traffic, then stopped beside us. Will opened the door, and I clambered into the backseat, Lil right behind me. We sat across from Will and Antonio, who both set to loosening their ties and opening wide their jackets. We all breathed a sigh of relief as the motorcar moved out into traffic, allowing air to flow through the compartment. Soon we reached the much quieter, narrower road that would lead us back to the villa.

I stared out the window, taking in the crumbling walls, perhaps hundreds of years old, and relatively new homes and other structures, all crowding right up to the road's edge, making use of every inch of space. The others were silent, perhaps because they didn't know what to say. Perhaps they thought I'd gone mad, giving a stranger every dollar I had on me. Perhaps they were moved.

I looked over to Will. "Do you believe it's real? The shroud?"

He paused, and his eyes drifted back and forth as if he was thinking. He leaned forward, elbows to thigh, fingertips tapping fingertips. "Does it matter?" he asked, staring into my eyes. "Regardless of whether or not it's real, it still serves God, yes? You were clearly moved."

"Indeed," I said, considering his words. "But then…you believe it a fake?"

He pursed his lips and tilted his head. "I wouldn't say that. I would say there are various accounts. Some say the Knights Templar held it for a time. But other scholars point out that Luke says in his gospel that Jesus was buried with two cloths, one for His head, one for His body. And yet…" He glanced over the side of the motorcar as we slowed to pass a farmer on an old wagon pulled by a donkey. Then Will looked back to me. "Wouldn't it be tender of God to provide such a miracle for those of us who benefit from the occasional reminder of His life? His Son? Is it not possible that Luke heard about two cloths laid upon Jesus, but another was beneath it? Or laid over the two?"

"Yes," I breathed.

"The cloth is very old. Scholars say that it could indeed be old enough to date from Jesus's time. But there's no way to be certain, is there? In the end, you either believe it's real, or you do not. Just like we believe in Him or we don't—that's what faith is. A step we take. Or don't. I consider the shroud a holy tool the Lord can use, as He clearly used with you today."

We drove for a time and then pulled over and parked, in order to see a famous fresco in the tiny local church. We walked up into a small hilltop village buzzing with the activity of an afternoon market. "Oh, might we shop?" I asked Will.

He chuckled. "With what? You've spent everything you had."

I smiled back at him. "If there's something I absolutely have to have, we'll have to come back for it."

"That can be arranged," he said. I took his arm, and we wandered, pausing before one stall and then another. There were women selling earth-hued pottery pieces, and others selling linens. Bottles of olive oil and vinegars. Casks of wine. Bits of Etruscan artifacts—"or so they say," Will said in warning as I paused over a piece, a primitive painting of a flying dove.

"And if they're telling the truth?" I asked.

He cocked a brow and smiled. "Then it's over two thousand years old."

"It's possible, right?" I asked, thinking again of the shroud.

"Certainly. Italy is full of such wonders." He moved on to the next stall, a watchmaker's, and picked up a gold pocket watch, admiring it for several minutes. I turned back and asked the vendor how much he wanted for the fresco piece, then borrowed money from Lil to purchase it.

When Will moved to the haberdashery stall to try on hats, I eased into the watchmaker's tent, hoping Will wouldn't see me. He'd left me under Antonio's intent gaze, and the older man's lips twitched as if he knew what I was up to. I picked up the watch that Will had admired and then fingered the tag. It was far more expensive than I'd anticipated—what I might have spent on a gift for my parents through all our Christmases combined.

Vivian joined me and saw my hesitation. She slid her eyes over her shoulder to Will, who was still engaged in conversation with the hatmaker, then back to me. "Oh, go on and get it," she said. "Why hesitate? Money is no longer a concern."

"I-I don't know," I stammered, feeling my belly clench up as I again stared at the enormous sum on the tag. It was beautiful, the watch, but such a sum would've kept me in Normal School for a good four months…

"Go on," she said, her eyes shining with glee. "You're in our world now, Cora. Money equals freedom. The freedom to buy anything you want. And Will has worked so hard. He deserves it."

"But I have no more cash. I already borrowed from Lil—"

"Please," she said, unclasping her small purse and pulling out a wad of Italian lire. After a quick glance over her shoulder at Will, she carefully passed it to me, hiding it in the folds of our skirts. "You'll pay me back. Go on. I'll distract him. Maybe *I'll* convince him to buy that hat." She smiled and squeezed my arm and moved away, leaving me to face the merchant, who eyed me expectantly.

It'd be the perfect surprise for Will, I told myself, handing the bills to him, even as everything in me screamed it was too much, too extravagant.

But he deserved it, didn't he? I wanted something to express all I felt for him. And he'd been through so much… It was the perfect gift.

I just had to find the right time to give it to him.

CHAPTER 7

~William~

He looked at Cora as she entered the motorcar and smiled as he noted the aura of pleasure about her. Gone was the vague mantle of weariness, worry. In its place was a new confidence in her step. Joy. Hope. Which made him feel worse about his own misgivings. Over her negotiating him out from under his debt holder's thumb. Over her instant fame—her wealth and position bound to increase her draw tenfold. Over her always and forever earning far more money in a year than he would likely ever earn in a lifetime.

He was glad for her. Truly.

It just didn't...*sit* well with him.

Add to that his concern that Andrew fairly seethed with jealousy. There was a new potential enemy within the group's very own ranks.

Will felt nothing but increasing agitation every time he looked at the woman he loved. And he did love her, with everything in him. *Please, Lord, help me find a way,* he prayed silently, watching as Felix helped her out of the motorcar. She leaned in to share a secret with Lillian and then laughed. She was so beautiful. So good. So innocent in all of this. Why did he feel any semblance of resentment? More importantly, how could he find his way past it?

"There you are at last!" Wallace said, emerging from the villa. "I want you all to meet Simon Grunthall."

They collectively turned and faced the newcomer, a small, broad-shouldered man in an expensive suit. He had brooding dark eyes that seemed to miss nothing.

"Mr. Grunthall is the company's new press secretary, just arrived from New York. He shall manage all correspondence and interviews with journalists seeking an audience with you young people." Wallace spoke to the group, but his eyes rested on Cora. One by one, he introduced Grunthall to Will, Antonio, the guards, and the Kensingtons and Morgans. Each shook his hand and greeted him. Cora was last. Will came around to stand beside her, and Simon's keen eyes flicked between them once, twice.

"So it's true? You two are courting?" he asked without preamble.

"Indeed," Will said.

"Be prepared for some competition," the man sniffed, unfolding an Italian paper to an inner page. "News is out about Cora being a Kensington, and many presume she is the one who shall prosper the most from the wealth found beneath Dunnigan." He eyed her. "They say that luck runs in the blood," he said, and gave her a smile of appraisal, as if considering it. "Add to that, this"—he handed her the newest issue of *Life*—"and you'll be bombarded. As soon as they can find you, that is." He turned to look over his shoulder at the heavily wooded hillside that rose above the villa, then out to the eastern vineyard, as if reporters might be lurking, even there, now.

"We aim to avoid that as long as possible," Will said. "Which is why we're now taking a rather unorthodox route on our tour."

"Take whatever route you wish. The Italians can certainly find you soon enough. And they shall sell their stories to the world press." He looked to Wallace. "It's good you brought me in."

"Yes, well, come inside and join us for luncheon. You can apprise our children of your goals. And your rules."

The two men turned and went inside, while the rest of the group shared looks of concern. It had to chafe for them all to be referred to as "children." All the light and freedom Will had glimpsed in Cora moments before seemed to disappear like air let out of a balloon. He squeezed her hand where it rested on his arm. "It'll turn out all right," he said.

"Will it?" she returned, lifting the issue of *Life* as if it were her obituary.

"Sure," he said with a smile. "If we got through the first article in *Life*, we can certainly manage the second."

~Cora~

We sat down at the long pine table and ate a hearty vegetable stew accompanied by crusty bread. It reminded me of something my mama made, and a pang of longing for her and Papa washed through me. How long until they received the message I'd sent? Did they know the good news now? I hoped so. Because there was surely a steep price to pay in accepting my father's offer, I decided as I looked at Mr. Grunthall. My eyes moved to Will. And yet there was so much that was a gift. Slipping free of our financial nooses came at a cost. But it'd be worth it. *It will be worth it,* I repeated to myself as Simon Grunthall droned on about the importance of guarding every conversation, of finding out the employ of each person we met before sharing personal details, of bringing him in whenever possible.

"But Mr. Grunthall," Lillian protested, "you are proposing we shield ourselves from every person we are yet to meet. Part of what the Grand Tour is about is meeting interesting and new people."

"And so you shall, young Miss Kensington," he said with a curt nod. "Only with my guidance. My goal is to protect you all."

He finished his last bite of stew and wiped his mouth with a cloth napkin. His eyes moved to me and then on to the others. "While I shall be available to all of you, my primary concern is Miss Cora." His dark eyes returned to me. "You have become quite the item of interest in America, my dear."

I shifted in my seat, not liking his uninvited use of my first name, the overly personal use of "my dear," or the implication that he would be watching me every moment. "I'm certain you are overstating their interest," I said. "Besides, I have no secrets now that everyone knows of my parentage. People will soon tire of me, even if I briefly caught their attention."

"Ahh, but we all have secrets, don't we?" he asked, his eyes penetrating, invasive. "Even now," he said with a flick of his wrist toward me, "you are inventing new ones."

"I'm sure I don't know what you mean."

He laughed, but no humor reached his eyes. "Women are complex and subtle creatures. It will take me some time, but I am interested in ferreting out any nuance of a story that might attract the undue interest of a journalist who wishes to exploit you."

"What on earth does that mean?"

"There is no rush," he said, taking a sip of wine. "We shall begin tomorrow with interviews."

"You mean to interview me," I said flatly.

"Most exhaustively," he said with a smile, raising his goblet in the air in a sort of mock toast.

"I don't care for your Mr. Grunthall," I said to my father when I found him outside. He was alone, smoking a cigar.

"You will in time, Cora," he returned tiredly. He took a deep draw on the cigar and let the smoke escape his mouth in a lazy cloud. "Trust me in this. I have become quite good at protecting my children. And while he might come across as overbearing, Simon Grunthall will protect you in ways I cannot. He comes with the highest recommendations from friends in the East."

Felix and Hugh came outside. They'd changed into more casual clothes. "The girls are changing and joining us for a game of croquet, Cora," Felix said. "Care to come too?"

"I'm afraid I need her with me," my father interrupted. "We have some work to do on the mine."

"Already?" I asked, blinking in surprise.

"Already," he said, drawing again on his cigar and peering at me with his bright eyes. "It's overdue, really. You'll find the mine needs our constant attention. So we must begin, even if it means you sacrifice some of your outings with the others on the tour—or a *croquet* game."

He was challenging me, intent on seeing how dedicated I was to my course. I lifted my chin. "Of course," I said. "There's nothing I'd rather do with my afternoon."

Hugh huffed a laugh. "Well, jolly for you. Can't say I'd agree."

"Someday, dear boys, you two shall have to accept a mantle of responsibility as well," my father said.

"Indeed," Felix said, already moving away, walking backward. "But we intend to put it off as long as possible!" He saluted me. "We'll play a ball in your honor, Cora."

"See that it wins," I said.

He returned my smile and walked down the hill with Hugh, and while a part of me wished I was going with them, I was also intent on seeing what it meant, working with my father and learning about this mine business. While I had thought my love of learning was leading me to teaching, couldn't the Lord have simply been preparing me to be ready to apply my mind to other matters? Just because I hadn't explored such things before didn't mean I wouldn't enjoy it.

Two hours later, as the columns of numbers swam before my eyes, my father droned on about the ethics of management. Another thick manila folder before me was neatly labeled "Kensington-Diehl Mine." There had to be over a hundred pages inside.

My father was silent at last, and I belatedly looked up at him. His lips gathered in a compassionate line. "I've overtaxed you. It's a great deal to take in. Perhaps a bit of tea outside, so you can get some fresh air?"

"That would be most welcome," I admitted, grateful for his kind attention.

"I'll have a maid fetch it for you. I must see to other matters anyway. It was a good start today. We'll pick up where we left off tomorrow." He rang a bell to summon a servant.

I nodded eagerly, as if I couldn't visualize anything more enticing, and then rose to leave. He and Mr. Morgan rose politely too, and when I left the room and entered the hallway, I took my first full breath in what felt like a long while. The house was very quiet—were the others still out playing croquet? Or had they all retired for afternoon naps?

It was just as well with me...I didn't wish to see anyone at the moment. Except that maid with my tea. My mouth was terribly dry, and a bite of something sweet might settle my oddly upset belly. I took deep breaths of the air, redolent with the scents of lavender and rosemary, the hot smell of summer in Italy.

I'd no sooner sat down—comfortably guarded by a wide umbrella from the full force of the sun—when Anna appeared, carrying a tray. "Your father said you were in need of some refreshments, Miss?"

"Indeed. That would be lovely." I watched her as she poured me a cup and used silver tongs to move a roll from a basket to the edge of my saucer. "Do you care to join me, Anna?"

"Ah, no, Miss. I'm afraid that wouldn't be entirely proper."

"Frankly, I don't care much for propriety," I said. "Please, sit."

She hesitated, but then looked down the long stone porch to where Mr. Grunthall stood, smoking. He lifted his chin in greeting, a slight smile on his face.

"I'm fairly certain he wouldn't approve, Miss," Anna said, wiping nervous hands on her apron.

"*I'm* fairly certain I don't care whether he would approve or not," I said crossly. But when I saw her face gather in increased consternation, I relented. "It's fine, Anna. Forgive me. Apparently I'm not fit for company anyway."

"Perhaps you need a bit of a rest?"

"I am more than a little weary," I said, sipping my tea and watching Simon Grunthall stamp out his cigarette and disappear inside. I'd glimpsed him working away at a desk earlier as I slipped through the hall to the restroom. Maybe he was off to continue his correspondence.

"Well, put your feet up," Anna said, looking out at the view from the expansive patio. "It's a lovely day. It's good for you to get some fresh air."

"Indeed." She disappeared, and I sipped from my cup, thinking about the overwhelming events of the last few days. Life-changing events. Was all of that the reason my head now pounded? I wished Will was here, beside me, so that he might help me sort it out. Distinguish what I was feeling. But he'd left me to my business and was likely accompanying the others. Or perhaps taking a rest himself.

My eyelids felt heavy as I placed my cup on the saucer beside the crumbs left from my delicious pastry, then set it on the table beside me. I did as Anna suggested and lifted my legs to the end of the chaise and leaned back, hands folded over my aching belly, eyes closed. Just a few minutes of rest, I decided. That would be all I needed…

"Miss Cora," said a low voice. "Miss Cora," the voice repeated, gently touching my shoulder. I blinked awake and immediately felt the heat of the afternoon sun.

"I'm afraid you drifted off," Mr. Grunthall said. He straightened and looked around as if seeking help, at a loss as to what to do.

"Oh!" I lifted a hand to my cheeks, hot with potential burn, and abruptly shifted my feet to the ground, embarrassment adding to the heat. "Thank you for awakening me," I said, rising and passing by him. I scurried inside, miffed that Anna had not come to fetch me. Then I laughed at myself and how I'd become accustomed to such coddling. I shook my head and walked down the cool hallway to my room, wondering where my traveling companions had gone to. Viv, Felix, and Lil. Even the Morgans. Mostly Hugh and Nell. Not Andrew. He could stay hidden. It was startling, the odd pang of separation I felt. I thought I was hungry for a little distance, the chance to breathe and move unencumbered by the group's needs or desires. But now even a couple of hours' separation struck me as…empty.

I entered my room, refusing to give in to a sigh. I'd been sighing far too often of late. I needed to concentrate on the bounty of gifts I'd been given, rather than on my trivial frustrations.

Anna was dozing in a chair in the corner, her small feet perched on the ottoman. I hid a smile as I opened an innovation trunk wider to find a suitable evening gown. She started as the heavy hinges creaked, rising so swiftly that I wondered if she had truly been asleep. "Oh, my goodness me! Forgive me, Miss, dozing off like that in your very own quarters." She straightened and looked me full in the face. "Oh!" she cried, her eyes rounding with her lips. "Miss! Did you go for a walk without a parasol?"

"No, no," I said ruefully. "I simply managed to doze off. In the shade at first, where you left me, but when I woke, in the sun." As I spoke, I moved to look at my image in the mirror, patting my hot cheeks. "Is it truly as terrible as all—" My words faded as I realized what Mr. Grunthall had seen. "Oh."

It was rather terrible. I didn't have the honest, sun-kissed glow or ruddy color I was used to from an afternoon in the fields. It was more of a one-sided burn, one that had singed my left ear lobe, most of my left cheek, and an odd portion of my nose.

"Oh," I said again, turning back and forth as I examined my face.

"Oh," Anna said, peeking at my reflection from over my shoulder.

"Oh," I repeated, but this time, I started to giggle, and Anna giggled too, and soon we were in hysterics, laughing at the silly predicament I'd gotten myself into.

"Perhaps," she said, trying to gather herself, wiping a tear of laughter from one eye with the back of a knuckle, "a bit of powder will help?"

"Yes," I said, blowing my nose in a handkerchief and wincing at the pain I felt on the left side of my nose. "Though I fear there will be no way to truly hide this."

I shook my head at my own folly. Why had I not taken my nap in here, as Anna had done? Although it had been so lovely…the gentle breeze, the heat of the sun on my lap, easing the pain in my head and belly…

Anna lifted a yellow gown from a trunk and smoothed it before her as if modeling it. "This one tonight, Miss?"

"I don't know," I said, taking a deep breath. "Might not that bright, light color make my face appear all the more burnt?"

"Hmm," she said, "perhaps. Let me see what else I might suggest…" She set to poking through the other trunks, as if she didn't know every stitch of my clothing as well as I.

I reached for a small brush and a jar of powder and opened it. I dipped the bristles in and tapped it twice on the edge so the excess would fall off, then began to cover my face. While it covered some of my burn, it was hardly concealed. I sighed, thinking about how merciless Hugh's teasing would be, and the patronizing smile that Viv was certain to send my way. I could almost hear their thoughts now. *The poor little country bumpkin, falling asleep in the sun. You can dress her as a lady, but you can't force her to act like one. Imagine that, dozing off in the sun, with so little care for her complexion! And she is supposed to help Father run a mine?*

Anna helped me out of my tan traveling suit and into a light periwinkle gown. But when I turned back to the mirror, I gasped. The burn extended down to my neck, in a slight *v* marking where my traveling suit ended.

As if it mattered at all. Such foolishness! How many times had my fair skin become pink from an afternoon of work in the fields, even with a hat on? How often had my hands and face and neck become brown over the summer, evidence of my place as a farmer's daughter? At one point I'd liked the color, until I'd gone off to Normal School and everyone seemed so intent on evading any brief kiss of the sun. Though their concern over it was nothing compared to the women in the circles I now moved…

That evening, Antonio took us to a lovely trattoria not far from the villa. It was on the very edge of Turin, and had only five tables. Our group filled all but one of them.

I was seated beside the window, which gave me a glorious view of the remains of the sunset, now a line of deep rose and orange along the horizon.

"I don't know if I'd venture so close to the window," Felix teased me as he passed by. "Haven't you had more than your fair share of the sun today?"

"Enough, Felix," Father said, taking a chair at the next table behind me. "You all have had your fun. Leave the girl alone."

Will squeezed my hand. "It isn't all that bad."

"Isn't it?" I asked, lifting a brow.

"Well, at least it won't be so bad tomorrow," he amended.

After conferring with Antonio, Will ordered food for us all. Antipasti of salami and cheese and bread. A tomato soup thick with basil. A full bass fish for each of us, with its head attached, which put off Vivian and Nell.

Will smiled at the girls as he finished the last of his own bass. "They believe you wish to see the fish's head," he said. "It allows you to confirm that the fish is truly fresh."

Vivian stuck her fork in the white flesh and looked rather sick. "I'd take their word for it."

He laughed under his breath and then sat back in his chair, chewing. "You look lovely this evening, Cora. Your color simply appears high. But how did you manage to get so much sun? I thought you were inside with your father."

"I was with him for a couple hours. Then I was feeling poorly, honestly. With the shade and welcome breeze, I fell asleep as soon as I thought about nodding off, I think. Then awoke under the heat of the full sun."

His eyebrows shot up and then knit together as he gave me a sorry smile. "Forgive me for not rescuing you in time."

"It was my own fault," I said. "But after our busy day, I was so weary, it felt impossible to fight it."

"Do you feel well now?"

I considered his question. "Mostly," I said, nodding when a waiter gestured to my plate. "I seem to be suffering a rather constant state of indigestion," I whispered. Even now my belly ached, and I felt light-headed. It was with some relief I saw the fish go, especially when the next dish was a wide plate filled with a scoop of risotto, which appeared appealingly bland. Perhaps I could manage some of that.

"Do you think we should summon a doctor?" Will asked quietly. His face was rife with concern.

"No, no," I said, waving him off. "I'm certain it's only the dramatic events that have sent my system in disarray. I'll be well soon enough." I took a bite of the surprisingly delicious steamy rice. "Tell us what you have in store for us tomorrow."

"Yes, do," Lillian said. She'd attempted to tame her curls into a knot tonight, and done a reasonably good job, but coiled tendrils still escaped all around her hairline. I thought it adorable, as bouncy and vivacious as her personality.

Will and Antonio shared a long look and then nodded at me. "We went to town this afternoon," Antonio said. "To confirm some options."

"We can go one of two directions," Will put in, loudly enough for all to hear. "Either to Cinque Terre, which Antonio mentioned to you. There is not much to see there in terms of history or art. Most tourists favor Pisa or Naples if you want to spend time by the sea. Antonio said that he thought that the group seems anxious for rest by the sea. Or would you all prefer Tuscany? Toscana boasts its own sort of rest, with her rolling hills and idyllic farms. And there are plenty of churches and monuments to explore, as well as loads of art."

I nodded. "I would love time in Tuscany," I said, suddenly longing for Dunnigan, for the smell of just-turned soil and water, fresh from the well, sloshing about a metal bucket. Idyllic, rolling hills, covered in crops of wheat or grapes, might be just what I needed.

"But to see the sea again," Lillian said dreamily. "Can we not go there first?"

Vivian nodded beside her, even as Andrew rolled his eyes and sighed heavily, as if this was all foolishness. He'd been exceedingly grumpy ever since Venice, and they'd taken a new track.

"Oh yes," I said, nodding encouragement to my sisters. The last thing I wanted was for Andrew to squash Vivian's desires. He could move on to Rome, as far as I was concerned, and wait for us to arrive, if it was all so tiresome. "I want to put on one simple day dress and stay in it all day long. To eat where the locals eat. To dip my toes in the sand."

"You might get a bit more burned," Will said, a teasing smile tipping up the corners of his lips.

"Well then, if it takes that to do as I've said, I hope so," I said, smiling back at him. "A little burn never hurt a body." I heard some defense in my own tone. "My papa said the Lord favored the echo of the sun on a man's face after a day of toil."

"Or a woman's?" he asked.

"Or a woman's."

We smiled at each other. I let my gaze linger overly long, but I couldn't resist him. It was so good to be openly *with* Will, without fear of others discovering our love. It felt good. Right. And I took that as God's encouragement that this was the path He wanted us on. Right here. Right now. And that was enough. *Thank You,* I breathed, sliding in the very last bite of risotto I could manage.

After declining dessert, my father settled our bill with the proprietor, and we rose to go. As we left, a woman at the other table caught my eye, and I immediately recognized her as the woman I'd seen at the church, the one who'd taken such an interest in me and the old beggar. She had a long, straight nose and wide eyes lined with dark lashes. We exchanged a polite smile as Will and I exited, but when I glanced back, I saw that she had caught Antonio and the two were chatting.

We waited outside for a moment as the others filed out, and Will glanced back in confusion, wondering what might be keeping Antonio. He arrived at last and pulled on his gloves. "That was Signora Eleonora Masoni," Antonio said, inclining his head back toward the door. "She saw what you did in the church in Turin, Miss Cora, and she was moved by your act of kindness."

"What's this?" Father said, overhearing our conversation. "What transpired in the church?"

"I only gave a poor woman in need a bit of money," I said.

"A great deal of money," Felix corrected.

Antonio's smile grew even as my father's diminished. "She's traveling too and hoped to host you tomorrow for dinner. But I informed her that we were likely off tomorrow to the coast. She gave me her card," he said, handing me an elegant calling card on thick cream paper. "She said that when we reach Toscana, we must stay at her villa near Montepulciano, at least for a few nights. She was most insistent."

Signora Eleonora Masoni, I read on the card, along with her address. "That was kind of her," I said. I smiled and then accepted Will's arm, walking—with a very full stomach—to our motorcar.

"One kindness begets another," he said.

~William~

Days later, Will alternately felt gloriously victorious, as if Cora was a prize he'd won after doing battle on multiple fronts—and riddled with guilt for exactly the same reason. But as they dug their toes into the sand beside the turquoise waters between Monterosso and Vernazza, two of the five cities that clung to the cliffs high above and made up the Cinque Terre, and she smiled at him from beneath the brim of her wide hat, he gave in to the luxury of joy.

Lord, Lord, how is it that You have given me such a gift as she? Over and over, the idea of it stunned him. That she had chosen him over Pierre. The shadow of Pierre's threat to meet them in Rome passed over him, but he ignored it like a potential cloud threatening the future sun in the light of today's bright orb. And then there was her fortune. He shook the thought off, not wanting to think of the complications that brought into their lives.

"What's the matter?" she asked, pouring a handful of coarse sand on his knee. "Why so distracted?"

"Hey." He smiled, brushing off the sand, then picking up a handful of his own and letting it drop on her hand, sprinkling each finger. "Nothing's the matter. I'm sitting on one of the prettiest coastlines in the world, with one of the prettiest women in the world. What could be wrong?"

She smiled, but he could tell by her expression that she knew he held something back. But what could he say? Why bring up his concerns?

Cora looked out to the water, and Will studied her profile. Long lashes, blonde at the tips, a perfect nose, an adorable chin. His eyes slipped lower, along her slender neck and over her bathing costume. She was small but strong. As strong outwardly as when he'd met her. But inwardly, now even stronger. And she was growing in strength, expanding in capacity.

Over the last days, she'd negotiated long meetings with Andrew and the family patriarchs, as well as a long interview with the bothersome Mr. Grunthall. It was clearly difficult for her, but she seemed to settle within, more and more, as each day passed. *If only I could do the same, Lord. Where do I belong in all of this? Where are You? Why do You hide Your face from me? Show me, Lord. Show me how I am to navigate these roads. How I am to protect her and yet be my own man in the midst—*

"Come," she said, suddenly rising. She reached down to him as if he needed help getting up. "Let's take a swim."

He took her hand and rose, glancing back at Mr. Grunthall, who was sitting beneath an umbrella twenty paces away, beside Pascal and Antonio. Antonio gave him a two-finger salute, his white teeth gleaming against his olive skin. Simon Grunthall looked grumpy, peering at them beneath the brim of his sun hat. For a moment, Will wondered if he should persuade Cora to stay under the protection of the umbrella, away from curious onlookers who might spot them and identify them to the press. He knew Grunthall had been inundated with inquiries once journalists learned he was traveling with them as secretary. The man went off to the nearest telegraph office every day to collect them from his assistant. But were any of them here? Off the beaten path of tourists?

Will scanned the beach, anxiously watching for any interloper. But when he glanced back to Cora and saw that she was already thigh-deep in the water, her bathing costume's skirt floating on the crystalline surface, he knew he didn't have the gumption to stop her. She grinned over her shoulder at him, and his heart seemed to actually stop for a moment, so lovely was she. So free. And he was again lost to the gift of this time with her. Exploring, experiencing.

Let me accept the gift for now, he prayed, wading in after her. In the distance, her sisters and brother splashed one another, and she was clearly angling in their direction. He caught up with her and took her hand. She paused, gasping as the cold water hit her belly and then higher, but forged onward, gradually getting accustomed to the temperature. He walked alongside her, unable to keep from grinning.

She was treading water before him, while his height afforded him more time on his feet. "Where did you learn to swim?" he asked, deciding she looked more like one of Homer's enticing sirens than a lady. She'd thrown her hat to the sand, and now, tendrils of her hair were coiling in the water around her, clinging to her neck when she lifted higher in the water. He longed to unpin the rest of it. To see it flowing all about her. To see her totally free…

"There used to be a pond on a neighboring farmer's land. There was a big tree and a deep hole. We played there for hours." Then, as if in a vision, she pulled the pins from her hair, letting one coil of hair fall about her shoulders and into the water.

"Cora, what will they think?" he asked in alarm, looking to the beach.

"Who? Silly Mr. Grunthall? Who worries about strangers on the beach? For once, let us not care about *others*." She finished her task and tucked the pins in a small pocket on her bathing costume, as if it had been made for just that. "This is what I long to do." And with that, she laid back, floating on the surface of the water. Her hair swirled in a glorious creamy cloud about her head. She looked up at him, with more than a hint of flirtation in her pretty blue eyes, like a reflection of the water itself. It startled him, because she was usually not given to flirtation. But then it sent a surge of pleasure through him.

He couldn't stop himself. He picked her up in his arms, cradling her close, featherlight in the water. She gasped and blinked in surprise. "Will…" she said, now glancing back to the shore in concern.

"I thought we weren't thinking of others," he said, smiling down at her. "Oh, Cora, how I love you. You are…" He looked up and then back down at her. "You are every kind of gift to me that I could imagine. So much more than any woman I ever imagined by my side."

She smiled softly. "And you are just the right man for me," she said. "Now come, float beside me, will you? Let us just be for a moment, you and I. Together."

He reluctantly released her back to the waters like a captive mermaid set free, and she immediately closed her eyes, bobbing on the gentle waves. He did the same, the water closing in around his face and neck, and he filled his lungs and allowed himself to float too, but he didn't feel nearly as light as she appeared. Their fingers brushed against each other as they floated, side by side, the sun beaming down on them, warming them, probably giving them new burns. But Will didn't care. Because in that moment, for a moment, life felt absolutely, gloriously perfect.

Even if it wasn't. He struggled to keep his mind on the moment, rather than letting it slip back to the quagmire of their future. Where could these paths possibly lead? How was he to marry a girl with such a vast fortune when he had so little? He would be an object of scorn. And what of his dreams to become an architect? Suddenly, he was free of his uncle's debts, but how was he to attend college if she had to be in Montana, helping to manage the mine? He doubted there was yet a university in the state that offered an architectural degree...and more and more, that was where he thought God was leading him.

It was then that Felix swam beneath him and pulled him under.

Will came up sputtering, half laughing, half mad. He went after his old college mate, remembering their wrestling match the day of their reunion in Montana. Again and again the two of them went under, until Felix, desperate for air, pulled loose of Will and rose to the surface.

"I give! I give!" Felix shouted, hands splayed outward, his lips just above the bouncing waters of the sea.

"Honestly, you two," Vivian said, shoulder-deep beside Cora. The others gathered around them. "When will you act your age?"

"I hope they never do," Cora said, eyes shining, grinning. "At least not entirely." She looked about. "Do you all know how I longed for siblings as I grew up? How I wished I were a part of one of the houses in my town that was brimming with children? Now, at last, I am."

Andrew groaned and looked sick to his stomach. "Heavens, it's all so sweet, I feel as if I'm floating on a sea of honey."

Vivian frowned at him. "You needn't be so nasty."

The rest of them frowned at him too. "Don't be such a lout, Morgan," Felix said, splashing him. "My sister is only trying to be nice."

"That's the trouble," Andrew said, rolling his eyes. "She's always so nice."

"I never knew that was a problem," Cora said, clearly not feeling pleasant at all toward him. "And haven't we been getting along the last couple of days?"

"You've been a gift to us too, Cora," Lillian said, taking Cora's hand to squeeze it.

"Yes, well," Andrew said. "Now that you all have bonded, perhaps we should go in now before Mr. Grunthall has a fit of apoplexy."

"He's right," Will said, glancing toward the beach. Sure enough, Simon was standing at the water's edge, shielding his eyes as he peered toward them. "We've had enough sun, too. If we're not careful, we'll all look like Cora did a few days ago."

"I resent that!" she cried indignantly.

He laughed and dived under the water when she tried to splash him, moving with long strokes a safe distance away. But as he rose, he knew he never wanted to be farther than this from Cora Diehl Kensington. Regardless of what it might cost him.

CHAPTER 8

~Cora~

I pored over the blueprints and architectural renderings of the Kensington-Diehl Mine, stifling a groan as the others in our party gathered, all merry, the girls in their peasant dresses and woven sandals, the men in plain shirts and trousers. The girls had their hair in braids, no hats in sight, and the men didn't don any covering for their heads either. They were off to hike the trail linking each of the five villages that made up the Cinque Terre, intent on blending in with the locals as much as possible and spending the night in the farthest village. But not me. My father and Mr. Morgan had made it clear that today we must make some critical decisions about the mine and telegram the foremen in Montana to let them know. And we were as yet at odds as to how to resolve a few key issues.

"I wish I could remain here with you," Will said when we paused in a corner of the grand foyer together.

"No, you don't," I said with a smile. "You wish I was going with you, just as I wish."

"Well, yes, that would be preferable. I hate it that you are missing this."

"Perhaps we can find some time tomorrow evening together, and you can tell me the region's tales."

"They're good ones," he said, arching a brow and brushing my bare hand with his. "Of pirates and fortresses and navies..."

"Please do remember the best ones for me, all right?" I said, wishing I could stand up on tiptoe and kiss him. But I knew that more than one set of eyes lingered over us.

"I will. Hold your own in there, Miss Diehl Kensington." He nodded to the two open doors that led to a small office. Already, Andrew Morgan stood in a corner, reading a document, the sun spilling over his shoulder. I stifled a sigh. Apparently he was staying behind too.

"I shall, Mr. McCabe," I returned. "Lead them onward."

"Only if it circles back to you," he whispered in my ear. And then he was gone, the happy chatter and laughter seeping out the house with the group. I pushed thoughts of grand views and remote villages and swimming from my mind and focused on the task at hand, squaring my shoulders and marching back into the office. Our fathers had not yet come down, but Andrew watched me enter. I ignored him and turned the blueprints on the large desk to the page that had kept me up late last night, thinking, thinking...

"It must be a trial for you, not being able to go with them," Andrew said from over my shoulder.

"No more so than it is for you," I said, my fingers running across the page, along the meandering line of the small river that split the vast area of rock.

"Come now. Admit it. This is a man's place. You belong out there. Frolicking."

"Frolicking," I repeated stonily. "Honestly, Andrew, you treat me as if I don't have a sound mind. Must I remind you that I was training to be a teacher before my father reentered my life?"

"Exactly," Andrew said, his voice uncommonly soft. "So why not go and pursue education? Become a teacher *of* teachers if you wish for something of more...*stature*." He shrugged. "But leave the family business to those who've been training all their lives to do this."

I felt the sting of his words even if his tone was carefully neutral.

I turned to face him. "This, in particular the Kensington-Diehl Mine, is none of your concern. Perhaps you can rejoin us later, after my business with Father is concluded?"

It was then that our fathers arrived, each carrying a stoneware mug steaming with what smelled like coffee. Behind them was Mr. Grunthall.

"No, no," my father said. "I want Andrew to be with us for this final meeting. He will be a support to you, Cora, in time. Won't you, Andrew?" he said pointedly.

"Why, I aim to be nothing but a support," Andrew returned, his smile catlike. I stifled a shiver. I really could not see any bit of what my sister saw in him. At least he hadn't been violent of late. But what sort of faint praise was that?

"The precious days of summer are slipping away," my father said, sitting down heavily in a chair and setting his mug beside him. He reached for a notebook and opened it. "Shall we get through what we must, without further ado?"

"Indeed," I said, leaning against the table and resting a hand on the blueprint. "We need to begin with this," I said, tapping the paper. "Your architect depicts the Gandy River flowing into the mine."

"Of course," he said. "We shall need to redirect the river and use the water to generate electricity."

So I had read it right. I'd asked Will to look it over with me too, and he'd confirmed my suspicions. But neither of us had quite believed it was true. "But we cannot," I said. "You know how dry that county is. How the farmers struggle to eke out a crop. If you take that water, how will they irrigate their fields?"

"Nonsense. It's already done," he blustered. "We've secured the water rights! None of those farmers have any sense if they remain. We're doing them a favor, really, pressing their hand."

"No," I said, shaking my head. "It isn't right. We either need to find an alternate source of power and water, or we need to buy their land at a decent price. It will be worthless after we divert the water and build this dam."

I heard Andrew chuckling behind me. Mr. Morgan and my father stared at me, while Mr. Grunthall scribbled notes on a pad. For what? His own article on me? He'd hinted that he would be writing such things. It was all so silly, so overwhelming...but this, this mission in my mind, was not. I was certain I must stick to my ideas. I could see my old neighbors in the small church with the white paint peeling from the sunbaked and snow-blasted boards. All fanning themselves as my old pastor rambled through a sermon. There was no way I could betray any of them.

"Every person in Dunnigan must gain from this strike, as we will most certainly gain," I said, crossing my arms. "It shall cost us more up front, but we shall gain long-term, just as you did in Butte. Don't you see?" I shook my head, boggled that they couldn't seem to grasp it, that they were hesitating over my apparently outlandish ideas. "I don't want to destroy my hometown. I want to build it to something even better than it was."

My father looked at me intently, and at last a hint of a smile tugged at the corner of his lips. "So there is a bit of empire builder within you after all," he mused. His smile faded. "But what you propose is most expensive. And not necessary at all. Darwin's theories on the survival of the fittest and all that."

"When we are clearly the most fit," Andrew said.

"We are most fit to *lead*," I returned, shooting him a dark glance. "Just because we *can* take advantage doesn't mean we should. Honestly, would you need a press secretary," I said, waving toward Simon, "if you were doing great, good things? Wouldn't the stories write themselves in a way that benefited you—if the people honestly loved you rather than feared you? If they wanted to help build up you and the company rather than somehow tear you down?"

My father was silent a moment, steepling his fingers before him. "What exactly do you propose?"

"Can we not find more water from another source?"

He shook his head, and his silver beard wagged under his chin. "Not enough."

"Then let us tackle it in a forthright manner. I wager you have squelched the news that we've brokered a deal for the water rights?"

He was still for a breath, then two. "I might have paid a few men the right amount to keep it quiet."

I sighed and pushed away from the table, pacing to the doorway and turning. How I wished Dunnigan wasn't so far away! That I could go and speak to my old neighbors and friends and tell them what I knew. Promise them that I'd make certain they were treated fairly. My eyes went to Mr. Grunthall, and I thought of his typing machine and sheaf of paper. He could help me! Get the word out to each and every one of them. I hurried back to the stack of blueprints and paged through them until I arrived at a broad-scale version that plotted out small homesteads and vast ranches, rectangles of land, alongside the miles of cliffs now owned by the Kensington-Diehl Mine.

My fingers traced one—the Ramstads'—then another—the Millers'. With each progressive plot of land, I could see weathered homes and derelict barns, failing fences. Very few of the ranches were successful enterprises.

"We will buy them out for a fair price. Allow them to start anew. Or stay right where they are and go to work for the mine. But they will no longer have to try and eke out a living from that soil."

A shiver ran down my back. Was I not proposing something awfully similar to what Wallace Kensington had offered my mama? Forcing my folks out by "buying" them out? "No," I amended. "We offer them more than twice the value for their land. Three times," I said, gaining steam. "And we allow them to keep the acres on which their homes and barns sit."

Andrew laughed, incredulous. "Thrice the value? Are you mad?" He turned toward our fathers. "She'll run us out of business before she's even begun!"

I looked back to my father, silently pleading with him to trust me in this, then back to Andrew. "This pertains only to the Kensington-Diehl Mine. And I am not in need of your vote on it."

My father studied me for several long moments, tapping his fingertips together. He glanced over to his old partner. "She was right in regard to our labor negotiations in Butte."

Mr. Morgan nodded. "There is a certain wisdom to it. Unconventional, for certain."

"It'd be quite a story," Mr. Grunthall said, lifting one black brow and shaking his head. "Your girl is already fascinating. This would ratchet her up to Molly Brown status. A Robin Hood figure, of sorts. Unconventional. Daring. But intrinsically good."

My father let out a scoffing laugh and rose to meander over to the window and stare outward, still thinking. "The Kensington name has seldom been tied to anything remotely considered 'intrinsically good.'"

I waited a moment. Then I said, "Isn't it then time?" I eased around the table and went to stand beside him at the window. "Wouldn't you much rather our name be tied to the good, the true? What if we led the country in showing how a business could succeed without treating our workers as cattle? What if every miner in America wanted to work for us over any other?"

His eyes shifted back and forth, searching mine. I knew he was running my words, our name, through his mind. It was echoing in my own. He slowly turned and lifted his hand for mine. After a moment's hesitation, I slipped my fingers into his and he covered it with his other hand. "My dear, you truly believe this is the best course of action?"

"I believe it is the only course of action," I returned steadily.

"Then," he said, cocking his head, "I say you are the majority share owner, and I shall support—"

"No, Mr. Kensington!" Andrew said. He came around the desk and stood near us. "You can't be serious. There's giving a horse a little rope, and then there's giving her the whole corral…"

"I am hardly a horse," I said, turning to face him.

"You are a wild and untamed filly," he bit back, staring down at me, "with no sense of a bit and reins. If we don't teach you what it means—"

"That's enough, Andrew!" Mr. Morgan cried.

"She will lose it all!" Andrew shouted, lifting his hands to his father, then mine. "This mine…"

He shook his head and then ran his fingers through his hair. He turned to my father. "I don't know what you're doing here. If you are so desperate to forge a bond with this girl"—he jabbed a hand toward me—"so desperate to make her beholden to you that you'd risk earnings that would help your *other* children in the future…"

My father's face became bright red, his eyes even more blue against the ruddiness of his skin.

"That is *enough*," he said with such vehemence that the last word became a shout. "I've said it before, and I'll say it again. This mine is only going to bring income because my daughter was raised on its doorstep. It has nothing to do with my other children."

"Doesn't it?" Andrew persisted. "Isn't this your mad attempt to level the playing field? To give your precious Cora an inheritance of her own? An inheritance that would rightfully be split with Vivian, Felix, and Lillian?"

"No," my father said, shaking his head. "They have more than enough with their inheritance that I will leave them through Kensington & Morgan Enterprises."

"But what of your forty-nine percent?" Andrew persisted. "Are those not funds that will filter into K & M? And is she not risking those funds? Quit thinking like a forlorn father and start thinking like the businessman I've always known you to be!"

"Andrew!" Mr. Morgan shouted.

My father was so angry that he couldn't seem to form words for a long moment. Then he settled on two: "Get. Out."

Andrew stormed out, then. A moment later, we heard the front door of the apartments slam shut.

The four of us—me, my father, Mr. Morgan, and Mr. Grunthall—stood in silence a moment.

"Forgive him," Mr. Morgan said tiredly, rubbing his forehead. "I fear he's been taxed of late, between these…changes, and his inability to, uh, come to an…understanding with Vivian." He met my gaze. "He'll come around."

"I don't know," I said. "He seems to loathe me."

"Loathe?" Mr. Morgan said, blinking. "That's a strong word…" But he didn't offer an alternative.

"I think it's enough for today," my father said, the fury all gone now, only a weary countenance in its place. "Let us reconvene tomorrow after breakfast."

I walked out, feeling stung and worn out and wondering if I was in the right place at all. Everything in me longed to be with

Will, with my siblings, out on the trail, exploring, laughing, having fun. Instead, I was in here, at an impasse with men I wasn't certain I wanted to spend my days with.

After making it to my room, I stood by the window and looked out to the green-blue sea until, gradually, my heart settled into a normal rhythm even if my head had begun another daily thrum of complaint. *Is this what You want from me, Lord? Is this the right path?*

Words from the basilica in Venice returned to me again. *Wait and trust.*

But what exactly was I waiting for?

CHAPTER 9

~Cora~

By the time the others returned the next day, I was desperate to see them...and even more desperate to be away from Andrew. We'd spent a tense morning in negotiation, cooped up inside the sweltering apartment, and then after lunch, Mr. Grunthall interviewed me again so he could continue writing his own stories. My father and I would review every story before it was sent out to the *San Francisco Chronicle*, which was then going to syndicate the articles to other papers. So far, the two I'd seen were fairly mundane accounts of our travels—exactly what Mr. Grunthall and my father wanted. The stories were our attempt to throw flour on a wild, spreading grease fire. Hard as it was for me to imagine, the world was hungry enough for word of our whereabouts and progress that they were willing to take whatever was sent to them, whether it was truth or not. Mr. Grunthall figured he could keep them appeased with what we sent them, and therefore stave off the more incendiary tales. Grunthall, of course, was careful to only send a story about our stay in a specific location after we departed that locale, and in this way, we stayed ahead of those who sought us out.

When I finally heard the travelers return, I rushed down the stairs and fairly threw myself into Will's arms. He laughed and hugged me in surprise, casting an embarrassed look around at the group.

"Cora!" Viv chided me.

"Aw, let her be," Felix said, giving me a brotherly smile and then winking at Will.

"I've missed you dreadfully," I said, looking about at the group. "All of you."

"We missed you too," Lil said, looping her arm through mine. "Wait until we tell you of the young men we saw," she whispered, giggling with Nell.

"The only young men you need to pay attention to are your brothers," Felix said, mock-sternly. The girls twittered a giggle again and moved off to change.

Will took my hand and led me through some French doors to a small balcony. "Are you all right?"

"What? Oh, yes. I'm fine, fine. It's only that…" I paused, suddenly feeling shy.

He bent his head, trying to get a good look at my face. "Only what? Was it as bad as all that?"

"Worse."

He wrapped me in his arms and held me close. "I'm sorry. Surely it will get better in time."

"I don't know. Andrew is simply awful," I whispered.

"He's only defending his territory. You keep defending yours." He kissed my head, and again, I was so glad that he was back. The rest, too. It would alleviate some of the tension, being in their company again.

"Will, do you think we might slip away for a walk together?"

"I'd love that," he said. "Let me change my coat, and I'll meet you in five minutes, all right?"

I nodded, and we kissed and parted. But soon, I hurried up the stairs too, knowing that this was the moment I had been waiting for. The perfect opportunity to give him his gift. In my room, I went to the bureau and opened the top drawer, sliding out the wooden box. I opened the lid and smiled over the gold watch. He was going to love it. What a joy it was to be able to give something so nice to the man I loved…

I slipped on my hat, pinning it with three long pins, and placed the box in a drawstring purse, then left the room. Will was waiting for me at the bottom of the stairs and offered his arm with a grin. Hearing voices approach, we quickly scurried out of the foyer and through the front door, closing it quietly behind us. Both of us were more than eager for a little time alone, and wished to slip out unseen in order to avoid a chaperone's company.

"I know just where to go," Will said, leading me down the street. "There's a place my uncle took me once, not far from here."

"Wonderful. Lead on."

Along the way, Will told me of their hike and the people they met, of the beautiful vistas, and of a fish fry for dinner down by the sea the night before. It all sounded so much more idyllic than my last two days, it practically made me cry that I had missed it. But such were the sacrifices I might need to make if I were to take on the mantle of responsibility my father had offered me.

Soon enough, we had turned the corner, and I saw where Will was taking me. We went down between two tall buildings to the very end of the street, which was capped by a waist-high wall. I leaned against it and over it, looking down the cliff face to the sea waves crashing against the rocks two hundred feet below. The sun was sinking in the distance, and the wind blew against my hat. I unpinned the hat and removed it, worried I might lose it, while Will looked up the quiet alleyway and then wrapped his arms around me from the back.

"Mmm," I said happily. "This reminds me of Carcassonne."

"Me too."

I turned in his arms. "I have a present for you," I said.

"You do?"

I nodded and slipped my purse strings from my elbow and opened it. "Will, I'm so happy to be with you. And I wanted to get you something special. When I saw this, I knew you had to have it."

He moved his head backward, as if he was both surprised and a little displeased, but he reached for the box and carefully opened the lid. His lips parted in surprise, and I grinned as he lifted the watch from its bed of velvet. But then he was frowning. "Cora, I can't take this. It's far too expensive."

"But you have to accept it!" I said. "I bought it for you! I can't take it back to the watchmaker…it's miles behind us now."

He looked at me in misery. "But I haven't given you a thing. It's not proper!"

"I don't want anything," I said, confused, taking his hand as he stepped a few inches away. "I have everything I need in you."

He looked to the sea and then back to me, and so much was going on behind his handsome light-blue eyes, it frightened me. Was he having second thoughts? About us? "Don't you see?" he asked, squeezing my hand. "This is what I fear most. You buying me gifts. And me, the pauper beau, unable to reciprocate. What will that look like to others?"

"To others?" I repeated, pulling him closer. "I thought we didn't care what others thought."

"Oh, Cora," he said, pulling away. "We all care, despite what we say. Don't we?"

"This is ridiculous! So I am to never buy you a present? Throughout our courtship?"

"No. I didn't say that. But this watch…" He held it up, and it glinted a warm, burnished gold in the evening sun. "It's an extravagance, Cora."

I shifted, uncomfortable. I'd known it was too much at the time. Why hadn't I listened to that note of caution in my heart? And all at once, I was thinking about the pearl necklace, the one Father had sent to me for my sixteenth birthday, as he had given Viv and Lil on theirs. But were such gifts the way toward true relationship? I shook my head—confused, embarrassed, frustrated, hurt, angry, all in quick succession. "Keep it or not. I don't care." With that, I shoved off, walking swiftly up the street.

"Cora!" he called, and I ignored him, continuing on. "Cora," he said again a moment later when he'd caught up. He took my arm and forced me to a stop. "Can we talk about this?"

"What, Will? Apparently I made an error of judgment. I purchased the man I love a gift. And that was clearly wrong." I hated what I was saying, *how* I was saying it, but couldn't seem to stop myself. I hurried off again.

He caught up with me again. "Look, it's not that I object to the gift. It's that I can't reciprocate. Is it too much to ask that we keep presents small? Trinkets, until…I don't know," he said, running an agitated hand through his hair. "For the foreseeable future?"

We were at the corner, and I paused to allow a curious couple to pass us. "Yes. I'm sorry I gave it to you, truly."

He stared at me in misery. "Please, Cora. Don't be like this."

"Like what? Generous? Loving? You're the one who is practically throwing my gift back in my lap. I didn't know it would offend you. Why do we have to reciprocate at all? Why can't I give a gift without expecting anything in return? And why do you think I expect it? I don't!"

"It's not proper," he resorted to saying. "It's a man's place to give a girl a gift, not the other way around."

I sighed and tried to gather myself. "What if this is the only gift I give you—for say…a year?"

He gave me a tentative smile and took my hand. "So…you anticipate being together for a year or more?"

I squeezed his hand hard and gave him a look of displeasure. "Now who is behaving ungentlemanly? What sort of question is that?"

His smile grew, and my tension eased a little, even though I was irked with him. "That was ungentlemanly of me," he admitted, holding on to my hand and covering it with his other. "Here is my proposal. You make the watch your only gift to me for two years, and I'll accept it."

Two years. I smiled. "Agreed."

He kissed my hand and tucked it through the crook of his arm, and we walked back to the apartments. But even as we settled into some semblance of a conversation, my stomach turned. Because something was now off between us. Just a little skewed. And I couldn't quite figure out how to right it.

~William~

They left the Cinque Terre and journeyed southward for a time, settling into sleepy Siena rather than the crowded Florence. The group traveled into Florence for the day, hoping to get in and out before they were recognized by any journalists or other American tourists, as they had done in Pisa and Lucca. That morning, they were touring the Uffizi in smaller groups—in an effort to attract less attention—gazing in rapt fascination at Botticelli's massive *Birth of Venus* painting. Time and time again, it surprised Will, seeing the famous works of art in Italy in person. But as they stood there, admiring the painting of a lovely naked woman arising from a clamshell, Hugh Morgan came up behind Cora and whispered suggestively, "Well, you all have found far more intriguing artwork than we have today."

"Really, Hugh," Cora said. "Must you always try and insert the devil in every tranquil scene?"

"Yes, *must* you?" asked his little sister, fanning her round face. "And why aren't you with your group?"

Hugh shrugged. "A man needs a little fun, Nell. Look," he said, glancing over his shoulder and around the room, "I realize it's a gift to see such famous works of art. But I have to say, if I never saw one more oil painting, it would suit me just fine. My head simply cannot take in any more facts of artistic methods or dates or titles. Can we not find a more entertaining method of learning about Firenze?" he asked Will. "Preferably something involving wine and women?"

"Much as I hate to admit it, I, too, seem about saturated," Cora said, giving Will an apologetic look. The younger girls bobbed their heads.

Will understood their weariness; by this time on the tour, almost everyone resisted seeing one more art museum or church, as they'd already seen so many. "Regardless of your weariness, Hugh, you'd best return to your group. You'll send Antonio into fits if he discovers you've disappeared."

"Not at all," Hugh said with a dismissive wave. "Antonio's in the next room. About to enter…now."

Will shook his head and heaved a sigh, then waved Antonio over as the other group did indeed appear. "I've changed my mind," Will announced to the reunited group. "I'll give you the short course of the Uffizi, then take you to see something rather more interesting… something few tourists can see. If I can manage a visit with no notice, of course."

"Well, *that* sounds intriguing," Vivian said, her eyes alight. But she wore a certain worry in the depths of her eyes. He wondered how she and Andrew were faring. Would she ever have the courage to break off her courtship with the man, once and for all?

"It is," he said, cocking one brow and nodding. "So, onward. I wouldn't be any sort of tour guide if you didn't at least see a fair number of Lippi, Titian, and Caravaggio paintings, as well as a few da Vincis and Michelangelos. Then we'll separate again outside and get some lunch, meet at the campanile, and I'll take you someplace special."

Antonio gave him a long look, questions in his eyes.

"I thought we'd stop by Signore Feliza's," Will said quietly. "See if he might grant us access to the warehouse."

Antonio's bushy black-and-gray brows shot up on his wide, wrinkled forehead. "You think it's possible? It's been years. Last time your uncle tried, he refused us."

"But he felt bad about that and now probably feels he owes Uncle Stuart a favor. I think I'll collect on it, since Stuart shan't be seeking to do so."

Antonio half turned to the group. "If your bear succeeds, you are in for a treat. A treat indeed."

"My man is most resourceful," Cora said, looping her arm through his and placing her other hand on it too. "I have every confidence he'll succeed."

Will blushed at her use of "my man," partially liking her claim but chafing over it too. Was he her man? Or was she his woman? Or both? He shook his head. *You're being foolish. Prideful. Move on, man.*

He loved her. And if he could afford a ring, he'd propose to her that very day. If she wore his ring, if he knew they were promised to each other, would that ease some of his agitation? He pondered that as they left the Uffizi, walking down the street and opting for a brief picnic of bread and cheese on the steps of the church and baptistery. It reminded Will of another place he wanted to take Cora. He lifted his head and checked the sun. It might be perfectly timed, if he was figuring right.

After eating, they moved back into the stream of crowds, passing vendors who sold leather goods and pottery, and crossed over the cobblestone streets to the Accademia dell'Arte. "Inside is the *David*," Will said to Cora, "which I definitely want you to see. But today I want you all to see something I like even better."

~Cora~

We passed the front entrance of the Accademia and moved around to the back of the big building, pausing at what appeared to be an entrance to a storehouse behind it. Will cast an anxious eye to the throngs of people heading to the famous museum that held the *David* and rapped on the door around the corner. After a minute, a short, older man with a bulbous nose opened it, wiping his mouth with a napkin. "*Chi è?*" he asked in irritation, squinting into the sun.

Then recognition softened his expression, and his face split into a wide grin. "William!" he said, lifting his arms out and offering his face for the common Italian greeting of a kiss to one cheek, then the other. The man I assumed was Signore Feliza squeezed Will's arms and then patted them, speaking rapidly in Italian. He cast an admiring glance over Will's charges, and then his eyes landed on me.

"*Bellissima! Chi è questa ragazza?*"

I didn't know what he said, but his expression and tone seemed directed at me, so I smiled at the man, who was about my height. He patted his chest as if my smile alone gave him heart palpitations and elbowed Will knowingly, chattering on.

"Signore Feliza *mi permetta di presentarle* Miss Cora Diehl Kensington," Will said. "Miss Diehl Kensington, meet Signore Feliza."

"How do you do, Signore?"

"Very well," he said, obviously proud of this little bit of English. "And you?"

"Very well," I said.

He seemed to remember there were others with us then and reached out to shake Antonio's hand and warmly greet the rest, one at a time. Then he cast a look of concern to Will again. "*Dove è Stuart?*"

"*Sono davvero spiacente di dirti che Stuart è morto più di un mese fa,*" Will said.

Even I could figure out that the two were conversing about Stuart's passing. The man's face contorted with sorrow. Then he said, "*Vieni, vieni,*" gesturing us into a small apartment. He and Will went on chatting. I decided that Will was telling our host about Stuart's death in Carcassonne, and after a moment, the two laughed over a shared memory, Antonio and Pascal joining in.

I didn't feel left out. I loved hearing the Italian language. And loved it even more when *my man*, as I'd earlier referred to Will, spoke it with such ease. It made me remember what had first attracted me to him—his knowledge, his ease, his demeanor, no matter what corner of the world he was in.

All of us stood about in our host's cramped little apartment, awkwardly taking up every square inch of room. Signore Feliza offered us coffee, gesturing to the stove, or wine, waving to a fat raffia-wrapped bottle. But Will declined and plunged in to what I guessed was his requested favor—still a mystery to me.

The man paused and tilted his head one way and then the other. He shrugged his shoulders, obviously uncomfortable with the idea. Will's tone changed to add a note of pleading, invoking my name first and then Stuart's, apparently calling in his favors—or his uncle's. Signore Feliza sighed heavily and then lifted one finger. "*Solo questa volta,*" he said. Then he turned to lead us through the end of his apartment, past a neatly made single bed, then down a narrow hallway.

Will wriggled his eyebrows at me and rubbed his hands together. I smiled over his self-satisfied pleasure. What was ahead seemed to excite him more than any other monument we'd seen yet. And judging from his face, Antonio, too. A thrill went through me as I stepped over a high threshold and through a small door.

It opened into a massive storeroom, and judging from the height, I wondered if the *David* might be directly behind the far wall. Shelf after wooden shelf held what appeared to be a hundred gravestone sculptures—men and women prone as if resting. Some of the women had veils over their faces and bodies—all carved out of stone. On the next shelf were a hundred busts, likenesses mostly of men, once prominent, now gone for decades or even centuries. Some had noses missing, but most were remarkably well preserved. I passed by them, a little unnerved by their wide, blank white eyes.

We reached the end of the shelves. In the very back, across the entire wall of the storeroom, were four massive blocks of white marble, each much taller than Will and wider than he could span with his arms. I gasped, seeing the first figure, nothing but a head, neck, and shoulder emerging from one of the blocks. Signore Feliza pulled off a canvas tarp from the next, and then the next, showing us each one.

Will stood beside me, hands on hips, mouth in a big smile. "It's even better than I remembered." He shared a look with Antonio, and the older man smiled back.

"Always a gift to see them here," Antonio said, nodding in thanks to Signore Feliza.

"What are they?" Vivian asked in wonder, walking around the third block for a better view.

"They're Michelangelo's unfinished sculptures," Will said. "Depictions of slaves, once meant for Pope Julius's elaborate tomb. They were supposed to be some of the fifty that Julius wanted, but the pope died sooner than expected, and the funding never came together to complete them. Two that were completed were in the Louvre in Paris. Do you remember seeing them?"

I nodded, but the Louvre, in its vastness, had been overwhelming. What came to me was only a dim memory. And I much preferred these sculptures still emerging, as if I could see the old master at work with his chisel and hammer, allowing each figure to find its way out of the stone.

"This one, they call the *Bearded Slave*," Antonio said. "It is the most finished of these four that remain."

And indeed it was. I liked the contrast of rough, untouched marble against the smooth finish of skin across shoulder, chest, and thigh. A wide band bound the slave, and his not-quite-finished face looked up and to the left, as if spying a far-off hopeful dream. Far more marble was at his back, waiting to be broken away. But my eyes were drawn to the next figure, in a narrower block.

"This is the *Young Slave*," Will said, stepping past it. "In the *contrapposto* pose."

"And that means…" Hugh said.

"See how he has most of his weight on one foot, and that throws his shoulders?" Will returned, emulating the figure. "How does that make him appear?"

"Relaxed," Hugh said.

"Rather bored, in a way," Lillian said.

"Indeed," Will said, staring up at the block. "Perhaps he's grown up as a slave. He seems settled with his lot in life, doesn't he?"

"And this?" I asked, moving to the third.

"They call him *Atlas*, since he seems to bear the weight of the world," Will said.

I smiled, because he was right. All that could be seen of the sculpture was the man's legs; his muscled belly; strong, wide chest; and burly arms. But his head and shoulders disappeared into the depths of the stone forever.

"Why did Michelangelo never come back to these?" I asked in wonder, a part of me dying to see them complete. And yet to see them in this state was a wonder too.

"Other commissions. Paid commissions. Even Michelangelo had to meet the bills."

We exchanged a smile of understanding. He took my hand and led me to the last one. "And this—this is my favorite. It's called the *Awakening Slave*.'" He said no more, simply waited while we looked on. I could see why it was his favorite. The figure seemed partially alive. Vibrant. Writhing, flexing, straining.

"Michelangelo saw himself as freeing his figures from the stone," Will said lowly, chin in hand. "But does not this one feel as if he's intent on freeing himself?"

"It *does*," I said, staring at the figure's wide chest. There was such raw power in it, I half expected him to begin moving, as if somehow, miraculously alive.

"He reminds me of you," Will whispered in my ear.

I started and peered at the figure anew. What reminded Will of me in it? Was I enslaved? Struggling to be free? Of what?

"Why are these not in a museum?" Vivian asked.

He laughed under his breath. "There is disagreement among the curators. Half find the stones vital, and half consider them trash. So here they sit. If my uncle hadn't befriended Signore Feliza, the caretaker here, we would never have seen them either."

"It's tragic, really," I said, practically whispering. "Out of all we've seen, I believe they are my favorites."

"Mine too," Will said, and we shared a tender smile. "Come. We should leave Signore Feliza before our intrusion is discovered by the curator."

"*Grazie*," I said to the man, heartfelt in my thanks, as were the others, and he waved a dismissive hand in the air, but his eyes said he was glad to share the figures. I wondered if perhaps he spent month after month near them, never uncovering them from their shrouds, forgetting the wonder they were.

We said our good-byes and left through his apartment. We emerged on the street, which was now several degrees cooler and darker than when we'd entered, and Will leaned in to share a word with Antonio. The older man's eyebrows lifted, and he smiled and nodded.

"It's been a full day," Will said to the group. "Antonio and Pascal are going to see you to the train and back to Siena, but I'm hoping to persuade Miss Cora to stay with me for a bit longer."

It was my turn to be surprised, but I tried to hide it as Felix scowled at his old friend. "Really, McCabe? Do you think it entirely proper? Without a chaperone at this hour?"

"Not entirely," Will admitted, with a crooked smile. "But I promise to be none but a gentleman in your sister's company."

Felix turned to face me and Will, arms crossed. "See that you don't break that promise," he said solemnly, making me smile. I'd always wanted a big brother... I kissed Vivian and Lillian and Nell on the cheeks, and they were off, guarded by their guide and a detective as well as Hugh, Felix, and Andrew.

"If Signore Feliza's is what you had up one sleeve," I said to Will, taking his arm, "I cannot wait to see what's up your other one."

He waggled his eyebrows and smiled. "Are you up for an adventure? Or are you weary? We could simply find a sleepy trattoria on the back streets and share a cozy supper if you're too taxed."

I smiled back into his eyes, full of mischief. "Oh, no," I said. "I won't be able to sleep until I see what you wish to show me."

CHAPTER 10

~William~

"So," Cora said, "why did you say the *Awakening Slave* reminded you of me?"

Will smiled down at her. "Perhaps it was his biceps…"

She laughed and shook her head. "No, really."

"Why do you think?" he pressed back. "Was there anything in the sculpture that reminded you of yourself?"

"Besides the biceps?" she said with an impish grin. She looked up to the red-tiled rooftops and evening sky, a pale blue above them, while Will kept an eye out for any reporters. The only trouble with escorting Cora was that she stood out in a crowd of southern Italians, with her fine clothing, blonde hair, and blue eyes. Everywhere they went, they drew curious looks. How long until someone connected her to the woman in Italy's own newspapers of late? It'd become a mystery, these last days, Antonio had told him. The Case of the Missing Heiress.

"I think," she said at last, "that you see me as freeing myself of the shackles that once bound me. Of claiming my identity, as a

Diehl, as a Kensington, and as a daughter of God—and exploring what that means." When he didn't say anything, she added, "No?"

"Yes," he said. "I've seen you grow in so many ways this summer, Cora. And I know that some of it has felt like freeing yourself of stone. It's been work, but you've done it. I admire that in you."

Once Cora had found her footing with her siblings—about the time they reached France—she'd seemed to blossom. Or had it been meeting Pierre that helped her over the hurdle?

Thoughts of the man—and his promise to meet again with them in Rome—darkened Will's sunny mood. Did she still think of him? Wonder about him? Hope for that day of his return—or dread it? Did she wonder what he might buy her as presents? Wonder if he might have reciprocated if she had given him as fine a gift as the watch?

"So why the sour face?" Cora asked, startling him out of his thoughts. "Do you not approve of this awakening slave?"

"Wh-what? Oh," he said, shaking his head. "Sorry. I'd moved on to other thoughts." He instantly regretted letting them creep in… At last they were together, alone, and he would ruin it by bringing up the watch again? Or Pierre?

"Care to share it?" she asked, leaning toward him as they walked across the cobblestones.

"No," he said quickly, more harshly than he meant to. She visibly recoiled. "Forgive me, but I can't."

"That's all right," she said. But she stared ahead, not looking up and around as she had a moment before.

Inwardly, he groaned. She felt cut out, and justifiably so. "Look, I was only thinking of Pierre," he confessed.

"Oh," she said, her delicate eyebrows shooting upward. "What brought him to mind?"

He put his hand over hers and slowed his stride. "I was thinking about how you've blossomed on our journey," he said quietly. "Like Michelangelo's sculpture back there, breaking free of your past and embracing your future. And I was hoping it was because of what you've seen, experienced at my side. Not because of meeting...Pierre. Or reaching a place of stature in terms of wealth."

She ducked her head as if in thought, and they walked in silence for a bit. Then she said, "Will, honestly, it has all impacted me—the entire journey and every person involved. But it is *you* by my side now, right?"

"Forever," he said gently. "I hope."

She gave him a soft smile. "As do I." And the promise in her clear blue eyes made his heart surge with pleasure.

"Forgive me, my love, for casting a shadow over such a brilliant day."

"I understand," she said lightly.

They entered through the tall doors of the duomo, into the echoing sanctuary. They'd already done a quick tour of the cathedral and baptistery with the group earlier in the day.

"You remember," she said slowly, teasing him as they walked beneath the dome again, "that we were here earlier, right? Or are you like Hugh in thinking that one church is like another, and you forgot we already toured this?"

"I wanted to show you the best part of this whole structure," he said, leaning close enough to smell the sweet scent of her hair, the subtle bit of lemon verbena on her skin. It made him long to pull her close, out and away from the crowds. To kiss her… He remembered her in his arms, in the water near the Cinque Terre, her hair spread in glorious waves—

"Will?" she asked, apparently for the second time.

"Oh, sorry," he said, feeling himself blush to be caught so lost in thought. "Come." He took Cora's gloved hand and led her to a side doorway. He spoke to the doorman and quietly paid him with a wad of lira, and the man allowed the two of them to slip through. They paused at the bottom of a long set of wooden stairs, and Will turned back to Cora. "This was my favorite place to go in Florence as a boy. My uncle brought me up these stairs the very first time we came here."

"Where does it lead?"

"You'll see," he said with a grin. He led her upward, and five flights later, they emerged onto a small walkway that ran around the circumference of the base of the dome roof. From here, they could see the fresco paintings up close.

"That's odd," she said.

"What?"

"They look distorted. All out of proportion. But from down below, they looked fine."

"Part of the mastery, isn't it? The painters had to figure out how it would appear below, and paint them wrongly, so they would appear *right* below. It's the same with *David*. If we were to stare at his eyes close up, they'd be looking in two separate directions."

"Amazing," she said, stepping down the narrow wooden walk.

"Careful," he warned, lifting his left hand to guard her as she looked upward to her right and leaned precariously close to the rail.

She glanced nervously to her side. To the church floor far below. "Well, that would be a nasty fall, wouldn't it?"

"Indeed," he said, swallowing an inner shudder at the thought of her falling. He shook his head. It was with some relief that they reached the next door on the far side and he told her to go through it. They entered a new stairwell that was rapidly growing dark as the sun set outside. He hoped there were some candles above—he should have considered it earlier. But they were this far. To turn back now would mean missing what he wanted to show Cora most of all.

They climbed one winding flight of stairs after another. "The dome that we're circumventing was a marvel at the time. A dome without external buttresses to keep it from collapsing under its own weight had not been built since antiquity. And this was to be even larger than the Pantheon's in Rome."

"Why not use buttresses?" Cora asked.

"They considered them ugly, and since their political enemies used them, the city's fathers refused to do so. It was a break with the Gothic pattern and the first of many of the Renaissance's hallmarks. And yet no one could figure out how to raise such a massive dome without buttresses. At the time, even the mason's mortar took several days to cure, and the weight put a tremendous amount of stress on the scaffolding, to say nothing of the stress to the structure long-term. So it remained unbuilt for more than a hundred years. Then came Brunelleschi and Ghiberti, competing architects, toward the end of the fourteenth century.

"Some say the two were given a test. Whomever could get an egg to stand on one end on a piece of marble would get the commission.

Ghiberti tried and failed. Brunelleschi took a long look at the egg, then cracked one end, making it stand in place."

"That's cheating!" Cora said.

Will smiled. "In a way. The other architects grumbled, saying they could certainly have done the same, to which Brunelleschi said, 'Well, yes, and if you could see my dome plans, you, too, could build a dome for Santa Maria del Fiore.'"

"He was so confident?"

Will shrugged. "Either confident or bluffing. But he managed to put more than four million bricks into this dome, and it's obviously still standing today."

"I can't imagine building such a structure. But I imagine *you* could."

"It must've been glorious to be an architect in such an era. Brunelleschi even invented a unique hoisting machine to get the bricks up to the masons. And he was granted one of the first patents ever in order to protect his idea."

"He must've been brilliant."

"Brilliant or simply willing to try."

"Likely both," Cora said. "I think I may have many willing-to-try moments ahead of me, working with my father. And Andrew Morgan."

"Indeed you will." Upward they went, single-file, hunched over in places in order to fit through. "I confess this was far easier as a child," he huffed after turning a particularly tight corner.

"I would imagine," Cora said, similarly out of breath. But her eyes shone with excitement, and he knew he'd made the right choice, bringing her. They climbed for another fifteen minutes before finally the stairs ended and they stood on a small platform. "Ready?" Will asked, his hand on the old brass doorknob as he looked down at Cora, who was only partially visible in the dark of the stairwell.

"Ready," she said.

"Close your eyes," he said. "I want to see your face the moment you see what I have to show you."

"All right," she said tentatively. He opened the door, took her by the shoulders, and guided her out of the stairwell, to the tiny cupola that served as the observation deck of the duomo. Here, the dome's roof descended in a gentle curve of cascading tiles in every direction. And here, on Firenze's highest building, there was a clear view in every direction. He looked about and then positioned Cora toward the last bits of the setting sun, now but a rose-hued glow on the horizon.

"Open your eyes, beloved," he said in her ear, smelling her perfume of lemon verbena again. He left his hands on her shoulders.

She gazed in wonder and, for the second time that day, gasped. In terror, she backed in to him, and he wrapped his arms around her. "It's all right. I have you."

She stilled and stared out from the small cupola. "Oh, Will," Cora said. "It's so lovely! I feel as if we're standing on top of the world!"

"It is, isn't it?" he smiled, kissing her hair, then her temple, and pulled her back against his chest, wrapping her tightly in his arms.

"You can see forever!" she said. "The closest I've been to this height was on the Eiffel Tower."

"Can you imagine being one of the original builders up here? None of them had likely worked at such great heights either.

Architects came from thousands of miles to study it and watch her crews construct it."

"It's marvelous. Astounding."

"Come," he said, dropping his arms and leading her to the other side of the platform so she could see the rest of the city and the mountains beyond it. The sunset's light was heavy with dew, layering everything they saw in a deeper, saturated color—from the green of the hills to the red of the tile roofs.

"It's so glorious," she said. "I could stay up here forever."

"You are glorious," he said, turning her to face him and tipping up her chin to give her a soft, lingering kiss. He pulled her closer, and their kiss deepened. Then he reluctantly pulled away, forcing himself to be content holding her.

But oh, how he longed to kiss her more.

"It's like we're the bride and groom atop a wedding cake," she said, leaning her cheek against his chest.

He laughed softly. "Yes, I suppose we are."

Her words echoed through his mind; he could hardly think of anything else. She was saying something, turning to him, a question in her eyes, but he was moving before he knew what he was doing.

Down to one knee.

Her hand in both of his.

"Cora Diehl Kensington," he began, his voice wavering at first, then gaining strength. "I have loved you from the moment we met. At every turn, I find myself deeper in love," he said, shaking his head and looking up at her. She was so utterly wonderful. And this was too… "I promise to forever love you and honor you and cherish you. I know this is sudden. But would you do me the honor of becoming my wife?"

"Oh," she breathed, bringing her other hand up to her chest, and he grinned up at her. "Oh, Will," she said.

It was then that he felt his first cold shiver of doubt.

He forced himself to wait where he was. For her to face him and say what she had to.

"Will, there's been so much." Her hand moved to her forehead. "So much these last weeks, months. I do love you," she said, reaching down to cover his hands with hers. "I do," she insisted, her eyes pleading. "But this step? Do you think it wise?"

That brought him to his feet.

He dropped her hands. "Wise? I suppose there are some who consider marriage a folly. But not I." His mind spun. His stomach roiled. Was it Pierre? It had to be—

"Will, come—" she said, reaching out but then letting her hand drop. "Of course I don't think… It's only that this is so soon…" She turned away and went to the rail of the cupola, looking out, while Will berated himself for acting on impulse. For not waiting. And inwardly, he crumbled that she wasn't immediately willing to say yes. That she wasn't as sure as he was that they were meant to be together forever.

She looked over her shoulder. "There has been so much that has happened these last months," she said. "I feel as Hugh does about seeing one more piece of artwork. One more thing, atop all the rest…"

"Well," he said stiffly, "I most certainly did not intend to burden you."

"Will," she said, her thin eyebrows furrowing in a frown. "Please. Don't do that," she said. "You know what I mean."

"Do I?" he asked. Even though he did, his anger, his humiliation was building. If Hugh and Felix found out about his proposal, he'd never hear the end of it... And Mr. Kensington? *What have I done?*

But overriding those emotions was a terrific sorrow, a sense of separation. Had he been wrong about her all along? Or had her change of station transformed how she saw him, after all?

"*Will*," she said, turning toward him and taking his hand, then looking up at him with pleading eyes. "I'm not saying no. All I'm saying is that perhaps this isn't the right time. Can we not simply enjoy each other's company through the remainder of the tour and discover where that leads us?"

He looked down at her, unable to summon the compassion to override his hurt. "Just tell me one thing."

"Anything," she said, desperation lacing her tone.

"Is it because I am below you in station now? Because I cannot buy you expensive gifts in return?"

She dropped his hand and took a step away. "We've returned to the subject of the *watch* again? And how can you ask such a thing of me?" She shook her head, fury bringing fire to her beautiful eyes. "How?"

"How can I not?" he asked, throwing his hands up.

"Clearly you and I do not know each other as well as I thought we did," she said stiffly.

"Clearly," he snapped back, but inside, misery washed through him. What was he doing? Driving her away on purpose?

She folded her arms and shivered. "It's chilly out here now that the sun's down. Perhaps we should get to the station and back to Siena. The others will be worried. Father will be worried."

He walked to the door and opened it, staring straight ahead as she passed by him and into the dark stairwell. She waited for him to go first, and he reached back for her hand. She reluctantly took it, and they made their way down the serpentine, oddly spaced stairs into the depths of the church, not another word shared between them. Here and there, light from outside spilled inward, giving them moments of respite from the dark. But even as they approached the final hundred steps, fully illuminated by gas lights, Will had never experienced a greater darkness. With each step, his mind screamed, *What have you done? Will McCabe, what have you done?*

CHAPTER 11

~Cora~

In all my traveling over the summer, I'd never done so in such utter silence. Someone had always engaged me, every single day. But our trip from Firenze to Siena that night was as dismally cold and silent as an abandoned cemetery.

Will and I sat across from each other for a while, each staring at the silhouette of the dark landscape outside as well as our own dim reflections. Over and over again, I tried to come up with the right words, the right rationale, something to help him see. But over and over again, I only heard my Lord say, *Wait and trust*. I hadn't been wrong in thinking it was too soon. I loved Will, but marriage was simply too great a consideration for me yet. I wanted him to come home with me. Meet my parents. For us to settle into our new lives, responsibilities, free of debt, and see where God led us. I formed one sentence of explanation after another in my head, but each time, I stopped myself from speaking. Everything I thought of would only add further insult or injury. I knew that all he could think was that I wasn't certain, that I didn't love him enough…

And was I certain? Would I have responded any differently if it had been Pierre who proposed? Most assuredly not. I loved Will. I had chosen the right man. It was merely that I was as I had said to Will…completely overwhelmed. Agreeing to marriage at that moment felt like it might very well break me. Could he not see that?

It wasn't until we reached the train station and saw Pascal waiting for us on the platform that Will looked me in the eye. "Cora," he said, my very name sounding like it pained him.

"Oh, Will," I said. I shook my head. "Clearly, what happened tonight was not what either of us desired, but can we not go on from here?"

"I'd like to," he said. He tried to quirk a smile, but somehow, it just made him look more hurt, which nearly twisted my heart in two. "At least you know my intentions."

I smiled gently in return. "Your intentions have been made most clear. And you've honored me. I only need more…time."

He nodded, then rose and offered me his hand. I took it, then his elbow as we made our way out of the car and down the steep stairs to the ramp. But even though we'd at least spoken, there was still a rift between us. *Please, Lord*, I prayed, even as I smiled and nodded at Pascal and he opened the door to the motorcar for us. *Help us find our way through.*

Because, I realized as we sped through the night to join my family and the Morgans, the only time Will and I'd been truly separated this summer was from Vienna to Venice, and every one of those days had felt like weeks to me. Whatever I had to do to mend this, I had to figure it out.

And soon.

~William~

Eleonora Masoni's villa was perfectly situated for their tour of Toscana, poised as it was on the crest of a hill between Pienza and Montepulciano, but even as they wound their way up to it, Will could see it was not as large of an accommodation as many they'd enjoyed on the tour. Instead of one massive building, it was a stately yet modest villa with several cottages about it. Would there be room enough for all of them?

They reached the turn into Villa Masoni, and the five motor-cars slowed, trying to keep from stirring up dust that would lift on the steady breeze over what looked like about twelve workers in the vineyard beside the road. All of them had been hunched over, prun-ing the vines, until they heard the cars, which made them all rise and stare. One woman in a broad-brimmed hat smiled and lifted an arm in greeting, and Will did a double-take, realizing it was the elegant Eleonora Masoni herself out with her field hands. He smiled in delight.

She pointed toward the villa, and the drivers moved on, tak-ing their charges to the top of the hill. They were all yet assembling when Signora Masoni entered their circle, calling *"Benvenuti!"*— welcoming them in with a broad, sunny smile. In a slightly tattered brown work dress that did nothing to diminish her beauty, she was even lovelier than Will had remembered. It took only seconds for

Hugh and Felix to angle their way forward, eager to be first to be introduced by Antonio. Each kissed her hand and vied to be most gallant. Will inwardly groaned. By her title and yet lack of ring, he knew she'd been married but was now either divorced or a young widow. Was she yet ready for such flirtation?

When she reached him, he shook her hand as he offered a single nod of his head. "*E' cosi' generoso da parte tua averci invitato a casa tua,*" he said. *It is most gracious of you to welcome us into your home.*

"Not at all," she returned in perfect English. "It is my joy to host new friends. Please, please," she said, turning to the rest. "Come in." She turned and lifted her skirts to climb the steps to the main house, then paused at the top. She leaned in to speak to a servant, gesturing to ours, and then spoke to their group again. "As you can see, I cannot house you all within this building, but there is plenty of room here and about. My foreman can direct your servants as to where to store your luggage, and we shall gather for some lunch. Come, come."

They followed her into a beautiful room full of aged but welcoming furniture surrounding a wide fireplace with so much soot, it looked like it'd enjoyed a century of continual use. The house was perfectly clean but far more rustic than anywhere they'd stayed yet. Will scanned the group, assessing their reaction, and saw that Cora was delighted, Vivian and Andrew clearly dismayed, the girls in shock—but game for an adventure—and Hugh and Felix…well, they hadn't taken their eyes off their hostess. The elder men had been dropped off in Pienza with Pascal to see to some banking business. Who knew how they would react to Will's bringing their children here? Would they object? Will sincerely hoped not. Signora Masoni had been more than kind to invite them all to stay with her, especially now that he knew what a stretch it would be for her.

She did not pause in the great living room, but moved on through an arched, open doorway, directly into a kitchen. He covered a smile when the younger girls shared a wide-eyed look at this new spectacle—no separation between a servant's domain and a lady's. Had they ever seen such a home? It was perfect, really. A true opportunity to expand their minds and help them understand how others lived.

"You must be famished," Signora Masoni said, wrapping an apron around her slim waist and bending to wash her hands in a massive sink beneath a window with one of the prettiest views of Tuscany Will had ever seen. "There's a washroom back to the right, or you can wash right here, if you like. I'll help Ita to get some food ready, and we can share a little lunch."

Will and Cora stepped forward as the others awkwardly paused. "It is most kind of you to have us here," Will said, rolling up his shirt sleeves.

"Not at all," Signora Masoni said with a smile, handing him a linen towel as he finished washing his hands. "I love to meet new people. And people from America?" Her brown eyes shone as she looked over her group of guests. "We shall speak long into the night as you tell me tales of your journey and home."

"Only if you share some of your own, too," Cora said, taking the towel from Will—the closest they'd been to each other all day.

"I like to tell a good story as well as hear them," their hostess returned. "Here, come," she said, gesturing to the vast aged-pine table in the center of the room. "Sit, sit." They sat down on the benches on either side after washing up, and Will looked up to see drying bunches of lavender, ropes of garlic, and peppers hanging from the heavy beams above them. In the corner of the room were three cured hams hanging in nets.

With one brief query from Signora Masoni, Hugh launched into a tale about their traumatic crossing from America, leaning against the counter as he spoke. Ita, a girl of about fifteen, moved swiftly and efficiently around him, dicing tomatoes with a practiced hand, then unwrapping a huge wheel of pecorino cheese and hacking off a chunk with what looked more like a small axe than a knife. Another servant girl appeared and silently set a cloth napkin and an ivory, porcelain plate in front of each of them, leaving three more for her mistress, Will, and Hugh—who were still standing—and then went about offering wine or water to each person. *"Vino o acqua?"*

They all opted for water, except for Hugh and Felix, who chose the wine. Andrew looked like he was suffering actual physical pain and kept shooting Will looks as if to say, *Surely you don't mean to keep us here.* Vivian, in turn, seemed to become more settled with this choice, since it was so obviously the opposite of Andrew's preferences. While she seemed to keep outwardly to her goal of sticking with their courtship, Will was as convinced as Cora—Andrew and Vivian belonged anywhere but together.

Antonio arrived, and Will moved over on the bench. Instantly, Ita had another place setting in front of him. Then came cold duck liver; grapes; a wedge of soft cheese; apple slices; and thick, crusty bread with soft-churned butter. In minutes, they were all eating, and Signora Masoni told them about the latest run of rain that had threatened the year's crop before letting up just two days prior.

"How long have you managed this place on your own?" Felix asked, careful to not look her way.

"You mean how long have I been without a man," she said, a hint of a smile on her lips but a direct challenge in her eyes.

"That too," Hugh said, lifting his cup to accept another bit of wine from Ita as she rounded the table. But his eyes were on their hostess.

"My husband passed two years ago," she said dismissively. "He was ill for a short time."

It was impossible to tell if there was any grief behind her words. She said them matter-of-factly, with no hint of emotion.

"I am sorry for your loss," Will said after an awkward pause.

The women murmured their condolences too, but Signora Masoni cut them short. "No, no. Don't be," she said, waving her hand. "I am far better off without him." She smiled. "He was not a nice man. The Lord spared me"—she crossed herself from forehead to chest, and across her shoulders, then placed her hands together as if in prayer, looking up—"when He took my husband from this earth." She shook her head, popped another bite of bread into her mouth, chewed, and swallowed. "My husband had a terrible temper. I did not wish to marry him, but my father insisted." She shrugged. "And so I did. We all make our mistakes, no?"

The group fell silent, none of them but Will daring to look down the table toward Andrew and Vivian. Andrew's eyes narrowed as he saw Vivian look to her lap.

"Take your ease, my friends!" Signora Masoni said, misinterpreting their collective unease. "I am young yet. And while my husband was far from kind, he left me with this, a home I love, and now, I share with you."

"Or rather, that we've now overtaken," Felix said, raising his glass in a toast. "Thank you for your generosity."

"It is my good pleasure."

They all began eating again. And while the conversation continued in amiable fashion, Will doubted any of them were thinking about anything but Vivian becoming entrapped by an unkind husband, just as Signora Masoni once had been.

The next morning, Will moved down the tiled outdoor hallway toward the main house, admiring the ancient fat timbers that crossed above, layered in vines. The Masoni villa was small but quintessentially Tuscan, and their hostess had put Will and Antonio in a separate small cottage, just off the southern corner of the larger, two-story villa. He thought it entirely satisfactory—and this brief respite, without any of his charges in view for once, even more so. Especially Cora. They needed some…time. Separation. Or at least he did.

Will put his hands on his hips and took in a deep breath, looking toward the morning sky, peach-hued and full of the promise of a warm day. "Thank You, Lord," he said.

A hat-covered head popped up from the other side of a four-foot hedge. Signora Masoni. She flashed him a smile, her eyes curious as she looked around. "To whom do you speak, Signore McCabe?"

"Ahh," Will said, feeling a flush of embarrassment. "To God, actually."

She gave him a confused, amused smile. "And do you often speak to God, Signore—*Mister* McCabe?"

"As often as possible," he returned, locking his hands behind his back. "And in retrospect, not nearly enough on this tour."

She rose, and he saw she'd been cutting sprigs of lavender and laying them in a broad, flat basket hooked over her arm. With the morning sun behind her on the horizon, warming the entire landscape with an ethereal, golden light, she looked more than a bit like an Italian angel.

"I'm surprised you look as rested as you do, Mr. McCabe," she said. When he hesitated, caught, she said with a smile, "Oh, yes. I know that you prowled the grounds last night." She came around the hedge of lavender and laid a featherlight hand on his arm, so quickly he wondered if he'd imagined it. She peeked up at him from under the brim of her hat. "I think it charming, Mr. McCabe. Most charming. You take good care of your tour group. Or is it Miss Cora that you worry most about?"

He studied her. Clearly she missed nothing. "I am concerned about the well-being of all my charges. And the first night in a new place…" He paused and shook his head. "Well, that never is my best night of slumber."

"They are fortunate to have you as their guide," she said, moving around him to his right shoulder and looking out to the valley with him.

"It is I who am fortunate to lead them," he said, "for I get to see lovely country like this and stay with kind hostesses like you."

She smiled and then paused to look out over a short wall. He stood beside her. The villa was situated on the crest of one of the highest hills around, affording a magnificent view for miles. The valley stretched before them. To the left was a massive olive grove that extended down and then up and over the next hill. To their right was a vineyard that covered five of the nearest hills in tidy rows of gnarled vines. "You have a sizable vineyard."

"Bigger each year is our goal," she said. "There are restaurants in Roma that only serve our wine."

"Truly?" Will said, crossing his arms and gazing down at the vineyards with renewed interest. "That is impressive. Most of the Toscana vintners I know only cultivate for their own tables."

"Well, that is a side benefit," she said, smiling again and giving him a wink. She turned to go and then glanced back at him. "Please find me at once if your people need anything at all."

"Thank you, Signora. You are most gracious."

"Please, call me Eleonora."

"Gladly. But only if you call me Will."

She placed a delicate hand at her neck and gave him a coy smile. "Will," she repeated with a slight *v* to her pronunciation. "Have a lovely morning, Will."

His eyes narrowed, even as he put a hand to his chest and gave her a slight bow. "*Grazie mille*, Eleonora," he said, then waited for her to turn and leave him, as was proper. When she finally did, he walked back down the stone path to his small villa, needing to get his thoughts in order before he faced the group.

Especially Cora. His eyes cut guiltily to Eleonora's back, almost inside now, then back to the path. What was that moment of attraction he'd felt? The easy connection to the young widow? In all of his years as an adult, that had only happened to him perhaps four or five times. One was Cora. And now...Eleonora as well? That could rapidly complicate things.

Antonio was outside on the small flat patio, arms crossed, admiring the morning sun. He looked to the right at Will as he came around the corner of the stone building. "Ahh, *buon giorno*, my friend. I'd be questioning your morals if I didn't know you'd returned to your bed off and on all night." He gave Will a sly smile.

"Come now," Will said, standing beside him, crossing his arms too. He knew Antonio assumed that he'd been romancing Cora. He hadn't told him what had transpired in Firenze. "You know very well how I must settle into a new place. No wine and long conversations for me."

Antonio clapped him on the shoulder. He looked out over the valley. "This is a good place, far from anywhere that Nathan Hawke might look for us."

"Indeed. With luck, we'll avoid him and any reporters in the hill towns, too."

Antonio eyed him again from the side. "And what of our hostess? Was she truly drawn in by our generous, thoughtful Miss Cora, or by her handsome guides?" He ran his hands down the lapels of his jacket.

Will smiled. "Perhaps both," he admitted. "You saw us up there in the walkway?"

Antonio gave him a smile in return. "I saw her cutting quite a bit of lavender for quite a long time. Almost as if she was waiting for you to pass by."

Will scowled at him. "You imagine things, Antonio."

"*Si, si,*" said his friend, slowly, pretending to agree. "I am an old man, given to fanciful ideas."

~Wallace~

After a brief reunion with the children, Wallace Kensington settled heavily into his chair beside Sam Morgan, who was smoking a cigar on the veranda of Villa Masoni, overlooking the valley. "Mighty far piece from Montana, aren't we, Morgan?"

The man nodded, took a deep drag on his cigar and then slowly blew it out. "Must we really follow the children along this tour? They seem safe enough, especially here in Tuscany. Business is piling up… It'd be advantageous for us to go to Rome straightaway. Look what we got done today. They could rejoin us there."

"I need to stay with them," Wallace said. "If you are so inclined, don't let me hold you back. We can go to the city as needed to keep things from the edge of disaster, but I…" He shook his head. "No, I need to stay nearby, even if you need to go."

"It's probably best," his old business partner said, waving in the air with his cigar. "I expect Andrew and Vivian will have good news for us any day now. If I wasn't here to witness it, Mary would have my hide."

"I expect she would," Wallace said with a humorless laugh.

The two sat in silence for a while. "Tell me the truth, Wallace," Morgan said, taking a slow look around to make certain they were alone. "Have you seen enough to believe that Cora has what it takes to run the Kensington-Diehl Mine?"

"She will," Wallace said, bending forward to cup his hand around a match and drag deeply on his own freshly cut cigar. He took a couple of puffs to make certain it was well lit and then settled back in the chair. "I aim to ensure that she's the most successful—as well as the richest—woman in America."

But even he could hear the sigh in his own tone.

"And are you hoping," Morgan said, taking a drag and then letting it out slowly, "that in filling her life with newfound duties, she'll turn away from young McCabe?"

Wallace gave him a sharp look and then gazed out to the valley again. "Let the chips fall where they may—that's what I say."

"Those chips might well cost you your daughter." Morgan paused and returned Wallace's frown. "Now hear me out. If you let this go…if it doesn't turn out as you wish, it will haunt you for the remaining years of your life. And as your friend, I'd hate to see you suffer through that."

Wallace let out a dismissive sound. "You make me out like a weak, desperate old man, Morgan. You know me better than that."

"Exactly," said his oldest friend, settling back in his chair and gazing outward. Wallace knew that he wouldn't say more. It was precisely what he liked about Morgan. He was a man of few words, and yet when he chose to speak, each syllable was full of wisdom.

The man's sons had fallen about as far from the tree as possible. Perhaps it had to do with being raised as sons of wealth, but they neither appeared nor acted anything like their father—with his steady grace, his kindness. And yet it was good that Andrew was so strong and forthright, given Vivian's stubborn spirit. While the two had been at odds of late, friction was bound to happen. In time, such friction created well-worn grooves, helping a couple fit together better. Hadn't it happened in his own marriage?

His mind cascaded back to those heady first days when wealth, true wealth, settled in and about him. They'd been in the house for five years, had hundreds of thousands of dollars in the bank, business was booming, and he and Georgina were still in that filing stage, working on their grooves, until one hardship seemed so nearly impossible to get past that they avoided each other for months.

And then Alma had come to work at the house.

Kind and sweet, direct in her gaze and yet respectful, she seemed to see through him from the first day onward. In her eyes, he felt known. Understood. Appreciated as a man. The very smell of her when she entered a room seemed to draw him, call him.

What was worse, she seemed equally drawn to him.

He ignored it for weeks, months. But after one particularly bitter argument with his wife, he'd gone to his library and settled into the chair to drink himself into oblivion. A footman came in at sunset to light a fire in the hearth, stacking the logs high as Wallace favored. And long after his bottle was empty and the fire had burned down to glowing embers, Alma came in to put away some borrowed tomes. He watched her, so intent that he lifted an empty crystal glass to his lips like an old drunkard, before he realized he'd long-since enjoyed his last sip. She didn't see him at first, sitting in his leather chair in the corner's shadows, and he watched her for a long, lovely minute as she quickly and efficiently shelved the books in just the right spots.

She was clearly as intelligent as she was pretty.

When she finally saw him, she was nearly beside him. She gasped and put a hand to her throat, then quickly bobbed a curtsy and took a respectful step backward. "I beg your pardon, Mr. Kensington. I would've waited had I known you were here."

She stepped away, intent on escape, but Wallace leaned forward and grasped her hand. "I'm glad you didn't," he said, covering her hand with a more gentle touch. "How I've longed for but a moment with you."

"Mr. Kensington," she'd said, pulling her hand away and shaking her head. Poor dear, she'd trembled. And he'd been a lout, pursuing her as he had. But in months, she was his. And gradually she loved him as he so desperately loved her. In many ways, she was far better suited to him than his wife had ever been. It was tortuous, knowing he loved her but could not keep her, especially when she became pregnant... It had never been fair to her. And then it had not been fair to Cora. He'd been a cad. But he'd done his best to do right by them...

Wallace blew out a thick cloud of smoke and rubbed his temples. It would have been best to do what he knew was right from the start. To honor his vows to his wife. To steer clear of the winsome housemaid with the direct gaze, a look in the eyes like he had not enjoyed since his days of building his fortune... But he hadn't had the strength to do it. He'd been weak, in the end. And for his weakness, everyone had paid a steep price. Alma. Georgina. Cora.

Before the day he sent Alma off on the train with Alan, he'd never known the meaning of a broken heart. Ever after, he had. And now, with Cora so near, and yet still not trusting him, there were echoes of that sorrow radiating through his chest. It was different now, as an old man. It was not a lover's love, but a far more melancholic tenderness, a father's fear that a beloved child might slip away.

"You are deep in thought," Morgan grunted, wrenching him back to the present.

"That I am," Wallace said, taking another drag on his cigar. "That I am."

CHAPTER 12

~Cora~

"So, tell me, my friend," Eleonora Masoni said, sitting down beside me, "how you find our Italia."

"I find it lovely," I said before sipping from my sweating glass of water as she poured her own. After enduring a couple of hours of mind-numbing instruction with my father about the nuances of hydraulic drills, I'd finally escaped to sit under a wide umbrella, shaded from the hot afternoon sun. Most of the rest of the group was out enjoying a game of badminton. Only Vivian was absent, claiming a headache after breakfast and returning to her room. "Of all the countries I've seen along our tour, I must confess that Italia keeps delighting me at every turn."

"It is a fine country to call home," Signora Masoni said with a smile.

I let my eyes slide to Will as he hit the birdie and felt Signora Masoni's gaze follow mine. "You've done a lovely job with your estate, Signora. I am impressed with how hard you work. I saw you out in the vineyard again this morning."

She gave me a casual shrug. "Please. Call me Eleonora. And I enjoy it. It's far better than staying inside and seeing to accounting and whatnot," she said, leaning forward on the table and gesturing with her chin to the main room, where she'd seen me and my father huddled over paperwork.

"Would it surprise you to know that I once worked long hours in my own fields, back in Montana?" I asked gently.

She sipped from her glass and studied me with her big brown eyes. Then she smiled, and her eyes lit up with recognition. "How could I have not known it?" she asked, smacking her forehead and then gesturing widely to me, then over to the group. "You…you are the grand tourists our papers follow! How could I have not known you from the start?"

"Indeed," I said, heaving a sigh. I'd hoped only to speak of a shared history, not my newest history.

Excitement lit Eleonora's eyes, and her hands moved to a staccato tempo now. "All my country… Ahh, Signorina Kensington—"

"Cora, please."

"Cora, all my country speaks of you! And the awful man who tried to get you in Venezia!" She shook her head and frowned. I could see her bright eyes piecing together the facts. "Is this why the papers have been silent about your progress of late? Why your Will has brought you to the countryside? To be safe?"

"That is one reason, yes. And why we are so grateful for your hospitality."

"It is my honor to be your lowborn hostess," she said, resting a hand on her bosom. She gave me a conspiratorial grin. "Imagine me running across you in Turino! It was meant to be, our friendship."

I smiled and let her shock fade a bit. "But I was going to tell you, Eleonora... I grew up working in the fields in Montana. It was hard work but good work. Honest work."

"Yes, yes," she said, studying me now as if I were a puzzle to figure out. "There is something about cultivating the land, coaxing it, wooing it to give you what you want, that is most satisfactory."

"Agreed," I said, looking out. "And on land like this...you get to see it season after season." It was my turn to shake my head. "I'm afraid my father's land was not so bountiful."

She frowned in confusion. "Did you try grapes?"

"Grapes? No, it is not the right land for grapes."

Her eyes lit up. "But it was! Bountiful, no? Not on the top, perhaps," she said, putting her hand out like a plank, then sliding another beneath. "But down below." She cocked an eyebrow and nodded, waiting for me to see.

I smiled. She was right, of course. The acres surrounding Dunnigan were going to produce a crop beyond anything any farmer had ever imagined. But hefting it from the depths was different than watching it sprout and grow and mature. It just...was.

"Sometimes," she said softly, "God answers our prayers in ways we did not expect. But it still is an answer to your father's prayer, and your father's father's, yes?"

My eyes met hers. "Yes," I said.

"There is much land here, Cora," she said, taking a sip and waving outward, "if that is what you miss. You are an heiress!" She splayed her fingers. "You can purchase what you want and play the farmer all you wish, and all will be well, yes?"

Her eyes slid to the group playing badminton out on the lawn. To Will. "So, my friend," she said leaning toward me to whisper, "are the stories true? Did your handsome Will steal your heart from that French nobleman? And did you truly never know you were a Kensington until this summer?"

My head started to slowly throb. I wondered for a moment if I'd caught Vivian's headache. Eleonora's smile faded. "I am sorry. Forgive me. I pry. And I know that is not the American way." She made a little movement to indicate a lock and key on her pretty lips.

"It is all right." I gave her a little shrug of my shoulders. "It is natural to wonder, after all that's been written… And you're right. We Americans like to hold our secrets close," I said, touching my chest.

"But you long to share them just as we Italians do, do you not?" she asked. "It is much better to share what is on your heart. Otherwise, it grows heavy, so full is it." She settled back in her chair and sipped from her glass, as if she was ready for me to tell all and yet cared not if I said a word. As if she was opening the door if I wished to walk through it. And suddenly I wanted to.

For some reason I didn't want to discuss Will with her. At all. But I longed to talk over what was happening between my father and me. I glanced over my shoulder to make certain we were still alone on the veranda. "You saw us working together, inside. But Father and I are like…oil and water."

"Ahh," she said, lifting a brow and nodding. "My father and I… we were the same. Oil and water. We had to learn to be kind to each other. We loved each other, you see." She looked out to the valley, then back to me. "I think God designed families in such a way. Some in each one set there to push out our borders," she said, making the gesture of drawing a boundary line. "And yet those people force us to see how far we ourselves are willing to go in order to stay together, no?" She studied me.

"Yes," I said, nodding. Suddenly my story was building within my chest, and I felt as if I might burst if I didn't share it. "My father has borders, as you say, that he fiercely defends. And his borders around me seem to be continually changing… I think a part of him wants to free me. Grace me. But another part of him wishes to control me. Manage me. And I am not to be managed." I set down my glass harder than I'd intended.

My hostess gave me a small smile. "So American women are as independent as they say," she said. "You sound like a suffragette."

I stared at her, blinking slowly. Was that who I was, what I wanted? And yet, what did the suffragettes long for? A voice of their own. A say in their own destiny. Autonomy. "Just because God created us female, does it mean we don't have a mind capable of making good choices? Following our own paths, as God guides us?" I found myself rising, then pacing. "Perhaps I am. A suffragette," I said, trying out the word in my mouth. It felt good. Liberating to state it rather than simply think it. As if I held up a sign against all the injustices I'd felt since my father had first driven up our farm road at the beginning of summer and changed my life forever. And yet, hadn't he also freed me to do bigger, grander things than I'd ever dreamed? Hadn't he led me to my sisters, my brother? To Will?

Will reached wildly to return Antonio's lob of the badminton birdie that came over the net and failed. Still, he laughed, and his response made me smile. If my father had never come looking for me,

I would never have met him. Or my siblings. Or even Pierre. My borders, as Eleonora had said, might never have been pushed outward. I would not have ever seen Europe. Perhaps never left Montana. Ever, in my entire life. And my future, my parents' future… Undoubtedly, I'd been blessed too, through all of this.

"The cause of the suffragettes is far from Italia, indeed," said Eleonora, jolting me back to the present. I'd been so lost in my own thoughts, a part of me had forgotten she was even with me. "Men of this country would have heart attacks and die if their women refused to stay at home and do exactly as they said."

"It is difficult for most of the men in our country as well. To imagine such a thing…women with minds of their own. Decisions of their own."

"And what does your Will say about such things?" my hostess asked, lightly eyeing Will and Antonio.

I gazed over at them in rapt appreciation and cocked a brow. "Honestly, I'm unsure. He seems to favor my strength. My determination." Hadn't he compared me to the *Awakening Slave*? "But he also struggles with my position."

"He is a good man," she said, looking away to the opposite horizon, then back to me with a smile. "You are fortunate to find him."

I realized that I'd been going on for far too long about myself. "What of you?" I asked. "Surely a woman as lovely as you won't be alone for long."

Her dark eyes shifted back to me. "We shall see." She took a deep breath through her nose and let it out slowly through her lush lips. She was truly beautiful. Exotic, in a way. Olive skin. Long, thick lashes rimming dark eyes that tilted down a bit at the corners.

I waited, not wanting to pry. And then I remembered what she'd said. It had been practically an invitation to inquire, hadn't it? "Was your marriage so very awful that you do not wish to try again?" I ventured.

Her eyes drifted to the side, making her appear even more sorrowful. "Ahh, he was nothing but an old, cranky man. It was… *advantageous*, as you say, for me to marry him. My father gained, my husband gained. The only one who lost was me."

I studied her. "What did you lose?"

Her chocolate-brown eyes centered on me. "My youth. My vitality."

"You are still young and beautiful," I protested, hoping to somehow reassure her with my shallow words. "And you live here," I said, lifting up my hands, waving outward.

"I'd sell it to you tonight, if you offered," she said, a hint of an honest offer in her tone.

Again I blinked slowly, my eyes roving over the horizon from left to right, from olive grove to vineyard. How my father longed for such fruitful land as this, all his life! "You jest," I said.

"I do not. To wander for a time on tour, as you Americans call it… To see the world, meet other intriguing people… What more could one ask for?"

I took a breath, then two. She was right. At one point in my life, I might have dreamed of such a trip as I'd taken but, awakening, would have considered myself mad for my imagination. And yet here I was, looking at this sublime land…

Green-gold grass waved in a gentle breeze. The hum of bees reached my ears, bouncing from lavender branch to lavender branch.

The sun, while warm, was tolerable in the shade. And the breeze smelled of sage, equally piquant with spice. "I would trade you," I said. "My American wealth. The expectations of my father. For this." I waved forward. "A solid piece of land that produces what one plants. The incredible smells on this breeze. A place to sit with friends."

She laughed under her breath. "We all bear our own cross, do we not?"

"I suppose," I answered easily, pausing. "But what is to keep you here? You have people to manage your land, your house. Have you not traveled yourself?"

"France, once," she said with a shrug. "Some in Spain." She leveled her dark gaze on me. "But it is Africa I'd love to see. And America."

I smiled. "Well, if you ever reach America's shores, you'd always be welcome as my guest," I said.

A slow smile spread across her face, her eyes glinting with mystery. "I'd enjoy such a visit. I would wish to see where a woman like my friend Cora, the suffragette, chooses to abide."

I lifted my glass of water, and she chinked hers against it. "*Salute*," she said quietly, her eyes again lost to the horizon.

To your health, the toast meant. And I thought that here, in this place of rest, surrounded by family, I should feel healthy. But so much pulled at me. My father's continuing demands and the nagging feeling that I was not measuring up to what was required to run the mine, that I might never measure up. My sister's ill-begotten relationship with Andrew Morgan and what I could do about it before it was too late. And most of all…Will.

My eyes moved to him again as he laughed at Antonio's antics. It was good to see him smile, even if it wasn't at me. Would he ever smile at me again? Would he forgive me for not saying yes to his proposal? Or even give me another chance to explain my hesitation? Would he ask again?

But it was up to him. Suffragette though I might be, in matters of the heart, a lady waited for a man to pursue her, not the other way around.

No matter how lowborn that lady might be.

~William~

Will and Hugh climbed the hill, each of them lugging a picnic basket over his arm. Ahead of them, Cora and Eleonora walked arm in arm, apparently already fast friends in the two days they'd been at the villa. They were the first in the entire group to crest the trail they'd been climbing for the better part of an hour. "It wasn't enough, making us prune our hostess's vineyards all morning, McCabe?" Hugh panted. "You had to make us climb a mountain, too?"

"Signora Eleonora says it's the prettiest view in Toscana. I wasn't about to miss that," Will returned.

"Thankfully for you, there's a carrot before us horses," Hugh grunted, nodding ahead at the women as they turned to each other and laughed. "Or rather, two. The prettiest girl from America with the prettiest girl in Italy. It's rather sly of you, really, McCabe," he said, sidling Will a look of reproach. "What man wouldn't follow along after them?"

Will wanted to deny it, put it down in some way, but he couldn't truthfully argue. Their trail leaders were indeed lovely. He looked back, to make sure the others still followed. They did, although they'd fallen behind. But Antonio and Pascal brought up the rear, and it felt far from dangerous here. Out on a warm summer afternoon, hiking the green hills of Tuscany, looking for just the right picnic spot…it was almost possible to forget about his concerns of the past and his fear of the future. Of the black, oily thought that he had ruined his chances with Cora and couldn't for the life of him find his way back to her. Every time he thought about reaching out to her, starting a conversation, it burned. Or felt wrong.

"Here it is!" their hostess cried, splaying her hands out and twirling. Will was caught for a moment, so taken aback by the glorious image of her, that it took him a bit to comprehend what she meant.

"Be still my heart," Hugh growled, shoving past Will to come alongside Eleonora. Will shook his head—he knew exactly what the man meant. She was as captivating as Cora, as attractive in her sultry dark looks as Cora was in her sunny beauty.

A few steps farther along the path, and he could see what Eleonora referenced. They had entered the barest remains of a castle high on a hill. Little but the base stones of small rooms and walls peeked from the tall grasses, the rest likely plundered long ago for other building projects in the region. He glanced at Eleonora again, then dared to meet Cora's eyes for the briefest moment before fully taking in the view. They'd driven for an hour to this place, then climbed for another hour, Eleonora cajoling them upward, farther, higher, as if she'd forgotten exactly where it was. But from the glint in her eyes, he could see that she'd known all along.

"From here, the Masonis ruled much of eastern Toscana for centuries," she said.

"The Masonis?" Cora asked, her pale eyebrows lifting. "Your family?"

"Indeed," Eleonora said, lifting the wooden lid on the basket Antonio brought her. The older man was huffing and red-faced. She pulled out a blanket, shook it out, and spread it across the grass, then promptly plopped down. "From here, they could see any enemies approaching for miles."

Will spread out another blanket and gestured for Cora to sit. "So when did they lose it?" she asked.

"A hundred years ago," Eleonora said with a shrug, "give or take. Times changed, fortunes were lost. My ancestors had to sell off much of the property, and this land hadn't been cultivated for generations. In the end, they chose wrongly. A terribly, rocky plot of land only good for a few rows of grapes. If it had not been for my husband…" She lifted a dark brow and shook her head. "We would've been beggars."

"Somehow I doubt that," Felix said, tossing her a wry grin. "Your suitors must have been lined up to the next town."

"Ah, there were plenty of poor boys with handsome smiles," she tossed back. "But only ugly, old, rich suitors…" She shrugged.

"But now you are your own woman," Cora said, sitting down on a blanket beside Lillian. "Free to choose whomever you want."

"*If* I want," Eleonora said.

"*If* you want," Cora repeated with a firm nod.

Will sat down and wondered about their exchange. He felt the heat of a blush. Had she spoken to Eleonora about his proposal? Of her turning him down?

He forced his dark thoughts away, focusing instead on the view, attempting to appreciate the moment, the day, not what had come before or might be ahead. This place had its own unique beauty, here. The hills were steeper, which was advantageous in times of war, but less so in times of peace. And it seemed more arid, perhaps part of the reason there had been less "cultivation," as Eleonora said. But to let it go… "Who owns this property now, Eleonora?"

She arched a pretty dark brow, and he noticed how it made her big brown eyes seem even more comely. "I don't know. There is never anyone about to ask. No one for miles." She opened the basket again, as Antonio settled beside her, and brought out a loaf of bread wrapped in a cloth napkin. Then cheese and grapes, the standard lunch in Toscana.

"How long has it been since you visited?" Cora asked. Her color was high, and she looked more beautiful than ever. Will forced himself to look away.

"A good many years. I used to love coming here on picnics as a child. Playing about the ruins of the walls, imagining the full castle and the like. My father liked it too."

Cora was silent a moment. Then she asked, "Did it pain him? That his ancestors had to sell this part of the property?"

Eleonora pursed her lips and frowned. "Pain him?" She shook her head, and a tendril of dark-brown hair pulled loose from her bun, down beside her neck. "I think not. He very much enjoyed his last years at Villa Masoni. To him, the day was what was offered, not what wasn't."

Will studied Cora for a moment, guessing that her mind was on her parents and the changes her mine was making in Dunnigan. But he was glad for Eleonora's words. He hoped they sank in. What more could anyone do than to appreciate what one had for the day, rather than fret about what was lost yesterday or what might be lost tomorrow?

His eyes moved back to their hostess. She was about his age, far too young to be a widow. How was it that she was still alone? Even an independent girl like her? And why was he taking such an interest?

She rested a hand on her chest and looked to the horizon. She looked like something out of a painting.

"But you lived on your estate, not his?" Vivian asked, accepting a clump of grapes from Andrew, who was sitting beside her. "It was always 'Villa Masoni'?"

"Ah, yes," she said. "I became the last of the Masoni family when my cousin died four years ago. My late husband"—she paused to cross herself at the mention of him—"had land but no name of record in Toscana. My father saw fit to join our fortunes. Toscana always favors the families that have been here for generations, regardless of their wealth."

Will frowned, adding up the years. She'd been perhaps sixteen or seventeen when she was married.

"You did not take your husband's name?" Antonio said, clearly confused.

"I did for a time. Legally, I am Eleonora Masoni Triguetti. But I no longer go by that."

"I see," Will's old friend said lightly. It was progressive of her, and Will doubted that many in patriarchal Italy would understand. And yet as she was the last living heir to the Masoni name, how could they not honor her choice?

Eleonora brought out a bottle of wine and then took out a corkscrew. He could see from the distinctive-shaped green bottle, pinched at the sides, that it was from her vineyard. She smiled over at him, following his gaze, and lifted it. "My great-great grandfather had hands gnarled by…" She paused, searching for the right English word. "Rheumatism?" Her expression eased when Will nodded. "And holding the bottle troubled him. He resolved it this way—by designing and having his own bottles manufactured in Murano."

Will smiled back at her. "Ingenious."

He saw Cora stiffen a little at their warm exchange, but he didn't mind that either. Perhaps Cora needed to see that he was attractive to others…

"Ingenious. Or lazy." Eleonora laughed lightly as she passed the tool and bottle over to Antonio's outstretched hands. Her face turned back to the horizon. "In his time, the vineyard was vast. My father intended to return it to its height of glory with the help of my late husband's infusion of cash. But he died shortly after our marriage, and then my husband took ill."

"Could you not invest in fulfilling that dream now?" Cora said, accepting a small glass of wine. Will could see the longing in her eyes. The burning desire to do the same for Alan Diehl, make something of the land he and his father had put so much of their lives into. But was that one of the obstacles that would keep them apart? Forever?

"I could," Eleonora said, reaching into the basket and pulling out a tray of cured sausage and a bowl of olives. The more she pulled out, the more Will understood why those baskets had been so heavy. But every morsel was more delicious than the last, so there was no room for complaint. "I intend for the vineyard to be at capacity within five years. I have an excellent vintner on staff, as well as a wonderful—how do you call it—man who manages the land?"

"Foreman," Antonio supplied. "Is that Mr. Triguetti?"

She nodded as she sliced the hard sausage, oily and red under the summer sun. "A second cousin. But I have plans for my fortune other than making more wine. All of Toscana produces wine," she said with a grin. "I wish to help others. Build an orphanage. Assist young widows to find a trade." She looked over to Cora. "That is what drew me to you. Your kindness to that woman in Turino."

"I assure you, I've passed far too many others. You simply caught me at my best."

"No," Eleonora said. "I see the goodness in you. And I knew I wanted to know you better." She waved at the others. "You and your family and friends. I knew I could consider you all friends, by that one act of Cora's."

"Well, here's to Cora," Hugh said, lifting his cup.

"To Cora," some of the others said, lifting their own.

"Or perhaps you saw our need, just as you see others'," Cora said lightly, casting her a grateful smile. "We are sincerely grateful for your hospitality."

"Please," Eleonora said, tossing out a hand, "it is nothing."

"It is much to us."

"Well, you are welcome to stay as long as you like. Here we are, two independent women, free to make our own way in this big, beautiful world. It is a lovely place to find yourself in, no? No man," she said, lifting a teasing brow at Hugh and Felix, "shall ever dictate how we live our lives again." She lifted her cup, and Cora lifted hers to meet her toast, clinking them together.

"That's the spirit!" Felix said, plopping down beside Cora. "That's what the world needs! More women in charge! So we men can relax at last." He rolled onto his back, his hands knit beneath his neck.

"As if you've toiled in the mines all these years, poor, dear brother," Vivian sniffed.

"Truly. You have no idea the burdens I've borne," he said with a dramatic sigh.

"I'm with Felix!" Hugh said, leaning down on one elbow. "You girls can take over the world. I'd be happy to go anywhere either of you two led me."

Eleonora laughed at him, and Cora rolled her eyes. She paused as her gaze met up with Will's, but Will looked away, picking at a blade of grass on his trousers and flicking it away in the breeze.

If Cora agreed with Eleonora, if she wanted no man to dictate her life… Well, was that how she saw him? A dictator? Someone else who sought to control her? He'd done nothing but support her, love her, want the best for her! Were those the actions of a dictator? Will bit into a slice of sausage and looked to the valley below, where on one hill, a shepherd was leading his herd, and on another two men on horses were riding away.

"It is supremely lovely," Cora said, sighing contentedly.

"Indeed," Hugh said. Without turning, Will knew he was staring at her and Eleonora, flirting as usual.

Will rose abruptly. "I'm going for a stroll," he said briskly to the group, who looked up at him in surprise. "You all will be in Pascal and Antonio's safekeeping, I trust."

Then, without waiting for a response, he turned on his heel and strode away.

CHAPTER 13

~Cora~

"Well, for heaven's sake," Felix growled. "What burr got under his saddle?"

I didn't answer him, but instead rose and followed after Will, down a narrow trail, up the next hill and over it. He was walking quickly, and I wondered if I'd lost him when I saw him leaning against a massive old oak, looking outward.

Tentatively, I drew closer, and it took him a few minutes for him to see me approaching.

"You remind me of the day I first saw you," I said shyly, feeling nervous. "In Butte. Leaning against that old tree in back of my father's house."

"Ah," he said coolly, leaning forward to walk partway around the tree. He lifted one hand up and rested it on a horizontal branch. Stubbornly, I refused to release him from my company and edged around the tree too, leaning one shoulder against the trunk.

"What do you want, Cora?" he asked softly, looking at me.

"I don't know." I shrugged and crossed my arms. "I want to go back to us. How it was a week ago, before…"

"Before you turned down my offer of marriage," he said.

"Come now, Will," I said, grimacing. "I didn't turn you down. I—"

"You didn't? It certainly felt that way to me."

"I merely said I wasn't ready. Can you not give me more time? Must it all happen now, on top of everything else?"

"I didn't intend for it to be another trial you must bear," he bit out.

I sighed and looked out to the valley with him. We stood there in silence for a few moments.

"Look, Cora," he said, his tone more civil. "I'm sorry. It's difficult for me to believe that it's only because of the chaos of your summer that you cannot promise your hand. It has to be more. It has to do with me."

"Well, it doesn't," I said. "The only factor that has to do with you, William McCabe, is that while I don't care for the way you're carrying on, I find myself terribly in love with you. Is that not the only factor that matters?"

His eyes searched mine. "You're certain of that. You love me, not another. Not Pierre de Richelieu."

"Will McCabe, I think you began to claim my heart that first night in Butte and have only steadily claimed more and more of it. Don't you know that?"

He cocked his head and shook it, as if he were struggling with himself. Then slowly, he moved over to me and tentatively reached out to run his hands down my shoulders to my arms, holding me lightly. I looked up at him, and his face was awash in pain. He shook his head and drew in a great breath of air. "I've been a fool, then.

Forgive me, beloved. It hurt that you could not say yes in Firenze. I wanted to claim you as mine. Crow the news to the world. Give the reporters something real to talk about...our love." He bent his head closer. "Will you forgive me?"

I nodded quickly. "Will you wait, Will? Wait for me to decide about marriage? Until I sort out the rest of my life? Get settled, to some extent?"

"If I can be where you settle." He tipped up my chin.

"But that's a question, isn't it? If I'm in Dunnigan, and you want to get your architecture degree..."

"We'll work it out. We'll find a way, Cora."

He pulled me into his arms then, cradling my head with one hand and kissing me on the temple.

"Oh, that is so much better than the last few days," I said with a happy sigh. I looked up at him. "So we're all right now? We can address the proposal...later?"

He smiled. "Consider it a standing invitation to be my bride."

I smiled with him. "Thank you, Will."

We forced ourselves to return to the others, recognizing we'd been alone for longer than was proper. But we did so hand in hand. When we appeared, over the crest of the hill, Felix stood up and, seeing us holding hands, began clapping. The others smiled, and a few joined in his applause.

"Oh, good. Our group will be far more jolly with you two not on the outs any longer," Felix said, nodding to me.

I hadn't really thought about our strain affecting the rest, but I imagined it had. Mama always said that a sour ingredient permeated the whole soup.

Eleonora accepted Hugh's offered hand and rose. "I wondered…" She shook her head. "No matter," she said, clasping her hands and bowing to me. "I think this calls for some dancing after dinner, no?"

"I always enjoy dancing," I said, casting a shy smile up at Will. We'd not been able to dance together much on the tour. Until now. If we were openly courting, it was entirely proper, especially if we were in the protection of Eleonora's home.

With the perfect, quiet strains of a villager's fiddle filling the air, Will danced with me, waltzing me across the broad stones of the patio among six other couples. Still more joined us, welcomed whether they were neighbors or off-duty servants, which made us smile all the more. This, this was where I belonged. In Will's arms, but in a village. Not high society. Would I ever be able to find comfort within the folds of the well-to-do?

My father and Mr. Morgan looked over the group, and I met my father's gaze when his eyes settled on me with Will. I dared him to object; I would not allow him to stand between us. But his disapproval settled not on me, but on Vivian, sitting alone on a stone bench, with Andrew off to who-knew-where.

"Uh-uh," Will said, pulling my gaze back to him. "Tonight's about us, not any of the others. No furrowed brows allowed, you understand?"

I pretended to object. "Wasn't I just declaring with Eleonora today that no man would dictate my life?"

"No man except a man who completely adores you and would lay his life down for you, right?" he returned.

I studied him as we turned. He wasn't teasing. He truly wanted to know where I stood on this. "Oh, Will, I was only joking."

"Were you? I know you have suffragette leanings, and that's fine by me," he said lowly. "You have a fine mind and solid spirit. I'd trust you with my life. But would you trust *me* with *yours*?"

"Of course," I said.

Still he held me, waiting.

"Of *course*," I repeated. "With my life."

"Good," he said, pulling me closer. He repositioned his hand on my lower back and looked down at me. His face was partially in shadow, his eyes shining in reflection from the numerous candles that lined the veranda. The combined effect of both the environment and the moment made me feel heady with love, so elated I was certain—absolutely certain—that all would be well. Forever.

"I love you so much, Cora," he whispered.

I smiled up at him and felt tears choke me. "As I love you."

"I'm the luckiest man in the world, to be here with you this night."

My smile grew, and I glanced around and then back up to him. "It is special, isn't it?"

"Indeed," he said, pulling me close. He smelled of soap and a hint of spice. It took everything in me not to pull him from the dance floor and find an intimate place to steal a kiss.

"Why are you grinning so?" he asked, narrowing his eyes in suspicion.

"That is not for me to tell," I teased.

"Oh no?"

"No. But I grant you this—I shall *show* you in time."

"Hmmph," he said, smiling.

We danced a bit, and then I looked back up to him. "There's a part of me that wants to stay here forever. Never leave. Never face our future. Our present is too marvelous."

He lifted a hand and brushed a tendril of hair away from my eye, tucking it gently behind my ear. "Let our future come. As long as I have you by my side, Cora, I can face anything."

"You promise?" I whispered.

"I promise," he whispered back. And then he dared to bend and give me a slow, soft kiss.

I pulled back in surprise, eyes shifting back and forth in fear we'd been seen. But the others were more interested in their own conversations and dancing than in us. Even my father seemed engaged in deep conversation with Mr. Morgan. Will grinned, pulled me close again, and whirled me in a tight turn, keeping time with the music. I leaned my head back and laughed, laughed with as much freedom and joy as I'd ever let loose. And I thought, *I want to feel like this every day for the rest of my life.*

CHAPTER 14

~Cora~

I awakened the next morning at a frightfully late hour. But what was worse was that I could not summon the impetus to care. I sat up and languidly stretched my arms out and rolled my head, my eyes drawn by creamy linen curtains dancing at the tall open window in a breeze that filled the room with the scent of Toscana. How I loved this land! Not since my time in Dunnigan had I felt such a visceral connection to a place. When I'd said to Will the night before that I wanted to stay forever, a part of me had meant it. Perhaps I could sell my part in the mine and buy a plot of land here. Will could find a job and, in time, go back to school to complete his education as an architect. He could build lovely Italian villas, and we'd spend our evenings watching sunsets over the hills and listening to bells toll from nearby towns...

I flopped back against my mountain of pillows, content in my idle imaginings, reluctant to let them go just yet. All my life, I'd been so practical, so set on reaching the next goal. Never disappointing others. Anticipating expectations and meeting them, surpassing them. But something in taking a stand with my father, something about having a position of respect and social standing, had made me feel somehow *free* for the first time in my life. As if I was now free to accept or deny any demands I wished.

Perhaps I really am a suffragette.

I sighed and rolled over. A serious part of me wanted to refuse the social expectations that urged me to rise, dress, and go out into the day. I stared up at the ceiling of plain plaster and dark oak beams, and thought of all the amazing painted scenes I'd seen along our journey. But it was here that I felt at home for the first time. It struck me, that. The sense of home. How odd to experience it so very far from my true home in Dunnigan!

I flipped aside the covers, swung my legs over the side, and eased off the bed, then stretched again. Suddenly, I was eager to see Will, to share with him my feelings of joy and contentment, my excitement over the future. How glad was I that he had been willing to give me more time to consider his proposal.

I went to the window and edged the curtain away. My room was on the second floor, looking over the patio where we had danced last night and down over the valley. Below me, I could see a man and woman bent over a table. The table had an umbrella over it, so I couldn't make out their faces, could only see that they were side by side. All at once, I wondered if it was Will and Eleonora. My morning smile faded. I'd caught his openly admiring look toward her yesterday. What were they doing together? Standing so intimately close?

I turned and lifted my bell to ring for Anna even as I perused my reflection in the mirror. I'd apparently had wild dreams all night, my hair was such a fright; it would take Anna a long time to get it into any semblance of order. I sighed and then stole over to the window again and peered over the sill. The couple below was still where they had been before, but the man had straightened. I could see his shoulder and was pretty certain it was Will's summer jacket.

My eyes shifted to the clock on the wall, and I huffed a sigh, irritated that Anna had not yet arrived. Had she not heard the bell?

I laughed under my breath and shook my head. Heavens, how entitled I'd become. When had I forgotten to dress myself? I grabbed my brush from the dressing table and began stroking it through my hair, even as I walked to the trunk and opened the lid. I lifted a rose-colored skirt and a rumpled white blouse with tiny roses embroidered across it. When Anna finally reached my room, I opened the door with it in hand.

"Sorry about my delay, Miss. I was out in the gardens. They had to come and fetch me."

"That's all right." I peered around the corner, and seeing that she was alone, opened it wider and handed her the blouse and skirt. "But could you give this a quick press, please?"

She eyed the ensemble, gave me a brief nod, and set off. I closed the door behind her and pulled out a clean shift and underclothes. Then I sat down on the dressing table stool and swiftly wove my hair into a long, thick braid. I didn't know where the day would take us, but I wagered it would entail a ride in a motorcar. I wanted the top down, wanted to feel the warm breeze across my face and not worry about my hair. The braid, while common, a peasant girl's style, was good enough for me.

I was tapping my booted foot in agitation by the time Anna returned with my clothes. Quickly, I pulled on the blouse, then the skirt with the wide waistband over it, smoothing it before the maid buttoned it down my lower back. She looked askance at me as I moved to the door, clearly unhappy with my braid. But I simply tossed it over my shoulder and left her behind me, intent only on reaching Will and discovering what our hostess and he were so intently discussing.

I hurried down the staircase and through the big common room, then carefully opened the door to the patio, slowly, as if I were casually emerging for the day, not intent on spying. Ahead of me, Will and Eleonora sat, deep in conversation.

"Well, good morning!" Will said, rising and turning toward me. Behind him, Eleonora rose too. She stretched out long fingers to keep the large papers on the table from blowing away in the wind. "I had about decided you might sleep through the entire day!" Will said. "The others gave up on you and set off for Montalcino with Antonio."

No wonder it was so blessedly quiet and still. The others had all left! Instead of abandonment, I felt nothing but relief. A little time alone with Will would be wonderful. *Alone*, I repeated silently, *without Eleonora*. "Even my father went?"

"Every one of them. Lillian was quite worried you'd taken ill. I assured her you were merely in need of a good rest."

I smiled and went to him, lifting my cheek for a kiss. "Actually, I haven't slept so well in years," I said.

He smiled down at me and ran his fingers down the length of my braid. "Don't you look fresh and pretty," he said. "Like a schoolgirl out for a stroll."

"I feel like a schoolgirl," I returned. "Ready to learn from my tutor all he can teach."

"Well, that sounds scandalous," Eleonora said with a laugh.

I'd almost forgotten she was there. I felt the heat of a furious blush rise as I repeated my own words in my mind. She'd taken a far different meaning than I'd intended. "I...I didn't..."

Eleonora and Will laughed. "Don't fret," Will said. "We know your heart." He lifted my hand to his lips, making me realize that I'd forgotten my gloves. Goodness, I had been in a hurry.

"What were you two studying so intently?" I asked, edging past Will to stand beside Eleonora.

Her deep brown eyes moved to the papers again, and here, beside him and Eleonora, I could see that they were architectural drawings. "It's the plans for our orphanage," she said proudly. "Will was sharing with me, over coffee, that his hobby is architecture, so I thought I'd show these to him and get his input on possible improvements." She crossed her arms and leaned closer to me to whisper, "Toscana's architects haven't thought of anything innovative since the Renaissance."

The breeze blew up again, and we both leaped to keep the sheaf of papers in place. "I assume he was of help," I said, glancing to Will. I felt a pang of guilt over my idle jealousy, when they'd simply been discussing a project of such import. But her next words sent me into a new wave of concern.

"He is a visionary," she enthused, her eyes shining as she gazed at him. "He thought of several different aspects that will make the building far more functional. The architect will not care for my meddling, but he'll do what I ask. In the end, she who pays the bills rules the day. That is, when I can pay it, he'll do what I ask." She sighed. "At the rate I'm saving, it will be a good two years before I can begin construction." She reached for several porcelain mugs and anchored the papers, then gestured for us to sit around the table.

I forced a smile. Even if she was looking at Will in ways I didn't care for, she was doing something wonderful. "It's so lovely of you, doing this for your town. Do you have a great number of orphans?"

She shrugged her slim shoulders and then began rolling the blueprints up again. "The community is good about taking care of her own. But there are quite a number of Gypsy workers who come for the summer and fall to harvest our grapes and olives, then move on come winter. Many leave behind children. Last summer, one left a baby on my doorstep."

"A baby! Did you keep it?"

She smiled sadly. "No. I wanted her to have two parents, and I knew a couple who had longed for a child for years. They welcomed her with joy. Others...older children who aren't quite as adorable, too young to work, too old to melt a person's heart, are more difficult to place."

Her eyes moved to the hillside, where six workers were patiently pruning the vines. It was only then that I noticed two were young, just barely older than children, not quite adults. She looked at me. "Giuseppe and Silvi, just fifteen and twelve. Two children left behind last fall when their widowed mother took sick and died." She shrugged. "What was I to do? Some of my Triguetti cousins took them in, thank God. But they cannot take in all my strays. Italian families are large, leaving many mouths to feed. I need a place to look after them until I can find them proper homes."

"It's a fine goal," Will said. "But does the government do nothing for them?"

"They are not Italian citizens, therefore they are not the government's responsibility. Or so they say," she said, splaying her hands in a helpless gesture. "Besides, it's the church's place to help orphans and widows." She lifted her arms. "And are we not the church?"

I stared at her, considering her words. "And if you can't find them all proper homes?" I asked. "What will you do then?"

She shrugged. "I will take care of the rest. Educate them, feed them, house them." She lifted her brows. "Love them."

I was overcome by her generous spirit, even if I was wary about her intentions when it came to Will. "I've never heard of anything so lovely," I said, lifting a hand to my chest. "To invest your own time, your own land and resources... Please, I'd be honored if you allowed me to help."

"Excuse me. What do you mean?" she asked, her long brown eyelashes blinking slowly.

"I want to help. Get you to construction now, not later, so that you can give those children and others a home," I said, nodding to the vineyard. The more I got going on the idea, the more it pushed my jealousy back into a comfortable corner.

"But I—" she stammered. "I couldn't..."

"Don't you see?" I said, taking her hand and looking into her eyes. "I long to do just this sort of thing. If I am to be a woman of means, I want to use those means for good purposes, wherever the Lord leads. And your purpose is a good purpose. You said it yourself. Are we not the church? You and I? Will?"

Still, she hesitated.

"How much will it take? How much do you need to begin?" I asked.

Her eyes set to figuring, looking to the sky. She named an amount in lire, and Will quickly translated the sum in American dollars. "That's it?" I asked, delighted. "I shall see that you obtain the funds you need this very week. I'll speak to Father straight away."

"I…I don't know what to say."

"Truly, you've made me happier than I've made you, allowing me to contribute to this project."

"What project?" Andrew said, arriving at the side table and pouring a glass of water. I stared at him in mute surprise. I thought everyone but Will had left for the day to Montalcino.

"Eleonora has an orphanage she intends to build. And I have just committed to assisting her."

Andrew let his glass drop a few inches as he stared at me, and then he rubbed his forehead as if I'd given him a sudden headache. "A word, Cora? May I have a word?"

Everything in me wanted to say no, but I didn't want to put our hostess into an awkward spot. Andrew took my arm, pinching it as he led me to the far end of the patio. "What are you doing?" he demanded.

"It really is no concern of yours, Andrew," I said, wrenching away. I looked back at Will and saw he'd risen in concern. But I waved him back. It was time Andrew and I had it out…

"You are giving away your fortune even before it is fully yours," he said, lifting a hand and looking at me as if I were ridiculous.

"Nonsense. I already have far more in my account than I can use in a year. I intend to put the rest to good uses like this," I said.

"Ways I can assist others. That is what the good Lord would want me to do."

"Spare me your moralizing sermons. Do you want to be a woman in business or a woman running a charity? Because we can certainly speak of a charity if—"

"Maybe both!" I said. "I haven't decided yet. And it really is none of your concern, Andrew. My father has made it more than clear to you that the Dunnigan mine is our affair, not yours."

"And yet he also expects me to tutor you along." He lifted his chin and folded his arms, giving me a cold stare. "I am your business partner, whether you like it or not. And I must insist you quit handing out money to every stray cat we run across until we know exactly where we stand," he said lowly.

"Eleonora is hardly a stray cat!" I whispered. "And I know where I stand financially, and I assure you, I have more than enough to do this!"

"Yes, well," he said with a sniff, "she is hardly the ilk of those we prefer to socialize with. If you insist on doling out handouts, there are more advantageous ways to do so."

"You are—"

He held up a hand. "All I'm asking, Cora, is that you return home and assess where you are *before* you begin giving away funds that might be better used to build the family business."

So there it was. He was afraid I would spend all available capital before *he* had the opportunity to make use of it himself.

"You listen to me," I said, reaching up to tap his chest. "I may be new to business, but I am not new to utilizing my brain. I am quite clear on what I have at my disposal, and I am not out buying one thing after another, as some of the other grand tourists are bent on doing. But I may very well invest in people. Projects, as God leads me to do. And if you have difficulty with that, well, you—you… Well, I assure you, I don't care!"

I turned back to the others, wishing I could've poured even stronger words on him, but I knew it was quite enough for today. Will, still standing, watched Andrew over my shoulder as I approached, his look silently daring the man to try to take it further.

"You are an uncommon woman, Cora," Eleonora said, rolling the blueprints into a tube. "I believe the world has just begun to see what our lovely Cora Diehl Kensington has to offer, no?" she asked Will.

He smiled back at her, his hard expression disappearing. Andrew went inside, slamming the door, but Eleonora ignored him. Her eyes brightened. "I have a plan for us today, since the others have abandoned you."

"Oh? What is that?" I asked, glancing toward Will. I'd hoped we might spend a few hours alone…

"Eleonora would like to take us someplace I've never been," Will said. "A place Antonio mentioned enjoying in the past. The baths at Saturnia."

"The baths?" I asked blankly.

"Toscana is dotted with hot springs, and in the south, the baths of Saturnia were those that many Romans favored," he said.

"Oh, it is divine," Eleonora said, reaching out to touch my arm. "But we must be off soon if we're to get there in time. It's quite a journey."

"As long as we can leave Andrew behind, I'm game," I whispered.

Several hours later, we arrived at Saturnia. I could hear the roar as soon as our driver pulled off the dirt road and turned off the motor-car's engine. My eyes widened. "Is that *water*?"

Will smiled. "I think so."

"Indeed," Eleonora said. "My cousin was raised in the town above and spent many an afternoon playing in these waters. What you hear is the waterfall—Cascate del Mulino."

Will opened the door for us. "The walls you can see above us are medieval, built by the Aldobrandeschi family. They surround an old Roman gate, dating back to the second century BC. As you'll see for yourself in a moment, this place is special, just as it was to the Romans and Etruscans before us."

We walked down the road and around what appeared to be an old stone bathhouse. And then I came up short, staring in wonder. Before us was a series of beautiful turquoise pools, steam rising from each. At the top was a twenty-foot waterfall thundering in a torrent over the edge and down into the pool below, which subsequently fed the others, each one pouring into the next. On the extreme right, the pools drained into a river below us. "Oh," I breathed. "This is lovely. So lovely! Is the water quite hot?"

"Deliciously hot," Eleonora said, taking my hand and pulling me along. "Come, let us change. I'm eager to sink into those waters."

We parted from Will, who went to the other side of the bath-house to change. I was struggling with the buttons on my skirt, and soon Eleonora was asking if I was ready when I hadn't even fully undressed. "Go ahead," I called. "I'll be out in a moment."

"Are you certain? Do you need assistance?"

"No, no. Just some stubborn buttons. I can manage."

"All right. See you soon."

She left, and in time, I managed to undress and don my bathing costume, a woolen short-sleeved dress that reached my knees, with pantaloons beneath that extended to my calves. I stuffed my skirt and blouse into my satchel and hurried out to join the others. But I halted at the doorway. Will held Eleonora's hand, helping her into the first pool. And the woman was in the tiniest bathing costume I'd ever seen—with no sleeves at all, a big bow beneath her breasts, and a skirt that stopped mid-thigh. Her hair was tucked into an adorable little cap, making her look chic. I looked down at my own bathing costume, suddenly feeling frumpy and out-of-sorts. I looked around for other women, but there were only two men in the distant pool beside a stand of cattails, looking with interest at my scantily clad hostess.

Eleonora took a step, then stumbled and shrieked. Will narrowly caught her and steadied her, laughing with her but clearly looking uncomfortable. My eyebrows rose, and the hair on the back of my neck stood on end. I stepped out into the light, and as if they sensed me, both turned to look toward the bathhouse. Will set Eleonora to rights and took a step away.

"Ready, Cora?" he asked, confused by my hesitation. "Come. It isn't too hot. It feels lovely."

I bet it feels lovely. Did it feel even lovelier holding her? I thought darkly as I set my bag with the others and then made my way to the rocks that were waist-high. Will trudged through the water and reached out a hand to help me over. I took it, not looking at him.

"Cora? Are you all right?"

"I'm fine, Will. Fine."

"Well, all right. You don't seem…" His words dropped off as I passed him.

Sharp rocks bit at my tender feet, and I abruptly paused and almost fell, just as Eleonora had done.

"Whoa," he said with a smile. "Perhaps not so fast?"

I shook off his hand in agitation, feeling first the weight of my ill-placed jealousy and then the assured righteousness of it. Was I imagining it all? "I'm all right."

He frowned and grabbed my hand again. "Cora, what is the matter?"

I looked up at him and then glanced over to Eleonora, who was two pools away now. I shook my head. I was being silly. Imagining things. She was simply being kind. Friendly. How could I begrudge her care for Will? Didn't he inspire respect from everyone he met? And she had likely just fallen, exactly as I had done, stepping on sharp rocks.

His eyes, watching me intently, widened in understanding, and then narrowed, one eyebrow lifting. "Why, Cora Diehl Kensington, are you *jealous?*"

"No. No!" I said, shaking my hand loose and moving toward Eleonora. I felt exposed and silly. In more ways than one.

He quickly overtook me, now smiling broadly, hands on his hips. But he at least had the sense to lower his voice before gloating. "I never imagined the day. I have to say, it feels grand. But, Cora," he said, cupping a hand around my neck and using his thumb to coax my face toward him, "you"—he leaned his forehead against mine—"have nothing to fear."

"Nothing?"

"Nothing," he said with a promise in his voice.

"You watch yourself, William," I said, lifting my head and staring steadily into his blue eyes. "Our hostess is beautiful and charming. Beguiling."

He smiled, as irritatingly pleased as possible. Then he took my hand. "Come on. I want to see something Antonio told me was here."

We pressed on, clambering over the next pool wall and then the next until we joined Eleonora in the deepest pool with the waterfall. She barely paid us any attention as she allowed the water to pound over her shoulders.

I sank deeper into the hot water. It smelled some of sulfur, but also of fresh grass and hot stones. Will went to his knees, letting the water cover his shoulders. His bathing costume was sleeveless, and I admired the broad strength of his muscles even as I smiled at the relaxation that stole across his face.

He opened his eyes and caught me staring.

I smiled, feeling suddenly shy, and he grabbed my waist under the water, turning me toward him. "Is this what you wanted to show me?" I said.

"No. I just wanted you to get used to the heat. This is what I want to show you." He took my hand, and we moved to the left of Eleonora. "Take a deep breath, and close your eyes."

I did as he asked, and he pulled me forward. I almost opened my mouth to shout, but he was moving slowly, the water pounding down on my head, my neck, my back, until we were under it. On the other side.

I blinked, and looked around. It was a grotto of sorts, a room of stone, hollowed out over the years by the water. "Oh, Will!" I practically shouted to be heard above the thundering falls. "It's so lovely." I turned to go back, knowing we shouldn't be here alone, in nothing but our bathing costumes, but he pulled me back around and into his arms, against his chest. He lifted me until our faces were at the same height as we sank down into the water. Then he bent his head and kissed me, long and hard and searchingly, demanding me, all of me. At first, I held back, but the longer we embraced, the more I gave in, wanting to be close to him as much as he wanted to be close to me. After a long moment, he pulled back and held my face in both his hands, tenderly, methodically kissing my eyes, my nose, my cheeks until I decided he wished to cover every inch of my face with his lips.

"Oh, Cora, Cora," he said, pulling me close until our noses and dripping wet foreheads touched. "Never doubt that you are the only woman for me. You were given to me by God Himself. I have eyes for no other. I promise you. Do you understand me?"

His intensity almost scared me, but it thrilled me more. I nodded and kissed him, taking my turn to pull him close. After another long moment, he took my shoulders and abruptly set me aside. He lifted a finger, looking pained at the effort, shaking his head. "No more."

I smiled, knowing he was doing his best to retain some semblance of gentlemanly distance. "No more," I repeated in a whisper, knowing he couldn't hear me over the thundering falls, but he could see the reluctant agreement in my eyes. For the first time, I had an even stronger understanding of what might lie ahead in the marital bed. And it took everything in me to keep from throwing myself at him. He just drew me...drew me in such a deep way, as if there was something connected between us already, and I only wished to deepen that connection.

I took his hand and moved to go, knowing we had been alone for far too long. What would Eleonora think of us?

I put my hands on his shoulders and lifted up to kiss him once more, softly, lightly. I cradled his face and mouthed, "I love you." And before he could say it back, I dunked under again and swam beneath the falls.

Eleonora, I saw, had moved off to the far side and, with slender arms outstretched across the rim rocks, rested with her face to the sun, eyes closed. She was so comely, so inviting, that I was glad again for the reassurance Will had just given me. He rose then, silently, barely breaking the water as he emerged beside me, a grin spread across his face. "Hello, lovely," he said, his hand against the small of my back.

"Hello, handsome," I returned.

"Come. Let us find some place to sit and rest," he said, dropping his hand and swimming for the far edge, on the opposite side of the pool from Eleonora.

I followed him, treading water, feeling like I was swimming in a vast tub.

"It's a bit warmer than the Rhône," I said.

He smiled at me over his shoulder. "Even the Mediterranean," he said.

He looked like he was searching below the water and then, apparently discovering what he sought, gestured for me to come closer. "Here. This should be the right height."

I felt the rock ledge beneath and sat down. It was perfect. Then he found a rock two feet away. He reached for my hand and pulled it under the water, entwining his fingers with mine, and leaned his head back against another stone, looking utterly at peace, as I felt. I wondered if there was any way for us to stay here in Tuscany. Forever. But I knew that it was an idle wish, a fantasy, an escape. And I wanted to find my way in the real world with Will, no matter what it took.

"Legend has it," Will said, "that Jupiter and Saturn were in a great battle. A thunderbolt fell from Jupiter, and it birthed the head-waters of these springs."

"A fitting legend for the place," I said, easing my head left, then right, stretching my neck. "You've never been here before?"

"No. I always wanted to come, but Uncle Stuart felt it was… unseemly."

"I see. But what a loss! This place is grand. Everyone should see it at least once."

Eleonora rose and swam closer to us. "If I stay in much longer, I fear I might fall asleep and never wake. Are you both ready for cooler waters?"

Will glanced my way, leaving it to me.

"In a moment," I said.

"All right," Eleonora said. She lifted a finger of warning. "But don't stay in too long. The Romans knew that a hot bath was to be enjoyed for a time, but too long and it became dangerous. Thus the move to cooler waters." She gestured toward the river. I understood the plan, then. We'd enter each successive pool below us, gradually getting cooler, until we entered the cold river water mixed with the last of the heat. It was perfect.

Eleonora clambered over one pool wall, waded through it, then climbed over the next. I inwardly shook my head at my silliness. She wasn't after Will. She might notice how handsome, how fine, how strong, how perfectly wonderful he was, but I could hardly begrudge her that.

Wouldn't I do the very same if I were in her shoes?

CHAPTER 15

~Cora~

We drove home, relaxed and sleepy as the wind and sun dried our hair. Mine flew around my face wildly, but I couldn't find it within myself to care. I knew it would be a tangled mess, but once at Villa Masoni, I'd brush it out and, if need be, wash it and begin again. I hadn't even finished buttoning the troublesome buttons on my skirt, figuring that two were enough to hold it and hiding the rest by leaving my blouse untucked. My shoes were on the floor of the car. I wiggled my toes in delight, feeling more content than I had in years as we turned through the stone gates and onto the long drive to the villa, which ran between two sections of the vineyard.

It was evening—we'd been gone all day—and we were all famished and eager for a casual supper on the patio as Eleonora had suggested. There'd been some talk of the others spending the night in Montalcino with some of Eleonora's friends, and they'd all taken an overnight bag. But as we pulled nearer to the villa, we saw that the four other cars were there. They'd returned. I looked in alarm at Will, and he frowned at me, even as I hurriedly tried to tuck my blouse into my skirt and pat down my wild hair.

We came to a halt. Will set the brake and looked over at us. We returned his hesitant look and then forced ourselves out of the motorcar.

They emerged around the side of the house. Clearly, the servants had settled them on the patio, and they'd heard us arrive. Viv and Andrew came first. Both visibly pulled back, Viv lifting her hand to her mouth.

I laughed under my breath and smiled over at her, cocking my head. "Surely it's not as bad as all that," I said, patting my hair.

She resumed her approach, but I could see that she was still stunned by my appearance. Her eyes traveled from my bare toes, hovered over my haphazardly tucked waist, then went up to my hair. "My goodness, Cora. What happened to you?"

I laughed outright then, as the others rounded the corner. Hugh and Lil, Felix and Nell, all looking as pristine and perfectly coifed as always. "By the saints, man," Felix said, shaking Will's hand, "from the looks of things, you've taken my sister and joined the Gypsies!"

"If only I had such courage," I said, smiling at him. "We were merely out to the thermal baths, and this is the result."

"I, for one, think you look wildly perfect," Lil said, giving me a long hug. "If only we could wear our hair like that all the time!"

I smiled and pretended to pose for a photograph. "All one has to do is go for a swim and then have a chauffeur drive you about under the sun until your hair is dry."

"Oh, I do wish we'd been with you for that swim," Lil said, a pout on her pretty lips.

"Indeed," Hugh said, eyeing me with a suggestive gaze and then moving on to study Eleonora as she approached. "For multiple reasons." He turned to Will. "How is it that you get all the luck, friend?"

We moved inside, and Viv and the girls followed me as I went to my room to change. As soon as we were out of the men's earshot, they began peppering me with questions. About Will. About me sleeping away the morning. About our wild outing to the baths. I did my best to answer them all, and eventually the girls went off to freshen up for supper. Yet Vivian stayed behind. I eyed her via my dressing table mirror. It had a long, jagged crack down the center and peeling backing. I still struggled with a few knots in my hair and resisted the urge to ring for Anna. "How was Montalcino?" I asked her.

"Oh, fine," she said, examining a broken fingernail. "Another quaint, ancient walled city, a fortress, a famous red wine, a connection with Siena's history. You know, more of the same. Aren't you weary of this? I long for the city. But mostly, I long for home."

"You do?" I asked, sitting down beside her, still trying to get the last knot out of my hair. I held a segment and furiously brushed at it. "That's funny. Because all day, I've been thinking about how I never want to leave."

"Well, that's because you're in love," she said, leaning forward to squeeze my knee.

We both froze, recognizing what her statement implied.

"And you're not," I said softly, staring into her eyes.

She rose quickly. "Don't be silly. I only meant—"

"Viv. I know what you meant. But don't you see what you said? What is in *your* heart?"

"Not everyone lives a fairy tale, Cora," she said, striding over to the window.

"Believe me, I know."

"Do you?" she asked over her shoulder. "Cora Diehl Kensington? The belle of every ball? Catching the eye of every bachelor?"

"I'm only interested in one," I said, frowning slightly.

She turned away, back to the window, and put a small hand on its frame. "But there are many more in the wings. If you turned Will away, Pierre would be there in a second," she said so quietly I could barely hear her. "And if Pierre wasn't, there'd be ten others."

I shoved off the bed and went over to her, leaning against the wall. She didn't look at me, so I stared at her profile. "Is that what you fear, then? That if you don't accept Andrew's proposal, there will be no others?"

"I don't know," she said, dodging my eyes, looking down, to the room, then back out again. "Perhaps. It's always only been Andrew. Other than…"

Other than the boy Anna had told me about. "You loved another, once. And it turned out badly."

Her eyes fluttered up to meet mine in surprise. "Anna told you?"

I nodded. "She was trying to warn me about Father's reaction to Will's pursuit. But it was a different time, I think," I said, taking her hand in mine, "for our family. When he drove your friend away, Father was different. Wasn't he?"

She paused, thought about it, then nodded. "Much," she said under her breath.

"Perhaps, Viv, it's time to trust your heart again. Rather than living in fear of Father or fear of being alone. What if you trusted in your heavenly Father's love for you? The inner strength He's implanted within you? You're a strong woman, Viv. Far stronger than you believe."

"Do you really think so?"

"I do." I bit my lip. "And you deserve love, true love. Not an arranged marriage. Aren't we past the era of such things? When women had no voice in their own future?" I pulled her away from the window, back to sit on the edge of the bed. "When I get home, Viv, I want to help make Montana the next state to accept the female vote."

"For national elections?"

I nodded, my excitement growing as the idea formed in my mind. "And if we stood together, Vivian—as friends as well as kin— well, our Mr. Grunthall would have quite the story to wield indeed." I studied her, my chin in hand. "You photograph well. I wouldn't be surprised to find a few bachelors turning up on Father's door- step in Butte, if they were to find out you were no longer Andrew Morgan's—"

"Shh!" she said with a frantic frown, gazing to my closed door, as if the lout was just outside.

"Do you honestly fear no one else will express interest? But who would dare with him around? Lillian told me he's always had a temper—I take it that's a well-known fact? Take him out of the picture, join arms with me as a suffragette, and you'll find an entirely lovely sort of man. A man who can lead and yet allow his woman to shine too." I smiled, thinking of Will. "Not someone who wants to put his woman in a cage."

"Do you really think so?"

"I do," I said firmly, squeezing her hands in mine.

She looked down, thinking for a long while, then back to meet my gaze. "I'm going to do it," she said in a whisper. "End it. Tonight." She looked wan, but she also looked relieved to have made a decision.

"You're sure?" I asked, stunned she'd finally decided.

She nodded.

"I'll be nearby," I said. "If you need anything. Or if Andrew gets unruly... Should I warn Will?"

"No!" she said, eyes sparking in alarm. "Please. No one else must know. If Andrew finds out from anyone else..." She shook her head. I knew what she meant. It would be terrible enough when she told him.

I agreed, and we walked out of my room and down the hall, arm in arm. We were silent, but all along, I was praying that the Lord would give her courage this night, strength to follow through on her decision. That He would give her encouragement and, most of all, that Andrew would peaceably accept it.

But as we came down the narrow stairwell, we could hear raised voices. After a shared glance, we moved down the second hall, into the great room and then outside to the veranda. Those gentlemen who weren't standing rose when they saw us. The last turned, and we recognized the press agent.

Mr. Grunthall had returned from his venture to Rome, where he'd gone to "pave the way for our arrival."

And apparently he did not have happy news to report.

CHAPTER 16

~William~

"Cora," Will said, offering his arm and ushering her in closer, "Mr. Grunthall has just told us that the newspapers are printing outrageous stories in our absence. He has asked us to hasten to Rome and complete our tour in public, giving reporters daily access." He frowned and rubbed his temple. "But I don't like it. It's not safe. It will take Hawke only hours to find us. He's certain to be awaiting us there, knowing we'll eventually show up."

"You *think*," Andrew said. "But why pay all these guards if we're going to continue hiding out in the country?" he asked, flipping one hand toward Pascal and another at the far corner of the veranda.

"It's true," Hugh said, crossing his arms and leaning against the villa wall. "So far, it's more of a vacation for Pascal and Stephen than any hardship."

"I don't regret keeping them on," Mr. Kensington said. "But are they enough manpower, William? For what is ahead?"

"In normal circumstances, yes," Will said. "But what Simon is describing seems rather chaotic. And he wants us—Cora—at the center of that storm."

"It's the only way," Grunthall said firmly. "Since we cannot leave before the ship sails, we may as well take hold of this story and steer it ourselves. Because what they are saying…" With a glance at Cora and Viv, he let it drop and shook his head.

Cora frowned. "Then let's get to it," she said, lifting her chin. "Do what we must. Speak to those we must. There are things I'd like to begin addressing myself, important matters, and perhaps this isn't a bad place to begin."

Will stared at her in surprise. "I don't know, Cora. I don't think you understand what it might be like. Gone will be your quiet escapes to the countryside. You'll be followed everywhere. Hounded."

"But won't that be good, in a way?" she asked. "If there are reporters about us all the time, wouldn't that make it more difficult for Hawke to get near again? He wouldn't dare."

Will sighed. "Perhaps."

"Why must it all center on Cora?" Andrew said to Grunthall, tossing back the last of his wine and reaching for the carafe to pour more. "I'm the rising leader of Kensington & Morgan Enterprises—why not craft a story about me?"

Will winced, hearing the pathetic, plaintive tone in the grown man's voice.

"While every one of you is of continued interest," Grunthall said, "it is Copper Cora that has caught the attention of the readership at large."

Andrew reached out to grab Vivian's hand, and she reluctantly stepped closer to him. Andrew seemed not to notice her hesitation. "What if we announced our engagement?"

Everyone stilled.

"Is that official, then?" Grunthall asked carefully, shifting his eyes to Viv and back to Andrew.

"I don't know, is it?" Andrew asked, smiling down at Vivian as if he expected her to immediately nod and smile. To Will's knowledge, the only proposal he'd made was a halfhearted attempt in Venice, which had ended badly. And judging from Cora and Vivian's glance at each other—

"No," Cora interjected too quickly, forcefully, surprising them all. She squared her shoulders and looked about at them, clearly trying to divert attention away from her sister. "This is my time. My moment. You all have had years of press. The public wants to know about me. Well, let's give them a story that will keep them entertained."

"Just as I thought." Andrew sneered, taking another swig of wine. "As long as our precious Cora gets what she wants—"

"Now see here—" Will said, stepping forward.

"What I *want*?" Cora cried, stepping forward too. "The only thing I've wanted is to be a part of this family, this company. To follow my heart but also the wisdom God gave me."

Andrew glared at her, then sighed heavily. "You vapid, silly woman," he muttered, shaking his head and turning away.

"Andrew!" Viv cried in dismay.

"What? She is! Thinking only of herself! You want the journalists to have a story, Grunthall? I have some stories. I think it's time the newspapermen focus not on the big, bad Kensington and Morgan families, but the treasure-seeking, manipulative little wench known as—"

Felix decked him before any of them saw it coming. Andrew staggered back, and his goblet went flying, crashing among the stones behind him. He cradled his jaw, glaring at Felix, and took one step toward him before Viv stopped him.

"I think you've said quite enough," Felix said, holding his clenched fist before his chest.

Andrew continued to stare at him for several seconds, while the rest of us held our breaths. "Come along, Vivian," he said, never letting his eyes drop from Felix.

Vivian went with him as he asked, visibly trembling.

"Viv," Cora said, reaching out to try and grab her hand.

"No. He'll stay away if I go to him." She looked at Cora, begging her with her eyes. Will thought she looked desperate. Frightened.

"*Viv…*" Cora tried again. And Will knew then for sure that something else had transpired between the sisters. Some agreement.

Something shifted in Vivian's eyes, and she bent her head and turned to follow where Andrew had gone, striding away down the length of the villa.

When they had turned the corner, the rest of the group sank to their seats, all feeling overcome with the weariness of the moment. Will took a sip of wine, and then he looked to Mr. Grunthall. "What on earth are they reporting that is so heinous? That causes these families such grief?"

"Some have said," Grunthall said gently, leaning forward again, "that Cora has been killed and buried so that her father can keep all the Dunnigan holdings for himself."

Cora gasped.

"There is much speculation as to whether your sisters or brother," he said to Cora, "or perhaps your future brother-in-law did it." He nodded toward the corner of the villa, where Andrew and Viv had disappeared.

Cora frowned. "That's easy enough to dispel. Put my picture in one paper, and all will see that it's foolishness."

Mr. Grunthall picked up a twig of lavender blown loose by the wind. "Others say that you and Mr. McCabe have entered an illicit affair, and the family has disowned you, and now you're all in hiding."

Cora shifted in her seat and glanced toward him. Will glowered at the press agent. But she had to know, had to be warned of what she faced. For the first time, Will acknowledged the wisdom in Mr. Kensington's decision to hire the press agent and looked at the older man. He'd been silent through the entire conversation and appeared to have aged as the details unfolded.

"Still others have suggested that Mr. McCabe himself orchestrated the events of your tour, to position himself as a hero, all in an endeavor to force the Kensingtons and Morgans to pay him significant bonuses, lest they look like cads if they didn't."

Will laughed under his breath and rubbed his forehead. "Lies! Such lies! And they call themselves journalists?"

"They do not report it as fact," Mr. Grunthall said. "They merely report the suppositions of those you've met—"

"*Met* being a loose term," Felix said, rubbing his knuckles and flexing his fingers as if they ached.

Everyone was silent, waiting on Cora. She turned to face Grunthall. "I'll do it. Whatever you need of me. But only if Will is beside me, all the way. I will not hide how I feel about him," she said, looking at her father.

Grunthall pursed his lips, considering her. His eyes flicked over to Will. "It will only intensify the scrutiny. If they find out that Cora has chosen Mr. McCabe over Pierre de Richelieu?" He rubbed his face and then shook his head, splaying his hands out on the table and looking down a moment, then back up to them. "I guarantee none of us have ever seen such a media frenzy as what shall occur then."

"Don't do it, McCabe," Wallace said to him.

Will stared hard at the old man.

"The girl has enough to handle without this, now," Wallace said, gesturing between them.

"No," Cora said, rising. "You do not get to decide this, Father. Not this. This is between—"

Wallace gasped and pulled his fist and right arm to his chest, looking stricken.

"Wallace?" Mr. Morgan said. "Wallace!"

Mr. Kensington leaned heavily to his right, his eyes bugging out. Felix and Hugh both rushed to his side as he slid partway out of his chair and helped him to the ground.

Cora knelt by his side and tried to take his hand, but his hands were clenched, as if he were frozen. "Father? Father, what is it? What is wrong?" She leaned over him, holding his face in both hands, then looked up with stricken eyes at Will. "Will! We need Eleonora! We must fetch a doctor at once!"

CHAPTER 17

~William~

Cora paced the hall of the hospital in Siena until the morning sun streamed through windows amber with age. Around the corner, her siblings leaned against one another or the Morgans in a line of straight-backed, uncomfortable chairs, most of them fitfully sleeping, the others staring straight ahead, dark rings beneath their eyes. Andrew brought small cups of soup for them all to drink—insisting they keep up their strength—and each took one, too dazed to fully consider the incongruity of Andrew doing anything of the sort.

Will leaned against a wall, arms crossed, one foot crossed over the other, and watched as Cora sipped her soup. He'd long since given up trying to talk her into sitting down, resting. She had it in her head that it was her fault—that she'd pressed Wallace to a point that his heart couldn't take. But Andrew's tantrum hadn't helped either. They'd been over it several times.

"I've been so caught up in my own drama, Will," she said, shaking her head in self-condemnation, "that I didn't stop to see him, really see him." She lifted a hand to her temples and shook her head. "What kind of daughter am I? What kind of woman am I?"

"Stop," he said, reaching out to grab her arm. "Cora, stop. Stop blaming yourself. None of us could see it coming. The man has been as strong as an ox for decades. He's looked a bit wan of late, yes. But we've all been through the wringer."

"It's because of me, Will… His worrying, over me, my safety."

"As well as your sisters, your brother," he put in.

"And then I've pressed him so, over the mine," she said, ignoring him. "Doubling his work, really, in having to teach me. Resisting Andrew's help. It's all been too much."

"Clearly," Will said. "For all of us, really." He took a deep breath. "Look, you couldn't see it coming," he repeated. "Life is not something we can manage or control. It's something we negotiate every time the path takes a turn. The turns just keep coming faster as we get older, right? Especially as a Kensington?"

"That's not what I want to hear, Will," she said, giving him a pained look.

"I'm sorry. But it's the truth. You've been berating yourself all night over this, as if you yourself made the man have a heart attack. You didn't. It just…happened. People of a certain age have things happen all the time. Look at your papa and my uncle Stuart." He took a deep breath and sighed. Getting irritated with her would only make things worse. "The only thing we can do is pray for wisdom on how we move forward from here. What's best for Wallace. What's best for the family. For you."

A nurse—a nun in her habit—passed by them, giving them a look of disapproval, he supposed for not staying with the others. They ignored her.

"You're right, of course," she said wearily. "We need to get him to Rome. The hospital there is supposed to be better than…" Her voice cracked, and she lifted a hand to her face.

"Oh, my darling girl," Will said. "Come." He pulled her into his arms and held her as she wept. Gradually it dawned on him. "It's a little too close to what you suffered through with your papa, isn't it?" he said lowly.

She nodded, and he pulled her closer, stroking her back. "He's going to be all right. Just as your papa pulled through, so will Wallace. You'll see. The man's too ornery to give up yet. He has fortunes to run, suffragettes to back, suitors to run off."

She giggled and looked up at him, a handkerchief to her nose.

They both belatedly recognized the sounds of a Kodak, the clicking they remembered so well from their time with Arthur Stapleton, and looked down the hallway. Three reporters were there, two on their knees, taking their photograph, one doing so standing. How long had they been there?

"Hey!" Will cried, pushing Cora behind him as the reporters continued to advance, calling out in Italian, taking more photographs as fast as they could. "*Fatela finita ora!*" Will shouted. *Stop it, right now.*

"We only ask you a few questions, Signore McCabe," said one in broken English.

Mr. Grunthall showed up then, on the run, looking disheveled and aghast. He rounded on the three men and stood between them and Will and Cora. "You may only interview Miss Diehl Kensington or Mr. McCabe with an appointment through me," he said in English, standing upright and straightening his coat. He looked over his shoulder at Will, mouthing a command for him to usher Cora out the other way.

Will nodded and put his arm around her, leading her quickly away, even as they heard another photograph being made. She was in no shape to grant an interview this morning, not after being up all night. None of them were. Was that where Grunthall had been? Shielding the others?

Obviously, someone had tipped off a reporter that the elusive Kensingtons and Morgans were in Siena. Now that the journalists were on their trail, they'd be nearly impossible to escape.

~Cora~

We were nearing the back exit when I heard Vivian's cry.

I paused and turned, looking down the long white hall to where my sister stood.

There was no mistaking her tone, nor the expression on my brother's face as he pulled her into his arms.

"No, no, no, no," I said, prying loose of Will's grip and practically running to my siblings while at the same time, inside, my heart seemed to thud slowly, as if asleep, separate.

Tears were running down Vivian's face. Andrew appeared and hovered, awkwardly, when she didn't turn to him. Felix's eyes, always filled with such mischief, held only pain, bewilderment. Gradually, I could hear others weeping, down the hall. Lillian? Grunthall, behind me, pleading with the reporters to have some common decency in this dark hour…

"Cora," Vivian said, reaching out to take hold of my hand.

"Don't say it," I whispered. "Don't say it," I repeated more loudly. "It's impossible."

"Cora," Will began.

"No. There's too much...I haven't...we didn't...we never..."

Tears choked my throat closed.

My father was dead.

And I had to get away.

CHAPTER 18

~Cora~

I ran blindly.

I couldn't breathe, and yet I couldn't stop either, turning one corner and then the other. If only I could gain a little distance, find a little space, I might wake from this nightmare.

With each step, I knew I was playing the fool. That I needed Will or a guard with me, that Nathan Hawke might be waiting for just this sort of opportunity. And yet Hawke was likely far away in Rome, right? My mind was spinning, my heart crying out for a moment alone, a moment to try and make sense of the insensible.

He's dead...he's dead... How can he be dead?

It was impossible. How could Wallace Kensington be dead?

I turned one corner and then the next, running again when a group of men came my way down one alleyway, then another when I heard my name called in the distance.

I arrived in a small piazza outside a massive cathedral that towered above me. Ornate gothic adornments clung to each crevice.

Gold and bright mosaics filled each arch. Behind the grand medieval structure, a massive bell tower climbed to the sky in alternating colors of white and black marble.

The duomo. The city's cathedral.

We'd planned to tour Siena in full but hadn't had the opportunity yet. There was something about the grand, sprawling church that called to me, welcomed me, like the arms of a warm grandmother waiting to cradle me as I wept.

"*Stai bene figliola?*" asked an older woman in concern. "*Dove è la tua famiglia?*"

She was practically as wide as she was tall, and she paused beside me, looking about as if I were a small child and she was searching for my mama or papa to look after me. Which only made me cry harder.

Mama. Papa. Father...

"I'm all right," I said, knowing she didn't understand English, breaking away and hurriedly climbing the steps as I pulled a handkerchief from my purse and blew my nose.

A man was exiting the cathedral. He held the door open for me, looking as concerned as the old woman, but I rushed past him before he could ask me a question.

Inside, the customary cool and hush welcomed me, but the visual impact of the interior held no measure of restfulness. The stacked granite alternated in black and white on every column. And before me, on the ground, was a marble mosaic, each section depicting biblical scenes or moments in Siena's celebrated history. I tried to concentrate on them, to get my whirling thoughts to settle, but over and over again my mind returned to my father.

He's dead. Wallace Kensington is dead. We didn't make our peace. Would we have, ever? Would we have ever found a relationship based on anything but…maneuvering?

I stared at a vast marble carving in the floor, white inlaid in black, depicting what I guessed was the Slaughter of the Innocents. Mothers crying out for their babes. Children in soldiers' arms. Swords. Bloodshed. Weeping. Above them were archways. The artwork had been done in such a way that it appeared three-dimensional, as if the arches actually descended, out and away, beneath my very feet. And in a way, I felt as if I were floating, ethereal, separate from this place.

I looked beyond it to the next, absently seeking a peacock Will had told me about, until I found it in the side nave. Sideways, his feathers spread wide, his eye wide and unseeing.

When we'd visited a church in Torcello, outside of Venice, Will had said that the peacock was an ancient symbol found in many churches. The people believed that it was a symbol for Christ. They thought the flesh of a peacock did not rot once it was dead and buried. He'd said we'd see many of them in other churches as we traveled, and it'd become a game of sorts, to be the first to spot one.

A peacock's body did rot, of course. But it set me to thinking about how we all died, but as believers, rose again. Was Wallace in heaven now? Looking about, bewildered? No longer a king in his own kingdom, but kneeling at the King's feet? Had he truly known the Savior? Or was he in some other place, far darker?

Tears came again, unbidden, my heart heavy with all the conversations I might have had, should have had, with Wallace

Kensington. My stomach turned so violently I thought I might retch. Conversations I'd never have the opportunity to have again. So much wasted time, so much effort in jockeying for position, power…

I moved on. Ahead was a prayer bench before a cascading group of candles, and a small woman, head bent in prayer. I went and knelt beside her, peering up at the figure of the Virgin Mary and her baby; mother in adoration, child at peace. The woman beside me finished her prayer and shuffled off, leaving me alone on the bench. For a moment, I felt as if I were the only person in the entire cathedral, so quiet it was. And with each breath I took, my stomach gradually eased. Candle flames danced in a draft I could not feel. Shafts of light illuminated dancing dust mites.

My eyes moved back to the sculpture of mother and child. The child that had grown into the Son of Man. *Our Kinsman Redeemer*, as my papa had always referred to Him.

Lord Jesus, Redeemer, I prayed, bowing my head against my clasped hands. *I am so lost. How could You take him now? When we had so much left to resolve, negotiate? How am I to be a Kensington if he is not here to teach me?*

The tears came again then.

I felt as if I'd been cast off the decks of the *Olympic* and set upon the waves to swim to an unknown shore. All my newfound confidence, my understanding of my place in this world, had abruptly disappeared the moment I saw Viv's face and knew what she had to say. *Father is dead. Dead…dead.*

I blew my nose into my handkerchief again, staring up at the sculpture, my eyes tracing the lines of the woman's hand on the baby's back. To the child's eyes.

"*You* knew," I whispered. "What it was like to belong to one family, and another one altogether." The thought made me smile through my tears.

Still I remained as another woman came to pray beside me and an older man lowered himself heavily to the bench on my other side. How had Jesus managed it, belonging to one family and yet to another Father? How did He keep it straight, to Whom He belonged, through it all?

I shoved away from the rail and moved along, gazing up to the sun streaming through the windows, thinking about it. He knew that He belonged to His heavenly Father. All along, He never lost track of that. It was His truest identity, from start to finish. *As it is ours.*

Chin in hand, I turned around slowly, repeating that thought in my mind. *My truest identity...* I shook my head. By some miracle, we were all His children, first and foremost. Forever claimed. My eyes rested on the cross.

Slowly, I sank to my knees.

Forever claimed.

A priest hurried up to me, reaching for my arm, but I waved him off. "I'm all right," I said dimly. "I'm all right." Tears poured down my face again as I stared at the cross. "I'm all right," I whispered.

I recognized that he was backing away—probably wondering if I was mad—but I couldn't take my eyes off the cross. Peace seeped through me, saturating me as if I'd become a living sponge, filling me so full I thought I might burst.

It mattered not from where I'd come. It mattered not what I'd accomplish in the future. All summer long I'd sought to fit in with the Kensingtons, gain their acceptance, and yet hold on to my Diehl heritage. But all along I'd missed the heritage that truly mattered. And that was as a child of God.

I looked up at the figure on the cross, and all I saw in His eyes was peace. Understanding. Love. How long had I missed this blessed assurance? No matter what I gained, what I lost, He was with me through it all. Unchanging. Unbreakable. Unending.

I forced myself to rise, to move. I walked past the high, ornately carved pulpit and looked up into the dome, admiring it as the high noon sun sent streaming columns of light through its windows. A few steps farther, and I slipped into a pew and knelt again, leaning my forehead against my clenched hands, wanting to remember what the Lord had given me here. Cement it in my mind and heart as I faced the future.

The last time I'd prayed in a church like this was in Venice. And the Lord had spoken so clearly, telling me to wait and trust. For this, I decided, this moment of clarity, understanding. Now, all I wished was to thank Him. Thank Him for drawing close, for giving me direction, just when I thought all was lost.

A man slipped into the pew beside me, uncomfortably near. Then another from the other side. Both bent their heads, as if in prayer, but they were too close. The hair on the back of my neck stood on end, and a shiver went down my spine. Were they dangerous? I straightened and then stood, and they did too, with me. The one closest to the end let me out, giving me a friendly smile, but then he seemed to follow me as I circled the altar again.

"There you are, Cora," Felix said in relief, grabbing my elbow. "We've been looking everywhere—"

He'd surprised me so much I let out a soft cry and yanked away.

"What's the matter?" he said, eyes narrowing at my jumpiness. He looked over my shoulder. "You. *Lexington*. Are you *following* my sister?" So Felix knew these men? "You'll have to make an appointment with Simon Grunthall if you wish to speak to her." He pulled me along toward the front door of the cathedral.

"Just doing a little scouting," said the stranger, pulling out a pad of paper and pencil and jotting something down as the lighter-haired man joined him. "Didn't know Copper Cora had a religious streak. That's a new bent."

I blinked in surprise, even as I digested the fact that not one, but two American journalists had already found me. And...Copper Cora? I'd heard Grunthall use that, but were others? I had a nickname?

"C-copper Cora?" I stuttered.

"It's catchy, isn't it?" said Mr. Lexington. He ran his fingers down the lapel of his jacket as if proud of himself. "I coined it. I realize that there's a fair bit of gold in Dunnigan too. But it just doesn't have the same ring."

"You didn't coin it," said the other journalist, pulling out his own pad of paper. "I did. Miss Cora, care to make a statement about what you think of this cathedral? Are you a churchgoing girl, back at home? Was it Wallace Kensington's death that sent you running here? Terrible thing, that. Please accept my con—"

"C'mon, Cora," Felix said, taking my arm and leading me out of the church, the journalists catching up to us in seconds, running down the stairs on either side of us.

At the bottom, Mr. Lexington turned, practically running backward before us, peppering me with questions. "Please. Give a guy a break. I'm only looking for a fresh angle. Are you a Catholic or a Protestant?"

"Protes—" I said.

"Miss Kensington will respond to you if you have an appointment," Felix interrupted.

"What flavor?" said the man, nearly tripping and narrowly recovering his balance.

"Excuse me?" I asked.

"What flavor of Protestant? You know, Methodist, Lutheran, Presby—"

"No more," growled Felix. "You fellows have no sense of propriety. We've just endured a terrible loss!"

"Propriety? I've heard you've kissed more women on the Continent than Casanova."

Felix barked a laugh. "You have me confused with someone else."

"Who? Hugh Morgan?"

"Right!" said the other, arching a brow in excitement and crowding in. "Care to make a statement about that?"

"No," Felix said, shaking his head.

"What if I go fetch a taxi for you?" said Mr. Lexington. "In exchange for an exclusive. A five-minute chat, just you and me," he said, giving me a begging smile. "Just five minutes, that's all I ask."

"And me. I want a part of that," Mr. Jefferson said.

Felix pushed me behind him and faced both of them. "You two have no scruples. Our father just died!"

"Look, I'm sorry," said the taller Lexington, hands up. "We don't want to push you in this tender time. Truly. But do you know how impossible it's been to try to speak to you? That Grunthall fella practically has a gag order on you all. Every story—and I mean *every* story—is written by him."

"It's as our father wanted," I said, realizing I sounded as distant as I felt. Was all of this real? Was I dreaming?

"You don't look so good, Miss Kensington," said the shorter Jefferson, looking suddenly, genuinely alarmed. "Maybe she'd better take a seat."

Felix gazed back at me in chagrin. "He's right." He reached out and grabbed hold of my arm as my head started to spin, my vision tunneling.

"Cora!" I heard Will shout behind me but knew if I dared turn around, I'd faint for sure.

"Felix…" I said, feeling sick to my stomach again, trying to gain a better grip on his arm but feeling impossibly weak.

And then my knees were crumpling, and I was falling, all the men seeming to lean toward me at once, making it worse. But it was Felix who caught me, lifted me in his arms. "I have you," he said. "I have you."

He stood upright as I fought the dizziness. The whole piazza was spinning now. "You two. Leave us alone, and I'll see Grunthall gets you an exclusive interview in Rome. But *not until then*. Give us a few days to mourn. Remember your civility, if you ever had a measure of it."

With that, he turned and walked away with me in his arms.

"Why'd you run, Cora?" he asked. "Why didn't you stay with us?"

"I needed…I needed to be alone. I'm sorry."

As he walked, the spinning in my head slowed. He paused beside a fountain, set me down on the wide edge, and reached out a cupped hand. "Here," he said, bringing his hand to my lips. I drank, embarrassed by my sloppy manner. But it was good. I was terribly thirsty, I realized. Will joined us there, sitting on my other side.

"You haven't eaten anything but that bit of soup Andrew brought us," Will said grimly. "You're feeling the effects of hunger, I take it, now." He nodded toward me even as Felix brought another handful of water to my lips.

My head was throbbing. "All right," I said, pushing away my brother's hand after drinking what I could. "You're getting more on my dress than in my mouth."

"Sorry," he said with a small smile. "Fresh out of crystal goblets here in the piazza."

"I appreciate it," I said. "Think you two can get me back to the hotel? I think…I need to rest for a while." I lifted a hand to my forehead, wondering if I was running a fever. But I felt no telltale heat.

Will nodded. "Your sisters are heading there now. And they need you, Cora. Felix, you, too."

I tried to rise, but Will was immediately on his feet and sweeping me into his arms. "Uh-uh," he said, shifting me slightly. "I'm not watching you run away from me again, Cora Diehl Kensington. Not today."

CHAPTER 19

~William~

Carrying Cora all the way to the hotel—once a grand palazzo—was not easy, but he refused to set her down. Just as she felt compelled to run—apparently in some vain effort to cope with the news of her father's demise—Will felt compelled to make absolutely certain she was restored to her family.

Felix opened the front door for them, and Will climbed the stairs and gently deposited her on the settee in the suite's central room, her sisters bustling in, bursting into new tears.

"Oh, Cora," Vivian said, kneeling beside her and taking her hand. "We were so frightened when you ran off like that! As if it wasn't awful enough... Please don't do that again. I can't take any more loss this day!"

"I'm sorry, Viv," Cora said. "And Lil," she added to her younger sister. "You're right, of course. I simply was...overcome." She shook her head. "Not thinking of anyone but myself. I'm terribly sorry. I'm not used to thinking about siblings." She looked around at them.

"It's all right," Lillian said, her eyes red and puffy from her tears. "Now that you're here and safe, we can get through this. Together."

"Together," Felix added, coming around the end of the settee. "We've been stronger since you joined our fold, Cora. We need you." He shrugged one shoulder. "Apparently, Father knew exactly what we needed when he invited you to join us," he said.

Andrew, in the corner with his father, let out a dismissive sound. Felix tossed him a furious glare and moved to engage him, but Cora reached out a hand to stop him. "No. Don't. It's not worth it."

A maid came and poured them all glasses of water and set out trays of cheese and bread, which they all forced themselves to nibble. None of them likely felt hunger, Will mused. But they had to keep their strength up.

"Children," Mr. Morgan said, tentatively entering the circle around Cora, "I'm afraid we must discuss what comes next. We can bury your father here, or they can prepare his body for the transatlantic crossing."

Cora looked at her siblings, clearly believing this was their decision, not hers.

Viv swallowed hard and lifted her chin. "He made his fortune and his name in Montana. That should be his final resting place."

Felix and Lil nodded, and Cora did too, then. It made sense. But it was an odd thought, Wallace Kensington making the crossing with them this time, but down in the hold in a casket. For a man who had wielded such power for so long, it seemed rather, well… powerless. But then, that was the end of every man and woman, wasn't it? The end of their own power. And the full recognition of where true power remained.

Cora, finally with a little color to her cheeks again, swung her legs over the edge of the settee and sat up, putting her hand to her head and blinking slowly, as if to fight a resulting wave of vertigo. "I imagine we all have a great deal of paperwork to see to, Mr. Morgan," she said, lifting her hand for him to assist her up.

He helped her and studied her in quiet admiration. "That we do. That we do."

"You rest," Andrew said, glowering as if he'd reached the end of his meager patience. "We can see to things, Father and I. No need for you all to be involved."

"No," Cora said stubbornly. "I will take my place where I ought."

"And I'll be with her," Vivian said.

Andrew's frown deepened.

"Do you have a problem with that?" Felix said, stepping up beside Viv. Lillian came to her other side.

Andrew's dark eyes shifted from one to the next, and then he tilted his head and forced a smile. "Not at all," he said.

~Cora~

We moved through the next three days in somewhat of a stupor, seeing to my father's airtight casket and embalming, choosing a proper suit for him, meeting with attorneys. I sent Will to inquire if we might get home sooner, regardless if the ship was less comfortable than the *Olympic*, but he returned with news that there was not a single cabin available. We would have to wait for our ship.

Settled into our new apartments in Rome, high on a hill, with a lovely view of the city's numerous church domes—including the towering St. Peter's—we sat down with Mr. Morgan, Andrew, Felix, Vivian, Lillian, Will, and an attorney, Kenneth Smith, who happened to be in town from New York.

I took a deep breath and forced myself to concentrate on the documents at hand. Upon my father's death, the Kensington portion of the Kensington-Diehl Mine had shifted to my siblings. With Felix taking part in today's meeting, I wondered if he might be ready to step up and take his rightful place in the company. Covertly, I watched him interact with Mr. Morgan and the antagonistic Andrew with some aplomb, exercising latent business skills that he'd carefully kept hidden. His presence relieved me. I knew he'd rather be anywhere but in that room, poring over document after document, but with him nearby, I felt less alone. Less weak in the face of Andrew's growing animosity.

Mr. Smith read through my father's will with all of us. Mr. Morgan had apparently carried a copy with him, as Wallace had done for him, in case the worst happened. Andrew was the only non-kinsman in the room, solicitously holding Viv's hand as she sniffled and listened. As I'd suspected, there was nothing in my father's will for me other than what had been promised—a certain amount set aside should I wish to go back to Normal School. The rest was to go to my three siblings.

"But you, Miss Cora," said the gray-haired man, peering at me over the edge of his spectacles, "are in more than adequate position to pay for your own schooling now." He smiled, obviously thinking it somewhat of a joke. And I supposed it was, given the meager sum Father had set aside for school, compared to what had already arrived in my personal account. "Still," he said, lifting the sheet and turning it over, "we'll be certain that it is transferred to you when and if you return to university or Normal School."

"Thank you," I said.

"The Kensington heirs," said Mr. Smith, looking over the documents, "shall be afforded a monthly stipend. When you graduate from university, Felix, it shall be doubled, and when the girls marry, theirs shall be doubled as well."

"And what if I choose to attend university?" Vivian asked quietly.

Andrew's coffee cup clattered to the saucer. "There is no call for you to go to university—"

"But if I did?" she insisted, eyes only on Mr. Smith.

His gray brows drew together in a frown, and he peered back at the documents. In a moment, he shook his head. "No, I don't see any provision for that. Did you ever speak to your father about a desire to attend university?"

"No," Vivian said. "I didn't get the opportunity."

Andrew let out a scoffing laugh. "Idle thoughts. There are better ways for the wife of a Morgan to spend her days than to have her nose in a book."

"Well, I am not yet a wife of a Morgan, am I?" Vivian said.

Everyone around the table stilled.

After a moment, Mr. Smith coughed and then turned the page. "I'm afraid, my dear, you would need to petition a judge if you wished to obtain a different settlement."

"I wouldn't stand in her way," Felix said. "Neither would Lillian." Lil nodded her eager assent.

"Be that as it may, it would still have to be revised in the will, and Mr. Morgan, as the legal partner, might have to agree to it. We'd have to review it with a judge."

Andrew smiled for the first time, as if that settled it. But Mr. Morgan folded his hands and bowed his head, obviously in deep thought. "I believe we'll need to discuss that further, Vivian," he said at last. Andrew scowled.

I could barely cover my own smile. There was hope yet for my sister. Although I highly doubted that the normal monthly stipend would be anything less than generous.

Mr. Smith proceeded with the reading of the entire will, and I excused myself, feeling I really had no business remaining. Will met me in the hall and walked out with me to the sprawling terrace that edged the third floor and afforded us lovely views of the ancient city. He came close and put an arm around me as we both stared at the horizon.

"I can't believe he's dead," I said. "Never coming back. I can't believe we're here. In Rome."

"It's a great deal to take in." He pointed out the tip of the Coliseum, just barely visible in the distance, and the various churches, as well as portions of the ancient wall built two thousand years prior. He talked about the places he wanted us to see while we were here but gradually saw that my mind was on other things.

"So," he said, "do you think you would like to return to Normal School?"

I smiled at him and then shook my head. "Running the mine will take every available hour."

"You could hire a manager."

"You seeking to apply?"

He smiled at me and dug his toe into the marble tile, as if to dislodge some dirt. "No. I don't know what a manager would need to know. And I still aim to become an architect, if God will smile on that plan."

"You'd be a fine architect. Maybe I'll give you the money, and you can simply get done with it."

His smile faded. "That'd be generous of you, Cora. But no. A man needs to make his own way."

"Oh, Will. I know it, but—"

"No." He shook his head and looked to the city again, standing beside me at the rail. "It wouldn't be right."

I stifled a sigh and then remembered our scuffles over the watch, and Pierre's warning. A man did not like to be kept. It was a matter of pride, I supposed. Would it stand between us, even if he made his own way? If the mine produced what my father had thought it would?

"Miss Cora," Anna said, appearing at the terrace door. "They're through with the reading and have requested you return to the table."

I did as they'd asked, begging Will to come along, moving back to the main living area of the apartments, and sitting down at the table. Vivian excused herself, and Lil went with her, and I tried to ignore Andrew's heavy gaze following Viv all the way out the door, as if he was still seething over her question.

"We've arrived at the Kensington-Diehl Mine documentation," Mr. Smith said, pulling out a heavy set of papers from a leather folder and sliding a second set over to me, and two other sets to Mr. Morgan and Andrew. "As Wallace stipulated, if Felix is not yet ready to take his place in the company, then the Morgans are to manage the Kensington portion of the mine."

I dared not look up at Andrew. I could feel him gloating from across the table.

"But it is still the case that I hold the majority share," I said gently.

"Yes," Mr. Smith said.

"And that means that if it came to a deadlock on a decision, that my opinion would rule."

Andrew stiffened at my words.

"Well, yes. But there is also a stipulation in the documentation that you institute a board of directors, should Wallace not be available for counsel."

"We can recommend some fine gentlemen for the board," Andrew said. "In fact, I have several classmates that would be most excellent—"

"A board of directors," I said to Mr. Smith. "What are the qualifications for a board member?"

"Well, usually it behooves a company to nominate men of stature. Men with business acumen. Experience. So that they might advise you well."

"So they could be men from Dunnigan. Men who know the land and—"

"What?" Andrew interrupted. "There can't be more than one or two from that godforsaken town that would have half the wits it would take—"

"Men who have sold the land to the mine and may be seeking a new way to support their families?" I asked.

Mr. Smith peeled off his spectacles, one ear at a time, and tapped them on the paper. "There is nothing in here that stipulates who should sit on the board, if that's what you're asking."

"That's what I'm asking," I said. I turned to face Mr. Morgan and Andrew and Felix. "We're radically changing the face of Dunnigan.

I want it to be a fine new start for the town, not the death of it. I was very serious when I said I wanted to pay landowners triple what the land is worth and leave them the land on which their homes and barns are on. Has that been done?"

"No," Andrew scoffed. "Your father thought you would come to your senses in time. He only pretended to agree with you in order to placate you."

"Andrew, please," Mr. Morgan said, lifting a hand. "That's not entirely true." He turned to me. "Your father thought we could address it as a *bonus* when the mine does well. So far, all land has been purchased at the current value. And all seemed happy to sell. However, he did honor your request to leave them their homes, barns, and five acres around each."

I shook my head. "I want to go back to them all and do as I originally was led to do. Don't you see? We have the opportunity to be a benefactor, a benevolent leader, rather than a company taking advantage of every citizen. Think of Zacchaeus, the tax collector. Once he saw the light, he went back and repaid everyone four times what they had paid."

Andrew rolled his eyes. "Now we're looking to the Bible for business practices? Let's leave such things to Sundays, shall we?" He turned to his father and Felix. "This is why women should not be allowed in business! They rule with their hearts, not their heads."

Will moved, and I worried that he'd pick up the man from his chair and toss him across the room. I set a hand on his leg, stilling him. I knew there wasn't anything that he could say to win Andrew over.

"This is exactly why women *should* be in business," Felix was saying, sitting back in his chair. "My sister is going to create a company like the world has never seen." His was a satisfied, proud smile. "It might not make the profits that others make, perhaps. But it will be a good company, a fine company, a company that any man—or woman—would be happy to call their own. She's going to make the Kensington name a proud one. Stronger for our association with the Diehls."

"Bah," Andrew said. "If you had paid attention at school in even your primary business courses, you would know such ideas are foolish."

"They may seem foolish up front," Mr. Morgan interjected. "But they will bear out long-term. Look what happened when we followed her advice in Butte."

"One instance does not make her the expert, Father," Andrew said.

Mr. Morgan shrugged. "It was a fairly significant moment. Did we not succeed in leading our workers away from a strike? Are they not far more productive than before? Is it not affecting the bottom line in a positive way?"

Andrew let out a dismissive sound.

"We must take into account," Mr. Morgan said, "that Cora is of Kensington blood and may very well have inherited her father's business intuition. The man was uncannily good at ferreting out potential growth in any business he set his mind to. He did so with an iron fist, of course, rather than the velvet hammer as our Cora may wield, but I see no reason to not give her a little leeway."

"A little?" Andrew asked. He waved a hand toward me. "She wants to triple the budget on land acquisition! Land that's already been purchased. Who would do such a foolish thing other than a woman?"

"I hear her goals clearly, Andrew," Mr. Morgan returned. "I wonder if you do. Have you bothered to listen?"

Andrew threw up his hands, sat back in his chair, and folded his arms. "Fine. Do what you wish. But don't say I didn't warn you."

"And I want at least half the board members to be Dunnigan men," I said to Mr. Smith. "Perhaps even a woman."

"No," Andrew said. "Absolutely not." His face was growing red.

"I am not seeking your permission," I returned. I looked to Mr. Smith. "I can decide this, now, right? Having majority holding in the company?"

"Yes," he said slowly. "But I would caution you to take care. There is a reason that Mr. Morgan wishes to place educated businessmen on the board."

"And we shall find them," I said calmly, even as Andrew rose. "Along with people who care for Dunnigan and its citizens as much as I do."

CHAPTER 20

~Cora~

The next day, I ignored my queasy stomach, assuming it was the clamor and the constant demands on me from all directions, and joined the group for a tour of Palatine Hill—once the Roman emperor's home—and below it, the Roman Forum. For days, we'd stayed indoors, and all of us were eager for an outing, to at least pretend we were something more than wrung-out people in mourning. We'd donned new black jackets and skirts in crepe; only our dickeys were ivory. Our broad hats were black, and Vivian even had new jet jewelry at her earlobes, matching Lillian's jet broach.

Over and over, we stopped to pretend to listen to Will's earnest explanations of scant remains of buildings gone for centuries, but we were each lost in our own thoughts. We saw ancient arenas, fountains, homes, baths and steam rooms, temples and gates, and gradually began to piece them together for a glimpse of Rome in her heady, grand days of power.

Halfway through the imperial remains on Palatine Hill, staring at a fountain in the shape of an Amazonian shield, Lillian broke down, weeping for Father, mourning that he wasn't with us. Viv and I sat with her for a while until she gathered herself, but her tears made each of us weepy as well. Vivian and Lil's grief was different than my own, I thought, even as I fished a fresh handkerchief from my purse for Lil. My sisters grieved a father they'd known all their lives. I grieved that I'd missed the opportunity to ever truly know him.

We moved on to the Forum. An hour later, I walked arm in arm with Vivian, marveling at the Roman road beneath our feet, the stones still in their place, wide enough for two chariots to pass by each other, according to Will. In some places, there were even grooves from centuries of wheels passing over them. "They were an impressive people, were they not?" I asked Viv, trying to get her mind on things besides our dead father. "Building so many roads to such distant lands."

"Indeed. It's dizzying to consider how vast the empire really was."

"Lucky for you," Andrew said, coming to her other side, "you needn't fill your mind with such facts. You can be free to contemplate the things that women should contemplate."

"So…history is not useful to women?" I asked.

"I did not say that," he said with a slight scowl. "Only that Vivian need not spend time thinking about things she finds perplexing. I'm here to do that for her. Perhaps at some point you will allow your suitor to do the same for you, Cora."

He strode off, and I fought the urge to grab his walking stick and club him over the head with it. "Why do you stay with him?" I asked Viv. "Why not break it off now?"

"It will be easier once we're home," Viv said. "He can go his way, I can go mine. Here..." She shrugged her small shoulders. And I could see what she meant. Here in Rome, and then aboard ship, it would be nearly impossible to avoid him. They'd run into each other again and again, making it all the more traumatic. Even back in Butte it would be difficult. But seeing her tolerate him until the end of the tour? It set my stomach to roiling anew.

~William~

Will and Cora were to meet with the reporters that afternoon. As he escorted her into the parlor, he took a second look at her. "Are you all right?"

"What?" she asked, as if confused by his question at first, then she shook her head. "Oh yes, why?"

"You look peaked. Is it your sorrow? Or are you feeling faint again?"

"A little," she admitted, repositioning her hand on his arm. "But I'll be fine. I need to get through with this."

He continued to lead her forward, as she clearly desired, but he watched her closely when she squeezed his arm as they turned the corner. She managed to greet Grunthall and the two reporters, Lexington and Jefferson, and then sit down primly on the edge of a chair, shoulders back, head high. She looked lovely, even in her drab black crepe mourning jacket and skirt.

Will braced himself. It had been a long time since he felt so utterly out of control. The story of their love was about to unfold as Cora decided, not him.

Simon Grunthall leaned forward. "Gentlemen, as I'm certain you anticipated, all questions must be asked of me—"

The two men began grumbling and speaking at once, but Grunthall held up a hand.

"—and I shall allow Miss Diehl Kensington to answer those that are appropriate."

The reporters exchanged tired looks but then forged on.

"Miss Cora," began Lexington, who was from the *Washington Post*, "tell us in your own words how you came to be a part of the Kensington clan."

Mr. Grunthall cast a raised eyebrow at Cora and gave her a nod. He had agreed earlier that the reporters would not rest until this point was verified and put behind them. But how would Cora phrase it?

"I only learned of my…connection to the Kensingtons at the beginning of summer," she said. "I was raised by my mother and a fine man named Alan Diehl. But after my school term finished, Mr. Kensington paid us a visit and invited me to join my siblings on their tour of Europe."

She blushed furiously under the men's intense gaze. But it only made her seem fresh and innocent to him, endearing. Inwardly, he prayed that she'd have the same effect on the reporters and they wouldn't pry any further.

Jefferson said gently, "So you did not know that Mr. Wallace Kensington was your true father until May of this year?"

Grunthall nodded. He probably knew it was inevitable, such questions. Cora had to get the truth out there now, or the newspapermen would continue to fabricate stories based on conjecture.

"I believe what I've discovered of late," she said, staring right at the reporter, "is that my truest Father is in heaven. But no, I didn't know of my biological tie to Wallace Kensington until May."

Jefferson and Lexington shared a look of surprise, but they continued to question her as Cora accepted a cup of tea from a kitchen maid.

"What sort of school were you enrolled in?"

"Normal School. I was working on my teaching certificate."

"Surely no longer, with your newfound wealth and position."

"I'm not certain," she said, glancing at Will. "Wealth comes and goes, but the thirst for knowledge is a perennial need."

The two men laughed at this.

"What of your bear, William McCabe?" asked Jefferson.

"What of him?" she returned without pausing to see if Grunthall approved.

Jefferson looked to Will and then back to her. "Is it true that you are in love?"

Cora smiled then, and Will thought she looked angelic. "Oh yes," she said, reaching for his hand. He stepped forward and took it, standing beside her, feeling a mixture of pride and awkwardness.

"What is your relationship, exactly, with Mr. McCabe?"

"Let us keep to Miss Cora and her family," Grunthall tried.

"What if Miss Cora would like to be a part of Mr. McCabe's family?" asked Jefferson cheekily. Lexington laughed, but Mr. Grunthall did not, which made Lexington abruptly sober.

"Is it true," Jefferson said, "that you turned away from Pierre de Richelieu in favor of a romance with Mr. McCabe? How'd a fellow like that swipe you from a powerful man like Richelieu?"

"Perhaps we can address Miss Diehl Kensington's romances at a later date," Mr. Grunthall said firmly.

"C'mon, Simon," Lexington complained. "You know that that's what most of our readers want to know about."

"Move along to another line of questions," Grunthall said.

"No," Cora interrupted, squeezing Will's hand. "I want people to know that I chose Will just as much as he chose me," she said, looking up at him. "And I'm blessed to be in love with him. I chose him because he's kind and loyal and strong and passionate."

"I'd love a photograph of the two of you right now," Lexington said. "Would you mind holding that pose?" He reached for his Kodak, but Grunthall waved him down.

"Photographs later. Of Miss Cora, alone."

"You're killing me, Simon," Lexington grunted, reluctantly ceasing his search in the leather bag he'd brought.

"What does it feel like to be the richest woman in America?" Jefferson asked.

Her blue eyes shifted left and right, then centered on the reporter. "It feels…new."

The men laughed and scribbled down her words on their pads. Once again, Cora was charming those around her. She had an uncanny knack for it, perhaps something she'd gained from her mother or her papa. Or perhaps even a bit from Wallace. Although she was far gentler than Wallace had been…

"How have you adjusted to the idea of having siblings?"

"I am far more grateful to my father for introducing me to them than I am for introducing me to any world of wealth." She smiled softly. "And they have been most gracious in accepting me."

"She makes it easy, as you can see," Felix said, leaning over by the door. The three other Kensingtons had come in unnoticed, and Grunthall scowled. He'd wanted to have tight control on this interview, Will knew. Additional people and answers to the reporters' questions might send them down paths he'd rather they not enter. But there was no stopping the Kensingtons from entering now, not without making a scene.

"We are as grateful for her as she is for us," Vivian added, coming near the table and pouring herself a cup of tea. "Not that it was easy at first," she admitted. "But in time, it was impossible to ignore."

Will studied Vivian, amazed by her candor. She truly seemed to love Cora now, and her love had made her somehow softer, approachable. Cora had been good for her. Lillian just beamed at them all, wringing her hands.

"You paint quite the cozy picture," said Jefferson, looking about. "But you've all been through a great deal."

"Sometimes," Cora said, without waiting on Grunthall's permission, "strife brings people together."

"But isn't a great deal of that strife due to your presence within their group?" pressed the man. "Perhaps Miss Vivian or Miss Lillian would care to answer that."

Grunthall hesitated. "I'll answer," Vivian said. "We have all made choices along our journey that have impinged upon our collective peace. Some we regret, and some we do not."

"Beggin' your pardon, Miss," said Lexington, "but we're looking for a story, not a Sunday school lesson."

"Perhaps there isn't as much of a story here as you all assume," Vivian said.

The reporters looked at each other and then raced to get in some more questions. "What about your choice to befriend a journalist who set you all up for the story of the decade?"

"Or Miss Cora's choice to fall for your guide?"

"Was it a conscious choice to send McCabe packing back in Vienna?"

"Enough!" Grunthall shouted, slamming his hand on the table. "Enough!" The room quieted. "You shall conduct yourselves in a civil manner," he said with a glare, "or you shall be ushered out of this house. You are guests, gentlemen, and I urge you not to abuse that privilege."

Lexington rose slowly. "We are reporters, Simon. Not a part of your press team. If you do not intend to allow the family to give frank and honest interviews, then we shall have no recourse but to seek our information in another fashion." He put on his hat and reached for his satchel. "Good day."

"But I am being frank and honest," Cora said, her delicate brows knitting together.

The man turned to her and took off his hat again. He gestured to her with it. "Miss Cora, perhaps you don't understand." He put a hand to his chest. "You are not only the richest woman in America, you are the most sought-after *story* in America, and," he said, gesturing to the windows, "beyond. If we don't get a story worth telling, then we shall lose our jobs. And the reporters that come after us…" He cocked his head. "You won't care for them much. They won't be the types that sit politely in a room, waiting to write down anything you care to toss their way."

Jefferson rose too. "Stanley is right. You can try to control the press, Grunthall. But this story is already far beyond any of us. There isn't a person able to read in America, or Paris—or Venice, for that matter—who doesn't know the name of Cora Kensington. *Life* was just the beginning. It's ten times as big now."

"Cora *Diehl* Kensington," she said, so softly that Will almost missed it. She looked stunned. Shocked. Like a china doll with her perfect makeup and pale complexion and stiff stance in her chair. And more than a little faint again.

"And they all want to know more," Jefferson said. "So it's us or them. Are you ready to give us a real exclusive? The exclusive we agreed to wait for?"

"No able-minded soul tells the press everything," Grunthall said. "Get out. This interview is over."

"No," Cora said, rising. She wavered, and Will reached out to steady her. "Mr. Grunthall, you are fired. Gentlemen, return tomorrow, and we shall discuss your exclusives." She lifted a finger. "But you only obtain your exclusive access to us if you persuade your compatriots that it's no use badgering us, we're only speaking to you two."

"Done," Jefferson said, eyes wide.

"Tomorrow at three?" Lexington asked, obviously eager to depart before Grunthall pressed for control. The man was red-faced and sputtering, looking as though he thought Cora had lost her mind.

"Three o'clock," Will put in. They all rose to say farewell, but a glance at Cora told him she truly was feeling terrible. Was that why she'd made such an abrupt decision on Grunthall? He moved closer to her.

The reporters nodded, and a maid showed them to the front door. As soon as they were out of sight, Cora fainted. Will narrowly caught her. Lillian gasped, and Vivian put a finger to her lips, gesturing to the empty doorway. Cora may have promised an exclusive, but they didn't need to make the story any more dramatic than it already was. This was the reason she'd taken charge—fired Simon in front of the others, agreed to more interviews. She'd known she was about to faint, and that would've just added more speculation to the stories reporters were printing daily.

Will set Cora on the settee and lifted her legs up, then stroked her face. "Cora," he whispered. "Cora."

His eyes shifted to meet Viv's. "Call Eleonora. We need the name of a good doctor here in Rome."

CHAPTER 21

~William~

"She didn't mean it," Grunthall said, as Will carried her past him. "She was clearly not herself. She didn't mean to fire me."

"Oh, I'm certain she did," he said over his shoulder. "Pack your bags. We'll handle our own press from now on."

Vivian and Lil rushed ahead of him and opened the door to her room. Will set her on the bed, and the others assembled. Felix and then Andrew, Hugh, and Nell.

"What was she *thinking*, Will?" Vivian asked, pacing. "Wasn't it the *exclusive* content from Arthur Stapleton that got us in this mess in the first place? And what on earth is the matter with her?" She gripped her belly as if the whole business had upset her stomach. "Is she ill?"

"She's not ill! She's only reached the limits of her feminine capabilities," Andrew said. "She's been sorely taxed. Asked to do far more than a woman should."

"I don't think that's it," Felix said, coming to the other side of the bed and sitting down on it. He reached for her hand and gently tapped her wrist. "Come on, Cora. Come back to us. Wake up."

"I don't know," Will said, stroking the hair back from her clammy, perspiring forehead. "Perhaps it all *has* been too much for her."

"That's what I'm saying," Andrew said.

"Please, Andrew, can you simply leave us?" Vivian said, turning and splaying her hands in agitation.

Andrew stiffened and straightened, his brow furrowing. "Certainly," he bit out, then turned on his heel and strode out the door just as Mr. Morgan rushed in.

"What has happened?" the old man asked. Nell went to him and told him. "Oh, for heaven's sake," he said, looking up at all of them again. "What other trial can befall our families?"

Vivian bolted from the room, clutching her stomach. Will and Hugh shared a look. "Maybe the girls caught a virus," Will said.

"If only there was a ship now, bound for home," Lillian said, wringing her hands, crying again. "How I wish we were home!"

"Oh, my dear," Mr. Morgan said, putting an arm around her shoulder. "Trouble is trouble, wherever you are."

Cora roused then and moaned, opening her eyes.

"Cora," Will said, turning toward her again.

"Wh-what? What's happened?"

"You fainted," Will said, holding her hand between his. "How are you feeling now?"

"Oh, I'm sorry," she said, lifting the back of her hand to her forehead and gazing around at all of them. "I've given you another fright. Forgive me."

"Never mind us," Hugh said. "How do you feel?"

"All right," she said, swallowing hard, as if she were lying. "It's my stomach again. I fear I am ill."

"We've sent for a doctor," Will said.

"That will give those reporters something new to wonder about," Hugh said, "if they see a doctor coming in. They'll be off and running with a story about Cora being pregnant." The girls shushed him.

"Really, I don't need a doctor," Cora said, struggling to sit up.

"Yes, you do," said Mr. Morgan. "Even if it's a touch of illness, we can't be too careful."

~Cora~

The doctor could find little wrong with me. While I felt feverish, my temperature was normal, and after a glance down my throat, he pronounced me free of any odd infection. But after listening to my belly, and then Viv's, with his stethoscope, he decided that it must be some sort of stomach bug. "Stay down," he said, in broken English. "Rest. Broth," he said, making the motion of a person eating soup, "through tomorrow. Should be better soon."

"*Grazie*," I said, smiling at him.

He gave me a shy bow and exited the room.

"How is Vivian?" I asked Lil.

"Much better. It seems to have passed."

"Power of suggestion?" Will asked, from a corner chair.

"Perhaps," I mused.

"Well, it's been a full day," Will said, rising and straightening his vest. "I'll let you sleep. I pray you'll feel much better come morning."

"Thank you," I said, accepting his kiss on my forehead.

Lillian smiled indulgently, watching the two of us, and her eyes followed him as he left the room. "He really is quite wonderful, isn't he?" she asked in a whisper, straightening my covers.

"He is," I said with a smile.

"Much better than Andrew," she said, mouthing the name.

"Agreed."

"So, how does one get two wonderful men to fall in love with her?" she asked, flopping down on her back beside me.

"I really cannot say. I'm as bewildered by it as you."

She turned to her side and perched her head on her hand. "I found something as I was unpacking your luggage today. I was helping Anna, trying to find your dressing robe."

"Oh?"

She gave me a devilish smile and leaped up and moved to the desk. With a look over her shoulder to the empty doorway, she slid open the top drawer and took hold of a sheet of drawing paper, then returned. Shyly, she turned it around.

It was the picture that Pierre had drawn of me in the garden. The one in which he had inserted himself, making us look like young lovers.

"Where did you get that?" I whispered. Now I, too, glanced to the door. If Will saw it…

"It was in with all your books. When I set the stack aside, they tumbled over, and there it was. So," she said, giving me a wicked little grin, "did he draw it for you?"

"Yes," I said, pulling it from her fingers and staring at the image. Pierre was truly a fine artist. The romance of it made me a little wistful, and that, somewhat guilty.

"You're not having second thoughts about Will, are you?" she whispered.

"Not at all," I said with frustration. "Now please, put this back in the drawer."

She stood up and took the drawing from my hands, and in that moment, I felt a twinge of the sorrow I'd felt at saying good-bye to Pierre in Venice. "Don't worry," she said, "he's coming back, right? Here, to Rome?"

"Please, stop," I moaned, putting a hand to my forehead. I truly needed to send him a telegram and ask him not to come. There was no need. It'd be a useless gesture. Just one more thing I needed to do among a hundred others. And undoubtedly, the paperwork was stacking up, what with our grief-distracted days and moving to Rome and now facing illness...

"I'll leave you now," Lil said. "I've worn you out."

"Good night, Lil."

"Sweet dreams." She left me then, closing the door quietly behind her, and I thought about her going home to Butte without her father, without her mother. Would I be welcome there? Would I live there with them? Or would I find my own home?

I fell asleep and was soon dreaming of being a rabbit, with a wolf fast approaching, but I was unable to find my rabbit hole...

CHAPTER 22

~Cora~

"Ah, there she is," Hugh said, as I entered the breakfast room the next morning. "Feeling worlds better, I take it?"

He was sitting with Andrew and Felix. I saw Andrew glance over the top of the paper, and then he snapped it taut, disappearing behind it again. Felix rose, came over, and kissed me on the cheek. "Well *done*, sister. No languishing in a sick bed for a Kensington!"

"A *Diehl* Kensington." Andrew sniffed, turning the page in his paper. "Vivian is still in bed."

"Probably avoiding you," Hugh jibed.

I turned away, uncomfortable with the likely truth in his comment. With no servant in sight, I took a croissant and poured myself some tea from the sideboard before sitting down with the men. The younger girls were apparently taking their leisurely time rising as well.

"Felix and I were just coming up with a plan to manage the press, now that you've chased off our Mr. Grunthall," Hugh said. "We believe we can so fill their column inches of paper with tales of our upcoming Roman escapades, that they'll leave the rest of you in peace."

"I see," I said, sipping my tea. My stomach was definitely stronger this morning. "So you seek to aid us," I said sardonically, "by sacrificing yourselves to the press."

Hugh winked at me. "We are ready and willing, my lady, to serve the families in whatever capacity we can."

"And get our pictures before all the socialites in Rome sooner than later," Felix added.

"We'll be invited to any party of importance," Hugh added.

"Aren't we weary of parties?" I said with a sigh. "And after what we've been through with Father—"

"Exactly the reason to indulge," Felix said. "It's time to shed our mourning cloaks and embrace the city before it's time to go. He'd want us to do so."

I shook my head. The idea of resuming the tour in a carefree manner felt…wrong. "What if we simply sightsee and spend these last days together before we embark on the *Olympic*? Surely, Will and Antonio could fill our days."

"I agree," Andrew said, still behind his paper.

Felix shot me a wry grin at the improbability of Andrew agreeing with anything I would say. I bit into my croissant.

"I'm not saying we stop our touring," Felix said. "During the day. But at night… At night, there is yet another side of Roma for us to get to know."

I shifted through the envelopes a footman handed to me and spotted a rich cream-colored envelope. "It appears we've received an invitation," I said, handing it to Felix.

"Excellent," he said, using his table knife to slice it open.

"And?" Hugh said, waiting for Felix to read it to him.

"Are you two men," Andrew said in disgust, folding his paper and rising, "or silly girls, waiting for the next invitation to the dance?"

Felix and Hugh shared a look.

"Um…yes," Felix said, with a straight face.

Andrew rolled his eyes and exited the room without a further word.

Felix tossed the card to Hugh. "Francesco Botticelli," he said, "the owner of *La Repubblica.*"

"Oh, yes," Hugh said in satisfaction. "It will be a most excellent party. Just the thing to shake us out of our grim doldrums."

"Don't you think it's too soon?" I asked. "After Father's death? Is it even appropriate?"

"No one follows the old rules," Felix said. "And it's time this family had a little fun."

I lifted the newspaper that Andrew had left behind. It was a French paper, dated three days prior, one of ten different papers on the table. I hadn't realized that Andrew spoke French, and then I wondered if he'd simply been paging through, trying to avoid us. I found myself doing the same, after so long on our journey— scanning the foreign press in an effort to gather some word of home or the world that I'd understand. I paged through the section and was folding it to set aside, when I paused and backed up a page.

There was a picture of Pierre de Richelieu in front of the Coliseum.

He was already here. But why had he not made contact? Was he waiting for me to reach out to him? Or just for the right moment to appear?

"Cora?" Will asked. "What is it?"

"Nothing," I said, trying to casually fold the paper and set it aside.

But he was watching me so carefully that he guessed I was trying to hide something. Slowly, he reached for the paper and quickly found what I had.

"So," Will said, setting down the paper, "he's here."

Felix and Hugh exchanged a look, rose, and excused themselves, clearly sensing the tension between us. We were alone in the breakfast room at last.

"It doesn't matter," I said. "Nothing's changed."

"Hasn't it?" he asked, squinting at me. "Then why hide the picture?"

"I…Will, I knew this would be awkward. I was simply surprised."

He shoved back from the table, rose, and walked to the window, hands on hips. After a long moment, he looked at me over his shoulder. "Have you seen him?"

I blinked. "Seen…*Pierre?*"

"Yes," he said, turning to face me. "Have you seen him?"

"No." I shook my head. "*You've* been with me every day since we arrived. Our days have been full. And why would I want to see him? In secret?"

"I don't know, Cora. Would there be a reason? Is there a reason he's here, other than that he doubts our love?"

I felt the heated flush of anger. "If he doubts it, then he must be sensing *your* doubt," I said, rising. "Not mine."

"So I won't find a paper with your picture in it, an article by Jefferson or Lexington detailing your covert romance in Rome."

I stared at him in mute fury. Then I turned to leave. I was too angry. I'd say something I regretted just as certainly as he'd just said something he'd regret. Or, at least, he should regret.

"Wait, Cora," he called, sounding sick and frustrated.

But I ignored him. Because for the first time in a long time, I wanted a good distance between us.

~Cora~

After an afternoon touring the behemoth St. Peter's basilica and an hour standing beneath the glorious Sistine Chapel dome, I was glad to return to our quarters. I had hoped that some makeup might disguise how exhausted I felt, but my black evening dress made me look all the more drawn. My stomach and nagging sense of weakness was better, but not entirely gone. And every time I thought of Will and our argument, I felt worse.

"As fun as this is," I said to Vivian, who was sitting across from me, next to Andrew, as we traveled to the party, "I confess I'm beginning to dream of our staterooms aboard the *Olympic* and a long, quiet voyage home."

"I can't stop thinking about home," Lillian said. She swallowed hard. "I really don't think I can stop thinking about Father until we get him buried, settled."

I nodded and looked outside the motorcar. Gas lamps cast a warm golden glow on ancient buildings deep in shadow. Rome felt more like a stage to me, I decided, than a city. And I the actress with all sorts of ill-fitting roles. The newest socialite. The grief-stricken daughter. The suffragette. The woman in love with the wrong man.

The gowns, the parties all were becoming more familiar to me, not nearly as frightening as when I began the tour, but they still didn't feel like the right place for me. Who I really was. These parties were all so much about being seen, about making a statement, desperate stabs at creating some idle identity. To me, it all felt hollow. What was the point? Did we all not have so much more to occupy our minds and hearts?

Lillian was crying again, quietly sniffling, and digging for her handbag to powder her face repeatedly. All of it combined made me want to call for the driver to pull over so I could run. But my days of running were over. Like it or not, I was tied to this family. And I would not put them through any further grief.

CHAPTER 23

~William~

The party was extraordinarily lovely, under wide Roman pines spreading their umbrellas of branches above the party attendees and littering the grass beneath their feet with needles and cones. The night was sultry, warm, and thick with the scent of pines and sage, and the wine and champagne were plentiful.

But it all felt so wrong. Not simply because he and Cora had quarreled. Because it was all too soon after Wallace's death. How had he allowed Hugh and Felix to convince them to come? Even those two seemed false in their frivolity, forced, as if determined to make it work.

Will leaned against a marble balustrade, drinking, alternately agitated and feeling the dark surrounding him, blanketing him, surrounding him, entering him. Cora had immediately been pulled into one circle and then another, everyone eager to meet the new American heiress who had captured so many headlines. He'd seen her look for him once or twice, but each time, someone new engaged her in conversation and he was apparently forgotten.

Terrible thoughts entered his mind.

She was slipping away… Her involvement with her family and their enterprise would not leave him any room… She thought them more important than she thought of him—she always had… She never was committed to him—a part of her still fancied Pierre de Richelieu.

"I never thought of you as a tortured soul before tonight," Eleonora said, suddenly beside him. Her scent wafted past him, over him, like a delicate net.

"Why, Eleonora!" he said with surprise, turning toward her and giving her a kiss on each cheek. "I'm so glad to see a friend. What brought you to Roma?"

"Francesco's party," she said, lifting a goblet. "Since I supplied the wine, he felt obligated to invite me."

"Nonsense," Will said, smiling down at her. "You clearly belong here. And now I know why the wine is so good." He lifted his goblet and gave her a quick glance as she turned away to survey the party. She wore a gown of cream, which made her skin seem exotic, olive-hued and lustrous. Her hair was pinned up in a sophisticated knot that allowed some tendrils to dance against her neck.

She smiled back at him, the dimple in her cheek deepening. She looped her arm through his, turning him to look upon the city instead of at her, as a true friend would. "Francesco has one of the finest views of the city. If you had to leave Villa Masoni, at least you're seeing vistas such as this."

They stood side by side, staring outward. "I guess there are perks to being a newspaper magnate," Will said.

"I suppose you are right. Perhaps I ought to forego my vast investments in the vineyard and try my hand at newspapering," she said.

"I think you could do anything," he said, looking down at her. He meant it. He'd watched her with her workers. Her neighbors. Her friends. And in every interaction, he so admired what he saw. "How is it, Eleonora," he said gently, feeling the heady buzz of the wine on an empty stomach, "that no man has yet claimed your heart?"

She gave him another shy smile and sighed. "There are not many in Italy who care to be with a widow who keeps her own counsel. Her own business, enterprise."

"Then they have missed a treasure." Will swallowed hard, knowing he'd said too much. What was he doing, speaking in such a way to anyone but Cora? And yet, how could he stay silent? Eleonora was beautiful. Passionate. Compassionate. Why were the fools not leaping at the chance to be with her?

He glanced behind them, over at the dance floor. "Have you danced tonight, Eleonora?"

"No, no," she said lightly, as if it didn't matter.

He frowned. "Would you care to dance with me?"

She laughed under her breath, and her white teeth flashed. "If you insist, Mr. McCabe."

He smiled and pulled her toward the dance floor—a wide stone patio surrounded by the soft brush of lavender and crisscrossed above with strings of lightbulbs. It reminded him of something else... It came to him, then. The dance floor in England, the first time he'd danced with Cora. His eyes searched for her and found her on a patio slightly elevated above the one where people were dancing. She hadn't spotted him yet with Eleonora. She was engrossed in conversation with...

Pierre de Richelieu.

Will's fists clenched, and he took a step forward, unable to believe his eyes. Cora was smiling, listening as Pierre said something to her and then to the reporter beside her. Lexington. The man had a notebook out and was furiously scribbling down notes as Pierre gestured in the air and then casually let his hand rest between Cora's shoulder blades.

Woodenly, Will turned from them and back to Eleonora, forcing a smile to his face. There wasn't any reason why he shouldn't dance with her, he reasoned. He needed to dance with her, to get his mind off his blind jealousy. But as the orchestra finished a fox trot and turned to a slow, elegant waltz, he paused and frowned, feeling a jolt of warning.

He ignored it. He couldn't leave Eleonora stranded now. It would be rude. Besides, a part of him hoped Cora would see them together. Feel the pain he'd just experienced himself.

He bowed to Eleonora and lifted his hand, casting aside his doubt.

She smiled and gave him a small curtsy, and then she was in his arms. She felt different from Cora, more stout across the shoulders, the hint of a greater curve at the hip beneath his hand, but about the same height. It pained him, feeling the longing within Eleonora, her need for love, companionship. Surely there was some good fellow here in Rome, even at this very party, who would make a great husband for her…

~Cora~

I managed to excuse myself from Pierre and our host, madly seeking Will out, knowing he'd misconstrue things if he saw us together. I looked up and saw the outline of the Roman pines against a starry sky and, down below, dancers flowing across the floor. In the distance, the lights of Rome cast a warm glow across the city, illuminating points like Saint Peter's and the Coliseum.

"Heavens, it's beautiful," I said to Hugh as I joined him on the stairs.

"Indeed. But no one will have eyes for the city with you in view."

I smiled at his idle flirtation. There was none of the predatory tone to his voice that had once made me leery of him. Only genuine admiration. "Thank you, Hugh."

He gave me a wry smile. "I do not lie. You are the prettiest woman here." He paused, waiting for me to turn to him. "Let me be the first to escort you to the dance floor?" He pushed his hair away from his eyes and over to one side. "Please, Copper Cora. Make me a star this night," he said. "Your reporters are about. Share some press with a young lad only seeking to meet some eligible heiresses."

I matched his teasing grin. "I'll do what I can," I said, well aware by now that other reporters moved through the crowds, following us. The relative darkness and constant movement on the dance floor would allow me a measure of rest, even under their watch. I knew that in such conditions, taking a photograph was nearly impossible.

Hugh lifted my hand as if I were some grand lady, and I swept down the wide marble stairs that sprawled wider with each step. I knew my new black gown fit perfectly, even if it made me look even paler than I had of late, and a part of me welcomed the admiring glances all about. How different this was from that terrible night at Syon House in England. When all had found out I was the illegitimate daughter of Wallace Kensington and cast me out. And only Will would dance with me.

Here, now, everyone knew exactly who I was and how I'd gotten there, and yet I felt accepted. Welcomed. Adored, even. It was much to take in. I nodded as others acknowledged my presence as though I were some sort of nobility. And oddly, I felt as such, as if I deserved it, as if I'd *worked* for it. There was something wrong in the thought even as I accepted it as truth. It was all so empty. So false.

Hugh and I reached the dance floor and waited as the last notes of the waltz faded.

And that was when I saw them.

Will and Eleonora, smiling at each other.

They looked beautiful, perfect. He in his black and white, somehow far more elegant than I'd seen him earlier, enhanced by Eleonora in his arms. And she in her ivory dress—like some fantastic bridal gown—looking up at him in shy admiration.

~William~

He caught sight of Cora as he lifted Eleonora's arm and twirled her one last time in their waltz.

He stopped moving entirely. Allowed Eleonora to flounder awkwardly as she turned from her spin. He could feel Eleonora stare at him, suddenly growing still beside him and then turning to follow his glance to Cora. Others stared too, at him, at Cora, and dimly, he was aware of a crowd gathering around her.

But his eyes were on Cora alone, three feet away.

She was impossibly elegant in that new black gown. But it was her lips, her lush lips, that captured his attention most. They were parted, as if she was stunned. As if he had hit her, hurt her. *Grief*, his mind belatedly registered.

"Here I was, looking about for you," she said lowly. "Thinking of Syon House and how we danced…"

Eleonora stepped away from him, as if guilty, and that made him angry. She had nothing to apologize for. It had only been a dance! Where was Pierre? He looked over Hugh's shoulder to the steps and spied Pierre watching them, casually bending his head to light a cigar. Looking…smug.

Cora was turning, fleeing, and he rushed after her. "Cora!"

Hugh put a hand to his chest, trying to stop him. "Don't, Will. The reporters—"

Will didn't care. He rushed after her, through the crowd, followed by men on either side, all with pads of paper and pencils out. "Mr. McCabe? Are you William McCabe?" they asked.

He glimpsed the top of Cora's head and redoubled his efforts as she neared the mansion. He had to see her, speak with her. It had only been a dance! Just a dance!

Or had it? Will swallowed hard at that thought humming within him like a giant bell resonating for a time even after being rung. "Cora! Cor—"

Two men grabbed hold of his arms and rammed him against a wall beside the door. "No, no," said one. "*La signorina gradirebbe stare da sola.*" The lady would like to be alone.

He tried to shake them off, infuriated, but they were strong. Guards, he figured after a second—the newspaperman's guards. "You don't understand," he said in Italian, trying to wrench even one arm loose. "I'm William McCabe. I'm Cora's..." What, exactly? Her beau? Her almost-fiancé? Her guide?

The reporters, six of them, all had pens out, hovering over their pads, waiting for him to finish his sentence. Will looked around in confusion. "Fine, fine!" Will said, pretending to give up and walk away. He had to catch up to her, speak to her, explain about Eleonora. But if he didn't get free, there was no chance.

"What did you want to say to Miss Kensington?" asked Jefferson, edging near.

"What would you say if you had the opportunity?" asked another.

"Have you two parted company?" asked Lexington, his keen eyes sidling over to Eleonora, who was watching from the edge of the patio. He fished a picture out from his jacket pocket and handed it to Will. "Do you have a comment on this?"

Will looked madly about and then finally to the picture in his hands.

It was a drawing of Pierre and Cora. In a garden. Looking like lovers.

"Where did you get this?" he sputtered, rage surging through him.

Lexington shrugged. "I have my sources."

"When was this made? Who drew it?"

"I was wondering if you would tell me," he said, grabbing it back before Will could crush it in his hand.

Will reached for the man's jacket lapels, but Antonio was there, grabbing his arms, pulling him back. "Mr. McCabe has no comment. Go, go," he said, turning to stand between them, making a shooing gesture. "Leave him be. This is a private party, not a press conference."

Guests in fine dress stared at him as they passed by, whispering to their friends.

Will considered an attempt at running around the mansion, intercepting Cora before she got to the motorcar. But the guards would likely tackle him to the ground, and that would only provide more humiliating fodder for the journalists.

Will let out a sigh of frustration and shook his head. The orchestra had resumed their playing, and Eleonora was soon asked to dance by a tall, thin fellow about their age. Will and Antonio walked back to the wall and stone balustrade, looking out over the city, which was growing darker by the moment. "What am I doing, Antonio?" Will asked. "What have I done?"

"I'm not certain, my friend."

"It was only a dance!"

"Was it?" Antonio asked, doubt lacing his tone.

Will winced and shook his head. "Did you see Cora's face?" he asked, so filled with pain by the memory that it made him want to cry like a boy.

Antonio leaned his hip against the balustrade and crossed his arms. "You must be careful with Eleonora. Her heart is…tender. And I fear she has feelings for you."

"I know." He slammed his fist in his other palm. "I didn't…until tonight. And then…when I saw Cora with Pierre." He looked up to the staircase again, then scanned the party guests, seeing Pierre nowhere. Will had the distinct feeling that things were playing out exactly as Pierre wanted. He put his hands on his head. "I'm such a fool."

"You're a man," Antonio said, putting a hand on his shoulder. "When it comes to women, we're all fools."

CHAPTER 24

~Cora~

"I simply do not see why we all must go, because Cora glimpsed her beau flirting with another woman!" Andrew said, pacing beside the motorcar. He wanted to stay at the party, but Vivian was insisting they return with me. Andrew looked at me as I got in the motorcar, but I ignored him. There was nothing I wanted more than to be away from them and their bickering. Felix got in after me.

"Flee if you must, Cora," Andrew said. "But do you honestly need us as your nursemaids?"

"Andrew, stop it! This instant!" Viv said.

I slid into the far corner of the backseat, knowing I had to leave. Immediately. I could barely concentrate on Andrew's nastiness, because over and over, all I could think about was how Will had stared down at Eleonora, in such wonder…such admiration.

The way he had looked at me.

And then there was Pierre. Smooth. Graceful. Wooing me in every way he could without overtly wooing me.

I swallowed against the lump in my throat when Felix patted my hand. "You don't know the full story, Cora," he said. "Men are men. A beautiful woman catches a man's eye. But that Will only has one woman in his heart. You."

I nodded quickly, wanting him to be quiet—to cease talking about it.

"This is asinine. We're staying," Andrew said, outside the car. "I'm done letting Cora dictate our schedule from morning until night." He leaned down and looked through the doorway at Felix. "You take her home if you must. Then send the car back for us in a couple hours, will you?"

"Sure," Felix said.

"You may stay, but I'm going," Vivian said, bending to enter the car.

"No, you're not," Andrew said, grabbing hold of her arm and forcing her to stand straight again. Felix and I shared a worried glance.

"Let go of me, Andrew."

"It is unseemly," he hissed. "Don't you know that all those reporters will turn their attention to us? And why *we're* suddenly apart?"

"Then come back to the apartment with me," she tried. "It's been a long day."

"Stop it! Stop arguing, and just do as I say." He shook her, and Vivian let out a little yelp.

"Stop!" I cried even as Felix moved toward the car door. I glanced through the small window behind us and saw Jefferson and Lexington acting as if they were casually smoking cigarettes, when I knew they were cataloguing every moment of this exchange. A part of me ached that Will wasn't running after me, but a part of me was relieved that the reporters wouldn't witness that private moment too. "Andrew, even now we are not alone," I said, peering up and out the open doorway of the motorcar. Felix was now standing beside the two of them.

We could all see Andrew shaking with anger. The veins in his neck pulsed. "Fine," he said, taking Vivian's arm and practically shoving her into the car seat across from me.

"Morgan!" Felix growled, grabbing hold of the man's arm. But Andrew was much bigger than Felix and easily threw him off. "There is no call for such treatment of my sister!" Felix insisted, doggedly stepping forward again.

"Your sisters—*all* of them, apparently—need to understand what it means to respect a man."

"And you need to understand what it means to respect my sisters," Felix said, pressing his chest against Andrew's. He was a foot shorter than Andrew, but he was scrappy. "Until you do, you can find another place to stay."

Andrew scoffed. "You're throwing me out? I would imagine my father would take issue with that."

"Then you don't realize what a dolt you're being," Felix said. "Find another place to stay tonight," he repeated, sliding into the car. The driver, obviously frightened beyond measure, tried to shut it after him, but Andrew caught it. Slowly, he leaned down, and I half expected him to yank Felix back out. "We shall resolve this tomorrow, after I spend the night elsewhere. If that is what Vivian wants."

"It's what I prefer," Vivian spit out. "Now let us go!"

Andrew straightened and slammed the door, making us all jump. The driver scurried around the car and entered the front; then, as the engine roared, we set off.

Viv looked as pale and as apt to cry as I did, but she rubbed her arm as if it pained her. We drove down the winding road, through several neighborhoods, before hitting a thoroughfare that would take us back to the heart of the city. I couldn't wait to get back. To put distance between us and all the confusion we'd left behind.

"Viv, he's manhandled you for the last time," Felix said, leaning forward, elbows on knees.

She looked to the side, out the window, one hand covering her mouth, her eyes wide and glassy. "He simply gets so overwrought…" she muttered.

"No, it isn't right," Felix said, flinging himself back against the seat. "No more excuses for him."

"He has no right," I said. "If he treats you like this now—"

"Please," she said, lifting a hand up and turning sad eyes on me. "Please. Haven't you…we…all had enough heartache for one night?"

I swallowed hard and leaned back, biting my tongue.

We drove the rest of the way in silence, our combined weariness and sorrow almost too much to bear. I thought about our neighbors the Stuggarts, back in Dunnigan. Mr. Stuggart had been given to too much drink, and on more than one Sunday, Mrs. Stuggart had arrived at church with bruises on her face that she explained away as falls or other mishaps but that my parents clearly took as abuse.

"Not a man on the face of the earth should treat a woman in such a way," Papa had said. Remembering his face, filled with sorrow and anger at once, made me long for him. I wanted him to wrap his arms around me and hold me, counsel me, comfort me. But he was so far away, and my father, here in Rome, was now in a casket.

I thought about the church in Siena, drawing comfort, warmth from the memory. About resting in my identity as God's own child, regardless of who claimed me here on earth. My folks. My father. Will. Pierre. I wrapped my arms around myself, suddenly chilled, and wondered what it would be like to climb up into God's lap, feel Him wrap His arms around me. The thought gave me a sweet bit of comfort, and I smiled as we pulled up in front of our building and the driver exited to come around and open our door.

Felix offered one arm to Vivian and the other to me. We entered the building and climbed the stairs, each separating to our own rooms. I said my good nights and slipped into my room, ringing immediately for Anna, so thankful to be with her again. She took one look at my face and said, "A hot bath would do you wonders," and set one to running without even waiting for my assent. I sank down on the dressing table bench and pulled off my dangling jet earrings—borrowed from Viv—then the black feathers and pins from my hair.

Anna returned and brushed out my hair. "Was it as bad as all that?"

"William and I...had another falling out."

"Oh," she said, waiting for me to go on. She unbuttoned the back of my gown and then rested her small hands on my shoulders, meeting my sad gaze in the reflection of the mirror.

"I saw Will dancing with Eleonora Masoni."

She frowned a little. "Are you not friends with the woman? Is it as odd as all that?"

"Their friendship is not odd," I said, my voice flat. "But they weren't dancing as friends."

"Oh," she said again. She bit her lip and looked to the window, then back to me.

A mostly full moon had risen, casting quite a bit of light into the room, so I turned off the electric lamp, which felt glaringly bright, and then felt my way to the tub and slipped into the water. When my skin was used to the heat, I slipped all the way under, allowing the water to cover my face and do its healing work against the tension that seemed to cramp every bit of my body.

Needing air, I rose and took a breath, then sank beneath again, liking how the sounds of my fingernails against the porcelain sounded bright and yet distant. I thought about all the places I'd been with Will over the summer that included water. Canoeing on the Montana lake. Wading in the Mediterranean. Walking beside the canals in Venice. Swimming beside the Cinque Terre. Sheltering behind the hot springs waterfall…

I rose, gasping for air.

How could he? How could he look at another after we had shared those moments?

I rubbed my face and took a cloth from one edge and a bar of soap from the other, knowing I had probably wiped my makeup into a broad smear. I set to sudsing my cloth, then rubbing clean every inch of my face, considering my disappointment, my fear, my fury.

How would *he* have reacted if he'd entered the party and seen me dancing with another? Looking at him like…like…

Like I had looked at Pierre countless times.

The thought brought me up short. Hadn't Will suffered moment after moment of strife, watching me with Pierre? When he longed to be with me himself? And then tonight...had he seen me talking with Pierre? Before he asked Eleonora to dance?

But all those shared moments with Pierre had been *before*. That was different. We hadn't made any promises to each other. Now... I thought of turning down Will's marriage proposal. I hadn't turned him down...exactly. That was different.

Wasn't it?

CHAPTER 25

~Cora~

I awakened before the sun the next morning, my first thought being Will. I wondered if he was still sleeping. If his waking thoughts would be of me—or of her. I groaned and tried to turn over and go back to sleep, but to no avail. Minutes later, as the sun rose, adding a delicate pink to the purple morning sky, I sat up, slid off the tall bed to the cold tile floor, and padded over to my dressing table.

I picked up my black crepe and then decided I couldn't take another day in it. Instead, I pulled on a rose-colored skirt and jacket with a lace dickey beneath, then wound my hair into a quick bun. If I hurried, perhaps I'd be able to eat alone in the breakfast room before the others arrived. My room, while lovely, felt stifling this morning. Perhaps, after a quick bite and a cup of coffee, I'd be able to awaken Viv or Lil and convince them to walk with me. Antonio was often up at this hour, so he wouldn't mind keeping watch over us. It sounded appealing to me, walking the streets as Rome stirred, seeing her people begin their daytime routine. A chance at a completely different sort of day than yesterday.

As I rounded the corner, a sleepy-eyed footman straightened with a start. He surprised me, too—there hadn't been a footman on duty yesterday. Given our late hours, our party was rarely up and dressed before nine, and my 6:00 a.m. arrival probably stunned the poor fellow. He forced a smile and pulled out a chair for me, helping me slide closer to the table before unfolding a cloth napkin and handing it to me. I spread it across my lap.

"Coffee, Miss? Tea?" he said in a thick Italian accent.

"Coffee, please," I said. He went to a side table and lifted a sterling pot, then came back and poured it for me. It was so hot, steam rose from the cup immediately. Perhaps it had just been brewed.

"Pastry?"

"Please," I said, and he immediately slipped a croissant onto my small plate, using silver tongs.

"Melon?"

"No, thank you. This will be quite enough."

"As you wish," he said, moving to the corner again and standing straight, with his hands at his side. I gave him a nervous glance. I hated that the servants were required to do such things—as if they were toy soldiers rather than living, breathing people who might be much more comfortable sitting or being in another room altogether. But I'd tried my hand at such suggestions—and usually neither my family nor the servants favored my ideas for change, looking at me as if I had every odd thought possible in my brain. It was as if they drew comfort from their routine, their understood roles and tasks and environments.

I sipped at my hot coffee, mouthing the bitter brew, willing it to fully awaken me, prepare me for the day. I split open my pastry, admiring the flaky layers, even as I slid a bite into my mouth, letting it melt. Tall French doors lined the far wall on the other side of the breakfast table, and I watched as the morning sun moved across the highest windows in a palazzo across a swath of greenery. The sky was now a rosy peach, and again I longed to go out and see it without the barrier of a window. To stretch my legs, give my mind space, my heart room.

I was eating the remainder of my croissant when Mr. Morgan arrived. I felt him pause at the doorway behind me, and instantly, without turning, I knew who had come.

"Good morning, Cora," he said, entering the room.

"Mr. Morgan," I returned.

"You've risen early."

"I couldn't sleep."

"I see." He went to the end of the table, to my direct right, and sat down. The footman immediately poured him coffee, unasked. Mr. Morgan asked for a soft-boiled egg and reached for the morning paper, which was sitting at the corner, neatly folded. *La Repubblica.* I sucked in a quick breath. While I knew Mr. Morgan spoke little Italian, I didn't doubt he'd page through the whole thing. Everywhere we'd been, he and my father had read every paper they could put their hands on, just as Andrew had with the French paper yesterday.

But not every paper had an editor who had hosted the party we'd attended last night. A party also attended by almost every reporter in Italy and beyond.

Nervously, I sipped my coffee, taking too big a gulp as he unfolded the paper and snapped it flat, reading the front page. On the back, from top to bottom, were several pictures surrounded by three columns of copy. One was of Pierre, shaking hands and posing with some Italian businessman. Another was of me and Vivian pausing before an archway in the Forum.

I struggled to swallow the hot brew as he lowered the paper and frowned at me. "Are you quite all right?"

"Fine," I choked out, nodding hurriedly.

I couldn't stand it. "Mr. Morgan," I said before I'd even thought it through. "Would you fancy a morning walk?" I nodded toward the windows, the morning sun illuminating the day with a golden glow.

"Right now?" he said, frowning.

"If you'd rather not…"

"No! No, I'd be delighted to take a morning constitutional. Perhaps a turn around the park below?"

"Yes," I said hurriedly, nodding. "I'd like that."

His eyes narrowed.

"I like to see how this city awakes," I added. "Will says that if you see how a city awakes, and how she closes down for the night, you get a good sense of her personality." *Will…* Never had he felt more distant, even while he was likely in this very building.

He stared at me a moment. "Indeed." He folded the paper again, never reaching the end, and dug into his soft-boiled egg. He cracked it open, then scooped into its soft center, rapidly reaching the bottom. The newspaper sat to one side of him, forgotten. I dared to take a breath as he swallowed his last bite. Would he pick it up again? He wiped his mouth with his cloth napkin and then finished his cup of coffee. "Well, shall we be about it then?" He didn't wait for an answer but merely shoved back his chair, rose, and came to assist me with my chair.

I hurriedly finished my coffee, wiped my mouth, and then rose, tentatively taking his arm. I'd wanted to distract him, as well as get out into the Roman morning. But now that I'd succeeded at both, I wondered what we'd talk about. In all our days together, never had we been alone for any length of time. He was my father's closest friend, but he was so terribly quiet, I doubted I'd heard him speak more than three sentences at a time.

He motioned to the footman and then waited for him to bend close to him, wishing to speak in private. After a word, he offered me his arm and led me outward. By the time we reached the front door, his directions had apparently reached a detective, because we were joined by the tall, broad-shouldered Pascal, who opened the door for us, then followed us by a few paces.

"Which way, my dear?" Mr. Morgan asked, gesturing down the thoroughfare beside the palazzo.

I nodded to the left, knowing there were several shops and coffee bars along the way. We walked half a block in silence, finding our pace together. We passed a coffee bar where several locals stood at the front, swallowing tiny cups of espresso, talking with their friends and neighbors. "Will would want us to step in there," I said. "Experience Roman dawn as the Romans do."

Mr. Morgan smiled, even as a shadow of sorrow covered his face. He nodded. "The McCabes are good guides. I rather miss old Stuart, don't you?"

"I do. But I think Will has done a fine job, assuming his responsibilities." *Will...*

"Indeed." He walked a few paces. "I thought Stuart and Wallace were both strong enough in constitution to last another good decade." He eyed me. "It must've been a terrible blow, losing Wallace when you were only beginning to know him."

"In more ways than you could know," I said tiredly. "We were at odds…constantly at odds. And I don't think either of us wanted that."

He shook his head, agreeing with me.

"And now there's no way to fix it," I said.

We passed a florist just opening her shutters and depositing her pots of fresh flowers, as if they were organically spreading out onto the street. She bent and lifted a broken bloom from the ground, offering it to me with a toothless smile, and I accepted it with a grin, twirling the white daisy in my gloved hand, admiring the flash of gold at its center as we walked on. We passed a grocer setting out a table with hard cheeses in several varieties, two of them in huge wheels, the rest in chunks as big as my head. Then we passed a produce market with baskets of zucchini, onions, and apples.

When we reached the corner, there was another coffee bar, and Mr. Morgan asked, lifting one silvering brow, "When in Rome?"

I blinked in surprise and then nodded. We entered just as a young couple left, opening a space at the small counter. "Espresso," Mr. Morgan said. "*Due*." He lifted two fingers.

"*Due espresso arrivano subito*," said the young man behind the counter, winking at me when Mr. Morgan fished in his pockets for his wallet.

I smiled and looked away.

The coffee merchant set two small cups on the counter, without even a saucer, smiling again at me.

"Watch yourself," Mr. Morgan growled in warning, setting several lire on the counter. His tone conveyed what his lack of Italian could not.

The young man, clearly stunned at the reprimand, took a step back, then turned toward others who laughed at him and called to him from deeper within, eyeing me and Mr. Morgan.

I picked up my tiny white porcelain cup, hiding a smile. The protective, fatherly stance he was taking made me feel cared for.

"I know just enough to keep the wolves at bay, my dear," he said, giving me a wise smile. "A wise business practice, if I may say so." He lifted his cup. "*Salute.*"

"*Salute,*" I said, gearing up for what was to come. I took a tentative sip and nearly gagged on the hot, intense brew. It was incredibly strong, as thick and dark as oil, and tasting the same as it slid down my throat.

Mr. Morgan's eyes grew wide, and he covered his lips with a gloved hand, staring at me in shock.

"Perhaps that's enough," I said, willing my tongue to unfold from its pucker, "of what the Romans do?"

He nodded and smiled, then took my arm and ushered me out. I was still smiling several steps later, and I thought it at once both odd and wondrous to be sharing such a moment with Mr. Morgan, in Rome of all places. There was a sense of shared adventure, camaraderie, that drew me and gave me hope that we might succeed, pursuing our shared enterprise together. And it was keeping me from having to deal with Will and the drama of last night. At least for a time…

It'd be better for him to hear it from me than to discover it on his own, I recognized. I struggled with what to say.

We turned the corner and moved down the block, back to the wide, green park that lined the back gates of the palazzos and buildings we'd passed. Once there, surrounded by green, the morning sky now bright, I took a deep breath and thought about what I wanted to say to Mr. Morgan. And what I didn't.

Grace, it came to me. *Trust. Honor.*

Those were the things that I had missed in my relationship with Wallace Kensington, things that my heavenly Father offered to me in spades. Things we had never worked out. Had I wanted him to give me more than what was humanly possible?

We strolled to the very center of the garden and then walked back toward our palazzo via the central avenue. Already the morning spoke of heat and dry. Densely planted azalea bushes flowered in a riot of purple and magenta near clumps of exotic-looking grasses taller than I could reach. Artfully placed benches were surrounded by specimens of an Italian horticulturist's dreams. Above us was Roman pine after Roman pine, each like a massive umbrella spreading its cover forty feet above us despite the lack of rain.

"So I gather you faced some difficulty last night," Mr. Morgan said at last.

I looked at him in surprise, wondering how he knew. He laughed softly under his breath, paused, and looked up at the trees, then straight to me. "After all this time, Cora, do you not know that fathers see everything?"

I stared at him. Then, "No, not really."

He gestured to the nearest bench, and I reluctantly sat down. He sat too, carefully, as if his knees or hips bothered him. "I believe that you were so intent in standing against Wallace," he said wearily, "that you might have missed that he was *for* you."

"For me?" I repeated. I shook my head. "It seemed as if he was standing against me at every turn."

"No, no," Mr. Morgan said softly, looking up again to the trees. He lifted a gloved hand. "Well, *yes*, I can see how you'd think that. But never, never had I seen him consider anyone as he did you."

"Truly?"

"Truly." He lifted a gray brow again. "I know that he stood between you and Will, favoring Pierre, but it was only because he could see what was coming. How your world would so radically change, for good, not just for a season. And he truly thought Pierre would be a better partner for you."

"I know," I said. And in that moment, I did. Father had done his best to control me, dictate my future, but at the heart of his actions, deep down, I had glimpsed a father's heart, his concern.

"And the manner in which he considered your suggestions at the mines… Well, that was unprecedented. It's one thing for a man to accept a woman's thoughts, but Wallace? Until you came along, he only listened to two others. Me. And the Lord God Almighty." He still looked surprised over this, but then he shrugged. "He could see you had a smart head on those slim shoulders. The apple didn't fall far from the tree."

I was silent a moment, absorbing this. "You said he listened to the Lord."

"Yes," he said, nodding.

"He wrote to me of his faith, but I didn't ever hear him talk about it."

"Well, like most gentlemen who don't wear a clerical collar, he didn't wish his faith to be overbearing."

Overbearing? From the outside, any faith the man had seemed a cursory thing, rather than something that was at the core of who he was. But Mr. Morgan was right. It wasn't fashionable to wear one's faith on one's sleeve. Not in their circles.

"He believed it was the godly thing to do, going to fetch you in Dunnigan. To try to make right what he had done wrong."

Done wrong. The words stung. And yet I knew what the man meant. "He gave me little choice in that fetching. Me *or* my folks."

Mr. Morgan turned partially my way. "And if he hadn't? What would have become of you and yours, Cora? Was it not the hand of Providence that he came to you after Alan suffered his first spell?"

"Are you equating Wallace with God?" I asked wryly.

Mr. Morgan huffed a quiet laugh. "The Lord knows that Wallace did try, on occasion, to give Him a run for his money."

I sighed, and we both sat in silence for a bit, lost in our own thoughts.

"Do you wish to tell me what transpired last night?" he asked. When I glanced at him in surprise, he gave me a small smile. "Young people do not rise at this hour unless they are suffering the ill effects of drink or a troubled mind."

"I *was* thinking about last night," I admitted, crossing my ankles. Speaking of Andrew and Vivian hardly seemed appropriate. But there were other things on my mind too. "Will and I had…a falling out. And Pierre de Richelieu has arrived."

His brown eyes seemed to pierce mine, and I looked away. "I see." I could sense neither victory nor empathy in his tone, just a simple acknowledgment.

"I thought such news would make you happy."

"Happy?" He shook his head a little. "I have no desire to see you hurt, Cora. Nor did your father."

His kind tone left me feeling raw, vulnerable. Why couldn't my father and I have gotten to this sort of conversation before he died? I was suddenly teary again, and I glanced warily about the park. I wasn't ready to break down here, not where some reporter might be lurking, nor with Mr. Morgan. We weren't close enough for such intimacies. "Shall we?" I asked, throat tight, my eyes blinking rapidly.

He rose and offered me his arm. We walked side by side for a time in silence. "Cora, it will ease in time, your pain."

I stiffened but kept on walking. "What do you mean?"

"With your father. I understand that things between you weren't ever quite…resolved. But then, don't you see that some things in life never are? Try as we might to place everything in its proper box, we must accept some things as they are and move on."

I nodded, not trusting myself to speak.

"I know that you were still in the midst of trying to accept Wallace as a father… But I want you to know…if you are ever in need…"

He gazed at me with such intensity, his age-rimmed eyes heavy with compassion, that I knew he was a man I could always trust, always go to.

I squeezed his arm. "Thank you," I managed, my throat thick with emotion. Because in that moment, I realized there was something more transpiring inside my heart. I didn't simply feel another earthly father's attention. In that moment, I knew the Father of fathers reached out to me, pulled me close, and whispered, *All will be well.*

CHAPTER 26

~William~

When Mr. Morgan and Pascal walked in with Cora, Will looked up at them in surprise. He'd thought they were all still asleep. He pulled out his watch from Cora and looked at the time. "You all are up early," he said.

He hated the nervous tinge in his voice and had to make his eyes settle on Cora.

She looked away.

"We went for a lovely morning walk," Mr. Morgan said. "Nothing like a stretch of the legs and a nice conversation to begin the day right," he said, smiling at Cora.

She gave him a tense smile and then nodded, as if excusing herself. "Thank you, Mr. Morgan." She turned to leave.

"We're gathering at eleven to go to the Coliseum," Will called.

"I won't be able to go with you," she said, glancing his way. "Regrettably, I have other things to attend to. It looks like a lovely day. Enjoy it."

She disappeared around the corner, and Will wiped his mouth with a napkin and hurried after her. He caught up with her just before she reached her room. The hallway was empty.

"Cora."

She paused at her door and bent her head, as if the sound of her name on his tongue hurt her.

He drew closer. "Cora," he said miserably. "We need to talk."

"Do we?" she asked, looking up at him with such pain in her eyes that it made him want to weep.

"It was only a dance," he said quietly. "One dance."

"Was it?"

They shared a long look. Defense and anger shot through him. "I would have been dancing with you," he said stiffly. "If you had not been...entertaining Pierre."

She took a deep breath, as if keeping herself from saying something she'd regret. "I was merely saying hello. Nothing more, nothing less."

"No?" he said, his anger now quickening his pulse. He put a hand on her doorjamb and leaned closer. "Lexington showed me something of interest too. A drawing. Of you and Pierre. In a garden. In a rather...intimate scene. Any idea where he got that?"

She looked up at him in surprise. "What?"

"A drawing. Of you and Pierre," he repeated, so close now that he could see the tiny beads of sweat on her forehead and upper lip, making him fear the worst. "Is it a scene of you two from somewhere here in Rome? Did you have an artist sketch it to remember some romantic moment?"

"Where...where did he get that?" Her expression turned from confusion to anger.

"So you admit it. It's yours?"

Cora shook her head. "It was mine, once. A gift from Pierre earlier in the summer. But Will, he sketched me, on a bench alone, and added himself later. It was what he wanted to be. Not what truly was."

"And yet you kept it."

She stared at him, aghast, her wide blue eyes searching his. "Will," she said, turning fully toward him. "What is happening to us?" She reached out and took his hand. "How have we become lost in…these jealousies?"

He stared back at her, his emotions warring within him. Part of him wanted to fight against his fears, his twisted visions of Cora with Pierre. Part of him wanted to press further, make her admit it. Admit that she still had feelings for Pierre. That she was going to leave him. Leave him as his parents had left him. Show him that risking his heart only would leave him vulnerable to the worst kind of hurt…

She lifted her small hand and touched his cheek. "*Will,*" she said again. "Please. Dig deep. Is this us? Is this what God wants for us? Or have we each given in to the worst possible distraction? Away from love? Away from light?"

He gazed back into her blue eyes, searching, searching, searching. And found his anchor point. She loved him. Loved him. And he was about to lose her, because he did as she feared…he gave in to distraction. Lies. "Oh, Cora," he moaned, leaning his forehead against hers. "But what about Pierre? Did you keep it because you still wondered yourself if you had made the right choice?"

"I don't know why I kept it," she said, shaking her head a little against his. She looked back into his eyes. "But Will, I haven't been with Pierre. I love you. I'm with you. Can you believe that? Or not?"

He took a breath, then took her hands in his. "I believe you," he said, throwing his trust outward as if he were tossing it over a cliff, hoping it would drift down into safety and not get crushed against the rocks below. "I believe you," he repeated more strongly. He bit his lip. Then, "And I need you to believe me. Eleonora is a friend. A friend I find comely. But nowhere near the attraction I have with you. Can you trust that?"

She stared at him for a long, silent moment. Then she nodded. "I trust you, William McCabe. Now *trust me*."

~Cora~

I closed the door, feeling bruised from my discussion with Will, but slightly relieved, too. As soon as my hand left the knob, I hurried over to my chest holding the books and rifled through them for the one that had held Pierre's drawing. The one he'd sketched for me in the garden, positioning us as if we were lovers, sharing secrets. The one that Lil had found.

It was gone.

Madly, I searched through the other books, until they lay in a pile at my feet, then through the bottoms of each trunk, thinking it might have fallen out. But it was nowhere to be found. Surely, that was the drawing Will referenced. How had Lexington gotten hold of it? Only Lil knew it was here, right?

I opened my door and looked down the hall. It was empty again, and I strode two doors down to the room Lil and Nell shared, and knocked. Lillian answered it, her head covered in rag curls. "Cora? What time is it?"

"Time to get up," I said, pushing my way in. I closed the door behind me and saw that Nell was still asleep in the big four-poster bed. "Lil, do you remember the drawing that Pierre made of us? The one you asked me about?"

She frowned and nodded, her rag-tied curls bouncing.

"Did you take it?"

Her frown deepened, and then she slowly shook her head. "No. Why would I do that?"

I bit my lip, considering her, but the girl appeared as utterly confounded as I.

But if she hadn't taken it and given it to a reporter, then who had?

"Are you going to the Coliseum with us?" Nell asked.

"Oh do, please," Lil said.

"I wasn't going to…but now I just might," I said. Someone in the house had betrayed me. Perhaps I could figure out who.

~William~

Andrew arrived as they were just assembling to depart. Will felt an urgency now. If they hurried, they might just escape the palazzo before the reporters came to lie in wait for them.

But Andrew insisted they pause for him. He brushed past, smelling of body odor and wine. "Please, Vivian," he said to her, taking hold of her hand. "Just give me today. I promise I'll make it up to you."

She sighed and looked to the rest of them. They all seemed to sigh with her and stand back, waiting for the man to go get changed and join them. If Vivian didn't break up with Andrew—once and for all—soon, Will decided he'd do it for her. He glanced at Cora.

She still refused to meet his gaze, fussing first with her gloves, then her pocketbook. Ill at ease in his presence. Making some excuse that sent her upstairs for a time.

Perhaps she was embarrassed for making such a fuss over him and Eleonora last night. Or worse, she was still angry at him. On his suggestion, the women wore colors, rather than their mourning black, to make them less conspicuous and perhaps to allow them to avoid the wandering reporters. While it was a superficial change, it made Will feel as if the group was somewhere near to what it once was, even if every relationship between them all had changed, deepened, divided.

At last, Cora and Andrew came back down the stairs, an incongruent pair, and everyone hurried into the waiting motorcars, the girls stubbornly sticking together, a bevy of massive hats that made it difficult to sit in one car.

They got out beside the Coliseum, and Will breathed a sigh of relief as the tension in the air melted into wonder. It was the same for everyone, it seemed, spying the structure, walking up to it. Pockmarks littered the stones of the front of the Coliseum, where metal pieces had been scavenged over the centuries. Roman officials had stopped masons from stealing the stones, at least, and had done a tolerable job at securing what remained so tourists could enjoy the monumental structure. If they hadn't, would there be anything left today? Uncle Stuart had often pondered that.

Will led them inside, lecturing on the various ways the ancient Romans had utilized the structure. They walked out atop a reconstructed stage on one end and peered over the edge, down to the Hypogeum. "For five centuries, no one saw that level exposed," Will said, gesturing to the complex series of tunnels and rooms. "It was there that the gladiators, as well as all the animals, waited to emerge on the Coliseum's floor, to fight for their lives."

The younger girls twittered. "Oh, Will," said Nell, "can we go down there?"

"I wouldn't be much of a guide if I didn't take you to both the greatest depths and the greatest heights of this structure, would I?" He smiled and dared to look at Cora, but she was looking away, as if he'd said nothing at all. He hesitated, again feeling the twinge of separation from her. "This way," he said, leading them to a small circular stairwell that led them downward.

In minutes, they stood below and walked along the walls as Will pointed out slices in the rock that indicated where capstans once were placed. "Four men would man each, and at the appointed time, they would turn it and raise a lion or bear to the arena floor."

"In a way, it was theater at its finest," Hugh said.

"A theater in which men were chained, awaiting their deaths?" Felix asked, running a hand down a stone wall.

"Indeed," Will said. "They were called the *damnati*—prisoners of war, criminals, for the most part." He paused where they could look up and see the Coliseum's upper stories rising high above them. "In later years, the Coliseum housed cobblers and blacksmiths. In the twelfth century, even a group of warlords. Pilgrim books incorrectly called the arena a temple to the sun, which attracted necromancers who came to summon demons."

"Boo!" Hugh said, tickling Nell. She screamed. Will widened his eyes at the piercing sound and waited for the echoes of it to fade as Nell turned to hit her brother.

"You stop that, Hugh," Nell said, "or I'll tell Father."

"Ooh, even *more* frightening," he said with a pretend shiver.

"Did they truly flood the entire floor?" Cora asked him, daring to look his way. "I've heard they flooded it for naval drama."

"They did. They removed all the wooden supports and diverted a nearby aqueduct to bring in enough water to flood the base of the arena to a depth of three to five feet. That ended after the first century, when all wooden supports were replaced with masonry."

The group was spreading out, dispersing as they explored. "Not too far," Will called. "Not much of the Hypogeum has been fully excavated and restored." He gestured to the guards to keep an eye after their charges.

"Is it true that they even brought in elephants and rhinoceroses?" Lillian asked, accepting his proffered arm as she stepped over a hole. She looked up at the walls as if they might turn into a menagerie intent on gobbling her up.

"That and more," Will said. "The Romans liked to bring in such spectacles because they thought it was symbolic of how they'd conquered far-off, wild lands—even nature herself, when you consider their aqueducts and roads." He peered around the hall, aware that the group had separated, ignoring his entreaty to stay close. He couldn't blame them, really. The place was fascinating. But he frowned when he saw that a number of them were out of sight.

Will was about to give a whistle—trying to alert Antonio—when he heard the worst sound possible.

Cora was screaming.

CHAPTER 27

~Cora~

I knew I was disobeying Will's request, wandering off. But I couldn't help it. I was agitated and needing space again. From him. From everyone. These rocks had stood for thousands of years; what could happen? I slipped around the wall and then scurried down a short hall and turned another corner, looking up at the glorious arena rising above, thinking about how it all would've worked together as an amazing theater back in the day.

I was about to take a step when I hesitated, sensing an abyss, and glanced down. My arms windmilled as I tried to regain my balance, and I narrowly caught it. Heart pounding, I took a breath, relieved I hadn't fallen into the hole, and it was then that I felt the shove at my lower back.

There was no time to see who had pushed me. I screamed as I fell, reaching out to desperately grasp at roots and bits of rotten timber. But nothing abated my descent, not until I hit the ground. I heard the crack of breaking bone, saw my arm turn at a terrible angle, and then a second later felt the resulting pain. I would've screamed again if the air hadn't been stolen from my lungs. I rolled to my side, dimly aware that my lovely hat was pulling away, most of my pins lost.

I blinked slowly as I lay on my side on the stone floor, watching as a cloud of dust mites flew through the air around me, swirled, settled. Reminded myself to breathe. Tried to tell myself the pain wasn't as bad as all that.

Until it was.

~William~

"Everyone, get up top and outside," Will told Felix, Hugh, and Pascal, gesturing to the remaining women. "Make sure everyone's accounted for," he growled to Antonio.

He turned and shoved through several groups who had arrived after them, trying to find where he'd heard Cora scream. It had been her, right? She wasn't in sight…

The two detectives and he ran down the corridor he'd last glimpsed her enter, then split up as they made their way through the various hallways. Will turned around at a dead end. "Cora?" he called. "Cora!"

He hated that it was so quiet, that he'd heard nothing but her initial scream. He turned to his right and ran down the next corridor, noting how overgrown it was.

"Will, over here!" called a voice from what sounded like two corridors away. It was Stephen, the lanky detective. Was he with Cora now? The place was like a maze, and Will had to guess at the fastest route. "Over here!" Stephen called again.

"Keep yelling!" Will responded. He ran to his left, cut across two corridors, and looked left and right. "Stephen?"

"Right here!" he called.

He was close. Will rounded another corner, and there he was, far closer to the entrance of the Hypogeum than he'd thought. She hadn't wandered far...

Will stopped beside him, at the edge of a pit that had probably once been covered by wooden beams and a thin layer of stone but was now a yawning chasm. Fifteen feet below, she lay unmoving. "Get some rope and some help," he said to Stephen.

He knelt in the damp grass and quickly pulled off his jacket, then eyed the overgrown walls—a living tapestry of plants—looking for anything that might hold his weight. There. A tree root, thin, emerging about a foot down on the right-hand wall. It wasn't much, but it was something. Without further thought, he leaped and grabbed hold of it, swinging to a stop and trying to gain purchase with his boots against the wall. Then he began lowering himself down. "Cora," he grunted. "Talk to me."

But she still didn't move. Her ivory hat lay beneath her head, the pins having ripped out much of her bun and sending her hair in a lush, golden wave over her shoulder.

Will had made it a couple more feet when he felt the root give way and fell to the ground. He hit hard and stumbled to his knees, panting, but his eyes were only on Cora. "Cora," he said, scrambling over to her. He hesitated, frightened out of his wits that she was dead. She was so pale.

The bottom of the pit was littered with old stones, which had obviously fallen from above. Had one of those hit her on the head?

He dared to stroke her face. "Cora," he said. "Can you hear me?" He moved his filthy fingers down to her neck to check for a pulse. "Cora!"

She blinked slowly just as he noted her heartbeat, and he let out a sigh of relief. "Oh, Cora!" he said. "Are you all right?"

She lifted her hand to her forehead, as if it were too bright in the dank pit. "Will…" she said, her voice raspy. "I'm such an idiot. I'm sorry I—"

"Shh," he said. "Don't worry about that now. Can you move your feet? Wiggle your toes? Is your other arm okay?"

The other men arrived up top. "Will!"

He waved at them, his eyes still only on Cora.

"I-I think so." She shifted more fully to her back and winced, and Will held his breath. "Oh," she said, her face draining of blood. "My left arm hurts."

"Let me see," Will said, moving to her other side. Gingerly, he picked up her hand. "Any of your fingers hurt?"

Her eyes, wide and blue, blinked several times. Then she shook her head, seeming to brace herself for what was to come. "It's higher up."

He moved his fingers up to her wrist and gently squeezed it. "Anything?"

"No," she whispered.

He ran both hands up her bicep and again, she shook her head, but her face was growing more pale. Carefully, he moved his fingers across her lower arm and felt the bump just before she let out a stifled scream.

Will immediately let go of her arm. "Broken," he said. "You must've done it in your fall. And you were out for a couple of minutes. I wager you have a pretty good concussion."

"Oh, Will," she groaned. "I'm sorry. If only I hadn't been such a dolt—"

"Shh, don't think more about it."

"I'll be thinking about it every day this arm is healing."

"True," he said, sharing a rueful smile with her.

"And now I've delayed the group's plans to—"

"Shh. Enough." He rose and waved for the men to toss the rope to them. As soon as the coils came flying through the air and then straightened into a line, he reached for the end and began tying knots, remembering Uncle Stuart teaching him various ones.

He quickly fashioned a harness for Cora, then knelt beside her. "Can you sit up?"

She swallowed hard. "I-I think so."

He took hold of her right shoulder and said, "If you can move your left arm at all, lay it across your belly so we can wrap it."

She gave him a horrified look.

"I'm sorry, sweetheart, but if we're to get you back up, there will be some jostling. I'd rather it be as controlled as possible. Just look at me, concentrate on me, while you do it," he said, taking her small right hand in his.

She bit her lip and nodded, her eyebrows pulled together in a frightened frown. Then she let go of his hand and reached across her torso for her left hand. Taking a deep breath, she pulled her left arm across until it rested on her belly, her lips parting in an agonizing cry that sent every hair on Will's neck on end.

He tried to swallow but found his mouth dry. "Let's get you upright," he said, repositioning his hand beneath her right shoulder. "Slowly," he cautioned.

She rose as instructed, letting out a slow "oh," as she did so. Then he stood to pull off his tie, setting it on a rock to his side, and unbuttoning his collar.

"Wh-what are you doing?" she asked, still panting from the pain.

"We need something to wrap your arm against you," he said, working down the buttons. Rapidly, he finished and shrugged out of his shirt, leaving only his balbriggan undershirt tucked into the waistline of his trousers. Her blue eyes belatedly moved away as he caught her gaze. He smiled as he knelt again, winding the shirt into a thick coil.

"Oh, your fine new shirt," she moaned.

"It's the least of our worries." He leaned forward and wrapped the shirt around her back, then fastened it gently under her arm. She winced at the pain.

"How's your head?" he asked, sitting back on his haunches. "Are you seeing double? Feeling faint?"

"No," she said, shaking her head. More of her hair pulled from her pins and fell around her shoulders. "Is it bad?" she asked, glancing down at her arm. "It's throbbing."

"That's for the doctors to tell us," he said. "Let's get you up top." He bent and lifted her, trying not to jostle her, then set her on her feet beside the wall. "All right?" he asked, waiting for her to affirm she wasn't going to pass out on him again. When he saw that she was standing on her own, he grabbed hold of the rope and looked up. "I'm sending her up in a minute. Pull it taut!"

Stephen did so, and Pascal moved behind him, each taking a span of rope to keep it steady, Pascal wrapping it around his own waist. Will bent and pulled it around Cora. "Just like on the glacier," he said with a smile.

She gave him a pained smile, clearly remembering their narrow escape from the crevasse. "If I were a suspicious person, I'd wonder if someone was trying to kill…me."

His eyes narrowed as she seemed to weigh her own words. "Cora?" he asked, tying the first knot, then the second, securing her in the makeshift seat.

"It's nothing," she said, giving her head a small shake.

"Are you certain?"

"Yes, yes," she said tiredly.

"Give it your full weight," he said.

She forced a small smile to her lips as he backed away to look at his handiwork. "Remember you're getting paid to bring me home in one piece. Even if," she said, pausing to wince as she sat down, "I keep getting myself into trouble."

"This is the first time you've gotten *yourself* into trouble," he said.

"I've done my best," she said. She frowned again at that, glancing up to the edge, as if thinking.

"Take her up!" Will called. "Slowly."

The men did as he asked, and Cora rose before him. "You all right?" he asked.

She nodded. "Will?" she said, three feet above him.

"What?"

"I wonder if…" She paused, frowning. "I think that…"

"What?"

"I didn't fall, Will. I think someone pushed me," she said just as she disappeared over the edge above him.

CHAPTER 28

~Cora~

It was with great relief that I saw Will come up over the edge soon after I'd reached it, especially once I decided that someone had pushed me. He moved over to me and began untying the knots that had held me in place, and then lifted me in his arms. "Let's get you to a hospital," he murmured.

I closed my eyes, my head now tilting and spinning in response to the pain.

Will began walking, with Pascal in front and Stephen behind us. "Cora," Will said lowly.

I looked up at him.

"Did you see anyone? I mean, someone who might've…pushed you?"

I shook my head, and then immediately decided that was a bad idea. Any movement of my head sent me into a whirlpool. I bit my cheek and breathed rapidly through my nose, fighting the wave of nausea that threatened to engulf me.

"Another…" I paused, trying to look around me. Seeing no one else, I said, "Another reporter? Trying to add spice to our story?"

I took a deep breath. The whole idea of another ferret like Arthur Stapleton in our midst made me weary. Was life not trying enough without having to negotiate those with nefarious plans?

"I don't know," Will whispered, frowning. "At the risk of your life?" He shook his head. "That seems foolish to me."

I tried to smile at him. "I'm of more value alive than dead?"

He returned my smile and arched a brow. "In more ways than one," he said, now climbing the tight spiral staircase that led out. I tucked my legs, but he still had to hold me partially over the rail to allow us room to move upward. "I'm so sorry, Cora. For bringing you here."

"It's not your fault, Will." I concentrated on his face rather than the growing height beneath us.

"I should have insisted…" he said, panting, "that you all stay close."

"We are stubborn charges with minds of our own," I said. "I should've stayed close of my own volition. I knew better." We reached the top, both sighing in relief. We didn't even make it all the way out the entrance tunnel before the rest of our group flooded in, surrounding us, all asking questions at once. As Will fielded them, and as my vision faded into a faint again, I saw two reporters taking our photograph, each with a clear view of Will holding me in his arms.

I knew how it would look. Will without a shirt, me with an impromptu sling, in his arms, our well-dressed cohorts all about us. *That will sell some papers*, I thought.

And the last thought, before I gave into the faint... *At least Father's not here to see it...*

The next morning, I awakened in a tidy, spare hospital room, my head groggy, my arm throbbing but neatly bandaged, my body in a crisp white gown. I turned and felt my pain like it wasn't quite my own. Drugs, I decided. *They've medicated me.*

I suppose there was much to be grateful for in that. I remembered coming to briefly, Will and Viv's faces above me, but then not much more afterward. Perhaps they'd administered some laudanum or the like at that point.

I wondered if I had screamed when they set the bone in my arm or if I'd slept through it. I wondered if the doctors were as skilled here in Italy as they were at home. I wondered if my arm would heal right or if I'd live forever partially lame, like some I'd known back in Dunnigan. From those I'd known, it all depended on the severity of the break.

I stared out my hospital window, the dome of St. Peter in perfect view, and ran the moment right before my fall through my mind again and again.

The more I considered it, the more I was certain.

I'd almost caught my balance, was leaning backward, righting myself, when I'd felt it. A hand at my back.

Where was Will? I needed him here. To answer some questions as well as comfort me. I'd feel better if he was near. Perhaps it wasn't visiting hours.

A nurse—or rather a nun—bustled about my room in her habit, straightening my clothes on a small chest, checking the water pitcher's contents, then eyeing me and speaking to me in rapid Italian. Her tone was friendly, concerned, but I had no idea what she said.

I lifted my hands. *"Mi dispiace. Non parlo l'italiano." I'm sorry, I don't speak Italian.* Two of the few phrases I knew.

She frowned at me and then grunted, lifting her hands as if asking my permission to touch me. I nodded, and she cradled my cheeks in her rough, fat fingers, tilting my face toward the window. Then she lifted my eyelids upward with her thumbs, looking from one to the other. She grunted again and released me, then went to write something on my chart. With that, she disappeared out the door, where I saw Pascal's hulking back, clearly guarding my door, and just past him…

Pierre.

Our eyes met right as the nurse pulled the door firmly shut behind her.

But soon he was through, carrying an enormous bouquet of flowers in an exquisite vase. Pascal came through the door behind him and watched us, his eyes wary.

"Mon ange," Pierre said, his brows knitting together in concern, his face full of nothing but devotion. "Is it very bad?"

"I…I don't know," I said, automatically lifting my cheek for one kiss, then turning for the second. "I believe my arm is broken, but I am uncertain what happened to my head. It aches quite a bit."

"I imagine it does," he said, setting the flowers—a dense combination of tiny red roses and purple iris—atop the chest beside my neat stack of clothes. "Mon Dieu, what you've been through." He pulled a chair close to my bedside and took my hand.

"It's all right," I said. "It isn't all that bad. But is there a doctor nearby? Is Will here?" I asked Pascal. "I'd like to hear my diagnosis."

Pascal nodded. "I shall see," he said, opening the door and peering outward.

Pierre's fingers tightened around mine, and I looked at him. He was frowning. "I will find out what they have to say," he said, brushing a tendril of my hair away from my eyes. He shook his head and stared at me earnestly. "If only I had come to you yesterday. I would have—"

"What?" Will said from the open doorway, a regretful Pascal hovering behind him. "You would have somehow saved her from falling?"

Pierre rose and straightened his jacket. "William. It is good to see you."

He held out a hand of greeting that Will ignored. "No. Say what you were going to say."

Pierre's lips twitched, and he sniffed. "Well, I would certainly not have allowed Cora to wander from my sight in such a rough and dangerous place."

"You're right," Will said, stepping forward to stand at the opposite side of my bed. "I made a grave mistake, allowing that to happen." The muscles in his cheek pulsed, and he looked like he was fighting the urge to toss Pierre from my room.

"It was no one's fault but my own," I said. "I'm a woman grown. Capable of making wise decisions when I'm not governed by emotions, as you two are at this very moment."

Pierre tore his glare from Will and looked down at me. He started to take my hand, thought better of it—with Will so near—and then folded his arms in front of his chest. "What was it, *mon ange*, that set you to wandering yesterday? What in your heart so troubled you?"

"It is nothing, Pierre," I said, dropping my eyes, remembering the odd separation I'd felt from Will, as well as the need for a little space in which to think…

"It appears I've arrived in Rome at an interesting juncture," Pierre said, his eyes shifting back and forth between us. "You two are…at odds."

"Who are you kidding?" Will asked, quickly poking out his hand, palm up. "You've been in Roma for days, just waiting for such a 'juncture.' I half expected you to show up at the Coliseum to see if Cora would run directly into your arms."

Pierre frowned and lifted his hands and shoulders as if unduly accused. "I have been seeing to my own business here in Roma," he said, "so that I might enjoy a respite with your group again."

"Yeah?" Will said, leaning forward across my bed. "Well, you're not welcome."

"Will!" I cried, aghast at his rudeness.

He looked down at me, furious. "What? You *want* him here?"

"No!" I inhaled sharply, not wanting to hurt Pierre. "I mean yes, it's fine that he's here, but…" I let out a groan of frustration, my head beginning to throb again. "Please. Enough of this. Both of you. Get out."

They both turned to face me.

"You heard me. Get out!" I cried.

Their anger toward each other turned into contrition with me.

"*Mon ange*—"

"Out!"

"Cora, really, I—"

"Out!"

The nun, hearing my cries, bustled in with a storm brewing behind her wrinkled brow. *"Cosa fate?"* she cried in Italian. *"Dovreste sapere di non disturbare una paziente!"*

Though I couldn't understand her, her expression and tone were unmistakable. She shooed them out of my room and returned to check my temperature, clucking to me in soothing tones and patting my arm like a doting grandmother. While I regretted reacting so with the men, in her care, I felt my heart settling back into a normal pace.

I sighed and looked out the window, remembering my mother caring for me as I battled a fever. Her thin hands neatly folding a wet towel into thirds, dipping it into a basin of water, fresh and cold from the well, wringing it out, then laying it across my forehead. Her pulling my sheet and blanket back in order, folding it across my chest. Her hand on my cheek.

How I wished Mama and Papa were here, now, with me, so that they could help me figure out what was happening. Another thought made my eyes widen. *Father. I'm missing Father, too…*

The nurse continued to mutter in Italian, her tone now calm and soothing. She turned and focused her coal-black eyes on me with a kind expression. I thought she might be telling me to rest, and she pointed to the door and shook her head, as if telling me that the men would not be allowed back in, but I was asleep before I could even try to cobble together a few of the Italian words I knew to respond…

CHAPTER 29

~William~

Pierre and Will set up a path for pacing, each stubbornly refusing to depart the hospital, each wanting to outlast the other, waiting for Cora to accept visitors again. Antonio took the rest of the group to see the crypts outside of the city, then out to Ostia Antica, the ancient Roman port, giving them a full day of touring. But they all returned to the hospital that evening on their way to supper.

"How is she?" Vivian asked without preamble, walking directly over to Will.

Will shrugged. "I don't know," he admitted with a miserable shrug. "She refuses to see me. Or him."

Viv's keen eyes ran to Pierre, who was chatting with Lillian and Nell, then back to Will. "When did he appear?" There was something in her tone that told Will she was inexplicably on his side. It surprised him. He'd figured she'd be like her father, encouraging Cora to take the richest suitor possible. But maybe he'd underestimated her.

"Today," he said. "Convenient timing, eh? Just after we had our falling out at the party."

"Hmmm," she said, tearing her eyes away from the handsome Frenchman. Was she herself interested in him? Perhaps she was day-dreaming of the day she could part from the troublesome Andrew and lure in another that Wallace Kensington would've approved...

Viv moved off to intercept the doctor, hauling Antonio along with her to translate. Will sighed and rubbed his face.

"Is it all that bad?" Felix asked, clapping him on the shoulder. Hugh came around his other side.

"For me, it seems. Pierre and I began to...bicker, and Cora threw us both out of the room."

Hugh guffawed at this, and Felix gave him a wry grin. "You should know by now," Felix said good-naturedly, "that my sister does not suffer fools gladly. It must be something she learned from the Diehls..."

Hugh laughed again at that, and even Will smiled. "I was a fool," he said, tiredly rubbing his neck. "Think she'll forgive me?"

"Of that I have no doubt," Felix said, clapping him again on the shoulder and looking back at his sisters. Viv gave him a nod. "Well, it appears my sister received word on our patient, and we can be off to eat at last." He patted his stomach. "I'm famished."

"As am I," Hugh said. "See you back at the palazzo tonight, William?"

"I imagine, at some point. Tell the others that we'll leave for Tivoli bright and early in the morning. Either Antonio or I shall lead you."

Hugh nodded and then left, unspoken questions alight in his eyes. The waiting room quieted as they left, like a hive full of bees all exiting to retrieve their daily nectar quota.

Will's eyes lifted to meet Pierre's across the room, and Will raised his hands in a gesture of defeat. "It appears our Cora shall remain stubbornly hidden away," Pierre said, daring to approach Will. They'd skirted each other all afternoon. He pulled out his pocket watch. "You have beaten me in this round," he said regretfully, "for I shall be late to a dinner obligation if I do not leave now."

"Perhaps she simply is asleep versus hiding from us. And she is not 'ours,' Pierre," Will said, folding his arms in front of his chest. "She is mine. I do not intend to share her with you."

"Hmm," Pierre said, pursing his lips and tapping them with one finger. "We shall see." Pierre moved to pass him, and Will reached out to grab his arm. He looked downward, rather than at the Frenchman, his eyes on the busy pattern of the terrazzo floor. "I want you to leave Rome, Pierre," he said.

"I know," the Frenchman returned quietly, his arm muscles tense beneath Will's grip. "But until I'm certain that Cora feels the same, I must stay."

Will reluctantly released him, despising his trembling hand, hoping Pierre didn't notice it and believe it a sign of weakness rather than rage. It took several minutes for his breathing to steady, and when he looked up, he saw Cora in the doorway of her room, dressed and looking reasonably well.

"Cora?" he said in a whisper. He coughed. "Are you free to leave?" he asked, walking toward her.

"The nurse doesn't like it, but I don't care," she said with sniff, stepping past Stephen. "I'm fine and will rest as well at the apartment as I would here." He saw, then, that Anna was right behind her. Had the others known this was the plan? He shifted uncomfortably.

Rarely was there forward momentum in his tour groups without him being the first to know. But this wasn't a tour group. This was…Cora.

Anna and Stephen stepped about ten feet away to give them privacy.

"Look, Cora. I'm sorry about what went on with Pierre this morning. It's only that the man makes me mad with jealousy."

"I know."

"But it's no excuse," Will said with a little shake of his head. He reached up to rub his temples. "And it shall not happen again. We both knew he intended to rendezvous with us here in Roma. I leave it to you to tell him to go…or stay," he forced himself to say.

"Thank you, Will," Cora said. "Now…might we go home?" She was already walking, and Will fell into step beside her. "I'd like to be there for a while before the others return from their evening jaunt. Perhaps even escape to my quarters before they do. I want to join you tomorrow for your tour of Tivoli."

Will blinked in surprise. "You believe you'll have the stamina for such a venture? Perhaps we should stick closer to the city and—"

"No, no. My arm should be fine, now that it's casted and I have some pain medication. And the doctor doesn't believe I suffered a concussion—that it was simply another of my troubling fainting spells of late." She shook her head and looked at him. "I don't know what's come over me. I never fainted a day in my life until the last month…"

"Perhaps it's the combined stress of what you've endured."

"Hmm. Perhaps. In any case, I've looked forward to seeing Tivoli. Don't alter your plans on account of me."

She turned to chat with Anna, who held firmly to her arm as they exited the hospital.

But all Will could think about was that he'd alter anything, anywhere in order to make things right for Cora. And that she'd never fainted before, up until the last month... What was truly going on? Was there some deeper illness lurking?

~Cora~

Outside, we made it through a small crowd of reporters and drove back to the palazzo in silence beyond idle chitchat, not because I was angry any longer, but because I wasn't certain how to delve into anything deeper with Will. But thoughts and questions swirled in my head, and as soon as Anna had settled me in the parlor, I couldn't stand it any longer.

"How did Pierre know I was in the hospital?" I asked.

Will stiffened and then shrugged as if it were an intentional effort. "He likely read about it in the paper. It was front-page news in *La Repubblica.*"

"Of course it was," I said with an embarrassed sigh. Anna brought me a cup of tea and asked me silently, with her eyes, if I needed anything else. I shook my head.

"And now it will be picked up by all the other papers around the globe. 'Heiress Appears Helpless,'" I said, thinking of headlines. "'Copper Cora Collides with Coliseum Crater.'"

Will smiled and sat down across from me, visibly relaxing. "Come now, I doubt it will be as bad as all that."

"No?"

"Well," he said, tilting his head back and forth as if weighing the thought, "maybe."

I let out a long breath and considered him. "Was I a fool, firing Simon? Perhaps he'd be helpful in this sort of situation…"

"No," Will said assuredly. "You will need assistance to manage in many ways, especially when you return home." His eyes met mine. "But you can decide when to speak to reporters and when not to. Even Simon couldn't have kept them from taking our photograph yesterday, out as we were, in public."

I hesitated, remembering thinking of how it would appear. "May I see?"

He leveled a gaze at me and then rose to walk over to the corner table. He snapped open a paper and then brought it over to me.

It was exactly as I'd imagined. But it was odd seeing myself looking so not myself, clearly in a dead faint, and Will, appearing virile and strong, easily carrying me out of the Coliseum. The combination of our modern clothing—or lack thereof, in Will's case—and the millennia-old building behind us was striking.

I sighed again, folded the newspaper, and tossed it to the coffee table. "Yes, that will be passed from paper to paper for certain. It's like catnip to the cats."

"Indeed," he said ruefully. He took a sip of his tea and studied me. "Cora, when it happened you said…" He paused, as if anxious about bringing it up again, perhaps fearing it would upset me.

But I knew exactly what he was going to say. "I said I think someone pushed me," I whispered.

His eyes held mine, looking stunned all over again. "Did you see anyone?"

I shook my head. "No. I was walking, looking around, but I sensed the chasm. I almost stumbled down into it. I had just managed to regain my balance when I think someone gave me the barest of pushes."

Will's frown deepened, and he set down his cup with a clatter. "Who? Who would want to do such a thing to you?"

"I don't know. All I can think of is…" I hated to say it. Aloud. It would make it real. Set things into motion that I—

"Andrew?" Will whispered, now behind my settee.

I looked up at him and then nodded, feeling shame for my suspicion. The man was a lout in myriad ways, but did he deserve this?

Will came around the corner of the settee and sat down across from me again, leaning forward, elbows on knees. "Let's think it through. Why would he do such a thing?"

I shrugged and then leaned forward so we could whisper even more quietly. "Because I've turned Vivian against him?"

"But Vivian hasn't broken it off with him, has she?"

"No. But he's certainly feeling the effects of my influence. Viv only manages to be civil to him, as far as I can see. It's as if she's playing a role. Andrew is smart. Surely he senses what's happening…"

"Is that enough for him to attempt to murder you?" he said, eyebrows lifted in disbelief. He cocked his head. "That's a serious, serious allegation."

"But think it through. If he gets rid of me so it looks like it's an accident, he can comfort Viv, maybe even win her back. Perhaps my portion of the Kensington-Diehl Mine would revert back to the Kensington estate."

"Would it?" Will asked.

"No. I made certain it would go to my parents. Only if my parents died would it…" My eyes shifted to meet his. "He… If something happened to me, he wouldn't go after my folks, too, would he?"

Will stared back at me. "I don't know." He rose and resumed his pacing. "I think that we might need to hire a private detective. Someone unassociated with the Kensingtons or Morgans heretofore."

"That's impossible," I said. "Andrew would pick up on our new suspicions. And that is liable to change every one of our relationships. We've come so far, Will. I don't want to end this tour with that in the air."

Will lifted his hands. "Tell them that you need additional security, given the media scrutiny and Grunthall's departure. Especially now, after this event at the Coliseum."

"And then what? Have the man accompany us all the way home to America and then pay for his return voyage?"

He looked at me with a wry expression. "It's not as if you can't afford it."

I laughed softly at myself. He was right. But still, it grated. I'd rather give that money to a charity than spend it on myself. I thought about Eleonora and her orphanage, but that led me down yet another troubling path. I brought my attention back to Will, who had asked me something.

"Who else could it be?" he whispered again.

"I don't know," I returned. "Another reporter, trying to enliven the story?" I gestured to the paper. "It certainly worked."

"Enliven the story at the risk of killing the subject?" he asked doubtfully.

"I know. But didn't Art Stapleton risk the same with us in France and beyond?"

He sighed and shook his head, continuing to pace.

I closed my eyes, pain suddenly making it difficult to continue.

He came around to me again and knelt beside me, picking up my good hand. "I've overtaxed you. Come. Let us get you something to eat and into bed. If you're certain you want to join us tomorrow, you need a good night's sleep."

The next morning, it was far more difficult to rise and dress than I had thought. *Perhaps it's the lingering remains of the medications*, I thought, cradling my head and opening my bloodshot eyes wide in the reflection of the mirror. Briefly, I wondered if it would be better to stay back and rest, but I couldn't quite imagine a whole day here in the palazzo, pacing the cavernous spaces, thinking, thinking, thinking about the things I'd discussed with Will.

After a quick knock on my door, Anna arrived, her arms full of a massive vase filled with three dozen red roses, and behind her, two other servants, both carrying identical vases.

My eyes narrowed. *Pierre.*

She met my gaze and hid a small smile, settling her vase on my dressing table, while the others set them on my desk and a small table between two chairs. The room filled with the sweet fragrance of the buds, just beginning to open, and I remembered the flowers he'd sent me in Geneva...and how I'd thought they were from Will.

"His note is in that one," Anna said, nodding to the vase on the desk. I saw it then, the envelope perched among the buds. "What would you like to wear to Tivoli today, Miss?"

"Mmm," I said absently, tearing my eyes away from the far bouquet. I wanted to read the card in privacy, and I briefly wondered if

I might get the maids to throw the flowers out before Will got word of them. But it seemed a sacrilege to do such a thing—the flowers had to have cost a fortune. Back home, even one flower, purchased rather than picked from a garden, would've been considered an extravagance…

"Miss?"

I started and turned to Anna again. "Oh, yes. I'll wear the navy suit. I imagine Will would like us to stay out of our black crepe so we can continue to blend in. Thank you."

She nodded and went directly to the third red chest and dug out the day jacket and skirt. "I'll return with it pressed, Miss," she said, her eyes shifting toward Pierre's note and then back to me.

"Thank you, Anna," I said.

The other maids had already left, and she closed the door quietly behind her. I turned back to the bouquet on the desk and hesitated, then moved over to it, as shy as if I were approaching Pierre himself.

My fingers traced the soft, velvety leaves of the nearest bud, then closed around the envelope—a rich, creamy ivory against the blue-red of the flowers. I cracked the red wax seal, slid the note out, and turned to the window in order to better read it.

Mon Ange,

How I have agonized over your well-being since your accident! Forgive me for my foolishness with William. But can you fault a man with a nemesis competing for his very heart? This time apart from you has left it clear to me that I must win you. I must.

Please do not send me away yet, my love. Not yet. Give me but a few days to persuade you. I know the course of your life has changed over this summer. With all my heart, I wish to be the man by your side to guide you. With your father gone, and your papa so very far away, it is plain to me that you have been like a boat without a captain. I can be your captain, steering your ship, so you can sit back and enjoy the pleasures of the life you're destined to have. A woman's heart is too tender to manage what you've been asked to do. I shall relieve you of responsibility.

Never have I loved a woman as I love you. And I believe we belong together, for eternity.

Forever yours,
Pierre

I lifted the letter to my chest and thought about his words. They were both heart-rending and agitating. Part of me longed for his relentless ardor, accepting his pursuit. But the bigger part of me grew tired of this game. I had made it clear that I'd chosen Will, and Pierre had not respected my decision. What sort of husband would he be? Likely one who would press for his way—seeking to *relieve me of responsibility* I wasn't certain I wished to lose—until I succumbed in exhaustion.

My eyes ran over his words again. It was plain he didn't think I could do it—manage the mine or my increased responsibilities as a Kensington or a public figure. He thought he should rescue me, squire me away, *manage* me…even as Andrew wished to.

So many men wanting me in a certain compartment, a neat and tidy box they could identify and place where they wished...all except for Will. With Will, I felt freedom as well as support. He wanted me to go where God wanted me to go, not where he wanted me to go. Clearly, it'd be best for him if I agreed to marry him and stay in Minnesota while he went to university. But he hadn't asked that of me.

I looked over Pierre's words again, the feeling of confirmation washing through me. I would tell Pierre. As soon as we had a moment together. Send him on his way home so that Will and I could settle again into a semblance of peaceful union. Every moment on the *Olympic* would be one I would want to treasure, soaking up our last days, our last hours together before we would have to part ways to see through the next year of our lives. And in those moments, I hoped we would plan on how soon we could be reunited...forever.

Because staring at these roses, so beautiful, so pristine, I knew in my bones that I'd prefer a single, scraggly bud plucked from a garden if it was from Will. He was the man that God wanted for me.

~William~

They spent the morning touring the dry, crumbling remains of Hadrian's Villa, hot under the summer sun, and discussing the height and breadth of Rome's power. Here, his clients were coming to understand the terrific reach of the emperor—his "summer home" was the size of a small town. They clambered through the remains of temples and past pools full of algae. Columns that once had supported roofs now stood alone in the hot sun. The cracked remnants of soldiers' and firefighters' barracks rose three stories high above them.

"Rome was terrified of fire, of course," he said, helping Cora and then Lillian climb across a small pile of rubble and into a hallway that once had held guest apartments, their elaborate black and white mosaic tile flooring still visible. "Under Nero, they'd seen the city fairly destroyed. Hadrian was determined to never leave such a legacy behind him. Only buildings upon buildings. And walls as far as the northern edge of England and Jerusalem. Everywhere you go, it seems, one runs across Hadrian's name... and his legacy."

"And he came here to escape the heat," Felix cracked, fanning his sweat-soaked shirt. He carried his jacket over one arm, as the rest of the men were doing. The women carried parasols, even above their wide-brimmed hats.

"Yes," Will returned with a smile. But his smile faded as he noted Andrew nearing Cora. His worry was silly, he told himself. There was no way the man would make a move against her here, in the center of them all. If he was culpable at all... "Much like your fathers have taken to moving you all to the lake during the height of summer to escape the heat of Butte."

"Are you comparing us to Roman emperors?" Sam Morgan asked, his gray brows knitting together in mirth. He shook his head. "Wallace would've loved that."

The others laughed, but Will noticed the shadow of pain on the Kensington children's faces. "In a way," he said gently. "But with all due respect, Mr. Morgan, I'm afraid Hadrian's wealth would've made you look like paupers."

The group looked to him in surprise. "Ah, yes. All of Rome's coffers were at Hadrian's disposal. There is good reason that few of Rome's emperors died of natural causes. That sort of wealth and power..." He paused and dared to look each of them in the eye, even Andrew. "Never take what you have been given for granted. There is great responsibility with the gifts your families have been given."

"Given?" Andrew said with a scoff. "Our fathers worked hard for what they've acquired."

"Indeed," Will said, unwavering. "As you must, in order to be wise stewards of it as it becomes yours." He circled around a figure mounted on a short column, looking up to its headless shoulders. "Hadrian was one of the few decent emperors Rome ever saw. He didn't spend time trying to figure out how to expand the borders Trajan forged; he spent his time traveling about the far reaches, getting to know his people, understanding their unique challenges."

He gave Andrew and Felix a meaningful look, ducked his head as if thinking, and then looked back up at the statue as if it had once been Hadrian. "Not that Hadrian was perfect. It was under his watch that the bloody Bar Kochba revolt occurred in Israel. He went to Israel, and at first was sympathetic to the Jewish concerns. Some say he even promised to rebuild the temple. But at some point, he received poor counsel, and his heart hardened against them. He outlawed circumcision and decided to rebuild the temple—and yet dedicate it to *Jupiter*. What followed was horrendous, not only for the Jews, but also the Romans. Over the next few years of war, hundreds of thousands died, and over a thousand towns and villages were razed. It's a sobering story of remembering it's important, whom we listen to."

Andrew stiffened as if unappreciative of the moral lesson, and the others moved off to the next stop in their tour, led by Antonio.

"My, the end of our tour is making you most courageous," Cora muttered to him as he helped her through another partially disintegrated doorway.

"Yes," he said, with a smile, "I suppose it has."

"Are you always so forthright with your tourists?"

"On occasion." He fell into step beside her. "How is your arm? And your head?"

"Both of them, throbbing," she admitted. "But I wouldn't have missed this. It's been marvelous. All of it has been marvelous, Will. Every step of this tour." She paused and looked out over the plains beyond the villa, where farmers had divided the rich, volcanic soil into neat plots of land, planted with alternating crops. "Other than our personal losses," she said, tearing up a little, "it's been grand."

He smiled, took her good hand, and looked into her eyes. "Grand?" he said wryly. "We've seen too much conflict, even beyond our losses, for that 'grand' assessment, haven't we?"

"Conflict is a part of all our lives, is it not?" she asked. "I admit, we've seen a greater share than I'd care to in the future, but…" She shook her head and looked at the ground, then back at him. "One learns a great deal about others in the heat of such conflict, do they not?"

"They do," he said with a nod. There was something in her eyes, something new when she looked at him. It was as if she had decided something integral, something that settled her inside. Whatever it was, he wanted to know more. He wished he could send the others on to tour the Villa d'Este while he found a quiet trattoria in which to speak with her at length. What had happened?

CHAPTER 30

~Cora~

We arrived at Tivoli, a town perched high on a hill above Hadrian's Villa and noticeably cooler. There was a lovely breeze that rustled through the Roman pines all about us and through the open windows of the Villa d'Este, an estate we toured—a sprawling, beautiful building full of frescoes, built by a wealthy Roman cardinal in the Middle Ages. Afterward, we moved out to the patio that extended over the gardens for luncheon, and I found myself counting the steps, more than anxious for some refreshment and a respite, feeling overtaxed.

To our side was a long wall with many different heads—gargoyles and wolves and distorted men—each opening their mouth in a wide "O" to spew water into the fountain trough below them. I was holding Will's arm when I saw Pierre first, rising with two others to greet us as we approached. I paused, and Will looked down at me, then back at him. That was when I noticed the red roses in a hundred tiny vases, up and down the two long tables, and even one in his lapel.

Will's arm tensed beneath my hand. "What is he doing here?" He spit it out, accusation in his tone, as if I'd invited him myself.

"I have no idea," I said, even then knowing he was here for me. Only me.

Pierre's eyes never left me as we approached. "Pierre," I said, the question in his name alone.

"Cora," he said, taking my hand and giving me a slight bow.

Our host, Signore Abramo Biotti, a bulbous, merry fat man, came up beside us. "When I heard your group was coming to visit the villa today," he said in a thick Italian accent, "I knew that my friend Richelieu would appreciate an invitation too."

"He's never one to miss an opportunity," Will said, halfheartedly shaking Pierre's hand.

"Did you see all you wanted of the villa?" asked Signore Biotti, waving upward at it.

"Indeed. It was most generous of you to allow us to traipse through your home," Will said.

"Please," he said, waving dismissively, then setting his hand on his chest. "It is my pleasure. You have come on a fine day, my friends." He looked to the rest of our group. "After luncheon, we intend to start the grand fountain, a spectacle that hasn't been seen in over a century." He waved down the steep embankment behind him. "Once, this entire hillside was one of the finest gardens of Italia. Visitors came from far and wide to see its exquisite layout and observe the fountains, fed by its own diverted aqueducts." His mouth opened in wonder as he gazed outward, as if he were seeing it for the first time himself. "There truly hasn't been anything in Italia like it since."

Pierre clapped Signore Biotti on the shoulder with familiarity and grinned us. "There is nothing like a passionate Italian," he said, then made the introductions all around. It was almost as if Pierre were more the host than Biotti was. I stiffened in frustration. Hadn't Will and I suffered enough strife over the last few days without Pierre interfering here? But the more I heard, the more I was certain. It was he who invited us to come to the table, he who decided who would sit where.

Ten others wandered in from the gardens and joined us at the long, dramatic table set symbolically with Pierre's red roses. We soon learned, via translation, that they'd been invited for this test of the grand fountain. But I felt that they were more a hired supporting cast in Pierre's latest play.

"It has taken us years to clear it," Biotti said, winding pasta onto his fork with the aid of a soup spoon, returning to his topic of favor, the fountain. "The brush and trees. Then we had to repair the tiles that had broken away, and *then*," he said, lifting his fork, mouth full, "we had to go to work on the aqueduct."

"I guess it was leaking in a hundred different places," Pierre said.

"Two hundred," Biotti muttered, still chewing.

I absorbed that with surprise. I had no idea what all it took to maintain a fountain, but it certainly sounded comprehensive. And expensive. It was no wonder the place had fallen into disrepair.

"How is it, Pierre," Will said, picking up his wine goblet, "that you know our host?"

"My father and he once did a great deal of business together," Pierre said, picking up his own goblet. "And now I hope to pick up where my father left off."

Signore Biotti laughed at this, winding yet another bite of pasta on his fork. It was delicious, I thought: linguine in a sauce bright with tomato and lemon and basil. And our host seemed to be enjoying it more than all the rest of us combined. I found his mood contagious. He obviously adored his home and was eager to share it. No matter how Pierre had finagled an invitation and how he might've decorated the tables just for me, I didn't want another argument between him and Will to interrupt it. I simply was too tired to deal with it.

Thankfully, Will did not press him, and conversation moved on to other subjects—the state of the government and their lackadaisical approach to European expansion of imports, a ball to be held in one of the noblemen's homes the following week, and on it went. As the food settled in my stomach, I closed my eyes and felt the lovely breeze cool my face.

"Ahh, the little bird with the broken wing is settling in for a nap, I see," said Signore Biotti.

My eyes flew open in embarrassment as all eyes turned to me.

"No, no," he said, lifting a hand of approval. "After you see the fountain, you shall rest, little bird. In the villa." He sat back in his chair, finished eating at last, and patted his chest. "Nothing like a siesta at Villa d'Este to invigorate the body." With the last of his sentence his hands turned to fists, and he lifted them in the air.

I smiled. "I confess, that does sound lovely."

"She was only discharged yesterday from hospital," Pierre said lowly to our host, a note of accusation in his tone as his eyes moved to Will.

"Shall we see the fountain now?" I asked Signore Biotti sweetly, quickly intervening. "I, for one, cannot wait."

Signore Biotti set down his napkin, his eyes alight. "Yes, yes, let us do so!" He rose, and the rest of the table rose after him. Then we moved down the walkway and learned that the fountain beside us was called the Hundred Fountains, even though only a portion appeared to be doing as they ought—casting small rainbows of water above. As we turned the corner, Lillian gasped. Above us was a tiny skyline, like a miniature model of an ancient city, broken in places, all of it eroded, but still breathtaking.

Will smiled. "It's a representation of Roma," he said to the group. "See there? Even a little Hadrian's Column, which should have more meaning to you all now."

Lillian clapped her gloved hands. "Oh, it's marvelous," she enthused. "Were I a small girl, I'd want to take my dolls up there and play amongst them."

"I'm certain that sculpture has seen its fair share of small girls over the centuries," Signore Biotti said, offering her his arm and then patting her hand in a fatherly way. His eyes grew distant. "For many decades this estate was abandoned. Can you imagine? Goatherds brought their flocks through here to eat the foliage. Perhaps their little sisters came along to play."

I noticed the fine mosaic paving beneath my feet—chunky tiles of purple porphyry, green granite, and other stones that, when a leaky fountain allowed their color to shine, made it look like a virtual treasure trove of rare rocks. I gazed around me and considered the estate anew. It truly must've been magnificent back in its heyday; the thought made me admire Signore Biotti's endeavors to restore it all the more.

Beside us, flowing down open channels, was water. And as we rounded the bend, we saw an ancient figure of a goddess, moss-covered and rising from the center of a half-moon of grotto dug out of the very cliff. "Yes, yes," Biotti said dismissively. "It's grand. But you must go down there, below, to see the big fountain in all its glory. If it works, I should say. No promises, no promises."

We turned and took the stairs he indicated, descending even more. Already I lamented all those we'd already descended, knowing I'd have to climb them again. Normally, it would be no issue, but my arm and head were truly throbbing, and I had little on my mind other than that promised nap in an airy room.

I had my hand on Will's arm, and Pierre scurried down the steps to catch up with us. I suppressed a groan and considered pleading my headache and returning to the villa now, entering a room where no one could disturb me.

"These gardens were truly the wonder of Italy," Pierre said, slowing beside us. "There was once a fountain with great clockworks that would ring out at the top of the hour, but Signore Biotti hasn't gotten to that yet. If he did, he'd make a veritable fortune in visitor's fees. Or at least have the grandest plaything for his parties." He moved forward and pointed out a hole in my path, as if I or Will might not have seen it, and we circumvented it.

At last we reached the bottom, joining the other guests at the far end of the rectangular, still pool and looking upward.

Signore Biotti appeared on the floor above us, leaning on a balustrade that sprawled the curved length of it. I winced, worried that the old stone would give way beneath his great girth. But he was rising then, lifting his arms and crying, "This is the day! This is a fine day, an historical day in the history of Tivoli! A hint of things to come!" With that, he put two fingers in his mouth and whistled.

We waited. And waited.

And just when Hugh and Felix both opened their mouths—presumably to break the tension with quick wit—we heard the water above us on the next level. With a tremendous rush, it spewed in a ten-foot-wide flow over one edge and down into the pool via twin waterfalls. A moment later, four waterspouts sprayed from the upper pool, and then three seconds later, water flowed from a second water-fall into the pool directly before us. I sucked in my breath, amazed at the sense of history unfolding directly before me. We heard a grumbling beneath our feet and felt a corresponding vibration. Then, two giant waterspouts rose, twenty feet high. We all cheered.

We stared in awe at the wonder of it, and Will stepped over to the nearest waterspout, plainly curious about how it all was working on gravity alone. Pierre leaned down and said lowly, "Do you like it, *mon ange*? Because I would gladly build you a replica as a wedding gift on our estate in Paris."

"A wedding gift," I said, turning to him in puzzlement.

But he was dropping to one knee and sliding a ring out from an inside pocket beneath that red boutonniere, all the while never dropping my gaze. He held my hand, and I felt Will catch sight of us and freeze, while everyone else turned from the spectacle of the fountain to the spectacle of us.

"Cora Diehl Kensington," Pierre said, love and earnestness in every line of his face. "You have stolen my heart as I pray I have sto-len yours. Will you do me the distinct honor of becoming my bride?"

I stared down at him as his eyes searched mine. I could sense everyone around us holding their breath. Only the fountain moved in that second.

I licked my lips. "Pierre! I…I cannot," I whispered.

Pierre's brows moved into a frown. "You…cannot? Certainly, you can, *mon ange.* Just think about what we could be together. Is this not the finest conclusion?"

"I cannot," I numbly repeated as if in a daze.

"You cannot," he repeated, rising, his face looking like I'd never seen it before, hard and…bitter. "Why?"

"Because," I said, "I'm going to marry Will."

CHAPTER 31

~Cora~

Felix let out a surprised cry and then bent backward in joyous laughter. He clapped slowly, a smile spreading across his face, but the others were shocked and uncertain as to what was proper in such an awkward situation. Pierre stared at me, stunned and hurt...and judging by the expression on his face, more than a little angry.

Will moved toward me, and the others parted the way for him. "Cora," he said softly. I wrenched my gaze from Pierre, hoping my expression told him how sorry I was as I turned to the man I loved most. The man who had claimed my heart from the start and was so right for me, in so many ways, took my good hand.

"Is it true?" he said in little more than a whisper, his eyes rife with hope. He led me a short distance away, still shaking his head. "You needn't allow his offer to—"

"No," I interrupted, unable to keep from smiling. "It's true. I choose you, Will. My heart has always known it, and today, I know it's right to give in to my heart's desire. It's you, William McCabe. I will marry you." A thought struck me. "Unless you've thought better of—"

He laughed, let out a little whoop, and bent down to pick me up at the waist and twirl me around above him. He was grinning, eyes wide, as if he couldn't quite believe this was happening.

Belatedly, we both seemed to remember Pierre. I looked over to him, even as Will slowly let me slide to the ground, taking care not to hurt my arm. Pierre appeared still stunned that when he actually offered, I could find it in myself not only to turn him down but to turn his invitation into an agreement with Will. His arrogance made me wince a little, confirming again that I had made the right decision. But I still felt sorry—desperately sorry—for hurting him.

"A word, Cora?" Pierre asked, pain etched into every syllable. His eyes moved to Will's, asking permission. "Just a turn around the garden," he said.

I nodded, moving forward, then stopped and looked back at Will, wanting to make sure he was all right with this. He lifted his chin. "No farther than around that bend, please, unless you want company," he said, gesturing toward Pascal and Antonio.

"There is no need for a guard," Pierre said stiffly, then awkwardly offered me his arm. I took it, feeling the lout again. Was he wanting a moment to try to convince me? Or to yell at me, releasing his anguish on me?

We climbed the sloping pathway in silence and, behind us, heard quiet congratulations being shared all around. At the turn, we entered a small building walled on three sides, set around a flower-shaped fountain pool beneath a woman's robust figure. This one did not yet flow, but there was water halfway up its walls, and the walls were wide enough to sit on. Despite the tension, I realized how weary I was and sat down first, concentrating on not fainting again, in order to give Pierre his due, once and for all. *And then be done with it.*

"Pierre, I'm sorry," I said, reaching across to take his hand. He allowed me to hold it, but he did not move. "I never wanted to hurt you. And I never suspected for a moment that you would make a public spectacle of your proposal."

"Forgive me if I offended," he said stiffly.

"No, no," I said with a shake of my head. "This is coming out wrong. I…I thought… I'm sorry," I finally said, knowing there was little else I could say that would make it right in any measure.

"How? How can you…" He paused, gathering himself before asking levelly, "How can you choose him over me?" His handsome green eyes were shrouded in pain.

"I…I simply know he will be a good husband to me. You and I," I said, with a squeeze to his limp hand, "have been mismatched from the start."

"But wasn't that part of the romance?" he said quietly, his eyes growing far away, as if he was imagining our first meeting aboard the ship.

"For certain," I said, slowly nodding. "But it was the start of an impossible romance, Pierre. A fantasy. Not a solid, God-given love."

He stilled at that. "I see," he said, pulling his hand away from mine and tapping his fingertips together. "You feel what you have with William is God-ordained."

"Yes," I said as gently as I could.

"And there is nothing I could do or say to persuade you otherwise?"

I shook my head slowly.

He rose, as if in pain, and offered me his hand. I took it and stood up, waiting for him to say what he needed to. "Then I bid you adieu, *mon ange*," he said, lifting my hand to his lips, and I saw that his eyes were wet with tears, which made me choke up too.

There was nothing to say but good-bye. No way to lessen the pain, nothing that wouldn't ring hollow in his ears.

But then a man behind Pierre, dressed in dark clothing, rose from an unseen doorway. He took Pierre in a choke hold, dragging him backward through the doorway and then disappearing altogether.

Stunned, I opened my mouth to scream. But it was impossible. Because a second man materialized behind me. He wrapped one arm around my waist and a hand around my mouth. He lifted me easily. I struggled, writhing back and forth, gasping in pain when the movement rammed my arm against the fountain. I was on my feet, desperately trying to gain purchase on the smooth tiles, trying to wrench away from him. I had to get away for more reasons than one. His hand now covered both my nose and my mouth.

My lungs burned with need, and I could feel my knees give way, ceasing their fruitless attempt at resistance. He was simply too big, too strong for me to fight off, especially when I was so recently injured.

My vision tunneled, quickly narrowing.

Will, I thought. *Will!*

And then all was black.

~William~

Will paced back and forth, twenty feet from the small alcove where Pierre and Cora had disappeared. It had been ten minutes or more.

Had they not had the time to say all they needed to say? Was the man trying to talk her out of her decision? Should he intervene?

He wrung his hands. She was his. She'd agreed to marry him! He couldn't get over his good fortune, God's grace, His mercy. After all this time, things were finally going to go his way. He could feel it.

His eyes moved to the end of the path again. Where were they?

He stepped forward, then thought better of it. He didn't want to be the cad, intervening when they'd only wanted a moment of privacy to say their good-byes. The poor man had just been turned down, humiliated…

But when his eyes met Antonio's and Felix's, and he saw that both men were clearly as anxious and concerned as he, he turned back to the empty path. He hurried up it then, Felix and Antonio right behind him, as he rehearsed one sentence after another as explanation for his intrusion and tossed each aside as inadequate. He finally faced the alcove into which Cora and Pierre had entered.

It was empty.

And it was only as Antonio joined him and walked around the far side of the fountain, then discovered the knob-less door, that the shout gathered in his throat.

"Cora!" Will cried. "*Cora!*"

He moved outside and around, shouting her name again and again as the others rushed to him. He turned to Antonio and said, "Stay with the rest, and get them safely up to the villa." Then he turned to Pascal and the other detectives and quickly dispersed them. He hoped, with everything in him, that Cora and Pierre had simply taken a path for a short walk, or gone upstairs to the villa because she was feeling poorly. Over and over, he banished thoughts of anything else. Of Pierre being a target for kidnappers himself. Of the two of them bringing twice the bounty—and thus being twice the attraction.

Will ran hard up the slope, past footmen clearing the luncheon table, past gardeners and fountain masters, calling Cora's name over and over again and even Pierre's.

But there was no response.

They had vanished.

"No," he muttered. It wasn't possible.

"Cora!" he screamed.

~Cora~

I fought back against the darkness, dimly recognizing that I was in danger, that men were carrying me, dumping me painfully into the back of a motorcar, then driving off with me. I blinked and blinked again, willing my vision to steady from a constant swirl that made me want to vomit, trying to decipher words as men shouted back and forth.

Where was Pierre? Was he with me?

Slowly, my vision focused, and I saw that I was bound hand and foot in the back of a motorcar, as I'd gathered. I was sitting tightly between two big men, both in the gardeners' uniforms I'd seen others in earlier. Across from us was a man with a large gun pointed at Pierre, who was also tied up.

We turned a corner too sharply and all moved to one side, the man next to me pressing against my injured arm. I yelped, and my vision became wavy.

"Oh, sorry," he said. *American*, I thought, and judging from the accent, East Coast.

"*Stai zitto!*" said the man with the gun, who was most definitely Italian. He waved his pistol at the American and made a show of clamping his lips shut and locking them. Apparently, they could not communicate beyond that.

"I don't suppose," I began, shrinking a little inside as the men gazed in my direction, "that you have anything to drink? I'm dreadfully thirsty."

The Italian with the pistol stared at me as if bored, then he waved at the American, apparently giving him permission to answer me.

"Nothing in here, sweetheart. Sorry. But it's not long until we get to where we're going." He reached up and pressed against the roof of the car, trying to keep from leaning against my injured arm again as we made another sharp turn. "Hawke!" he cried. "Ease up on those turns! There's no one behind us!"

I froze at the sound of the name, and the man looked over his shoulder briefly to meet my gaze. "Nice to see you again, Miss Cora," he crowed. "So pleased that you could drag your Frenchie into the mix one last time so that I could quadruple my earnings on a certain exchange."

He smiled at the man in the passenger seat, and my eyes shifted to Pierre. He looked terrible, oddly gray-skinned and with a bruise rapidly forming beside his right eye. Beneath it was a small cut with a short smear of blood, as if he'd brushed at it with his hands. He looked woozy, his head nodding down, then jerking up, then nodding again. "Pierre..." I tried.

His head jerked up again, and he looked over at me, grim and in obvious pain.

What scared me most was that he didn't say anything. No words of comfort, no light joke to try to ease my tension.

Because he was clearly as frightened as I was.

CHAPTER 32

~William~

When they reached the top of the hill, a footman looked over to them as if stunned. "They came so fast," he said, lifting his hands. "They had them," he said, gesturing toward William, Antonio, Pascal, and Felix, surely meaning Cora and Pierre. "They dragged them into the motorcar and *vroom*, off they went."

"Did you recognize any of them?"

"No, but two or more spoke English."

Will's heart paused and then pounded painfully. "Did one have blond hair, about this tall?"

The footman, eyes wide, nodded.

Nathan Hawke.

Pain and fury flooded through Will. How had he managed it? To track them here to this private estate and find the rare moment when Cora was unprotected? And not even that, she had been with Pierre...

The others had already begun running toward their motorcar, and Will did the same. He yelled over his shoulder, "How long ago?"

"Three or four minutes!"

"What color was the car?"

"Black!"

Black didn't help him. Nearly all motorcars were black. And three or four minutes? Was that enough time for them to make it to the main road? Or another road he wouldn't think to follow? *Cora*, he cried internally, anguished, as he jumped into the car beside Antonio, who pressed on the gas even as they were shutting the last two car doors. The car lurched, almost died, and then chugged up the hill and over it.

They drove pell-mell through town, dodging wagons and pedestrians and even a goat, and when they finally began to descend the mountain—and Will could see the upper half of the serpentine road exposed—he swallowed hard.

Because it was empty.

~Cora~

"Look out!" someone yelled up front.

We were all thrust forward, almost out of our seats, as the brakes were applied and then, abruptly, the gas. We fell back.

Up front, Nathan laughed and looked back at me. "There went your last hope! One lone police car, now off the road!"

We had finished trekking the last of the switchbacks down the small mountain, it seemed, and now Nathan was driving faster and faster. Clearly, he knew the police weren't my only protection. Did he think they would still be standing in the gardens, gazing at the fountains, wondering how long Pierre and I would tarry? I knew

Will wouldn't have been too patient. I wanted, with everything in me, to look back and see if I could spot his motorcar somewhere on the mountain road, chasing us, but I dared not. If Nathan wanted to believe he'd escaped them, so be it.

I was still hoping Will and the others would somehow appear behind us when the car lurched to a halt and the men roughly dragged us out, separating me and Pierre into two cars, half the men entering one, half entering the other. Pierre and I shared one last fleeting, grim glance. In a matter of seconds, we were off again.

This time, I did look back, watching in chagrin as our original motorcar pulled out behind us, going slowly, as if he wanted to be seen or wanted to create a physical barrier. I straightened and tried to gather enough saliva to swallow, thinking. *A decoy. He'll lead Will onto the wrong road...*

My eyes flicked up to see Nathan gazing back at me, a sly smile on his face. He did not have to say anything for me to understand.

Pierre and I were in deep, deep trouble.

There was one man to my left and one across from me. Two up front, including Nathan. I thought there was likely an equal number in Pierre's car, but I couldn't be certain. *Pierre...* I thought in anguish. It was all on account of me that he was in this mess. Why couldn't I convince him in Venice that we weren't meant to be? Why had he insisted on coming to Rome at all? And Tivoli? I shook my head. An arrow of guilt shot through me that I was glad I wasn't alone in this, glad he was in this with me, even if we weren't in the same car for the moment. *Pure selfishness*, I chided myself. I didn't want anything to happen to Pierre.

I knew that if Will caught up with us, or if I managed to escape, that was when it'd become most dangerous. Nathan wanted me and Pierre alive so he could extract a double ransom. Why else would he have taken us? It was why he'd tried before. But if I escaped, he'd want me dead. Because this time, he'd certainly be caught or hunted down. I would pay a hundred detectives myself to find him.

Nathan glanced back at me and then did a double take. "What is this?" he asked in a patronizing tone. "There is something new in your eyes. I do believe you're angry with me. But I didn't believe sweet Cora Diehl would ever look at me as if she wanted to kill me. You've changed since Vienna."

We went over a bump in the road, sending nearly all of us to the roof and back down, hard. It made my arm ache. I finally looked back at him. He didn't need to know that I didn't want him dead. Let him think what he wished. "You will pay for this, Hawke."

"Ooh," he said, poking fun at me. "I like this new turn in you. Beautiful *and* tough." He slapped the man next to him on the arm. "Is there anything more intriguing in a woman?" He looked at his cohort, then back at me.

"They will find us," I said. "And you will spend years in prison."

The motorcar slowed; we turned left, Pierre's car turned right, and the decoy car continued on straight. Hawke's grin grew wide. "No, Cora. They will not. Not where we're going."

We passed the next hour in relative silence. Once in a while, Nathan would try to engage me, but I ignored him, unwilling to give him the satisfaction. The men in back with me stared out the window. I considered trying to open the car door when we began to slow down, attempting an escape at the corner, but with my injured arm, the mechanics and viability of it seemed impossible.

Thinking of my arm made me consider how I broke it and my belief that someone had pushed me. Were the two events related? Hawke would've gained nothing by having me killed. Or had they only meant to weaken me, do exactly this—break an arm or a leg, making me an easier target? My stomach roiled at the thought, which made me also consider how often I had felt weak and queasy these last weeks. The fainting spells…could someone have been poisoning me? Could Hawke have paid one of our servants? Even one of the detectives who had pledged to protect us?

Nathan slowed our car, and the man to my side took my arm, as if anticipating my idea of leaping to freedom. "Stay back," he grunted, leaning forward, clearly not wanting people on the sidewalk to see me. Nathan had tucked his blond hair beneath a hat and kept his eyes low. Where were we?

Anxiously, I watched as we passed groups of people, caught fleeting glimpses of women holding babies, of old men and women. The streets were busy, but I had no idea where we were, even after spotting a couple of street signs.

"*Girare a sinistra*," said the other man up front, obviously giving directions. He went on directing Nathan up and through a neighborhood, then over a hill—at which point I saw a brief glimpse of the sparkling sea, a jarring contrast to my dark circumstances—and then through a few more turns.

We came to a quick stop, and one man got out, paused, then turned back to motion me out. The other car was right behind us, and I felt a surge of relief to see Pierre, to know that we might be together or at least in the same location. Nathan took my arm and ushered me down a side path, and again I saw the sea. We were high up, on a hill again, overlooking the ocean. But then the water was hidden by walls and the back of a villa. We entered a small structure, which appeared to be an old garden shed, about ten by fifteen feet.

Nathan took a length of rope and tossed it over a thick, ancient beam and then back down. Then he took my good arm, wrapped a slipknot around my wrist, and pulled it to the small of my back and around my waist.

"May I sit?" I forced myself to ask him, though requesting any favor at all burned. But with my fainting spells of late, I didn't want to break my other arm.

"No," Nathan returned rudely just as Pierre was led in by two men. They tied him in a similar fashion ten feet from me, across the room.

"Give her a chair, man," Pierre insisted. "We may be your captives, but she is still a lady."

Hawke gave us a sly smile. "But I am no gentleman."

"Clearly," Pierre muttered as Hawke left the shed and shut the door. We heard the crossbeam latch slide into place, and for a moment, I was transported back to Dunnigan, sliding the barn door closed.

I looked in misery at Pierre, well aware that I was very far from home. Perhaps never more so than this moment. "I'm sorry, Pierre. Had you not come to Tivoli, you wouldn't be here."

"But then you would be alone," he said, eyebrows knit together. The bruise beneath his eye was darkening. "I am glad I am here to help you. Together, we shall escape."

"Escape? Do you think it's possible? Or will we risk getting shot?"

"I'd rather be dead than pay that scoundrel a penny," he said, gesturing toward the door with his chin.

"Truly?" I asked.

"Well, perhaps I overstated it…" He gave me a slow smile. "But we must see that he is not paid. If we pay one kidnapper, we are doomed to a life of others coming to collect more of the same."

I took a deep breath and looked up to my tied hand, which was turning white from lack of circulation. I flexed my fingers and tried to not upset the slipknot as I wriggled my wrist, wondering if I just might free myself, but it only grew tighter. I assumed Pierre's bindings were the same. "How do you propose we make such an escape?"

"They want us alive," he said in a whisper. "Soon, they will bring food, drink, or release us to use the bathroom. At the least they will surely bring us something to sleep on. However you get free, when I give you the signal, you run."

"I run," I repeated. "What about you?"

"I will divert them."

"But what if you cannot escape?"

"Then you shall find someone to help me." His eyes shifted to the doorway and back. "Whatever happens, Cora, run. Hide. Agreed?"

I didn't like it. Leaving him behind, vulnerable to whatever abuse Nathan would mete out in his fury. The thought made me sick…but what choice did I have?

If one of us had the opportunity, we had to run for help.

CHAPTER 33

~Cora~

I'd been thirsty before, but as the minutes ticked by, I became desperate for something to drink. Pierre and I had stopped talking an hour ago, since every word seemed to make our throats drier. And I could no longer feel my hand. There was no window in the shed, but we could tell the sun's position by the light streaming through the slats of the door. It was getting toward evening; hours had passed.

"Do you think they will return today?" I asked. "Or do they intend to leave us this way for the night?"

"I don't know."

I couldn't wait any longer, even though pride demanded I do so. "I need some water, Pierre."

"I do too." He nodded at me and turned his head toward the door as he barked, "Hello! *Ciao*! Come!"

For a moment, there was no response, and my thirst seemed to triple. Had they left us altogether? Were they in another building? My panic grew.

But then we heard the scrape of worn wood, and a man appeared in the doorway, his hand on his pistol at his waist. "What is it?" he asked in a heavy Italian accent.

"We need some water," Pierre said. "We are no good to you if we die of thirst. And the lady is in need of a lavatory."

My cheeks flamed as he added this last bit. But I managed to nod, understanding now what I had not at first—the guard could place a glass to my lips for a drink, but he would have to untie me in order to get me to a lavatory.

The guard grunted and then disappeared through the door, sliding the board-lock closed again.

"No matter what happens, Cora, you go as soon as you have the chance. Do you understand me?" Pierre whispered, his tone urgent, his green eyes staring at the door. When I did not respond, he frowned and looked to me. "Do you understand me? If you are free and can get—"

The guard was back. He came through the door and left it partially open, since his hands were full of a tray with a pitcher and two glasses. He set it down on a workbench beside Pierre and then came to me. After some effort and grunts, he managed to untie my wrist. Then, keeping a firm grip, he guided me to the tray. "Pour yourself some water."

"I can't," I said. "My good hand is numb." I shook it and winced. "And my other is…" I gave him a plaintive look.

With a sigh, he poured me a glass and lifted it to my lips. Feeling like an infant but grateful nonetheless, I quickly swallowed it down, draining the glass. "Another?" I asked as sweetly as I could. "I'm so terribly thirsty."

Clearly irritated, the man poured a second glass.

"I-I think I can manage it," I said, even as I noted that my hand was filled with a thousand prickles, the circulation returning. I reached for the glass and tried to grab hold, but as soon as I attempted to lift it, the goblet fell.

The man swore and, without thinking, bent to grab the biggest piece.

That was all it took. I turned and ran to the door, but one thought made me pause. *Pierre.* It felt so wrong to leave him! But when I glanced back, I saw that the guard had straightened, a dumbfounded look on his face.

Pierre had managed to pull himself up by the rope and was swinging his body up to try to get the man's neck in a leg hold. "Go!" Pierre growled even as the guard struggled to keep his feet. Clearly, Pierre did not want me to try to free him. We had only seconds before others in the main villa—which I could see now—recognized that the guard was taking overly long in retrieving me for the lavatory run.

Another guard, carrying a pistol, rounded a corner, and as smoothly as I could, I moved around the shed's far wall. I could hear the struggle going on inside, the crashing of a glass, which was bound to draw the other guard in seconds. Without a thought beyond getting away, the desire to flee exploding within me, I pressed through the tall hedge, squeezing between big branches, hearing my jacket rip, feeling it scratch…

But in seconds I was on the other side, and having any sort of barrier at all between me and my captors made me glad. I held my breath and crouched as I heard a shout, and then another. I turned to look over my shoulder and almost gasped aloud. Because below me spread the corner of an ancient city—clearly an archaeological dig now—with entire streets exposed. It was empty at this hour, the sun setting across the sea in the distance.

I scurried down the short hill and then took a footpath between some trees, glad for anything that blocked me from the villa's view. I heard more shouts and broke into a run, panicked that I'd been spotted.

Around a bend, I dared to glance back.

They were after me. I took in three men tearing down the hillside, not bothering with the path—and then Nathan Hawke burst through the hedge.

I ran as fast as I could, jumping up onto a crumbling old stone half wall that surrounded the archaeological site and running down the eerily quiet, empty street that had to be thousands of years old. I dodged to the right, and then after a block, to the left, then right again, praying I was putting distance between me and my kidnappers.

Out of breath, I turned into a larger building with taller walls and slowed to a hurried walk, sliding from one room to the next. I paused periodically to hold my breath and listen but heard nothing. I saw the earth-hued frescoes and figures in Romanesque dress, confirming that this was indeed an ancient city. I thought about our location, near the sea, and it came to me then. I scanned the room hurriedly, and as I moved to the next, and out into an alley, I caught sight of the jagged, cratered tip of an old volcano shining in the setting sun.

I was in Pompeii.

Not wishing to be in a thoroughfare for too long, I moved to the next building, trying to make sure Mount Vesuvius was to my right every time I glimpsed it. In this way, I made my way steadily across the spooky abandoned town. With each passing minute, I thought I might have lost my captors.

But then I hit a broad expanse, an open area, with the remains of a temple on one end. It reminded me of the Forum back in Rome with its remnants of buildings, only a few remaining identifiable. I heard a shout behind me and started. Did I dare risk running across the grassy field? Or was it best to head to the side and use the remaining buildings to hide?

Another shout, unexpectedly close, pressed me into action. I ran across the field, trying to crouch, praying that God would shield me from view. But I heard a man exclaim behind me just as I reached the other side. I didn't stop to look. I continued my wild pattern through the city, taking a left, running a block, then taking a right again. Over and over I looked to Vesuvius, gaining my bearings and hoping that the men who followed me were too stupid to do the same. With luck, I'd send them into endless circles.

I passed another small temple, one with a small piazzalike area before it, and stopped to catch my breath again. That was when I saw him.

Nathan.

He was only two blocks away from me. He ran with frightening speed in my direction. I dived into the nearest room and through its window, then down an alley. I went into a larger home, through its open courtyard and into another room. On and on, until I wondered if I would ever reach the end of this city. How large was the site? Had Pompeii really been this big?

I'd just turned a corner when a hand grabbed my broken arm, wrenching me about. I screamed in agony, the pain threatening to make me drop in a faint. But then he had my throat in his hands and drove me back to the nearest wall.

We both stood there, panting, glaring at each other.

"Do you have," he began, "any idea…what trouble you…have caused me?"

"Sorry…to have…*inconvenienced* you," I returned.

Nathan smiled, and I glimpsed the handsome man I'd once met in far-off lands, connecting in our shared knowledge of Montana. And yet at that moment, I couldn't think of anyone uglier. He was ugly on the inside—a leech bent on sucking me dry. A parasite.

"Say I make certain you are paid," I said, still trying to pry away his choking fingers.

He abruptly dropped his hands, and I crumpled to the ground. He put his hands on his knees, clearly trying to catch his breath.

"Go on," he said.

"You cannot live a life in society," I said after a moment, rising to my knees. "You'd be recognized."

"Society does not have such a great hold on me," he said. "You mentioned making sure I was paid?"

"But you would live knowing you'd gained by ill-begotten means."

"I am not riddled with guilt by past sins as some are." He straightened and stepped nearer to me.

I stiffened, my back against the wall.

"Nor do most of us wake to find we're wealthy, rather than poor," he said.

He lifted me to my feet. He was terribly close. I looked to the right, as if he were a wild dog and I feared antagonizing him into biting me.

"You have some means. To travel to Europe. Enough to track me down," I spit out. I dared then to look him in the eye again.

"Some," he allowed. "But not nearly enough. You"—he took my arm—"are going to rectify that."

CHAPTER 34

~Cora~

Nathan hauled me to the nearest thoroughfare, one of Pompeii's ancient streets, where he spotted one of his men several blocks away. We turned and were heading toward him when a man came barreling out from between two buildings. He tackled Hawke, and the two of them fell to the ground, very nearly pulling me into the melee with them.

It was Pierre! He had escaped!

I stared at him in relief and hope, even as they wrestled, but when he pinned Nathan to the ground, he frowned at me. "Go, Cora, go!"

Hawke made use of his distraction and turned over, managing to pin Pierre to the ground. But then they turned over again. With the other man coming fast, I did as Pierre said, running back into the maze of buildings. Instinctively, I knew the second man would follow me, and my running would give Pierre more opportunity to keep the upper hand.

Out of breath, I made my way through another block, then turned a couple of corners and put my back against the wall, gasping for air, trying to gain control so I could be silent in a moment if he came near. My heart pounded in my chest.

If they got me this time, something told me I wouldn't get free again. I'd be under constant guard. After waiting another minute, and then fearing my pursuer had gotten ahead of me, I moved out again. But now I was cautious about turning each corner, my heart hammering in my chest. Would I ever make it to the end of this city that still echoed of death and memory and lives snuffed out in an instant?

I had just glanced up again at Mount Vesuvius, now glowing with a faint pink reflection of the last of the sunset, when a hand closed around my mouth.

I struggled, but the man shushed me and held me tight, and in a moment, I knew it was Pierre. I melted and then turned in his arms. He stroked my back, murmuring comforting words in my ear. "It's all right, *mon ange*, it's all right. They think we went to a different part of the city. We are almost to safety. I saved you." He leaned back and took my face in both of his hands. "You are all right? Do you need to get to the hospital?"

I shook my head, and he again folded me in his arms and kissed me on the forehead. "I was so frightened, *mon ange*, so frightened that something would happen to you."

"And I, you," I said, tears coming. They made me feel like a little girl, weak and dissolving, now that we were reunited. Now that I was no longer alone.

"Shh," he crooned, pulling from his pocket a handkerchief dusty from his scuffle with our kidnappers and handing it to me.

I wiped my eyes and blew my nose, but still the tears came. It was all too much. Pierre backed away and held my face again, his expression one of compassion and relief.

He smiled at me, his handsome eyes crinkling at the corners, and put an arm around my shoulders. "Come. We must get out of here and to someone who can get us to the police. Hawke may still have others looking for us." He took my good hand and led me down the street, pausing at the corner to scout it out, and then we went down another. When we finally reached a modern road with motorcars and horses and wagons and people, I dared to take a deeper breath and then two, but I knew what Pierre did—with Nathan about, there was still an imminent threat. We could be taken, kidnapped, right here, just as neatly as we'd been taken in Tivoli.

When we reached an empty storefront that had a big IN VENDITA sign, which I assumed translated as *for sale*, in the front window, we slipped inside. Pierre moved to one corner of the muddy window; watching and trembling, I stood close by, drawing comfort from his proximity. The rest of the rectangular room was bare, with cement walls. There was a door in back.

"Come," he said quietly, pulling me close to him again and stroking my back. I couldn't stop shaking. I was not cold, but my teeth chattered.

He kissed my temple again and gave me a squeeze. "It is all right, Cora," he said. "From here, we can keep watch for Hawke and look for a policeman."

"And if we do not see the police?"

"Then we shall go to the next store to see if they have a phone."

I nodded. Then I stepped away from him, suddenly aware that what I was doing was building an intimacy between us that belonged to me and Will alone.

Pierre's green eyes watched the flow of traffic, but more and more returned to me. He cocked a smile. "Now you have seen what I am made of, *mon ange*. I am not just a man who can throw the best parties in Paris or run a successful business."

"No," I said slowly, uncertain what he meant. "I've always known you were more than that."

His eyes moved to the street and then back to me. "And now God has shown you that I can protect you. Fend off your enemies."

I nodded, but my eyebrows knit in confusion. Hadn't we fended them off together? Yes, there was no doubt in my mind that I couldn't have done it alone. But what was he trying to say?

He turned away from the window and toward me, putting one hand around the back of my neck. I backed up toward the wall, feeling a wave of warning shoot through me, but he followed, his eyes filled with compassion and care. But also desire. That was what God was warning me about. Pierre had not yet given up his hope—thought he could convince me…

"Pierre, I—"

"Shh," he said, drawing close. He lifted his other hand to stroke my cheek, to push away a coil of hair falling over my left eye. Then he bent and kissed me, softly at first and then more demanding, his right hand moving to the small of my back, pressing me to him. Through it all, I froze and stood there like a dress mannequin.

After a moment, he backed inches away and looked at me, frowning. "What is it?"

"Pierre, no," I said. "I can't do this. I have pledged my heart—my life—to Will."

He let out a scoffing huff. "*Will*. Where was *he* through all of this? It is I who saved you," he said, pulling a thumb to his chest and leaning toward me. "I was the one."

"Yes," I said carefully, the hair standing up on the back of my neck, fear growing in the face of his sudden anger. "And I am grateful."

"Don't you see?" he tried, his tone softening to pleading. "Surely, we are as 'God-ordained' as you and Will are. Providence has seen us through." He picked up my good hand and studied it. "You must choose me, Cora. *Me*," he said firmly, nodding so earnestly, it was as if he believed he could talk me into it. "Be my bride, and I will never let anything bad happen to you again."

I gave him a wry smile. "Pierre, no one can promise such things. Bad things happen all the time. To everyone, rich or poor. All we can do is to promise that we will find our way through together."

I belatedly saw my mistake. He thought I was speaking of us, and he was kissing me again, joy and passion in his movement. But again I stood there, and when his lips no longer locked mine in place, I turned my head and waited.

He froze and then, a second later, dropped his hands, but he stayed as close to me as he'd been before.

He let out an exasperated sigh and then looked at me, bitterness lining his expression. "I have given you every opportunity."

"You have," I said, willing to accept blame if this would end it.

"Never have I pursued a woman as I have you."

"And you honored me with your pursuit," I said, shaking my head, still surprised that he'd done all he had over the summer.

"Papers around the world now wait for the outcome of our romance."

"Yes, I know," I said, feeling guilty for pulling him into my world at all.

"But still you would turn from me. Pierre de Richelieu."

His superior tone brought my head up. "It doesn't matter to me, Pierre. Your titles, your wealth. You could've been a fisherman on that boat crossing the Channel, and I would've been drawn to you," I said, pointing to the window. "But always, always, it was Will. You see, at the beginning, his uncle wouldn't allow—"

Pierre held up a hand as if every word out of my mouth burned him.

But I had to try to explain myself, help him understand why I gave him an opportunity even as Will and I were fighting what we felt for each other. I swallowed hard. "And my father—"

"Stop," he said, grabbing my shoulder.

His sudden movement scared me, and my lips clamped shut.

He looked down and shook his head. "Do you know how this shall appear?" he asked. "In the press?" He looked at me. "I shall be a laughingstock."

"Surely it won't be as bad as all that."

"So that's how you send me back to France?" he said with a sarcastic laugh. "After all this? With the hope it won't be as bad as I fear?"

I frowned. "What else can I do?"

He lifted his head then and looked at me, moisture in his eyes. Then he nodded, and relief flooded through me that at last, at last, he had accepted it. He took my hand, gently, and led me to the back door. I wondered why he'd abandoned his plan to wait for a police car, but I wasn't willing to question him about anything at that point, not when he was so…raw and…different. He opened the door a crack, its hinges squeaking their complaint, and peeked out.

He looked back at me. "I'll go for help," he said. "You stay here where it's safe."

I shook my head, not liking the odd expression on his face. Misery, I understood. The poor man had a broken heart. But was that guilt? "No, Pierre. Let's stay together."

"No," he said, shaking his head and lifting his brows. "We were apparently never truly that. *Together*." He was slipping out, and his words confused me.

More than that, the idea of being alone in this cement room terrified me. "Pierre…" But even as I reached for him, he pulled the door shut firmly behind him, almost catching my fingers. I bent my head to listen, worried I'd hear a shout, or worse, a gunshot. But then a second later, a different sound made me draw back in surprise.

He had whistled.

Or had it been someone else? A passerby, perhaps? Or maybe the police?

I scurried over to the front window, thinking I might see a policeman on horseback or on foot. Maybe even in a motorcar. But traffic was sporadic and slow as the evening waned. Only two cars and a wagon passed.

I thought I might take my chances and flag down one of them. Plead for help, even in English. I'd seen the Italian word for police back in Roma, on a building, nearly the same as our own: *polizia*. Even uttering that word would be enough.

I reached for the handle, deciding that Pierre had chosen his path but I would choose my own, when the back door slammed open.

I turned and saw Nathan Hawke pointing a pistol in my direction.

I blinked, not willing to believe what my eyes told me. He waved me forward, to him. "Come, Cora. Step away from the window."

The hope of a ransom no longer shone in his eyes. Instead I saw murder there. Which made no sense. What good was I to him dead? Or was that his angle now? Shoot me, and be long gone with the ransom money before Will and my family discovered my cold, dead body?

But I could see it in his flat expression, his mechanical movement. To try to escape would certainly mean getting shot. Was I willing to risk that?

No, it was better that he thought me beaten, cowed. Perhaps he'd forget whatever fury had changed his demeanor and return to his plotting to squeeze thousands of dollars from my siblings. Bending my head, I moved toward him. The big man from the car came through the door behind him, opening it wider.

"That's a good girl," Nathan crooned, pleased that I was being so compliant.

Pierre. It had been he who had whistled. He was the one.

He had left me for them, a sheep offered to the wolves.

No. It wasn't possible. It made no sense.

Why would he do that?

"Where are you taking me?" I asked meekly, not really interested, just buying a second. My tone sounded pleasingly beaten.

"Somewhere—"

I shoved Nathan then, pushing his gun arm upward. The pistol fired, setting my ears ringing, but I ran through the open door and started to turn left, saw two others, and veered right.

I tore down the alleyway, Pierre nowhere in sight, drawing on my fury at him to strengthen me. I felt the impulse to weave, in case Nathan was aiming again, remembering how hard it was to shoot the darting antelope back home, who turned one direction and then the other as they ran. A second later, a bullet hit the brick wall just over my left shoulder, sending a cloud of dust into the air, and a second after that, another to my right.

Thank You, Lord, I breathed as I ran, trying to hold my injured arm close to my chest. *Help me escape these men, Father. Guide me! Save me!*

Even now, I could feel them gaining on me, but I was nearly to the next street. If they wanted to kill me, they'd have to risk an audience.

I was not going to give up.

I was not going to give in.

I was not going to wait for someone else to save me.

God, I trust You alone to see me through this! Guide me! Show me!

I turned the corner, and the only person I saw was a fat old woman sweeping the front porch of her shop, closing up for the night.

My heart sank.

I need a policeman, Lord! Or a lot of men! Help me!

But I felt inexplicably drawn to the woman.

I continued on toward her, slowing my pace, feeling as if I were lost to my enemies already. Hopeless.

"Signora, I need help!" I cried in English. "Help!"

She looked up at me and frowned, her chin settling firmly in the rolls of fat at her neck. She wasn't even as tall as I! What was she to do? Fend them off with her broom?

I saw the men, just a block away now—Nathan and the big man from the car—then looked back to the shopkeeper. "Help! They're after me!"

I hoped my tone and the sight of the men pursuing me would leap our language barrier. Perhaps we could take refuge inside the store, place a call, if she had a phone…

She lifted a hand to my shoulder and glared at the men coming at us, her broomstick before her like a sword. *"Fermate subito!"* she yelled at them. *"Ci sono dei disordini qui fuori,"* she muttered to someone on the other side of the screen door, barely turning her head.

"Come, signora," I said, desperately pulling her arm toward the door. "Come inside!"

But she remained where she stood, unwavering. Her dark brows lowered as the men pulled to a stop but five feet away. I straightened my shoulders and stood slightly behind her. I didn't doubt that these men would pluck me from my spot, but I wouldn't give them the satisfaction of seeing my fear.

"It is all a misunderstanding," Nathan said, lifting his hands, gesturing to me. The woman surely couldn't comprehend his words any more than my own, but he was playing it as charmingly as possible. The role of the spurned boyfriend, or husband, perhaps.

She frowned and glanced back at me, probably wondering if she was entering a marital spat, but I shook my head. And the presence of the second man seemed to steel her resolve against them.

When a motorcar drove by at the end of the street, Nathan lost his patience, stepping toward me, but the woman lifted her broomstick and made a *tut-tut* sound.

Nathan grunted, sneered, and then reached for his pistol. But just as he drew it out, a man came through the store screen door, a rifle in his hands.

He leveled it at Nathan's temple, just inches away, and my attacker froze. "Whoa, whoa, whoa," Nathan said, lifting his arms, the pistol slack in his hand. His partner behind him began to reach for his weapon, but the old woman again made her *tut-tut* sound and nodded toward the glass.

Directly behind the window was a teenaged boy, also holding a rifle.

I took my first breath in what seemed like ages. "Is it true?"

"Is what true?" Nathan said.

"Was Pierre…somehow *in* on my kidnapping?"

Nathan looked away, clearly not wanting to say anything on the matter. But the fact that he didn't immediately dismiss it told me all I needed to know. Pierre *was* in on it, somehow. How could he? How could he be a part of all this when he purported to love me? And to leave me behind… His only thought had to have been that I would end up…

Dead.

No other supposition made sense. I shook my head. His words of going for help were said only to placate me, give him time to exit. But he never intended…

"*Polizia*," I said to the old woman. "I need to get to the *polizia*."

~William~

They had driven for miles on the roads about the hill town, desperate to find any semblance of a clue as to where Cora and Pierre had been taken. But all they discovered was the police pushing a car back onto the road, and the kidnappers' abandoned black motorcar. When they found it, and Cora's hat discarded in the back, Will thought all was lost. A part of him wondered if he'd ever see Cora again, alive.

Desperate, they returned to Tivoli to meet with a whole roomful of police officers—who were clearly thrilled with a case of this magnitude—and to make a plan.

But the police's plan was for them to stay put and let the authorities do their jobs.

The group had spent a large part of the afternoon and evening running back through their story, trying to summon patience as the officers took notes. Will paced, and paced, and paced some more. He was still pacing when a servant whispered in their host's ear.

Signore Biotti gestured to him. "Come, William. There is a phone call."

Will hurried over to the man and tried to suppress his frustration as they lumbered through the doorway of one room to the next, making their way to their host's office. Cora's sisters and brother followed behind, hanging back as if they feared they were intruding but sensing what Will did—they might finally gain some word of Cora. Signore Biotti handed him the telephone. Will moved so the mouthpiece was close to his lips as he placed the earpiece up to his ear.

"This is Will McCabe."

"Mr. McCabe, this is Captain Giovanni Russo in Napoli," said the man in Italian, his voice deep and raspy. "We have Signora Kensington here."

Will held his breath. "You do? Is she all right?"

The captain paused. "A bit worn from her ordeal, but she is all right, yes. A doctor is seeing to her now."

Will felt the blood pool to his toes in relief. But fear sent prickles over his scalp and down his neck. "Please, Captain. Can you please make certain she is under armed guard at all times?"

The man let out a scoffing noise. "We are in a *police* station, signore. I assure you, there is no place more safe for the woman."

"I know. But Signora Kensington's enemies…the men who kidnapped her—"

"Two of them are in our cells now. And the rest…I assure you that we have every available man on the hunt for them."

They caught them? "Who? Whom do you have? Do you have Nathan Hawke?"

"Yes. Come, and we shall discuss it further in person."

"*Grazie*," Will breathed in relief. To have Nathan…"*Grazie mille*. We will be there as soon as possible." He took down the address of the police station, and then he paused. "Captain, one more thing. You said you have Cora. But do you not have Pierre de Richelieu?"

"No," he said. "Pierre de Richelieu…escaped, it seems. We are still searching for him. Come, and we will tell you all of it."

"Right away. We'll be there soon."

They all hurried to their motorcars and made their way as fast as possible to Napoli, but the miles seemed to drag by. When at last they pulled into the police station, Will did not wait for the women—he ran inside, taking the steps two at a time. Madly, he looked about, hurrying past an inquiring secretary, down one hall and then another. At last, he saw her.

"Cora," he said from the doorway.

"Will!" she cried, leaping up and running to him.

He pulled her close, stroking her hair, which was wild and out of place, but she was well—she was whole. And they were together. "Cora, how I feared for you! How those men managed to grab you—in the space of an instant—" He leaned back and shook his head. "I'm so sorry I could not protect you."

"Will, no one could have protected me. Us," she corrected, but then she looked to the side, appearing confused. "They were intent on taking us. And I believe they had help," she whispered, looking up at him. "From inside our group."

Will frowned. "One of Biotti's guests?"

"No." So beautiful, so earnest, she took his hand and stared into his eyes. "Will, I think Pierre was a part of it. Somehow," she amended, as if she weren't quite settled with her suspicions herself.

Will's frown deepened. "P-Pierre?" he spit out. "But Nathan Hawke was caught and arrested, right?"

"Yes, but—"

The others found them then, surrounding them, hugging and giving kisses, the girls full of nervous chatter, the men shaking hands and clapping one another on the back as if they had personally been a part of bringing Cora here. The detectives had no doubt taken up position as Will had directed earlier—one at the back, one on each side of the building, and two at the front. If those who wished to do Cora further harm dared to come here now, they would die trying. Will had every man's word on it.

With everyone asking her at once, Cora sat down and related what had transpired, which sent the girls to gasping and the men to grumbling. The longer she went on, the more Will admired this girl he so loved—her tenacity, her inner strength, her courage when all seemed so set against her. But there she was, holding something back, racing over what exactly had happened with Pierre, particularly at the end...

What on earth had he said, done, to make her suspect him so?

"And then the most unlikely angel appeared," Cora said. "I had prayed for someone to help me, picturing a big, strapping man like our bear." She smiled shyly up at Will, then turned her face back to the Kensingtons and Morgans. "But no. It was the shortest, fattest Italian *mamma* you've ever seen! I thought I was lost. But she did it. She saved me with nothing but a broom!"

"Truly?" Felix asked, arms folded. "Nothing but a broom?"

"Well, that, and her husband and son pointing rifles at Nathan and his man," she added reluctantly, and the others laughed in approval.

"You will pull that story out for years," Hugh said, pointing at her in satisfaction. "Mark my words. People will beg to hear it, once the reporters get wind of it."

Cora's smile faded. "Always the reporters and their stories." She sighed. "I think I wouldn't resent it as much if they represented who we truly are. But there is only so much of us that can be placed in a column inch of newsprint."

"Perhaps we should be grateful for such limitations," Vivian said.

At that, Cora smiled and quickly agreed.

"Well, can we get you out of here?" Felix said, rising from his perch on the arm of the couch. "To someplace more comfortable for the night?"

Will nodded. "We'll go to a hotel I know about. My men can easily guard it because it has few entrances and exits. And I myself," he said, pointing to his chest and turning toward her, "will be sleeping at Cora's door. No one shall disturb you this night."

"But what about poor Pierre?" Lil asked. "What if he is still lost and looking for aid?"

"I don't think he is lost," Cora said softly, looking to the window.

"What?" Viv asked. "Do you know where he is?"

Cora shook her head. "But I think he is all right."

The room was silent.

"Ladies and gentlemen," Will said quietly, "do you mind waiting for us out in the lobby for a minute? I just need a word with Cora alone."

The others did as he asked, filing out, murmuring together. He closed the door and turned back to Cora, folding his arms. "So…tell me what you must."

She swallowed hard and looked to the window again, then back to him. "Will, I need you to think about how it would be, if you'd been in my shoes, in a dangerous spot, alone against so many…"

It was his turn to swallow hard. But he managed to nod. He thought he understood what she meant. That it had made things more…intimate for a time with Pierre for her. It made sense. She had to have been so frightened…

"Pierre thought…when we escaped Hawke's men for a time, when we'd made it to town…" She gathered herself and seemed to force herself to say the words. "He thought that I would be grateful. And I was, of course, but…"

"So, he…stole a kiss? Made an inappropriate assumption?"

"Well, yes, but…"

"Cora, please," he said. "This will be far less tortuous for me if you simply tell me what happened."

"He said that now I could see him as I saw you. As a hero," she rushed to say. "That *he and I* were as God-ordained as I had told him you and I were."

He took a breath. "I see."

She shoved away from the desk and walked a few paces, wrapping her good arm around her waist, and then turned to him. "But when I told him again, as I've kept repeating for days now, that I was yours, that I'd always been yours, he seemed…different. Angry. *Livid*, in fact. And utterly humiliated."

Will didn't know why this so surprised her. "That seems like a logical reaction. It's a man's response to—"

Cora shook her head. "He said he'd be a laughingstock. And then he seemed to turn away from me, inwardly. That's the only way I can describe it. As if we'd been in a theater, and the curtain came down, and he was on the other side. He said he was going for help and left through the back door."

"Perhaps he thought you were safe there, and he could find a policeman in time to—"

"He left me, Will. He pulled the door shut behind him, and he left me." She walked over to him, and he put his arm around her, waiting for her to go on. "And then he whistled, as if giving a signal. A minute later, Hawke and his man were there."

Will's blood seemed to stop. "He *whistled*. You think he *intentionally* gave you up to Hawke?"

Cora turned fearful eyes up to him. And then she nodded.

"But why? He loves you! Why would he *do* such a thing?" Will asked. It made no sense.

"I don't know," she said, shaking her head.

"You said he was humiliated. That he feared being a laughing-stock," Will said slowly.

Cora nodded.

"Could it be… Might he have set out to be a hero of sorts? Maybe he whistled for the police and inadvertently summoned Hawke and the others? If that's how it transpired—even if he sought to generate a story about his valor rather than as the spurned suitor—at least he didn't set out to see you harmed."

"I suppose it's possible," she said slowly, as if it didn't quite square with her memory. "It's better than thinking that he intentionally threw me as a sheep to the wolves."

"What about Hawke? Has the captain interrogated him?"

"He's with him now, I think," Cora said.

Will stared into her eyes a moment. "Let's go see if he's made any progress."

CHAPTER 35

~Cora~

Nathan Hawke was not talking to the police or anyone else when we left, nor the next morning when we stopped by the station again.

"He could simply be protecting himself," Will said quietly as we departed.

"Or his employer," I said. But after a night's sleep, I doubted my wild thoughts, wondering if I was so collectively exhausted I was liable to see a wolf behind every door.

"Has anyone heard from or seen Pierre de Richelieu?" I asked the captain. Will translated our conversation.

"No," the man said with a firm shake of his head. "Either Monsieur Richelieu is in hiding, or he is…indisposed. If he was still seeking assistance, he would be here by now."

Indisposed. I knew what the captain meant, and Will's look confirmed it. I blanched at the thought of Pierre, dead, regardless of my suspicions. "You will call us in Rome if you hear of him, in any way?"

"Si," he said.

I had persuaded the rest of our group to let Antonio take them on the long-awaited tour of Mount Vesuvius and Pompeii, but I elected not to go—the mere thought of getting anywhere near it sent me into a cold sweat. There were only two days left in Italy before we boarded the *Olympic*, and a hundred things to occupy a tourist's time. Yet I wanted to do nothing but hole up in our cozy palazzo apartments back in Rome—knowing that we were well under guard—and sleep, preferably with Will just around the corner.

I was so dreadfully weary, but I couldn't seem to doze more than minutes at a time. As he'd promised, Will had spent all night sleeping in a chair set firmly against the outside of my door. My sisters had insisted on sleeping with me, and we'd all crowded into the bed. And while I thought it endearing, I also listened to Lil snore softly and Viv smack her lips all night, which hadn't helped my fitful state.

Will and I arrived at the palazzo again that afternoon, and three or four reporters staked out near the front leaped to their feet. They rushed at us, all calling questions at once, but they all spoke in Italian. I didn't even look up. One word I could easily make out—*Tivoli.*

So word had already spread of this latest chapter in our story. It was sure to ignite additional fires and send others to our door.

"We can only hope," Will said to me, as he shut the ancient, heavy front door in their faces, "that none of them have passage on the *Olympic.*" Pascal moved into the main hall, away from us, giving us some privacy. Stephen had accompanied the rest of the group with Antonio.

I smiled up at him, new hope surging through me. He was right! We ourselves had done our best to book earlier tickets; perhaps any reporters hoping to ride along with us, once they found out our departure date, would find the *Olympic* equally full. "With luck, their only hope would be as a stowaway," I said.

"Bite your tongue," he said, cradling my cheek and tracing my lower lip with his thumb. He quirked a smile. "I want those six days of passage to be nothing but an idyllic pre-honeymoon. Long, languid dinners, good conversation, dancing…"

I kissed his thumb and smiled up at him, wrapping my arm around his waist. "That sounds perfect to me. Although I don't know how I'll fare on the dance floor with one arm strapped to my chest."

"We'll manage," he said.

I was turning to follow Pascal when Will caught my hand and turned me back around. "Cora…"

"Yes?"

He looked suddenly bashful, all traces of his flirtation a moment ago disappearing. He put his other hand atop mine. "Back in Tivoli, you said…" He paused and broke off, tilting his head as if summoning the nerve to continue speaking.

"I said I was going to marry you," I said softly, stepping closer and looking up at him.

He stared at me as if he didn't trust he'd heard me correctly. Or couldn't believe it.

"Yes," I said, nodding. "I want to marry you, Will. I don't know when or where. But after all we've been through, I know that life is fleeting. That we must take what we know to be true, right, and hold tight to it. And Will…you are the truest, rightest man I've ever met."

We shared a long smile, each of us trying to say with our eyes all we felt.

"I have so little, Cora. I—"

"Don't you see, Will? You have everything I've ever needed. I would sell Andrew Morgan all my shares in the mine in order to be with you. And I shall, if that's what it takes for us to be together. But I want more than anything to marry you, Will McCabe," I said, tapping his broad chest, "even if we were as poor as church mice." I stepped away from him. "My folks were as poor as church mice, all my growing-up years. Life was a struggle, hard." I shook my head. "But Will, oh, how they love each other. It's a good love. A right, true love. Like ours. And *that* is all I need."

He smiled and stepped toward me again. He bent to kiss me, softly at first, then deeply, searchingly. When he released me, I felt slightly breathless. "Let's do marry, then, love," he whispered. "Soon. Even aboard the *Olympic*. Would you like that?"

My heart skipped a beat at the idea of it, that soon. As soon as next week? But then, why wait? "Perhaps. It'd certainly be romantic…"

"But you want your folks there? Or perhaps a ceremony in your church in Dunnigan?"

I shook my head and looked up at him. "Honestly, Will, I don't think it matters to me." I stared into his eyes then, feeling such love and intensity that my eyes began to fill with tears. "As long as I have you…it's all I need. We can have a tiny ceremony with the captain alone, as far as I'm concerned."

He laughed in surprise. "Oh, my dear, practical girl. Your sisters would be sorely frustrated with us if we did that."

He pulled me over to a settee, sat down, and then urged me into his lap. "So we've established we want to marry. And soon. But we also want to be together afterward, right? How do you foresee us doing that, given our disparate goals, and that my life is in Minnesota and yours is in Montana?"

"Perhaps we could settle in North Dakota," I said with a smile.

"That'd be an awfully long train ride to school every day," he returned, smiling back. But his eyes remained troubled.

"Our goals are not all that different," I said. "And I've been involved in enough of the business of the mine this month to see that I don't want to fill my *life* with it. I want to be involved, influential, but Will, I don't want it to claim my life. I think that's what happened to my father…his business became him, overcame him. He loved it." I shook my head. "What I've done so far…I do not love. Endless numbers, tiresome legal documents…"

Will considered my words. "So what, then? You want out?" He sounded guardedly hopeful.

"No, not entirely," I said, rising and going to the window.

He waited where he was, for me to continue, and in my mind, I saw myself in Dunnigan again, and even in Butte. "I want to establish sound goals and fair work agreements. Hire a board of directors that won't let Andrew run roughshod over those goals. Hire an attorney I trust, to speak on my behalf when I am not in Montana, because I want to be free to leave Montana."

This made him smile.

"I think," I said, looking back at him, "Father gave me controlling interest because he thought it would keep me in Montana. Close to him."

Will nodded and rose. "He was…something. Your father."

"Indeed." I gave him a little smile as he wrapped his arms around me again. "He was imperfect, for certain. But in an odd way, I find it heartwarming that he wanted me close to him."

Will kissed the top of my head. "He was still discovering how smart you are. He would have been both confounded that you managed to find your way out of his plans and yet delighted. Perhaps you were more similar than you imagined."

At first, his words chafed, but then I smiled. The sun was shining on me and Will through the window, making our reflections dimly visible in the glass. And in that reflection, I studied my face; my lips and cheeks and nose so much like my mother's, but my eyes… my eyes were my father's alone. From the start, I'd recognized that unmistakable connection with him, with Felix. The deep blue that ran in the Kensington genes.

Was Will right? Did I take after my father in other ways? I'd spent so much of the summer resisting him, resenting him. But I could see what Will meant. There was a part of me that was surprisingly tenacious, that liked to consider all avenues toward a goal, then pick the best and champion it. I figured that if Father had lived, we would have often argued about the best avenues.

"I think," I said, and then faltered. "I think that I spent too much time being angry with my father and his attempts to control me that I lost sight of God's grace in the midst of it all." I put my good hand over Will's arms, which were wrapped around my waist. "I wish…I wish I'd spent less time standing against him and more time getting to know what was good about him. Because there was good in him."

"Some," he said, a smile in his voice, and I smiled too. "He made it…challenging to concentrate on the good, though."

I sighed. "Yes. But I think part of that was all the years he spent building one business after another, fighting for them, making him into a hard man. My mother," I said, dropping my voice to a whisper, "could've never fallen for a tyrant."

Will said nothing for a moment, only held me tight. But I'd needed to say the words. Not to condone the sin, but to recognize the humanity and fallibility we all shared. Even our parents.

"I'm glad your mother found lasting love with Alan," Will said.

"Sometimes," I said, turning toward him and looking up, "it takes a woman a little time to see who is best for her. Thank you for waiting for me, Will. For loving me, even when my heart was fickle."

"You," he said, leaning down to touch his forehead to mine, "have never had a fickle day in your entire life. Trust me, I know fickle women. And you are not one of them. You were simply…" He lifted his chin and smiled. "Misguided."

"Ah, yes," I said, smiling too. "I see." But thoughts of Pierre made me sober.

"What is it?" Will must've seen the change in my face.

"How can I leave, Will? Leave Italy without at least knowing he is alive? Without knowing what really happened?"

I could feel Will stiffen. "You wish to see him again?"

"What? No," I said right away. "Not see him in *that* manner. Only to make certain he is alive. To put to rest my crazy thoughts about him somehow being tied to our kidnapping in Tivoli…"

Will took a breath and stepped away from me. He cocked his head. "He'd best tell us he had nothing to do with Tivoli, or he won't be alive for long."

I laid a gentle hand on his arm. "In any case, we should pray for him."

"Pray for a man I may very well wish to tear apart limb from limb?"

"Yes, him, most of all, then."

~William~

When Cora fell asleep at last that afternoon, exhausted from her ordeal, Will quietly covered her with a throw, then slipped from the room and spoke to Pascal. The man agreed to take up watch right outside her door—and Will set two guards downstairs, outside the palazzo. No one would get in or out without them knowing. "And I don't want anyone save the Morgans and the Kensingtons to enter while I'm gone. Not even anyone you've seen enter this palazzo before. Understood?" Will asked.

Pascal nodded once.

Will knew the man didn't need to be told. But he was taking no further chances. He walked down the stairs and cautiously peered out, afraid he'd be accosted by reporters. But they all seemed to have given up on Cora emerging again today and perhaps had elected to make the most of an afternoon's siesta, as their favorite source of material had elected to do.

Will made his way down the street, moving quickly, anxious to get back, and then turned left. Another block down, he spied the wire office, and his heart began pounding. Was it there? A response to his query?

Inside, it was dark and quiet, except for the bell that rang as he walked in and shut the door. No one was behind the counter.

He grimaced, knowing that the man was probably taking a nap, as was customary, but that he was obligated to remain open because of the nature of his business. *"Buongiorno?"* Will called. *"Mi scusi. C'è qualcuno qui?"* Hello? Pardon me. Is anyone here?

"Si, si," grumbled a man from the back. Will could hear the telltale sound of squeaks and rustling, confirming his suspicions.

"I'm sorry to disturb you," he said to the man in Italian, trying to hide his smile at the man's hair, which was sticking straight up in back. "But I must know if I've received any telegrams in the last week."

"Name?"

"William McCabe."

The man turned and began looking through his cabinets, which were set up in alphabetical order. "Signore McCabe," he muttered, moving to the end.

Will's neck prickled with anticipation, and then he felt his heart sink as the man began to shake his head. *It isn't here. It hasn't arrived yet. What—*

But then the man perked up. "McCabe!" he said, pointing one finger up in the air as if he'd just thought of something. He went to the corner of his desk and riffed through another file. Then he pulled out the yellow paper.

Will grinned. He'd found it! "I'm so glad," he said in Italian. "I've been waiting weeks on that."

"Yes, yes," said the man nonchalantly now that the thrill of the hunt was over. "It came in last week. These," he said, waving dramatically at the row of cubbyholes, "are all from this week."

"Ah." Will gestured to the corner lamp. "May I?"

"Go ahead," said the man, already sliding on his spectacles and looking at other papers on the counter.

Will swallowed hard and went over to the light. He slid his finger beneath the small seal and opened the telegram and read it. Then he lowered it, grinning like a Cheshire cat at the waning sun that streamed through the window.

Will left the telegraph office, whistling all the way back to Cora.

CHAPTER 36

~Cora~

I awakened disoriented, the room in deep shadow. "Will?"

"I'm right here," he said from the wing-back chair in the corner.

"Oh! It's so dark in here I thought I was alone."

"I wondered if you might be sleeping through the night," he said, coming over to sit beside me as I pushed myself up.

"How long did I sleep?"

"Well, let's see now…" Will made a great show of pulling out his pocket watch, which made me smile. It was the one I'd given him—the one that had very nearly broken us apart. It all seemed so long ago. "About three hours," he said, snapping the lid closed.

"And I have the groggy head to prove it," I said, blinking, determined to fully rouse myself. We had only tonight alone; the others were not due back until late from Pompeii. I didn't want to miss a minute more of my time with Will.

"Well, let me see you to your room, Sleeping Beauty," he said, taking my hand, rising, "and ring for Anna to attend you.

I'd very much like you to freshen up and join me on the terrace for dinner."

I smiled, my heart alight at the thought. He'd planned supper while I was asleep? How utterly thoughtful! All summer long, I couldn't remember a single night that at least some of our group weren't with us, aside from that lovely few hours in Florence that ended so dismally. I practically skipped up the steps, despite my head being full of cobwebs from the nap.

Will rang for Anna, kissed my hand, and asked me to be ready in an hour. I shut the door as if I had all the time in the world, then hurried to my trunks, looking for the right gown—the pink one that I'd worn in Paris. I hadn't worn it much since. Anna arrived, helped me out of my day coat and skirt and dickey, then pulled the pins from my hair and began brushing it out. I wiped my face with a damp cloth—which did considerable work to awaken me.

"Oh, this arm," I said, frustrated by my bandages and how every movement still hurt.

"If you'd just sit ladylike and stay put for a while, the arm would heal well enough," Anna chastised me, still brushing. "But that isn't your way, is it?"

I met her gaze in my reflection in the mirror. "I never was much of a patient," I said. "There wasn't time for such things on the farm. You had to be running a mighty big fever to stay in bed."

"And breaking an arm isn't reason enough?" she asked, biting down on some pins, preparing to twist my hair upward.

"Well, clearly, that would have been a wise decision," I said, feeling the heat of a blush at my jawline. "Had I stayed back, not insisted on going with the rest of them to Tivoli after just getting out of the hospital, I might've avoided so much pain…"

Anna put her hands on my shoulders. "I was not chastising you, Miss, about Tivoli. You made your decision with the best of intentions—to remain with your sisters, your brother, your friends. It was evil men who turned it into something terrible."

I met her eyes, saw her sincerity, and nodded. She resumed pinning. In a minute, she was done, finishing with my pearl comb. "Lovely," I said, turning my head this way and that.

"Indeed," she said, cocking a brow.

I rose and followed her to the bed, where she helped me slip on the gown—an awkward, lengthy endeavor, given my arm—and then I bent to slide my feet into the delicate ivory slippers that matched. I rose and took in my reflection in the full-length mirror just as Will knocked.

Hurriedly, as Anna went to answer the door, I pinched my cheeks to add some color. I turned and gaped at Will. He was in tails, his shirt crisp and white, his tie perfect at the neck. "M'lady," he said with a flourish and a bow, then left his hand outstretched for mine.

"M'lord," I returned, taking it and grinning.

He tucked my hand around the crook of his arm and led me down the hallway, then up one flight of stairs, and still another. There, he opened a narrow door, and we climbed upward, single file. I gasped when I reached the terrace. "Oh, Will."

He grinned and looped an arm around my back, resting his hand on my hip. For a moment, we stood there together, looking out over the city of a hundred generations, cobbled together and yet somehow fitting exquisitely. Romanesque, Gothic, Baroque, and Neoclassical—all architectural styles I could now readily identify, thanks to the tour and Will's training. Domes and arches, columns and obelisks, loggias and rusticated building blocks. Far below us, in a small piazza, was a fountain of a reclining Nero, water spurting from his mouth into the pool that covered him to the hips. He was big and vibrant, like Rome itself. In the distance were the hills of Rome, and in the far distance, bigger hills moving into green mountains.

"It is beautiful," I breathed.

"You are even more so," he said, looking down at me.

I smiled, and he took my hand again and led me to a table for two set with cloth and crystal beneath a canvas-covered portico. I glimpsed him then: Pascal stood watch at the far corner and gave me a small nod and smile. He, too, bless him, was in formal attire.

"Even here we cannot be alone?" I asked Will softly as he moved in my chair.

"I will not have my fiancée"—he paused to give me a triumphant grin—"plucked from my hand again." He sat down across from me. "Even if my enemy comes on the wings of eagles, Pascal and I shall fight him off. You, Cora Diehl Kensington, shall remain with me."

I smiled and waited as a footman poured water into our goblets and then wine into our glasses. Another served escargot and tiny crostini with delicate wedges of cheese and tiny slices of basil. I was famished and ate everything on my plate.

"Breakfast was some time ago, wasn't it?" Will said, obviously similarly hungry. The footmen brought soup then, a rich minestrone, and then pasta. But I laughed aloud when they brought the most monstrous steak I had ever seen and set it between the two of us.

Will grinned at me. "*Bistecca*, a dish best served in Florence," he said. "But given that we left Florence in haste, I never had the opportunity to introduce it to you."

I gave him a wry grin. "This would feed an entire family in Dunnigan."

"But tonight, it is solely for the two of us." He gestured to it and rose. "May I cut a portion for you?"

"Please. And then I'm afraid you'll have to cut it into bites for me too, given my arm…"

"Of course," he said, more relaxed than I had ever seen him.

We ate. And talked. And ate some more, until I could not eat another bite. I leaned my head back, closing my eyes against the splendor of the city at twilight, memorizing the smell and sounds and tastes of Italy, a country I might never see again.

My eyes shot open. "May we return one day, Will? To Italy?"

He looked like a contented cat, across from me, chair shoved back from the table, tie loosened, eyes half closed. He met my gaze. "Of course. Whenever you like. Cora," he said, reaching across the table. "Don't you understand it yet? You are a woman grown. A woman of means. A woman of power. This tour has brought about changes in you—internally, externally—just as it does for everyone. Except in your case, it's tenfold. A hundredfold!"

I laughed under my breath. "I suppose you're right. But even given all that, I'd only want to return if you would come with me." I looked out at the city, then back to him. "It's where we finally found our footing. Together."

He smiled and nodded as he lifted his glass. "To our next trip to Italia."

"To our next trip," I said, lifting my glass and clinking it against his. I sat back again, sipping for a while, then set it down. "Will."

"Mmm?" he said, lifting one brow.

"You spoke of my means, my power."

"Yes," he said, now waiting.

"I would like to use some of that means and power to lobby for change in Montana, or Minnesota. Wherever we might be. So that women might obtain the vote." I held my breath. I thought I knew where he stood. But I had to be sure…

He considered me for a moment. "I take no issue with that." He turned the stem of his goblet in a circle, thinking. "I've told you before, Cora, that I believe women should have it. That women are far more capable than men give them credit for."

"I appreciate that, Will. It's important to me." I thought a moment and then went on. "And I don't need a big mansion. Servants. I mean, I suppose some might be necessary, but, Will"—I leaned across the table and took his hand—"I'd rather spend money on people. On projects, like Eleonora's orphanage, but in our hometown as well as here. I want my wealth to be a gift that benefits many."

He studied me for a long moment and smiled a little, silently acknowledging that I intended to keep my promises to Eleonora and more. "So you're telling me not to become used to being a kept man, with fancy watches and fancy duds and fancy motorcars. That you might give it all away?"

I smiled. "No. Don't get used to it."

"Okay, then. We'd best see to those university degrees then, especially me," he said. "I apparently still need to make a living wage."

"It's always good to have something to fall back on," I said, enjoying our game. I sobered then. "But honestly, I don't think you'll be satisfied until you get that architectural degree. Set about building your own portion of Rome," I said, gesturing outward.

"With my own funds," he said, pointing softly at me. "It must be with my own funds, Cora. The remainder of my schooling, getting set up in an office. A man can handle a wealthy suffragette for a wife if he has his own means of getting by."

"I understand," I said.

A footman arrived with dessert, and we both groaned. It looked wonderful and yet horrible, all at the same time. Confused, the man set them down and left, clearly wondering if he'd somehow brought us the wrong dish.

I rose, picked mine up, and carried it over to the long-suffering Pascal, who probably was sick with hunger by now. "Here," I said, lifting the plate and fork up to him. "Thanks for taking such good care of us, Pascal."

"It's a pleasure, Miss."

"We'll miss you when we leave."

"And I, you. This tour has been the most eventful duty I've ever had the privilege to experience. Vienna will be a bore after this."

I smiled. "Well, you never know whom you shall guard next. Perhaps it will be an even grander adventure. Eat up. I'll ask a footman to bring you a sandwich."

"*Merci*, Mademoiselle Cora."

The sound of strings brought my head around. A trio had entered the terrace floor and sat in one corner, warming up. Will strode over to me. "Would you do me the honor of a dance, Miss Cora?"

I gave him a wry grin. "If you don't mind dancing with a one-armed stuffed pig." Heavens! Had I said that aloud? When had I become so free with my speech around him? So ready to say whatever I thought?

He laughed, a great belly laugh, even as he led me to the open space of the terrace directly in front of the musicians. "Even 'full as a tick,' as Uncle Stuart used to call it, you are nothing short of sublime." He lifted his hand in order to take my good one, then wrapped his other arm around me. We waltzed through one song and then another, and still another, as darkness finally claimed the city and the footmen cleared the table and set out candles all about us.

"I'm sorry I don't have a ring for you yet, beloved," Will said. "I wish to purchase one at home."

He wanted to use his own funds, I understood, purchase it once he received payment from Mr. Morgan for the summer's duty. "Will," I said, leaning my head against his chest, "I'll be happy to receive it, whenever you find the right one. But I'd prefer a plain band."

"A plain band?" he repeated, leaning back to get a look at my face.

"Yes. My mother had a plain band. It was good enough for her, and it shall be good enough for me."

"I must say," he said with a dumbfounded sigh, "that you still manage to surprise me, even after being together all summer long."

"Maybe I'll surprise you all our lives."

"I wouldn't mind that," he said.

The longer I danced, the sleepier I became. The movement eased the ache in my belly, and by the time I walked downstairs with him, I thought I just might be able to sleep rather than stay up all night moaning.

At my door, he hugged me gently. Downstairs we heard the foyer door open and the noise of the rest of our group returning. He lifted a finger to his lips, obviously intent on keeping this night our own treasured little secret, then he bent to kiss me. "Thank you for the most marvelous night of my life."

"Oh, Will. Thank *you*."

"One more thing," he said. He reached inside his coat and pulled out a telegram. "Read this," he said, "when you are alone."

I gave him a puzzled nod. "All right."

"See you in the morning, my future Mrs. McCabe," he whispered in my ear, sending shivers down my neck and shoulder.

"In the morning," I agreed, then reluctantly pulled away from him and shut the door.

"Well, you two had quite the evening," Anna said from a corner chair, startling me out of my wits. "Oh, sorry!" she exclaimed, seeing my reaction. "Forgive me, Miss. I'd just come up, thinking I'd help you out of your gown and to bed, and then nodded off myself. I'm doing more and more of that of late. Perhaps my days of travel have come to an end. Best stay put in Butte next time your family decides to summer in Europe."

"Unless we stayed in England, yes? Then you could see your family."

"Yes, yes. If you decide to only go to England, I'd come along for that."

She attended me, and I soon locked the door behind her and slipped under the covers, telegram still unopened. He'd wanted me to be alone. And at last I was. I turned up the flame of my gas lamp and slowly unfolded the paper.

It was from my papa, I saw, my heart skipping a beat. FROM ALAN DIEHL it said, right there at the top.

MR. MCCABE – STOP – THANK YOU FOR DOING US THE HONOR OF REQUESTING PERMISSION TO MARRY OUR DAUGHTER – STOP – WE ARE CERTAIN THAT ANY MAN WHO MEETS CORAS APPROVAL IS GOOD ENOUGH FOR US – STOP – IF YOU WILL TRULY LOVE HONOR AND CHERISH HER YOU MAY PROCEED WITH OUR BLESSING – STOP –

Tears ran down my face as I read and reread the words, hearing my papa's gentle, firm tone, imagining Mama at the telegraph office, making certain it was all said right. I collapsed back against the goose-down pillows, thinking about how grand it was of God, to sort out the glittering promises of my life and make it clear what was truth and what was a lie. What I could cling to, count on, and what I could not.

And Will, Father. Will! Thank You for bringing me a man I could count on from the start. A man who knows where I came from and can see where I'm going, a man who is willing to walk beside me forevermore. You've blessed me, Lord. Far more than I could've ever imagined. But most of all in the love of this man.

I turned down the flame of my lamp until it was almost out, clutched the telegram to my chest like a hug from my folks, and in seconds, I slept.

CHAPTER 37

~Cora~

"Wake up, Cora," Viv was saying, shaking my shoulder. "Wake up."

"What? What is it?" I asked, sitting up, trying to get my bearings.

"I'm sorry, but you need to get dressed." Behind her, Anna bustled in, carrying my freshly pressed tan jacket and skirt.

"What's going on?"

Viv leveled her no-nonsense gaze at me. "Pierre de Richelieu showed up at the police station here in Rome, claiming men still pursued him. He said he's been on the run since he left you and hoped he'd given you the opportunity to escape."

"He did?" I scooted to the edge of the bed. An arrow of guilt shot through me for thinking the worst of him. "Is he all right? Is he hurt?"

"He's all right," she said, sniffing, "but when you hear what Nathan Hawke is now claiming as truth, you might not care."

I shook my head in confusion. "Why? What is he saying?" I asked, wrapping my dressing robe about me and moving to the chair to brush out my hair. Anna held out her hand for the brush, and I assented, but

I had to grip the table. "What is it?" I met my sister's gaze in the mirror. "I trust Anna to keep confidences," I assured. "Say what you need to!"

Vivian stood over my left shoulder as Anna stood over my right. "Perhaps it'd be best if Will told you."

"Viv!" I frowned, turning toward her. Her neck was so stiff, her tendons stuck out. For the first time, I felt fear. "I've never known you to hold back a single word from me! Even those I wished you had! What *is* it? You're frightening me!"

She grimaced and then shook her head, flinging out the fingers on both hands. "All right!" She knelt and tried to gather herself, then took my hand even as Anna continued to brush madly. "Nathan's story," Viv said, "is that he was after you for some time."

"R-right. I knew that. We *all* knew that." I winced as Anna tugged through a knot at my neck.

"But Cora," Viv rushed on, "he says he was working for Pierre de Richelieu. Since Venice. That Pierre told him to meet him in Rome."

Anna stopped brushing. I stopped breathing. But in the corner of my mind, for a moment, I felt triumphant. I'd been right about the whistle!

Then just as quickly, I crashed into confusion. What was this? How could it be true? How could Pierre have...*sent* Nathan after me? Were my worst fears true?

I rose, and Viv hastily did too, stepping away from me but following me, wringing her hands. "Cora..."

"Quickly," I said to them both, having trouble focusing. "My skirt, my jacket, my hat." I had to get ready quickly. Go and see these men, the police. Because if my suspicions were true, I wanted to witness the moment Nathan and Pierre were charged.

~William~

In the end, Cora wanted only Vivian and Will to come with her. Felix looked frustrated and Lil hurt, but Will knew the police wouldn't allow the entire Kensington-Morgan crew entry. Or at least close enough to hear anything, anyway. So he persuaded the rest to stay back, doing his best to distract and entice them with a visit to the great Roman Baths of Caracalla. Even Will doubted they'd listen to a single word Antonio uttered.

As they drove across town in silence—each of them too pre-occupied to chat—Will considered the marvel of the tour. How it could unite such disparate people as Vivian and Cora, women who had been so distant from each other in May, now as bonded as sisters raised together. Or was it God who deserved the credit?

The driver pulled up the motorcar outside the police station, and Will got out, assisting Viv and then Cora. Pascal had accompanied them, and he was last to come out, carefully scanning passersby for any sign of an enemy.

But Will knew what Cora now knew. Her enemy was inside.

He couldn't believe what the detective had come to tell them.

It was impossible. Pierre de Richelieu had loved her, right? Will had been as certain of it as Cora.

They climbed the steps, and Will was glad the chauffeur had been able to leave the reporters behind. Undoubtedly, the press would soon learn of this delicious new angle of Cora's story. But for now, they were in a bubble of blissful privacy.

Introductions were made, they were shown into a small office heavy with wood, and Will began translating for the women.

"Nathan kept up his silence for the last two days, refusing to say a word," the officer said. "Until he heard that Pierre had arrived here. That was when Nathan admitted he worked for him."

Will listened to the short, wide detective with a thick neck and bald pate go on for a while in Italian, then he turned to summarize. "They've brought Hawke up from Pompeii. They think that if they bring the two men together, and if you're here, the whole story will spill out." He narrowed his eyes at what the man said next. Reluctantly, he turned to Cora. "Whatever they say, they want you to go along with them." He shrugged. "Play the part. Are you all right with that?"

Cora looked at him, seeming alarmed and a little afraid, then gave a tiny nod of her head.

Will took her hand. "We have to see this through. To find out the truth once and for all. And hopefully be free of any known danger. Agreed?"

She nodded her head again. But he noticed that her face had grown paler. Vivian wrapped an arm around her shoulders. The sisters rose together and followed the detectives out into a bigger room with a long conference table in the center. Cora and Viv sat in the center, with Will between them and Pascal standing behind. The fat-necked detective sat next to Cora. A secretary came in to take notes and sat at the very end of the table.

"May I have some water?" Cora asked, looking even more wan than before.

"Of course," Will said, pulling a sweating pewter pitcher nearer and pouring her a glass. "Are you feeling faint again?"

"No. I think I'm only nervous, not sick." She lifted the glass with a trembling hand, and it made Will angrier than he already was.

Pierre had better deny any wrongdoing, or Will was liable to leap across the table and beat him senseless.

At last the door opened, and Nathan Hawke and Pierre de Richelieu were both led into the room.

"Cora!" Pierre cried, nothing but relief and joy in his tone. She stiffened, and Will saw Viv take her good hand under the table.

Only Nathan was chained, at the ankles. He shuffled forward, dragging the chain across the wooden floor. Pierre was simply attended by a broad-shouldered policeman, who kept a hand on his shoulder and pulled out his chair for him.

"*Merci*," Pierre said to him quietly. Will narrowed his eyes. Why the French when the man spoke passable Italian? Had he paid these policemen off? Was this all just a farce?

Pierre tried to catch Cora's eye. "I am so glad you are well, *mon ange*. It has all worked out!"

"Are you?" she bit out, surprising all of them with her vicious tone. "Has it?"

"*Aspettate,*" said the lead detective. "*Non parlate a meno che non è richiesto da voi una domanda diretta.*"

"He doesn't want us to speak unless we're asked a question," Will translated.

The door opened again, and a new detective entered, this one slim and elegant in his posture. He had a thick file that he tossed casually onto the table next to Nathan. They could all see clippings from newspapers peeking out the edge, as well as pages upon pages of notes. "I am Detective Bonaventure Beluzzi," he said in heavily accented English, with a suave smile all around. "We shall continue on in English, but I ask you to speak slowly and clearly, so that our pretty secretary can take good notes." He nodded down the table to the young woman, who looked like she might be blushing a little. "Her English is good, but not as good as mine."

"You still have not told me what is going on," Pierre said disdainfully.

"That is what we are here to ascertain, Lord de Richelieu," Beluzzi said, moving around the table. He walked with his head bowed and his hands together, touching at the fingertips. Will shifted back to watching Nathan and Pierre alone.

"Do I need an attorney?" Pierre asked.

"I don't know," Beluzzi said casually. "Do you?" He kept pacing. "Here is what we know so far. You and Miss Kensington were kidnapped from Tivoli. You were held by Mr. Nathan Hawke"—he gestured down to Nathan, continuing his slow circle—"and managed to escape. When you and Miss Kensington were in an abandoned store, she said that when it became clear that she did not return your… *feelings of love*…you left, ostensibly to go for help. But she had the distinct impression that you were handing her off to Mr. Hawke again."

"What? That is ridiculous," Pierre said with a shake of his head. He looked at Cora in horror. "I was going for help!"

"It is not ridiculous if what Mr. Hawke has said is true. That he works for you. That he was your 'last resort.'"

"I've told you already. That is a blatant lie. I've only seen this man once before our kidnapping—at a ball in Vienna."

Hawke was rubbing his index finger over a groove in the wood of the table, reacting to none of the conversation.

Beluzzi went on, unruffled, "Thankfully, Miss Kensington was able to escape Mr. Hawke again and was rescued by some shopkeepers. You"—he waved at Pierre—"made your way to us here." He frowned and looked puzzled, lifting a hand in the air. "And yet you did not summon the police in the two days you've been missing."

"I was afraid for my life!" Pierre said, waving his hands in frustration. "Two men were chasing me. I narrowly escaped them, again and again." He looked to Cora. "Only my desire to draw them away from Cora kept me going through these long days and nights."

"But did you not fear for her, leaving her, clearly injured, traumatized, alone?"

"Of course I feared for her! That is why I had to run. To give her a chance, possibly her only chance."

"Or was it to give your partners, just around the corner, theirs? Is that why you whistled?"

Pierre frowned, but Will thought he detected a brief shadow of guilt. Pierre's eyes flicked to Cora's again, and then he repeated, "Whistled?"

"To tell them to come? Miss Kensington heard a whistle outside the door after you shut it."

"No," Pierre said, shaking his head. "I don't know of what you speak. And I had no agreement with this man."

"You did," Nathan said at last, looking up at him with deadly calm. "It was exactly as they say. If you hadn't caught our attention, we might never have found Cora."

Pierre shook his head and lifted his hands. "He is lying. A liar and a cheat, trying to bring me into his game."

"We met in Vienna," Nathan said. "He knew he was losing his hold on Cora. That McCabe was stealing her heart." He seemed to relish saying that, tossing it at Pierre like a grenade. "He was desperate to hold on to her. And when they reached Venice…" He shook his head and quirked an odd smile. "Men in love do mad things." He sat back in his chair and stared at Pierre's profile, then resumed tracing the groove. "When we met again in Rome, Pierre discovered that Cora and Will were somewhat estranged. He hoped to widen the gap by making her doubt Will further." He sniffed, mischievous pride in his eyes. "With only a couple of moves we'd sparked jealousies that erupted into an argument, just as Richelieu had hoped."

Will thought of the night of the party in Rome—of Pierre's arrival when he'd been in the city for days, on the exact night that he saw the drawing.

"The sketch," the detective said, obviously on the same track. "How did you get it from Miss Cora's room? Shall we add thievery to your list of offenses?"

Will could feel the muscles in his jaw tense.

"I didn't take it," Nathan said, smiling without showing teeth. "It was given to me. Then I simply handed it along to another interested party."

Pierre scoffed. "I did not know this was story time for the children," he said to Beluzzi, who was still pacing in a slow circle around them, now with chin in hand. "Fables! Lies! How much longer will you allow him to go on?"

Beluzzi ignored him, eyes still on Nathan. "Are you telling us that you even went as far as to push Miss Cora over the edge of the pit in the Coliseum?"

Nathan remained silent, but his tracing of the wood groove paused for a telltale second.

"You were under a great deal of pressure," Beluzzi went on, now turning to Pierre, "weren't you, Lord de Richelieu? With your public pursuit of Miss Kensington. No one has ever spurned you. You've surely left a trail of broken hearts, but for a woman to leave you?" He shook his head. "Most men dislike such treatment, but the great Lord de Richelieu?" He paused behind Cora and looked over at Pierre. "It might have made you feel even… murderous."

Pierre's eyebrows knit together, and he lifted a hand to the detective, palm up. "And now it is you who begins to knit a fable."

"It is not a fable as much as words from your own mouth. Did you not tell Miss Kensington that you would be a laughingstock if it got out that she had turned away from you?"

Pierre looked at Cora, and Will saw a shadow of fury in his eyes. As if she had betrayed him! Will's hands tightened to fists beneath the table, and he reminded himself to breathe.

"Did you not wish to look like a hero to Miss Kensington, saving her from the kidnappers, just as Mr. McCabe had done for her in Venice? Were you not trying to level the playing field, as they say, Lord de Richelieu?"

"We are done here," Pierre said in disgust, rising. "You may speak to my lawyers. In France."

"You're not going anywhere without me," Nathan said, his fingertips resting over the groove.

"You and I are not tied in any form," Pierre protested, drawing away as if Nathan were clinging to him, though the man had not even moved. "I tell you, I never knew him outside our brief meeting in Vienna! When we *all* met him."

Nathan sighed and looked over at Will, Cora, and Vivian. "All I wanted was a nice ransom. A tiny sliver of the bounty in Dunnigan," he said to Cora, his tone bitter and indignant, as if she could've paid him off from the beginning if she weren't a miser. "And then I was stuck in Venice. I'd spent what money I had to get there. How was I to get home?" He lifted his hands in the air as if that were an acceptable explanation. "I was going to make another attempt in Venice—at Nell or Lillian at least, when Richelieu tracked me down. Set me on the task to meet you all in Rome and make certain that you'd practically fall into his arms."

Pierre leaned on the table with one hand and poked it with his other, emphasizing each word. "He is a liar. He cannot prove a thing!"

Hawke stared at him, even while he spoke to the rest of the group. "One man can tell you that I'm telling the truth, and that Richelieu lies when he says he is not involved."

Pierre shot him a deadly gaze.

"Who?" Beluzzi said.

"What do I get if I tell you?" Hawke asked.

"What do you get if you don't?" Beluzzi returned. "There is more than enough evidence against you, Mr. Hawke. If you want Lord de Richelieu to share some of the blame, to level the scales, you'll need to provide more evidence."

"I have no physical evidence," Nathan said plaintively. "Richelieu and I only had three conversations, nothing in writing. But we had an accomplice. Someone with his own reasons to take part."

"Who?" Beluzzi demanded.

Nathan's eyes flicked from Cora to Vivian. "Andrew Morgan."

CHAPTER 38

~Cora~

I stared hard at Nathan. "What did you say?"

His eyes moved to meet mine, and for the first time, a sly smile stole across his face. "You heard me. Miss Vivian's intended."

We all sat still, temporarily rendered mute. Even Detective Beluzzi stopped his ceaseless circling for a moment.

"This is preposterous," Pierre said, leaning forward. "This man may be in cahoots with Morgan, but I am not."

My mind spun. But for me, it was like the ingredients in a loaf of bread coming together and rising. More and more, I could see it. How these three men came together and conspired, all for their own purposes. For Hawke, it was money. For Andrew, it was power. For Pierre, it was for…

"How could you?" I said, shaking my head and looking up to stare at Pierre. "Regardless of your rationale, how could you put me through what you have? How could you risk my life?"

"*Mon ange—*"

"Don't call me that!" I cried, my voice sounding high and shrill.

Pierre looked as if I had struck him. At first, I caught a glimpse of frustration and pain, then in quick succession, anger and…remorse. It was gone as fast as it appeared, but I'd seen it.

He was in on it. I was certain.

Wearily, I rose, avoiding Viv's gaze. I didn't know if she had regained some secret hope for her relationship with Andrew in the last weeks, or if she was still biding her time to break it off, but this would certainly prove to be a key factor. She had to know just as surely as I did.

"Detective Beluzzi, it is as Mr. Hawke says. We will not know the truth until you question Andrew Morgan." I straightened in my chair, striving to appear every ounce the person in charge as my father once did. "Send men to search Andrew's belongings. Then meet us this afternoon at our rented palazzo, with these two in custody."

"This is ridiculous," Pierre said.

"If it is ridiculous, then we shall all soon know it," I spit back. "But I think you're afraid. Afraid of admitting the truth."

"Andrew could simply deny the whole thing," Will said.

"But he cannot deny a bottle of poison in his belongings," Hawke said, a smug smile on his face.

I gripped the back of my chair and stared at him. Once again, the entire room was silent. Slowly, Will rose. "Are you saying that Andrew has been poisoning Cora?"

Hawke looked even more smug. "Not enough to kill her. Richelieu here didn't want her dead. He only wanted her weakened, distracted from you."

Pierre scoffed at this and lifted a hand but said nothing. Will stepped forward, as if to dive across the table at Pierre, but Beluzzi grabbed his shoulder and arm. Will resisted a moment and then regained his composure. He wrenched away his arm, clearly seething.

But it was nothing compared to what I was feeling. "The fainting spells...the nausea, the weariness. He was putting the poison in what? My tea? My food? Upon *your* direction?"

Pierre only shook his head and looked up at me as if I were the one who was mad.

"Send men with us now," I said to Beluzzi, rising. "Otherwise, I might tear through every inch of Andrew's room myself."

"Don't do that," he said with empathetic eyes. "If he's guilty, we shall need the evidence."

"His father..." Vivian said, standing at last, looking sick. "It will destroy him, to find this out."

I wrapped my good arm around her shoulders. "Trust Mr. Morgan, Viv. It will hurt him deeply. But he is stronger than you think."

"Cora," Pierre called as we turned to leave. *"Mon ange!"*

I glanced back. "Do you know who recognizes angels, Pierre? The devil."

We were all waiting in the grand salon that afternoon when the others returned from touring the Baths of Caracalla. Even Mr. Morgan had elected to go with them. Eight officers in uniform stood about the room and straightened as they entered. Only Beluzzi was in a suit. Nathan and Pierre were in the corner, seated in two chairs, with a policeman on either side.

"What's going on?" Felix asked, stepping forward. Those who came through the door behind him ceased their conversation and turned to see what had so captured those in front. Andrew moved between the girls and detectives. His chin came up, and his nostrils flared at the sight of the men in custody.

Vivian rose from the settee, holding a brown paper bag, every movement looking like it pained her. She went to Mr. Morgan, whispered a word to him, squeezed his arm, and then stood before Andrew. I could see two policemen move between Andrew and the door. No one would escape this house.

"Andrew, Nathan Hawke has accused you of poisoning Cora."

He scoffed and lifted a hand. "What's this?" He gave her a confused look. "I have a temper, but I'd never resort to murder."

"You weren't trying to murder her," Viv said quietly. "You were trying to remove her. From Montana. From Kensington & Morgan Enterprises. From Dunnigan. You wanted her married to Pierre, just as my father wanted her to marry him, because it was good for business. And moreover, it was good for you."

"You've been reading too many dime novels," he said disdainfully. But his eyes moved to Nathan and Pierre. Clearly, he wondered what they had told us already.

"No, Andrew," Vivian said, her voice growing stronger. I knew his refusal to tell the truth was steeling her anger. "You have thought too much of yourself, thinking you were so above all of us, so in control, that you could even dally with my sister's *life*."

Lillian moved over to me, and I wrapped my arm around her shoulders. Felix moved to stand beside Viv.

"Where is this all coming from?" Andrew said, looking angry now. "From him? Hawke?" he said, flinging a hand toward Nathan. "You're going to believe the word of a man who has attacked and kidnapped Cora and Lillian? *Him* over me?"

"Kidnappings that you may have known about," Beluzzi said, stepping forward between Vivian and Andrew as Andrew's agitation grew. "Or at least…silently cheered on."

Mr. Morgan took a faltering few steps farther into the room, looking wan. He slowly pulled off his hat. "Tell us, my boy," he said softly. "Tell us it isn't true." Hugh and Nell moved to stand beside him.

"It isn't! They have no proof besides that lout's word!"

We all stilled.

Calling for proof…was that a partial admission of guilt? If he were innocent, would he not simply insist on his innocence? And he had looked to Pierre again, as if wondering if he'd told us more.

"Actually, we do have some proof," Viv said, holding up the paper bag. "Or evidence, anyway. Inside this bag is a bottle. A poison that would make Cora feel nauseated, weak, even lead to fainting." She looked back at me, and I could sense the others putting it together too, their memories of me feeling ill these last weeks, fainting. "And all over the bottle are fingerprints. Detective Beluzzi will make certain of it, but we suspect that they will match yours."

Andrew was silent for a moment. "Why are you doing this, Vivian? Why are you standing against me? You are my future wife!"

"No. No, Andrew," she said, shaking her head. "I am not. Regardless of what the fingerprints tell us, I will not marry you. Our courtship is over. Our promises broken—all the promises you made me over the years were nothing but empty lies. You've proven to be everything I feared and nothing of what I hoped."

The veins on Andrew's neck bulged. "It's her fault, Vivian!" he said loudly, looking at me. "She is the one who has poisoned you against me! We were fine until she came into our lives this summer. Everything was going as it should."

Viv stared hard at him. "So you felt that if you removed her, it would return to what it had been. What we had been."

"I'll freely admit to wishing Cora would go away. We were all better off without her!" he said, looking to his siblings and mine. "Don't you see? Weren't we better off without her?"

"No," Felix said, shaking his head and looking back at me. "I, for one, am a better person for knowing her. I'm glad for this summer. Glad she's entered our family."

"Me too," Vivian said. Lillian just squeezed me and laid her head on my shoulder.

"Us, too," Hugh said, looking at his sister. "Do not tie us into your ill will."

Andrew looked disgusted.

Vivian lifted the paper bag. "Isn't it best to admit guilt before you are convicted of it? Tell us, Andrew. Tell us why you did it."

When he still hesitated, Mr. Morgan said one word. "Andrew."

Andrew tore his eyes from Vivian, then looked over to his siblings, then to the Kensingtons, and finally back to his father.

"A month's pain for a lifetime of good," he muttered. "We all have to press through hard times in order to get what we want. And what I was arranging for Cora would hardly have been a trial for most women. To be the wife of the great Pierre de Richelieu. To live in a mansion in—"

"Cease your idle chatter, Morgan," Pierre growled. "I want an attorney present. Immediately." He turned to Beluzzi.

"For what?" Andrew said. "All is lost. All on account of your precious Cora. She's brought us down." He stared at me with venom in his eyes. I had to remind myself to breathe. "You couldn't simply accept what was being so freely offered to you. You had to do things your way, even if it harmed our families."

"She has not taken anything from our family!" Mr. Morgan cried, wrapping an arm around Nell. "It is you who has harmed us."

"Don't you see? I did it for us," Andrew said. "Even for her!"

Pierre groaned and put his face in his hands, but Andrew ignored him, only looking to his father.

"You can't see it, but I can!" Andrew went on. "She wanted to do business in ways that were foolish. Giving money that was rightfully ours away to the workers. Tripling the Dunnigan landowners' payment. What she plans might increase our future holdings, but for now, it will greatly reduce what Kensington contributes to our company in terms of cash flow. What opportunities will we have to bypass because of that? What will I be held back from conquering," he said, tapping his chest fiercely, "because she has crippled us? It simply makes no sense, Father. And consider Viv… Cora was pulling us apart. And haven't you always wanted us married as much as Mr. Kensington wanted it?"

Mr. Morgan looked up at him, clearly aghast. "So you did it?" he said in barely more than a whisper. "Poisoned her. Collaborated with Pierre and Nathan."

"Morgan…" Pierre warned.

Andrew ignored him, his eyes solely on his father. "I did it for us! Even for Cora. Don't you see? It was better for *all* of us."

Mr. Morgan's mouth parted as he stared up at him. "I have failed you, son, if you can somehow rationalize this evil deed. I'm sorry."

"Don't say that, Father!" Andrew cried, even as Detective Beluzzi handcuffed him.

Pierre and Nathan were lifted to their feet, and this time, I saw that Pierre was handcuffed too. "It is as Andrew said, Cora," he said. "I did it for us."

"And when you knew we weren't going to be together, you left me to die?" I sputtered.

"No! *No.* Hawke was to kidnap you and take you to Greece, then release you on ransom in a few months. *Mon ange*, I could never bear to see you harmed. I only sought a…diversion for a while. So that I could preserve my reputation and resume my life. Just as I hoped you would, in time."

I stared at him for a long moment of mute rage. *A diversion. For a few months. Preserve my reputation.* "And now we know why you and I were not meant to be together," I said, shaking my head. Such madness!

The policemen hauled Pierre, Nathan, and Andrew out of the grand salon.

Detective Beluzzi turned to us. "I am aware that you depart tomorrow on the *Olympic*. I must obtain comprehensive statements from each of you before you go. Some may need to return to Italy if this leads to a trial. May I return in an hour with a secretary to obtain your statements?"

When we only stood there, too numb to respond, Will said, "Give us two hours, Detective. All of this has been…a lot to take in."

The man nodded curtly, checked his pocket watch, and said, "I shall return then."

CHAPTER 39

~William~

His clients all gathered at the tall windows on the far side of the salon to watch as Pierre, Andrew, and Nathan were led out onto the street below them, and into two waiting police motorcars. Mr. Morgan sat down on the edge of a wing-back chair, as if he meant to spring up and run after them, if he could only figure out the right solution…

The younger women were crying, but Cora and Viv were oddly stoic. Perhaps too traumatized to shed another tear.

"How could we not have known?" Nell said, looking to Hugh.

"How could he do it?" Lil asked. "And think he was in the right?"

"Which one?" Felix said. "Andrew or Pierre?"

"Both of them," Lil said, shaking her head. "I can't believe either of them wouldn't have persuaded the other to…" She lifted her hands and paced away, then turned back, hands on her hips. "I don't know. To do right, instead of such wrong?"

"Do you hate me?" Nell said to Lillian, tears streaming down her cheeks. "Is our friendship over?"

"What?" Lil asked, wrapping her arms around her best friend. "What are you talking about?" She leaned back to see her face.

Nell cried with such intensity, it was difficult to make out exactly what she said. But it was clear she thought her brother's devilish choices, and an end to the courtship between Andrew and Viv, would tear the families apart.

"Never," Lil said. "Never ever! We are like sisters! Would you cast me aside if Felix had done something similarly dastardly?"

Nell shook her head.

"There, you see?"

"Still," said Mr. Morgan behind them, rising. He walked over and took Cora's hand in his. "I owe you an apology on behalf of the family. Had I known…"

"But you didn't," Cora said, giving him a sad smile. "I trust you, Mr. Morgan, no matter what your son tried to do. I know you as a man of principle. I know my father trusted you. And so do I. I need you more than ever, if Andrew is…indisposed."

Mr. Morgan nodded and patted her hand. "Thank you, child. You can count on my assistance. Don't you worry about that." He glanced over to Hugh. "I'll need you to step up, son. With Wallace gone, and Andrew…" He looked Hugh in the eye and set his hand on his shoulder. "I need you."

For the first time all summer, Hugh looked daunted. Yet he nodded, reaching to pat his father's hand. "I'll try my best, Father."

Mr. Morgan gave Nell a squeeze. "I think I'll go and rest for a while. I'm awfully weary after the day's events."

"Most of you must feel the same," Will said. "Detective Beluzzi will be back for those statements. Until that time, I suggest we rest and try to remember anything relevant to the case."

"But that feels terrible!" Nell wailed, and Lil embraced her again. "If I tell my story, isn't that like betraying my brother?"

"No, child," Mr. Morgan said from the doorway. Will thought his slim shoulders looked more stooped, as if he carried the weight of Atlas. "Andrew must see through what he started, even if there are repercussions for his part in it. We are all family, the Kensingtons and the Morgans. And Cora is a part of that. Everyone must face the consequences of their decisions. And everyone must be honest in his statements with the detective, even if we feel it hurts Andrew's case. We owe the truth to Cora, not lies to cover Andrew's sins. Do you all understand me? Tell the detective nothing but God's honest truth, or you shall answer to me."

Their last dinner in Rome, up on the terrace of the palazzo, was a somber affair. Every group that Will had ever been a part of had made it a celebration, often in this very place. But even Hugh and Felix were distracted, halfhearted in their attempts to keep conversation going and, for once, short on wisecracks and comments under their breath. Each was going home to a very different situation than he had left—Sam Morgan clearly expected Hugh to step into Andrew's place, and Felix had new responsibilities of his own.

As Will took a sip from his goblet, he considered them, then the horizon of Rome's rooftops. He doubted he'd ever seen a greater difference within a group after a solitary summer. Every traveler returned home changed, he mused, in small or big ways. And most went home to meet expectations. But these travelers were returning transformed.

When the footmen had cleared the last of the dishes, he looked down the table to Mr. Morgan, at the far end, and then around at the others. Antonio shot him a knowing glance, suspecting what was coming.

"On this night, it is the McCabe custom on the tour for each member to share what you think you will remember most about the summer. Much has happened for us all, these last months. For me, too." Will smiled and lifted his goblet in a silent toast to Cora. "I'm well aware that you all have suffered painful losses. But I'm confident you've gained, too. So give it a moment of thought, then let's all contribute what we think we will be taking with us in memory, into the future."

The table fell silent. Far below them, they could hear the *clop clop clop* of a horse's hooves on cobblestone and, in the distance, the beep of a motorcar horn. Shouts of greeting and laughter echoing up the stone faces of the grand buildings. Will pushed his chair back from the table and looked out to the skyline in coral-hued twilight. He so loved this city, as his uncle had loved it. But he was eager to return home, to let the next chapter of his life—alongside Cora—unfold. He wanted to meet her folks and determine how he and Cora might both manage her responsibilities in Dunnigan and Butte and make their way toward what God wanted them to do.

"I mostly don't want to remember this awfulness with Andrew," Nell said first. All eyes moved to her. "Is that terrible of me?"

Will glanced down to Mr. Morgan, who had bowed his head, and then back to Nell. "Obviously, it's unavoidable," he said gently. "But I'd be very glad if you remembered other things too."

She nodded a little and looked to her lap for a moment, then again to him. "Then I shall remember the grand parties in all the grand places we've stayed, and all you've taught us, Will. It will stay with me forever."

Will smiled.

"And while this was the place we lost Father," Lillian put in, "I also think I got to know him better here. He worked hard, of course, but here and there…I don't think he and I ever chatted more than we did these past weeks. I'm grateful, in a way." She gave a little shrug. "You know. For the difficulties we faced, because it brought him and Mr. Morgan here. If Father had died…" Her voice broke then, and she paused to gather herself. "If he had died at home, alone, it would've been awful, I think."

Felix gave her a sad smile and covered her hand with his. Then he looked up to Will. "I think I'll remember jumping into the Rhône the most."

"Hear, hear," Hugh said, lifting his goblet. "And the women of France. And Italy. And England. And—"

"*Hugh*," Mr. Morgan interrupted.

Hugh lifted his hand and smiled his apology. "The women have been extraordinary," he dared to add as he quirked a smile. "But, McCabe, you've been a fine guide as well. I know we've not been the most attentive students, but you've been more than attentive as a bear. As Nell said, I will remember much of what you taught us in the years to come."

Will smiled in surprise. "Thank you, Hugh."

"I believe," Vivian said, twisting her glass in a slow circle over the linen cloth, "that I'll remember this summer as the one in which I gained a sister." She looked up at Cora. "One I didn't want at first but can't imagine being without, now. And if it weren't for the tour, journeying through the good and bad together, I don't know if that would have happened at all."

Cora smiled, and tears immediately welled in her eyes. "Oh, Viv. Me too. You, and Lil and Felix... I never imagined..." She shook her head and wiped away an escaped tear with the corner of her napkin, then looked at each of them. "I'm so grateful. So grateful you all are my family."

"As are we," Felix said.

Cora looked at Will. "This will forever be the summer I lost everything I thought I had—my home, my proximity to my folks, even a sense of who I was. My identity. But it will also be the summer that God used the tour to rebuild all of that into something eternal, regardless of what happens in the future. And it will be the summer that I found new love." She smiled softly at him, and he thought he'd never seen her look more becoming than she did in that moment. "The love of a fine man, and the love of family I didn't know I had."

The table fell silent, except for the sniffling of the women.

"Wallace would be so glad to be here, hearing all this," Sam Morgan said quietly. All eyes shifted to him. "He would have been proud of his children." He nodded to them all. "And he would've shared in my pride over you, Nell, and you, Hugh. He would have shared in my sorrow over Andrew's choices, but then he would have stood with me in seeing him through the consequences of that, too." He heaved a sigh and then looked up again. "We sent you off on the *Olympic* as children. But as we embark tomorrow, I know that I am in the company of a fine group of adults." He lifted his glass and looked down the table at Will. "We owe a debt of gratitude to you, Will. And to you, Antonio. Thank you."

"Hear, hear," Felix said, raising his, too.

"Hear, hear," the others echoed.

CHAPTER 40

~Cora~

The next morning, I wore my dreadful mourning crepe, as did my sisters. On board the ship, Will thought it would be satisfactory to wear black arm bands, but in attendance with our father's body, nothing but the formal black seemed right.

My eyes moved to the men carrying our father's casket past us, in solemn procession, up and into the ship. People parted before them, frowning or looking distressed, as if recognizing the import of the casket's presence for our family. Many, despite the good seal on the casket and the embalming of my father's body, lifted handkerchiefs to their noses.

But then Antonio was before me, a welcome distraction, giving me a hug and a kiss on both cheeks and taking my hand. "Cora," he said, smiling at me. "I will anticipate hearing about your progress through young William's correspondence. He will be a fine husband to you, and I know you will be a fine wife for him. I look forward to greeting you as Mrs. McCabe."

"Thank you, Antonio," I said, feeling the heat of the blush at my cheeks. Discussing our marriage made it seem impossibly real. I was going to marry William McCabe! The thought of it left me with nothing but joy, and I hoped with everything in me that we wouldn't have to wait long. Even the prospect of parting in New York left me feeling melancholy.

"I would very much like to have a photograph of the two of you when you do marry. I know you will be a beautiful bride."

"I will remember that request," I said. "It makes me smile, thinking of you returning home to family and friends after this sojourn with us, Antonio. Thank you for taking such good care of us this summer."

"It has been my pleasure." He kissed my hand and then reluctantly let me go, moving on to say farewell to the others, along with the rest of the detectives, who would now be free to return to their homes in France and Italy. Seeing Nathan Hawke escorted away by the police had done a great deal to settle our fears about potential kidnappers. And for the next six days of the crossing, we would have no one but Will, Felix, Hugh, and Mr. Morgan to protect us. It felt sufficient to me. The sooner we could get back to a semblance of normalcy, the more content I would be.

Our farewells said, and our belongings already aboard, we followed the rest of the first-class passengers. I looked to the dock halfway down the ship, where a multitude of third- and second-class passengers stood waiting to do the same. They looked upon us as if we were heroes of some sort, some actually waving, and I lifted my hand to wave back.

Vivian looked to whom I waved, the jet stones of her broach flashing in the sun. She lifted her eyebrows. "Must you?"

I laughed. "Three months ago," I said with a sigh, "I would have been fortunate to be in *their* number, affording a ticket aboard the *Olympic* at all. Is it truly so unseemly, sister?"

She shook her head as if too weary to argue and edged ahead to join Felix. I sighed. For as far as we'd come, we still had a distance to go.

Mr. Morgan took the place she'd left beside me. "Does it trouble you, leaving?"

"No," I said, looking his way. "I am eager to see what lies ahead."

He walked with his hands behind his back. "You take after your father, that way. Wallace was always wondering what was around the next bend in the road, what business opportunity might arise."

I thought about that for a moment. It still surprised me to think I was in any way like Wallace Kensington, but that forward-thinking drive was not anything I could pinpoint in my mama or papa, so I supposed he was right. "Do you mean not to say your last words to your father until the funeral?" Mr. Morgan said, stopping beside me, as those in front of us hit some unseen delay.

"Pardon me?"

"Your father's body. The others, your sisters, your brother, saw him at the hospital. But you, child...I've noticed you avoid it. It's important to say your piece, say your good-byes."

I grimaced inwardly at the thought. Why was it so important? Could I not say my farewells while staring at the swirling waves of the sea rather than beside the empty corpse of my father? But it seemed important to my siblings, too, that I do this dark deed. Almost as if they could not close that particular chapter of our tale until I had read the part as they had.

"I admit I've avoided it."

He took my elbow, and we began moving again, up the gang-plank. "May I ask why?"

"I'm not entirely sure."

He nodded. "Wallace's casket will be in a private hold, to which I'll have access. Perhaps you'd like me to accompany you at some point on the journey? We could each say one more good-bye. Though I think we'd best keep the casket closed."

I nodded hurriedly, but inside I railed against the idea. Visiting a casket in the loud bowels of the ship seemed more like something out of a scary tale than some peaceful, meaningful moment of parting.

~William~

Two days into their crossing, Will passed the *Olympic* Mercantile & Fine Goods store. He had gone fifty paces when he stopped, drew himself up, and turned around. There, in the corner of the window, he saw it. A beautiful white satin dress overlaid with gossamer-thin lace. Atop the mannequin was a matching crown and veil, and at the bottom were tiny slippers also covered in lace. Beside the slippers was a card that read, *Why Wait? We Can Arrange Your Romantic Shipboard Nuptials. Inquire Within.*

Will smiled and tapped his lips. She'd said she'd like to marry whenever, wherever, but had she really meant it?

He altered course and took the stairs nearest to him, heading to Lillian and Nell's room. Five minutes later he reached it and knocked on the door, then straightened his jacket, hoping he didn't look as feverishly excited as he felt.

"Who is there?" Nell asked, as he'd instructed them all to do before unbolting the door.

"It's Will. May I see you and Lil for a moment?"

He heard the bolt slide aside, and then the door swung open. "Come in," Nell said, gesturing to the tiny sitting room with three chairs that blocked off the rest of the first-class cabin. "Please, sit," she said. "I'll go and fetch Lillian. She's just changing for a walk about the decks with Vivian."

"It's a good day for it," Will said.

Nell left him alone, and in a few minutes she and Lil both returned and Will stood up, just as Viv came to the door.

"Perfect," Will said. "I wanted to speak to you all, actually." They all sat down. "I have an idea," Will said nervously, wondering if he was making the biggest mistake of his life. "Downstairs, in the merc, they have a bridal gown for sale. And…"

The younger girls leaned forward slightly, eyes wide. They looked at each other and then to him. "Cora's seen it!" Lil said, grinning. "She loves it!"

"Sh-she does?" Will said, both surprised and pleased. "Well, I was wondering…what would you two think of a surprise wedding? Could we pull it off? A wedding in a few days? Do you think she would like it?"

All three moaned with pleasure and began speaking at once.

"I could take care of the flowers!"

"And the cake. I adore cake!"

"I imagine the captain would perform the ceremony."

"Or would you think Cora would prefer the chaplain?"

Will laughed under his breath, watching as the three of them fired questions and comments at one another and, on occasion, him.

But it was clear that they were off and running. After a while, he interrupted. "If this goes as I wish, it would happen on the last night of our voyage. A late-afternoon ceremony, a private dinner in the dining room, dancing."

"Oh!" Lil said. "It would feel as if the entire ship were a part of it!"

"One grand party!" Nell added.

Will nodded with a smile. But then he sobered. "I only have two hesitations."

"And those are?" Viv asked.

"Would Cora want to plan it? Be a part of it?"

Vivian tapped her lips. "I don't think so. She's a practical girl, at the core, and I know she wants only to be your wife. I think she'll consider it romantic, this surprise."

Will smiled, feeling a jolt of excitement as the word *wife* echoed through his mind.

"What was your second hesitation?"

Will shifted uncomfortably and swallowed hard. "I…I, uh… Well, you see…"

Viv smiled in understanding. "If your second hesitation is in regard to funding…"

"Well, yes," Will said gratefully. "You see, I don't get paid until the end of our tour. I could reimburse you when—"

"Nonsense," Viv said, dismissing his thought with a wave. "We are Cora's family. It's only right that we prepare her trousseau as well as get her everything she needs for the nuptials. The girls and I will see to all of that."

"Thank you," Will said.

"Cora went to the hold with Mr. Morgan, so we could go to the mercantile now!" squealed Lil. But her words gave Will pause.

"To the hold?" Will asked, frowning in puzzlement.

The smile slid from Lillian's face. "Yes," she said with a sigh. "Cora agreed to visit Father's coffin." She looked to Nell. "Mr. Morgan felt it important."

~Cora~

Mr. Morgan slid a key from his jacket pocket and unlocked the heavy door. Inside was a narrow room barely wide enough for a person to walk beside the casket, which was set on the wood floor and strapped into place to keep it from sliding in heavy seas. He let the door shut behind him after I pulled the string on a single bulb hanging above us.

I swallowed hard against the faint stench. "Why?" I whispered. "Why are you forcing me to do this?"

"Because it's important," he said gently. "You only met the man a few months ago, and now he's gone. He was a hard man, and he put you through hard things, Cora. If you don't do this hard thing, it may haunt you for the rest of your life."

He poured a few drops from a bottle of cinnamon oil onto a handkerchief and handed it to me to hold beneath my nose.

I hesitated and then took his crisp, clean handkerchief with the initials SJM embroidered on the corner, shaking out the folds. I held it to my nose and mouth and concentrated on breathing in the sweet, spicy scent, which was strong enough to cover the odor, then nodded to Mr. Morgan, signaling my readiness.

I ran my hand down the length of the coffin made from rich mahogany, which had been sanded and finished to a fine sheen.

My father lay inside. He'd swept into my life and fairly overpowered me in so many ways, and yet now here he was, powerless.

Mr. Morgan looked down to his shoes, then back at me. "When I was a boy, my father died, far from home, and was buried there. For years, I felt like he might come home at any moment, come through the door, be somewhere that I could go and talk to him. I think if I'd had a moment…" His voice cracked, and he looked down and to the side as if embarrassed, sniffing. "If I'd had a moment to recognize that someone who'd been so powerful, so forceful in my life, was no longer present, that he'd moved on, I wouldn't have been so haunted by his memory. I could move on, knowing he'd given me what I needed to work, to succeed. After I'd said good-bye."

He looked down at the casket and then back to me. "Wallace was a powerful, forceful man, like my father. Part of him is evident in you." He paused before adding, "Now say your piece, and I'll wait for you outside the door."

With that, he left me. The heavy door made me jump a little as it shut. I wished I was outside, with him, rather than trapped here with the shell of my father's body. I didn't have anything to say to him, did I? Hadn't I said all there was to say?

I licked my lips and cleared my throat, imagining Wallace Kensington nestled inside the casket, serene, his skin waxy and gray. I coughed and tried to gather my thoughts. "I suppose I want to say that…"

What mattered? Now? To me? After all we'd been through, after all that was done?

"I suppose I wish you were still here. To teach me what I need to know about the mine, about running a mine. I'm glad Mr. Morgan is with me. But I wish I could say thank you," I said. "Thank you for doing what you didn't have to. For giving me and my parents a part of the mine. For providing for us. Whatever your reasons…" I ran my hand along the edge of the coffin again and looked back at where I imagined his head was. "Thank you. I wish…" My voice cracked, and I frowned. "I wish we'd had more time. To find our way with each other. Whatever that was supposed to be."

I paused, but there was no more to say. My mind was utterly blank. I decided Mr. Morgan had much more he wanted to say to his father than I did to mine. I started for the door when it came to me. I rested my hand on the edge again. "Oh, and I suppose I wish to say I'm sorry. That I was stubborn for so long. That I wasted some time that we could've had. I know it wasn't all your fault. And also that I forgive you. I mean…I'm still rather angry about some of the things you did and how you did them. I'm angry that you tried to control me rather than love me. But I forgive you."

I shook my head and swallowed hard, tears now rolling down my face, surprising me again. "I don't want to live life as a bitter woman, Father. And so I choose to forgive you and move on." I nodded. "That's it," I added, shrugging and feeling like a little girl who had gone on and on, now embarrassed. It awakened other memories, and I shifted my weight to the other foot, frowning. "I also didn't like that you treated me like a little girl at first. That you didn't respect me or my mother when you came to the farm. You simply took over. That was not right. You took advantage of us at a weak moment, to get your own way."

I leaned back, rocked by my own anger. "And yet you gave me so much," I whispered, shaking my head. It boggled my mind, thinking of what he'd left me. What he'd brought me into. "Mostly, I'm grateful," I said. "In spite of the trouble between us. Mostly I'm grateful." I repeated the words, nodding, the feeling clarifying inside me. "Thank you. Thank you, Father." And as I said those words, I could hear an echoing prayer in my heart, for my heavenly Father, who had seen it all, led us all, whether we recognized Him in it or not.

With that, I dropped my hand from the casket and turned toward the door.

The door cracked open, and I could see Will peeking in. "You all right?"

"Yes," I said, my chest feeling light and free as I took my first deep breath in what seemed like ages. "Better than all right."

He opened the door wider, and Mr. Morgan's eyes met mine, gently curious.

"Turns out I had more to say than I thought," I told him, taking Will's arm.

"That's the way of it, most times," he said. "And that Wallace…" He cocked his head, then shook it. "He cut a wide swath. Which was sometimes good and sometimes bad. But mostly good."

"Mostly good," I repeated, smiling at him. "That's how I'd summarize it too."

CHAPTER 41

~Cora~

It was a lovely day to be aboard the *Olympic*. The seas were calm and the air brisk but warm as we steamed toward the eastern coast of America. I was getting excited to be home, on US soil tomorrow, and soon to be reunited with my parents in Minnesota. How good it would be to see them, to hug my papa and feel strength in his embrace again. To hold my mother's hand and tell her I understood, at long last, about mistakes and making the best of past decisions. I wanted to take them shopping and see them purchase at least one item simply because they wanted it—something I'd never ever seen them do. I wanted to make sure they were in a soundly built, comfortable home.

All this I was telling Will as we took a midmorning stroll about the decks, and gradually, I noticed that he had become grim in countenance.

"Will? Is everything all right?" I wondered if he was worried, if things were changing between us, now that the reality of reaching home was upon us.

He turned to me, a very serious expression on his face. "Cora, I fear I've done something terrible."

My heart sank. "What is it?"

He hesitated, and I wanted to shake him for making me wait.

"I think I've made a terrible mistake."

"What? What happened?"

He took my good hand in his and looked down at me, his brows knit in concern. "I thought it would be romantic... You see, I was walking along past the shops downstairs and..."

"Will. What is it?"

He seemed to gather himself and took a deep breath. "Listen to me. We can call the whole thing off. Do this whenever and however you wish. But I took the liberty of...Cora, I planned a surprise wedding for us today."

I stared at him. "You did *what?*"

"We bought you a gown. And veil. And slippers! Your sisters and I organized the ceremony and a small reception. Scheduled the captain to come and do the honors." He bit his lip, studying my face. "But listening to you talk about how excited you are to see your folks..." He shook his head and ran a hand through his hair. "I was an idiot. All I could think about was marrying you, Cora. Of spending the last night on the *Olympic* together as man and wife. Of how romantic it would be...I wanted to leave this ship, step on American soil, together, united forever. But I was a fool."

I smiled up at him and shook my head. "Why'd you think yourself a fool?"

He hesitated, and in that moment, I'd never thought him more adorable. "Well, now I'm thinking you'd rather have the wedding in

Minnesota," he said. "Or Dunnigan. That every girl likes to plan her own wedding. And after all you've been through this summer, you'd probably really like to plan something yourself, rather than be thrust into another's plan."

I looked out to the sea for a moment, then back to him. "William McCabe, I think that out of all the amazing events of the summer, marrying you will be the height of it all. I want you as my husband. And I think marrying you today and returning to America as your wife would be a marvelous idea."

His sorrow-filled face turned to such utter joy, it made me grin too. "Are you certain?"

I nodded, and he picked me up by the waist and turned me in a small circle, grinning up at me. I was aware of other strollers pausing, or giving us a wide berth, but I kept my eyes on Will. My fiancé. My *husband*, as of tonight.

He set me down gently, then leaned in to kiss me, not caring who saw us. Then he offered me his arm and we set off on our stroll, feeling like we were already walking an aisle. "So would you have liked to be surprised in a couple of hours instead? Did I ruin it, confessing?"

"No," I said with a laugh. "A couple of hours' preparation for a girl's wedding is probably a good minimum."

"We could have another ceremony—or a reception!—with your folks."

I paused and turned to him. "Oh, Will, my folks will be delighted that we are together. They will love you and celebrate our love, rather than worry about the wedding."

"You're certain?"

"I'm certain," I said, nodding. "Now, you'd best escort me to my room. I apparently have a wedding to dress for. And you've already seen the bride on her wedding day. That's bad luck!"

"No bad luck that God's blessing can't cover. And Cora, my darling girl," he said, stroking my cheek, "all I can feel of late is that blessing, flooding over and around us."

"I think I know exactly what you mean."

I felt like I was practically floating down the stairs and down the hall to my room. I fished a key from my purse and realized my hands were trembling. He took it from my hand and slid it into the lock, opening the door for me. "Luncheon will arrive for you at noon. And your sisters will come and collect you when it's time." He lifted my hand to his lips. "Think you can get ready quickly?"

"I think I can manage that." I turned to enter, but he grabbed my hand and turned me back around. He leaned down and kissed my cheek, whispering, "Next time we enter this room together, it will be as man and wife." Then, with a mischievous smile, he closed the door, and I was alone.

I stared at the door a moment, trying to collect my thoughts. I was getting married. *Married.* Within hours! Then I slowly turned around and looked at the gown that had been carefully laid out on my bed.

It was beautiful and must've cost a fortune. His sweet gesture, and the idea that he had planned all that lay ahead, made me tear up. Thinking about it, I didn't know if I would've had the strength to plan our wedding in the coming months anyway, on top of everything else. I picked up the gown and laid it against me, turning to the mirror. It looked like it would fit perfectly.

I set it down again and moved to the veil, which was attached to a heavily beaded crown, and set it on my head. I'd have to get Anna to work with it, to make my hair more sleek and smooth, with a knot low on my neck, but the veil was beautiful too. Even the slippers looked perfect—I doubted Will had known my shoe size. Anna or my sisters must've helped him with that. Perhaps with all of it. Whoever had done it, they had done a smashing job, and I couldn't wait for it all to begin.

Suddenly, I wished we had married weeks ago. Perhaps it would've circumvented all the nastiness with Pierre and Nathan if I had simply said yes in Florence when Will asked. But I hadn't been ready then.

Now, I felt completely, joyously ready. There wasn't a shadow of doubt in my head or heart. There were challenges ahead, logistics to negotiate, but nothing we couldn't do together. Of that I was certain.

Anna came with my luncheon at noon, a light salad and soup with a roll and tea. "I thought you wouldn't want to eat much," she said, setting the sterling tray down on my table.

"Heavens, I'm not certain I can eat a thing," I said, rubbing my belly. I'd managed to get out of my morning ensemble of the skirt and jacket and lace dickey and into my dressing robe.

"Well, you need to eat something," she said, straightening and smoothing her jacket. "You may no longer have poison in your system, but if you don't eat anything, your knees might give way beneath you during the ceremony. We can't have that."

"No, I suppose not," I said tiredly, sitting down before the tray. I took off the dome over the soup, and steam rose into the air. Perhaps I could manage a few bites of it, even with my jitters.

Anna moved swiftly into brushing out my hair and smoothing it into exactly the kind of knot I'd envisioned at the base of my neck. I watched her in the mirror, wondering how she'd managed to read my mind. "So you're ready to become Mrs. McCabe, are you?" she asked, winking at me.

I sighed. "I think I've always been ready to be with Will. It is like we were meant to be."

"I'll say," she said, lifting her brows and beginning to pin. "It was as if everyone could see it but you. When that Pierre came sniffing about, it took everything in me not to scream."

I was silent a moment. "So you could see him for what he was?"

She frowned and glanced at me from behind my shoulder. "What? No. None of us knew what a ne'er-do-well the man was. I only knew that *William* was right for you, Miss Cora. Knew it in my bones."

I smiled, relieved that I hadn't been a complete idiot in thinking Pierre was a man to consider, even if he distracted me from Will for a time.

"No, you've crossed your bridges and suffered your share of losses to get to this day," Anna said. "Even Mr. Kensington would bless your union, child."

"You think so? If he were here?"

"I know so," she said, resting her hand on my shoulder a moment.

I did my best with just one arm to fuss with powder, some kohl liner around my eyes, and a pot of rouge, applying just a little color to both my lids and cheeks. Happily, after the days of rest at sea and the distance from the trauma behind, I found that I was looking far more robust than when I'd left Italy. Had Will surprised me with a wedding in Rome, I might've needed far more assistance.

In the end, I attempted to screw on the rouge lid, but Anna had finished my hair. "Ach, let me see to that," she said and took the pot from me. She glanced at my reflection in the mirror. "You've done a fine job, Miss."

"Thank you, Anna."

"Now let's get you dressed. The minutes are passing at frightening speed."

I looked to a wall clock, and my eyes widened in alarm. She was right. It was only a bit of time before my sisters would come and escort me to the chapel…

Anna helped me into my gown and gingerly worked the delicate lace sleeve over the clumsy cast. "My, my, this gown is so lovely, and you so lovely in it, no one will even see that cast," she said, intuitively relieving my concern. I knew she wasn't entirely right, but as I turned to the full-length mirror and she buttoned up the back, I knew she wasn't completely wrong. With a bouquet of flowers…

But I truly didn't care then. I was marrying William McCabe. He loved me, and he didn't care a whit if I was a broken-winged bird at the moment. He wanted me as his bride. Me.

The glory of it, the honor of it, made me misty-eyed.

Anna finished her buttoning and smoothed out the shoulders. She came around me and clasped her hands together to her chest. "Oh my, Miss Cora. You are so completely lovely that our dear Will might stumble overboard when he sees you."

I laughed. "I hope not!"

But then I turned back to the mirror, to memorize my image, to remember this day always. The beautiful silk draped over my shoulder and ended in lace at my elbows. At my waist was a wide, gathered band of silk and a wide silk rose on my left hip. The skirt was several cascading layers of the silk, cut at a diagonal and edged with six inches of lace. Each progressive layer grew progressively tighter, and yet from the back, an elegant, small train trailed behind me.

"Oh, he did choose well with this gown, didn't he?" I said, delighted.

"Better the girl inside than the gown upon her," Anna said, setting the crown and veil atop my head. She lifted a pouf of my hair above the pearled crown, leaving the knot low. I sucked in my breath. How had she known how to do that? I looked like the most chic of women in Paris!

A knock sounded at the door, and when Anna opened it, my sisters and Nell came in, all murmuring their appreciation over my appearance. Vivian wore a deep green dress with black lace at the bottom edge, a white collar, and a fanciful black hat that reminded me of something an artist might wear. Lil wore a gorgeous butter-yellow gown with black stripes on the edges and a tiny band of black in her hair with a long, black feather. And Nell was in burgundy, with ivory lace and long lace sleeves. All three wore black arm bands just below their right shoulders.

"Well, don't you all look glorious too!" I said. "Far better than the mourning crepe."

"My father," Nell said proudly, still fingering the lace of my dress as if it were an exotic animal, "said that *your* father would turn over in his grave if he saw us all in black on such a happy occasion."

"It's true," Viv said, taking my good hand. "He'd want us to be celebrating in every manner. And so we shall," she said, offering her arm to me as Anna knelt before me, obviously intent on helping me into my shoes. I stepped into the white slippers and marveled that these, too, seemed to be meant for me. I might even dance in them this night and not form blisters! But I felt so reckless that I thought that I might even go barefoot, should I feel the first rub.

Another knock, and Nell pulled open the door. In walked two footmen, each carrying two bouquets of flowers. For the girls were sweet nosegays of ivory roses, and for me, a giant bouquet of ivory and white roses with delicate, fragrant lilies of the valley interspersed between. I wondered over the amazing resources of this fine ship—every night, we had fresh flowers on our tables in the dining room, too.

"Oh, aren't they lovely?" Nell said, dipping her nose into the nearest. "Utterly delightful." She turned to me. "A man who could choose so well will certainly be a delightful husband, too."

"I believe so," I said.

The footmen left, and we spied Hugh and Felix in black coats and tails outside the open door. "May we escort you lovely women to a wedding?" Hugh asked.

"Oh!" I said, covering my mouth with a hand. "I hadn't even thought of it," I murmured, almost to myself, thinking of Papa, so far away.

Hugh raised a brow. "An escort down the aisle?" he said, reading my expression. "I know you'd like to ask me, but I think you really ought to ask your brother."

I smiled and turned to Felix, but he was already stepping forward. "No need to ask, sweet sister. It would be my honor," he said, with a smart, short bow.

He straightened, his smile wide, and offered one arm to me and the other to Viv. Hugh escorted Nell and Lillian, and we stepped out of the cabin, Anna right behind us. I made sure of it, and she nodded, looking like a proud mama as she followed. Other passengers stopped to admire and nod at us, parting and standing politely at the side to let us pass by, murmuring their congratulations and good wishes. For some reason, that alone made me want to burst with joy, having strangers wish nothing but well upon us.

By the time we'd descended a flight of stairs and made it partway down another aisle, I was slightly out of breath. But we could already hear the music—a string quartet—playing inside. Felix turned to me. "Ready?"

"In a moment," I said, trying to regain my composure. I turned to Viv and Anna, wishing I could touch my hair, make sure it was all right. But as I turned, seeing their smiles, I knew nothing was out of place. All was well. And it was time.

"All right," I said, taking a deep breath.

"I'll go in and stand with Father and Will," Hugh said. "The musicians will know you're ready then."

I nodded.

He touched my arm and bent to give me a swift kiss on the cheek. "I'm so glad for you, Cora."

"Thank you, Hugh," I said, looking up at him. Then he slipped through the door. The song ended, and another began.

"It's our cue," Vivian said. She nodded to Lil and Nell, and the two lined up. A footman opened the wide door and kept it open. To me, it felt like a curtain on a stage. Inside, the small group of guests—people we'd met aboard ship, along with the captain—all rose. But my eyes sought out Will, blocked in a frustrating way for a time by my sisters, and then, as the music moved to "The Wedding March," beautifully visible, staring at me alone.

He was so handsome, looking so smart in his black tails and white bow tie. And the way he looked at me as Felix and I came down the short aisle…well, it was so intense it made me want to laugh and blush all at once. How was it that I was so blessed to be given a man like this as a husband?

He forced himself to look at Felix as Felix stubbornly held me back. "Take close care of her, man," Felix said gruffly, "or you shall have me to answer to."

The two shook hands, each hiding a grin, and then Felix placed my hand in Will's.

And in that moment, as I felt the heat of Will's palm, the fast pulse in his fingertips…as we moved through the vows to love, cherish, and honor for all the hours and days of our lives…I knew it.

I knew hope.

I knew the power of promise.

I knew who I'd been, and who I now was, and who Will and I would be together.

And above all, I knew love. In me and beside me and around me. Behind me and before me.

Love so intense it moved me to tears. But I smiled as the tears rolled down my face. Oh, how I smiled.

... a little more ...

When a delightful concert comes to an end,

the orchestra might offer an encore.

When a fine meal comes to an end,

it's always nice to savor a bit of dessert.

When a great story comes to an end,

we think you may want to linger.

And so, we offer ...

AfterWords—just a little something more after you

have finished a David C Cook novel.

We invite you to stay awhile in the story.

Thanks for reading!

Turn the page for ...

- **A Chat with the Author**
- **Historical Notes**
- **Discussion Questions**

A Chat with
the Author

Q: Given the fact that you love Italy so much, was this your easiest
book to write?

A: Easiest in terms of locale, but not in general writing. This was a
pretty traumatic year for my family due to health struggles and tran-
sitions, and I was fairly exhausted already after writing five books in
one year—not a great way to start. God reminded me that I do best
if I work from rest rather than rest/collapse from work. I'm trying to
get my rest rhythm back on track, so I can live my life—professional
and personal—in a healthy way. Writing always flows better when I
operate out of a sense of peace rather than panic.

Q: What are your favorite memories about visiting Italy?

A: An intimate Vivaldi concert in Venice with my daughter Olivia;
walking around the glorious Piazza Navona in Rome at night with
my daughter Emma; and a week with my husband in the most picturesque, romantic villa in Tuscany you can imagine. Celebrating my
fortieth birthday in a trattoria in Florence with my parents, hubs,
and kids. Seeing it all for the first time with our dear friends Darren
and Sarah. I swear every acre of that land is magical ... and most of
what you "experienced" in *Glittering Promises* came from my own

experiences while there. I wished I could've put it all in the series … but you're probably happy I didn't. The book would've run five hundred pages.

Q: What about your own spiritual journey informed Cora's arc through the series?

A: Thanks to the ministry of 3DM, I've been exploring what it truly means to be a child of God over the last few years, absorbing my identity from Him rather than the things we usually rely upon to give us a sense of identity. In some ways, what Cora externally experiences helps her discover new aspects about herself. Life and its challenges have that capacity to mold us. But the most important thing for her is that internal, eternal Force that never changes, always calls, always loves … the God she can rely upon regardless of what comes to pass. That's what I hope readers absorb from her spiritual journey. That's what I've been leaning into myself.

Q: What's next for you on the writing front?

A: Well, related to your first question, I'm slowing down a bit. My readers know I can never do the same thing for long, so I'm rolling into a genre-bending dystopian-spiritual-suspense-epic-romantic tale called *Remnants*, a three-book series for teens and YA-friendly older readers.

Historical Notes

As I understand it, the Cinque Terre was little more than a group of sleepy fishing villages until the latter part of the 1990s, when Rick Steves began touting their beauty and charm. I doubt many Grand Tourists would've thought to go there. But then, my tourists were trying to escape notice and get off the beaten track! These days, it's a prime stop for anyone wanting to visit Italia.

Michelangelo's unfinished sculptures in the Accademia in Florence were personal favorites, because seeing them was truly like stumbling into the artist's workshop and discovering the master-pieces in process. I'm uncertain where they were in 1913—if they were already on display or elsewhere—and I devised the "warehouse" behind the gallery for fictional purposes.

The Hypogeum in Rome's Coliseum was not unearthed/excavated until the 1930s. I moved up the date because I wanted to share that perspective of the marvelous structure with my readers and for obvious dramatic purposes. If you ever get to Rome, be sure to sign up for a tour that includes a visit belowground (special tickets required). We went with Dark Rome and were impressed (with *that* particular tour, *not* the one to Pompeii and Mount Vesuvius, an entirely different experience).

In Tivoli, the Villa d'Este's amazing gardens were neglected and overgrown for centuries, her fountains broken. I loved the *Secret Garden* aspect of that site! There was a period of renewed attention during the tenure of Cardinal Hohenlohe at the end of the nineteenth century, but full restoration of the gardens and fountains didn't happen until well after World War I, and I've gathered that some of the amazing waterspouts were later additions. Again, I moved up the date of restoration for dramatic purposes. We took a tour out of Rome with Context Travel to escape the heat and crowds of the city for a day and to see Hadrian's Villa and the Villa d'Este in Tivoli—highly recommended for serious history hounds.

Discussion Questions

1. Do you ever wish you could travel? If money wasn't an issue, where would you go and why?

2. How does traveling with someone help you understand that person better? Discuss your own travel experiences with others, good and bad.

3. Cora is on a journey of self-discovery, and part of that is finding her footing with her father. When he dies, her budding hope that they might establish some sense of relationship dies with him. Why is that good … and bad?

4. What was Wallace Kensington's prime motivation for inviting Cora into the fold and along on the tour? At the core, was he a good guy or a bad guy?

5. Name a person in your life who has helped shape your identity. How did he or she do so, externally or internally?

6. Do you find you move through life more as a child of God or as a child of your parents? Discuss the benefits of both.

7. In 1913, women were on the verge of voting for the first time. Some places allowed women to vote in school elections, and many saw even that as edgy territory. What would your life likely be like if social norms were still the same as they were in 1913? Would you be married? How many kids would you likely have without birth control? Would you be working (as a teacher or nurse, most likely)? Would you be happy/content? Why or why not?

8. Discuss one hard decision you've had to make that went against what your family wanted you to do. Was it a good decision, in hindsight?

9. Cora gradually becomes accustomed to wealth and privilege and exhibits some of the same traits that initially bothered her in the Kensingtons and Morgans. How would you avoid or have you avoided absorbing characteristics you've objected to in those who surround you?

10. In the end, Cora finds closure in visiting her father's coffin in the hold. How important has it been for you to have closure with those who've died? What is it that keeps us from saying important words to people while they're alive?

Acknowledgments

Some books are harder than others, and when you have a year of personal struggle as I have, they become nearly impossible to complete. Specials thanks to Traci DePree and Caitlyn Carlson for putting their arms under my shoulders and practically carrying me across the finish line. Thanks also to the rest of the fantastic pub team at David C Cook—Dan Rich, Don Pape, Ingrid Beck, Marilyn Largent, Jeremy Potter, Ginia Hairston, Karen Stoller, Amy Konyndyk, Karen Athen, and Michael Covington—the publicity chicks of Litfuse, and Steve Gardner and James Hall, the design team that gave me another gorgeous cover. I truly appreciate your support for the Grand Tour Series.

Also, thanks to Amber Galik for her help with translations, as well as the darling Eleonora Masoni, who both allowed me to swipe her name for a character and helped me with Italian translations. *Grazie mille!*

Still Want to Know More?

Find out more about Lisa and connect with her by visiting:

Web: LisaBergren.com
Facebook: Facebook.com/LisaTawnBergren
Twitter: @LisaTBergren

THE GRAND TOUR SERIES

GLAMOROUS ILLUSIONS

GLITTERING PROMISES

LISA T. BERGREN

GRAVE CONSEQUENCES

LISA T. BERGREN

LISATAWNBERGREN.COM

@LISATBERGREN

LISA.T.BERGREN

As she travels with her family to Europe in 1913, Cora faces the blessings as well as the curses of the family name. An unseen enemy is closing in fast. Yet torn between the love of two men—one she cannot have and one she cannot turn away from—her heart may need guarding too.

David C Cook®

transforming lives together

THE
HOMEWARD
TRILOGY
-COLORADO 1883-
BREATHE
A Novel of Colorado
SING
A NOVEL OF COLORADO
CLAIM
A NOVEL OF COLORADO
BEST-SELLING AUTHOR
LISA T. BERGREN
— THE HOMEWARD TRILOGY —
A love story, a coming-of-age story, and an embrace-your-life story—join three siblings as they find their way home in this Western epic.
800.323.7543 • DavidCCook.com
David C Cook
transforming lives together